Lucky Shot

ALSO BY REBECCA JENSHAK

Holland Brothers Series

Burnout

Playbook

Comeback

Spotlight

Wildcat Hockey Series

Wildcat

Wild About You

Wild Ever After

In Your Wildest Dreams

Forever Wild

Campus Wallflowers Series

Tutoring the Player

Hating the Player

Scoring the Player

Tempting the Player

Campus Nights Series

Secret Puck

Bad Crush

Broken Hearts

Wild Love

Smart Jocks Series

The Assist

The Fadeaway

The Tip-Off

The Fake

The Pass

Standalone Novels

Sweet Spot

Electric Blue Love

Lucky Shot

REBECCA JENSHAK

Cover design by Lori Jackson
Cover illustration by Sarah Jane (@illustriousjane)

ISBN: 979-8-3470-3657-8

Published in 2026 by Podium Publishing
www.podiumentertainment.com

Lucky Shot

Chapter One

RUBY

They say be ready when opportunity knocks, but in my experience, opportunity is rarely that polite. In the best of scenarios, it trudges in wearing a cloak of uncertainty (that undoubtedly wears off on you) and takes up residence on your couch for months on end. Worst case, opportunity sprints by so fast you barely recognize it or the lifeline it tosses in your direction.

I have a sneaking suspicion that this moment is the latter. Because in what world does your literary agent email you on a random summer Friday with news that your dream publisher wants to meet?

Okay, for other people maybe that isn't that rare. Me two years ago wouldn't have even thought it was remarkable. But that was before . . . well, a lot of things.

I pull my hair down out of the messy top knot and finger comb the red tangles into some semblance of a tidy hairdo, then pull it back up. I don't have enough time to make myself more presentable before the meeting alert chimes. And really, what should they expect? I'm an author. My idea of business casual is a nice shirt paired with my most comfy leggings.

My stomach is in knots as I click the link to join the call. Molly, my agent, is already present. So is Doreen, an editor for a top publishing house and my final hope of selling this book before I'm forced into retirement.

"Hi," I say as I adjust my laptop so I'm centered in the screen.

Both women smile at me while my pulse kicks up enough speed that my watch buzzes and asks me if I want to record a workout.

"I am so thrilled to talk to you," Doreen says, leaning back in her cushy, leather office chair. Her gray hair is pulled back into an elegant bun at the nape of her neck. She wears silver hoop earrings, and a scarf tied around her neck. She has that timeless style of a woman in her fifties that has found what she likes and sticks with it.

"You are?" I ask. My voice betrays me by wavering a little.

"Of course." A small laugh leaves her as she rests one elbow on the arm of her chair. Her fingers absently touch one earring as she adds, "I'm a big fan of your work. You have been a big part of the resurgence of vampire romances, and no one does it quite like you. I've read every single one and I'm smitten with them all."

"Even the last one?" I ask before thinking better of it.

Over the past five years, my career has rocketed. The first two books did well, but it was the third that launched my career to the next level. I hit bestseller lists in three countries, accepted foreign publishing deals, optioned movie rights, and had more ideas than I could possibly write in my lifetime. All that came to a screeching halt a year ago. My fourth book flopped, I went through a messy breakup, and then I was hit with writer's block so hard I couldn't come up with a single good idea. I haven't sold anything since, but hopefully all that changes today.

Doreen lets out a hearty guffaw that somehow still comes off sophisticated and chic. "Was it my favorite? No. But your talent shines through even when the story isn't compelling."

I'm not sure how to take that. I know she meant it as a compliment, but I'm hung up on the whole "the story wasn't compelling" part. She isn't wrong.

"But none of that matters. Publishing has a short memory. And the most recent book Molly sent over shines like nothing else I've read from you."

"Thanks," I say, relief flooding me. I'm shocked, honestly. It was painful to write, and it was only a proposal and the first two chapters. If I manage to sell it, I'll have to figure out how to get my mojo back—something I need to do regardless.

"It's surprising and fun, and the tension between the main characters jumps off the page. What made you want to change things up? I mean, a sports romance from Ruby Madison?!"

I'm nodding along and smiling, eating up her words, until the last part clicks into place.

"Wait. Sports romance?"

"Yes." She laughs again, smiling at first, but then she must read my confusion. She reaches for a pair of tortoiseshell glasses and pulls them on, then glances at what I assume is a second monitor. "*A Sporty Romance* by Ruby Madison. That *is* you, right?"

A memory of me typing those words on the title page before sending it off to Molly flashes in my mind at the same time I inwardly cringe. Not my most original title, which is probably why that book was shelved *two years ago*.

While Doreen waits patiently for an answer, I glance at Molly. She somehow continues to beam while I shoot lasers out of my eyes at her.

Silently, I panic scream, *"You gave Doreen Walters my old manuscript!?"* While she seems to say, *"Just go with it, Ruby. We need this!"*

The quiet stretches out for several tense moments.

"Yes, of course I wrote it," I say as heat blooms in my face. "I'm sorry, I thought we were meeting about the vampire royalty book."

"Molly sent over the proposal and chapters for that one too. It isn't bad." She pulls off her glasses and holds them in one hand, then motions toward her monitor. "But this is the one I want."

"Why?" The question bubbles over and slips from my lips.

She lets out a laugh as she arches a brow. "I *thought* I liked it."

"I'm so sorry," I apologize again.

My brain reels. Two years ago, before the worst year of my life, I wrote a sports romance. It was fun. My sister, Olivia, had just started dating Flynn—a professional baseball player. I was going with her to games, completely caught up in their love story. It was inspiring to watch them fall in love. So inspiring that I wrote an entire draft faster than anything before or since. It was different from what I'd written previously, but my early readers all loved it, including Molly, who I trust implicitly. She pitched it to my publisher at the time. They passed, noting they liked the book, but it wasn't right for them. Then two more editors at different publishers did the same.

I shrugged it off because I was getting plenty of requests for more paranormal or romantasy. Publishing seemed to be telling me they wanted me to do more of what I was already doing, and I listened. We shelved *A Sporty Romance* (still a terrible name), and I wrote another vampire book—the one that flopped.

My agent continues to smile through the screen, but I note the tension bracketing her mouth. Why wouldn't Molly tell me she was shopping this manuscript around again?

Doreen continues. "I know the book is different, but it's precisely why I love it. Not everyone can pull off switching genres like this, but I think you can. Your writing is gorgeous. The hero is charming, and your heroine is nuanced and lovable, if not slightly chaotic. The book has all the charisma and wit that your readers adore."

"But my readers aren't expecting a sports romance." My readers may not be expecting anything, honestly. It's been over a year since I've published, which wouldn't be all that concerning if I were promoting or teasing something to come, but I'm not.

"If you partner with us, then I will make it my mission to convince your readers and everyone else that they *need* to read this book," Doreen says without a beat of hesitation in her tone. She's launched so many careers that her confidence is well-earned.

"I don't know what to say." She's not known for her flattery, but she's handed me several compliments in the span of five minutes. I try my hardest to let them land and soothe the previous rejections for this book. Even if she did call my heroine chaotic. Not exactly what I was going for, but I can smooth that out in edits. Oh my god, am I actually considering this?

"There's just one little thing," Doreen says in that way that foreshadows the little thing is going to be a huge pain to fix. She places her glasses back on the bridge of her nose. "We'd like you to change the sport from baseball to hockey."

Her words rattle around in my brain like a pinball machine. Baseball. Hockey. What's the difference?

In the small image of me on the screen, my brow furrows. "Excuse me?"

"We have another baseball romance on our list this summer. Besides, baseball is harder to sell in this market. Hockey romance is what readers want right now." She grins like we're in on a secret. "And the sport is such a small part of the story."

That's true, but there's one more thing she's failed to account for. "I don't know hockey."

I barely know baseball. I had Olivia and Flynn helping me get the sport's details right, but it was a huge undertaking.

"Oh." Doreen gets the first flicker of disappointment on her face, and instantly I get the feeling that I've ruined everything. And judging by Molly's face, she thinks so too.

There goes opportunity sprinting by.

I've wanted to work with Doreen since before I finished my first manuscript. She's smart and powerful. She navigates publishing like a badass boss bitch. Her eye for picking out books from the slush pile and making them bestsellers is impeccable. If there's anyone that can help revive my career, it's her.

But hockey?

And if I say no, then what? I could have Molly send this book back around to editors. To be honest, I'd forgotten about it. I shelved *A Sporty Romance* (*such* a terrible title) in my metaphorical box under my bed with a dozen other manuscripts.

Maybe someone else would take it as is. Or I guess I could write another book, but, well, that hasn't been very successful the past six months, i.e., I've written nothing except proposals.

"What Ruby means is that she would need additional resources in order to make sure she gets the hockey information correct," Molly interjects. "I can help with that. I'm originally from Upstate New York. I know lots of people in the hockey world."

I shoot my agent a look that I hope communicates my skepticism. Meanwhile, Doreen's smile is back and wider than ever. "Great."

"Great," I mimic, with a lot less enthusiasm.

"I'll send over my offer this afternoon. Take time and think it over, but not too much time." Doreen quickly transforms back into serious editor mode, steepling her fingers in front of the camera. "We want to turn this around quickly and get it out with our winter catalog. You're attending the Delaroche Book Fair this fall, right?"

I nod. It's the one event Molly absolutely refused to let me cancel this year—otherwise I would have.

"Perfect. We'll announce it then with big, flashy signage and advanced copies." She gets that hopeful smile on her face again.

Panic rises in my chest, sending a flood of warmth through my body. "You want me to rewrite the entire book by the event in September?"

"Of course not. We'd need it by the end of August," she says with not a single drop of teasing in her tone. "We'll rush to print advanced copies for the convention."

Several seconds pass where my entire body is frozen with a mixture of hope and terror. I want so badly to believe this is the chance to turn things around, but it's so unexpected. Lying low in my apartment, plotting books, and writing bad first chapters over and over again has become almost comforting.

"Okay." Molly gets that look in her eye that tells me she's heard all she needs and doesn't want me to put my foot in my mouth. "Thank you so much, Doreen. I'm excited about this."

"Me too," Doreen says.

I can't seem to speak, so I force my mouth into what I hope is a smile.

"We'll talk soon." Doreen leans forward and then ends the meeting.

Two seconds later, Molly calls me.

"Don't panic," she says by way of greeting.

"Don't panic?" I ask, parroting her words but with so much anxiety I can feel it vibrating through me. I stand and pace back and forth in my small living room. "Why didn't you warn me?"

"Honestly?" She pauses, then adds, "I was afraid you wouldn't take the meeting."

"Nobody turns down a meeting with Doreen Walters," I whisper-hiss as I squeeze my eyes shut.

"She is a legend," Molly says. "And she loves the book."

Even Doreen must get it wrong occasionally.

As if she heard my internal dialogue, Molly uses her stern, lovable tone. "So do I. I believe in this book. I always have. I wouldn't be pushing it if I didn't. Maybe now is the time to finally get it out there while you figure out what's next."

Or it could flop like the last one. I swallow the words, but they burn all the same. I stop pacing and inhale a steadying breath.

"How would this even work?" I ask. "I wasn't exaggerating. I really don't know anything about hockey."

"Let me worry about that."

A tiny scoff leaves my throat. This is crazy. I can't do it. I'm the least sporty person I know. My knowledge of hockey is nonexistent, unless you count fifth grade physical education class where we played scooter hockey. And the only thing I remember about that is how painful it is to have your fingers run over by a scooter wheel.

"I promise I will get you the support you need. Your character will be deking and chirping, putting up hat tricks, and shaking out his glorious lettuce," Molly adds confidently.

"I have no idea what you even said."

"Me either, but I love *Shoresy*. Have you seen the show? It's hilarious."

My throat constricts, and a fresh wave of panic ripples through me. I shake my head, but no words come out.

"You can do this!" Her enthusiasm is contagious, and finally a small laugh escapes. If I don't laugh, I may cry.

"Oh, she's already sent over the offer," Molly says, then gasps.

"Is that a good gasp or a bad gasp?" I ask. Maybe it's so bad it doesn't justify learning an entirely new sport. We can go back to pushing the vampire royalty book, and I can figure out how I'm going to write it, if and when someone wants it.

"I just forwarded it."

I hustle back to my laptop and pull up the email from Molly. When the attachment loads, I let out my own gasp. I have never, and I mean *never*, seen an advance even close to this number. It would be the biggest deal of my career.

I straighten and blow out a breath. "What does lettuce have to do with hockey?"

Chapter Two

RUBY

"Six weeks." Molly's voice, filled with unwavering finality and a dash of hopefulness, comes through my headphones. "That should be plenty of time for you to interview him, get through edits, and still be able to enjoy a little summer fun at the lake."

"Here's hoping," I reply as I make my way through the small Montana airport.

"You don't need hope. You've got this."

I can almost see her, sitting at her desk, covered in books and coffee mugs, pumping her fist into the air. Fueled by too much caffeine and a competitive spirit. She's the single hardest-working person I know and on top of it, somehow a constant ray of sunshine. We're a lot alike, actually. Only, my optimism is on a temporary hiatus.

She's one of the best agents in the business with more than fifteen years of experience in publishing. It's not a world for the faint of heart. I've questioned if I'm cut out for it more times than I can count. Including every second since I got on a plane in Arizona to fly thousands of miles to learn hockey and rewrite my book.

If it weren't for Molly's belief in me and the lure of hiding away to lick my wounds, I'd still be curled up on the couch in my apartment binge-watching another reality dating show. Instead, I'm in Montana, weaving through men in cowboy hats to find the baggage claim.

"Ruby?"

"Yeah," I say. "I'm here. I will get it done."

"That's the spirit! Did you look at the videos I sent you? He's cuuuuute."

It probably says something that my immediate reaction to a guy being cute is to wrinkle my nose. I'm having a hot girl summer, and a cute guy isn't getting in the way of that.

"No, not yet. It's on my to-do list."

- Fly to Moonshot ✓
- Meet Mike at the cabin I'm renting for the summer
- Research the hockey expert I'll be interviewing
- Interview said hockey expert to learn sports puck stuff
- Spend a week editing the hell out of my manuscript
- Come up with new, fabulous book idea
- Sell fabulous book idea

Easy peasy, lemon squeezy or whatever. I've got this.

"I better go," I say as I swivel around, realizing I've walked the wrong way.

"You have Mike's number?"

"Yes," I confirm with more sureness than before. I'm hesitant about my ability to finish this book, but I distinctly remember putting Mike's contact information in my phone. Plus, the dozens of emails Molly has sent over, confirming and reconfirming all the details.

Six weeks in Moonshot, an adorable lake town in western Montana, working with a local expert to edit the book that will hopefully reignite my flailing career. At worst, I'm going to spend my summer reading with a killer view. But I don't say that to Molly. She'd fly out here to hold my hand, and that would be beyond pathetic. I'm a grown-ass woman, I need to pull my shit together.

Just . . . not quite yet. I need to figure out how to write again first while editing a book I never thought would see the light of day. I really must be desperate. And is hockey really all that different from baseball anyway? I mean, I know they're different. One has a bat, the other a stick. Hmm . . . now that I think about it, aren't those sort of the same thing? I'll add that to my list of questions to ask my hockey guru.

"Great!" Molly's unending enthusiasm keeps me going. "I hope the cabin is as great of a find as it looked in the pictures."

That makes two of us.

"I just know it's going to inspire so many great, romantic stories. Who knows, you might get your next book idea while you're there."

"I'm sure you're right," I say because, dammit, I can do this. My steely resolve won't let me throw in the towel, only toss it into the corner and let it collect dust. And isn't that almost worse? If I were the type of person who could walk away and get a different job, then I already would have done it. I love putting words down, creating characters, and weaving stories. I know that I *can* do this, but that fact doesn't make it any easier to do the damn thing.

"Text me when you get there, and send me the new first chapter at the end of the week."

"Will do," I say as my stomach dips. One chapter. Totally doable.

Probably.

Maybe.

Fingers crossed.

After saying goodbye and ending the call, I let out a long breath.

"As if the first chapter isn't the most important," I mutter quietly. I try really hard not to go all tortured artist, locking myself away and existing on coffee and angst, but the first chapter is *so* important. I usually save it for last. After I've written "The End" I go back and rework it ad nauseam. The idea of sending it to Molly and the publisher without knowing the new ending of the book is incomprehensible. Unless I can somehow figure out how to work a grand-slam victory kiss into the grand gesture of my hockey book.

It needs charm and excitement. *Sparkle.* Three things I've felt very little of lately.

My steps slow as I approach a bookstore. Like all airport bookstores, it has a table display in the very front with bestselling authors and popular books stacked artfully and strategically to drive people inside.

It's an occupational hazard, noticing books everywhere I go. I love seeing what people are picking up on shelves or flipping through while they wait for their flight. The first time I saw someone reading one of mine, I hid like I'd been caught doing something terrible. It was so surreal.

I smile, pride zipping through me, when I see my friend Lily's newest release stacked up on the far-left side of the table. I snap a picture and text it to her. Seeing friends' books in the wild is way better than seeing your own somehow. Less debilitating imposter syndrome perhaps.

Before I've repocketed my phone, my gaze lands on another book. One I'm far less happy to see. The familiar white cover with red foil details is impossible to miss, unfortunately. Since the first edition of the book sold out, the second edition has the words, "An instant NYT Bestseller!" proudly stamped across the top, along with splashy praise from well-respected media. Adjectives like "refreshing" and "genius."

My stomach sinks, and my cheeks warm with embarrassment or possibly rage. Yes, definitely the latter.

I turn on my heel, like fleeing as fast as possible will erase that book and that author from my mind. Unlikely.

In my haste, I nearly collide with a man walking in the opposite direction. I screech and somehow manage to run over my own foot with my roller bag while he gracefully dodges me, sidestepping to the left as his brows rise in a confused, startled way. Whether at my ear-piercing vocal range or the frazzled, clumsy reaction, I'm not sure.

I'm not known for my grace. Okay, fine, that is a gross understatement. I'm easily the klutziest person that I know. And the klutziest person that most anyone who knows me knows. My sister Olivia blamed it on me being top-heavy once. She was going through her preteen mean-girl phase and was pissed that I got boobs before she did. Regardless of intent, her words stuck with me. I often wonder if I would be less accident-prone if I had smaller breasts or perhaps a bigger butt to even things out.

"Sorry," I wheeze out as I lift my gaze to his face.

He's taller than average, easily over six feet tall. His hair is tousled, possibly from travel, although he has that look about him that suggests he's always a little bit unkempt. It's working for him. From the dark, wavy locks, to the scruff on his face paired with black athletic pants and a gray T-shirt that hugs his broad chest and muscular arms. There's something about his clothes or the way he stands that refuses to be categorized as disheveled. It's so annoying how men can roll out of bed and put on whatever clothes they find lying around and still look this hot.

I'm still staring at him when the backpack slung over my left shoulder slides off and throws me off-balance again. The heavy weight of it hits the ground next to me with a *thunk*, thankfully not on either of our feet. I packed way too much.

I flash an apologetic smile that I hope comes off cool and collected despite all other evidence. My hot girl summer is getting off to a shaky start.

Green eyes lock on me. His lips are pressed in a distinctly annoyed line, but he lingers like his manners won't let him walk off before assuring that I'm not a danger to myself. Fair, I suppose.

Slowly, he leans down and picks up my bag. His brows arch, possibly in surprise or judgment as he realizes how heavy it is.

"I promise it's not a dead body," I say with a nervous chuckle. "I mean, not that an entire body would fit."

The way he stares at me is so impassive, like I could literally tell him anything and it wouldn't faze him. It must be for that reason that I keep babbling.

"I guess it could be just the head, but I'm too squeamish for dismembering bodies, let alone transporting them through an airport. I'm more of a 'plot your demise but never act on it' kind of girl."

Hmmm. There's an idea.

"A woman flees thousands of miles from home with a head in her backpack," I say like I'm pitching the story concept.

If this man were in charge of judging my idea, his face just told me "that's the dumbest thing I've ever heard."

Regardless, I make a mental note to give Lily this story-nugget idea when I text her next. In the world of suspense and horror novels, dead bodies—even dismembered ones—aren't anything new, but I still like to pass plot ideas on anytime I have one. You never know what will strike a writer at any given moment. Plus, she'll be impressed by my depravity. My brain is way too Pollyanna for her liking. Sometimes I have to remind myself that it's okay to be pissed or mad or anything other than happy. Toxic positivity is a real thing.

Even still, it's my default mode. Like right now I'm already wondering if the woman in the story will have a happily ever after. Another occupational hazard, I suppose. Maybe she's been set up.

I snap my fingers and point at the man as I share another brilliant nugget. "A handsome stranger in the airport swapped out her bag!"

"What's happening right now?" he asks, looking over his shoulder like he expects cameras and a celebrity host to jump out and say, "Gotcha! You're on *America's Most Awkward Encounters*!"

"Nothing," I mutter, shoulders slumping. My optimism is on a teeter-totter, and he just sent me plummeting back to the bottom with his apathetic demeanor.

"O-kay." He has this deep, sexy voice, but his tone is all boredom. He extends my backpack toward me. "Here you go."

"Right." I take it from him, struggling a lot more with the weight of it than he had. "Thank you."

I get a nod instead of "you're welcome" or "no problem" or even "I'm calling security." Why is indifference the most frustrating response to be on the receiving end of?

He steps past me and rejoins the steady flow of foot traffic. I watch him retreat, head and shoulders above the crowd, until he turns a corner.

Jerk.

Sure, he was nice enough to stop and help me, but would it have killed him to pretend I'm hilarious and charming instead of awkward and klutzy? Whatever. Hot girl summer, take two.

My next stop is the car rental line. The guy working behind the counter moves at an impressively slow pace, and everyone shifts their luggage from shoulder to shoulder, inching forward with heavy sighs. When I finally make it to the front, his lips curve slowly.

"Hello. Welcome to Moonshot Lake," he says like I'm the very first customer he's had all day, and the greeting is a novelty.

"Thank you. I have a reservation—"

"How are you today?" he asks, leaning forward with something like genuine curiosity on his face. He looks like he's in his early twenties. His light-brown hair is cut in a fade that reminds me of Billy Matthews's second-grade picture and sends a wave of nostalgia over me. The friendly smile he continues to aim at me takes me by surprise, while also making me feel like an impatient asshole.

"I'm doing well. Thank you. How about you?" I summon a little patience as I set my backpack on the floor between my feet.

"Not too shabby." With that same slow, unrushed pace, he stands straight. He's a big guy. Tall, although to be honest everyone feels tall to my five feet, three inches, but it's more than his height. He's wide-shouldered and sturdy. He looks like the kind of guy who could wrestle a calf to the ground or block a doorway by simply crossing his arms over his chest. Admittedly, I may have binged one too many episodes of *Yellowstone* in preparation for this trip.

"Do you have a reservation?" No hint of an accent and didn't call me darlin'. Pity.

"Yes. Ruby Madison."

"Ruuuby." He draws it out, finally hitting me with just a little of that Montana charm I was anticipating. He grins at me as he begins to tap on the keyboard. "Cool name."

"Thanks." I glance at his nametag. "Curtis."

One side of his mouth lifts higher at my use of his name. "I've got you in a mid-size for . . ." He pauses. "Six weeks?"

"That's right."

"Cool. Cool. Plenty of time to see all that Moonshot has to offer. You're in luck, it's beautiful this time of year. It's a little hot now that we're in July, but better than shoveling snow, am I right?"

"I wouldn't know. I'm from Arizona. We don't see a lot of snow." Certainly not enough to shovel. Once, when Olivia and I were both still in high school, we got almost two inches at my parents' house, and we were able to make snowballs and a very short snowman.

"Then you should feel right at home here." He continues tapping as he adds, "I am going to hook you up with my favorite car on the lot."

"Wow. That's so nice."

"I know," he says in a matter-of-fact tone as he grabs a set of keys off a hook on the wall beside him and drops them on the counter in front of me. "You're all set, Ruby. I hope you have an amazing time in Moonshot."

"Thanks, Curtis." A wave of fresh excitement washes over me as I pick up the key fob and flash him a grateful smile.

He leans forward over the counter. His dark eyes twinkle with amusement as he says, "My name isn't really Curtis."

"It's not?" I feel my forehead crinkle as the guy stands tall again, still wearing an expression that is all boyish humor with a tinge of arrogance.

He shakes his head, then holds one hand up to cover the side of his mouth so no one can read his lips. "It's Bobby but can't have angry customers reporting me."

For a change, I can't think of a single thing to say. So, I wave the key fob, pick up my backpack, decidedly not filled with a human head, and leave the airport.

The first thing I notice in the rental car lot is that it is not, in fact, hot outside. Maybe it's Montana hot, but it's Arizona sweatshirt weather.

Cool wind whips across my bare shoulders. I'm not sure if I'm excited or stunned by this development. I don't exactly love summers in Arizona, but I'm rethinking all the tube tops I packed.

I stop and let my hair out of its ponytail. The long strands cover my back and shoulders, and I lift my head to the sun. A smile spreads across my face at the clouds dotting the sky. Big, fluffy white clouds that look like they've been crafted out of cotton balls and placed lovingly amidst the painted blue sky for aesthetics.

A car alarm beeps somewhere in the lot, bringing me back to the present. It hits me then that I have absolutely no idea what car I'm looking for. I glance down at the key fob. Attached to it is a plastic keychain with the words "Mini Convertible" scribbled in permanent marker. I look up and scan the lot.

"No," I say at the exact moment I spot the vehicle that I am certain is mine for the next month and a half. I hit the unlock button and beam as the lights flicker on the car.

Curtis's, aka Bobby's, favorite vehicle on the lot is a lime-green MINI Cooper with black stripes down the hood. In a sea of mostly black, white, and the occasional blue or red vehicles, it most definitely sticks out. It screams summer and fun and adventure, carefree days, fun nights. It's over the top. It's flashy. It's the kind of vehicle that is impossible not to notice. In any other situation I would be horrified, but not today. And not this summer.

It feels like a good omen. The perfect car to turn things around—metaphorically, although I bet it turns like a dream too.

"I think I misjudged you, Bobby," I say quietly as I approach the vehicle.

Somehow the closer I get, the more in love with it I fall. Even as I struggle to fit my large roller suitcase in the trunk. If I had to choose between all my packed essentials (tube tops are absolutely an essential) and this car, I'd . . . pick my essentials, but I would be sad about it.

Once my luggage is stowed, I pull out my phone and snap a selfie of me standing next to the vehicle, then fire it off to my sister with the words, "Hot Girl Summer Has Commenced!"

Chapter Three

NICK

"Dad?" I call as I step into the house from the garage. It's silent, but the lights are on in the living room, and the smell of fresh coffee hangs in the air.

When I don't get an answer, I peek in to see if he's asleep in my favorite recliner. The one I bought even though he told me it was too big for the room and that he now sits in more than I do.

There's no sign of him as I drop my duffel bag on the floor of the entryway and cross through to the kitchen.

Exhaustion from a week of conditioning camp and the red-eye flight home hits me hard. I'm pouring a cup of coffee when I finally hear footsteps coming down the stairs. I turn with my mug in hand as he appears in the doorway. He has on headphones, the over the ear, noise-canceling ones we got him for Christmas last year. Aidan picked them out, so they're bright red—my son's favorite color—and the sight of my un-tech-savvy dad wearing them still brings a smile to my lips even six months later.

His eyes widen when he spots me, and his steps falter. He recovers quickly, pulling the headphones down around his neck.

"Son. What are you doing here?" he asks with a smile that falls almost as fast as it forms. "You aren't supposed to be home until tomorrow."

"I took an earlier flight." Amusement threatens to lift one corner of my mouth, but I'm too tired. "Good to see you too."

"Sorry. You surprised me. Welcome home. How was Texas?"

"Tiring." Four days of grueling workouts with one of the best sports trainers in the business will do that.

"And the shoulder?" he asks.

Instinctively I tighten the muscles on my right arm. It's been months since I broke my collarbone and dislocated my shoulder in a season-ending injury. Surgery, plus rehab, was not how I planned to spend the first half of the summer, but at least I'll be ready come October. Physically, I feel stronger than ever.

"Good. It didn't give me any issues."

"That's great news." Genuine relief is apparent in his expression.

I guess I wasn't the only one worried I wouldn't come back from it. At this point in my career, every injury has me, and I guess my dad too, questioning how much longer my body will hold out.

"How's everything here?"

"Great. Is Aidan coming back early too?" His brows draw down and his lips purse as he waits for my answer. If I didn't know better, I'd think he's bummed out at the prospect of seeing his grandson. Which makes fuck-all sense.

"No. Just me. He's staying at his mom's until tomorrow."

"Good. Good."

I narrow my gaze to study him closer. He's back to acting strange, but I can't quite put my finger on why. My dad and son are tight. Arguably closer than I am with either of them. All of Dad's overbearing and frustrating mannerisms soften around Aidan, and my son is more like the sweet kid he was before his preteen attitude took over.

"Well, you probably want to get unpacked," he says in a happy tone that feels fake as hell.

"I thought we could grill tonight. Chicken, veggies, maybe we could do kebabs." Sitting on the back deck with a beer in hand sounds perfect right now.

"Sure. That'd be nice, or you could head into town and enjoy a night out before Aidan gets back." His reply is so predictable I'm embarrassed I didn't see it coming.

"We can go out to eat if you prefer." I dodge the blatant attempt to get me out of the house like I'm a forty-year-old single man still living with his parents. I'm thirty-one, my dad lives with me, and I happen to like being unattached.

"You don't need your old man cramping your style. I have leftovers in the fridge. Go. Have fun." He brushes past me, missing the eye roll I throw in his direction.

"It's about two hours too early for dinner."

"Get drinks first," he offers, upbeat, like it's the best idea he's ever had. "What's Travis up to? I'm sure he's game for a night out."

My teammate Travis is always up for a night out, so it's a good guess.

"Why are you trying to get rid of me?" I cross my arms over my chest. "More than usual."

"I'm not." He doesn't quite meet my eye, but he waves off the idea with one hand. "I only want to make sure you're having some fun. You've spent all summer training instead of letting loose."

It's an argument we've had many times before.

He picks up a dust rag and a bottle of multipurpose cleaner. "Anyway, go or don't. I'll be down at the cabin if you need anything."

"You're moving into the cabin?" My voice climbs with surprise. Six months ago, my father had a heart attack. He was already staying with me and Aidan, on and off, but that scare was the catalyst for him to move from my childhood home in Kansas City to live with us.

My house is plenty big enough for all three of us, but I worried he might like to have his own place. When the small cabin next door went up for sale a week later, I took it as a sign. It needed work, so it took some time for it to be renovated, but in the nearly three months since it's been ready, Dad has refused to move out there. He claims he likes hearing me and Aidan moving around the house (even as he's started wearing noise-canceling headphones most of the time to drown us out). It's become a sore subject, and neither of us has mentioned it in weeks.

There are a lot of things we don't talk about. The Galaxy family motto is to keep your emotions to yourself—good and bad. I'd forgotten how much it annoyed me. Partly because it reminds me I'm just as bad about holding things in, and partly because I can now recognize when he's doing it.

To say it's taken some adjusting to him being here is an understatement. I thought I knew what I was getting into since before he moved in he was already visiting us a lot, especially during the hockey season. He'd fly in and stay for a week or two at a time so someone would always be here with Aidan on my weeks. I was grateful to have him around. Still am. Not just because I want to keep an eye on him and make sure he's doing everything he can for his health or because it's convenient to have someone I trust around here while I'm gone, but because I want Aidan to grow up with family nearby. It's a tough life being traded from team to team, uprooting his life repeatedly and taking him away from friends and routine.

Moonshot is the third team I've played for since I joined the league, the same year Aidan was born. Three years in Chicago, then four in Minnesota. Moonshot is finally our chance to build a home and a life.

I signed a contract that will keep us here for seven more years. Assuming I can get a couple of one-year extensions, Aidan can finish out high school here, and I can play out the rest of my career in Montana.

"No," he says, igniting a twinge of annoyance in me with that one word. "I, uh, just don't want it to get dusty in there after all the work you put in to making the place so nice."

I bite back my first retort, *"What the hell does it matter if no one is going to live there?"* and instead say, "Larry and Pam clean it every other week."

As if he didn't hear me, he continues on, adding Windex and paper towels to the cleaning supplies in his hands.

Exhaustion washes over me. The only thing I want to do is shower and sit outside on the patio with a beer. Instead, I push off the counter. "I'll give you a hand."

"Nonsense. I've been looking forward to this all day."

"You've been looking forward to cleaning the cabin?" I ask instead of outright calling bullshit.

"A little fresh air. A new audiobook. When you get to be my age, it's all about embracing the little things."

"You're sixty-two."

"Exactly."

I shake my head, prepared to give up this fight. What do I care if he wants to clean the place? Maybe he'll start to feel at home there the more he's in it. It's a nice cabin. Closer to the water than my house, with a wraparound porch and a great view of the sunrise over the lake every morning.

Dad heads for the back door, but before he pushes it open, there's a knock on the front door. I wait to see if it happens again. Few people come by, and even fewer knock instead of walking right in.

"Are you expecting someone?"

He looks from me to the door and back. His mouth hangs open, and his expression morphs to something that looks a lot like dread.

"Dad?" I ask again at the same time whoever's outside finds the doorbell. They ring it three times in rapid succession.

He smiles, then quickly drops all the cleaning supplies onto the counter. "I got it. It's probably a solicitor or that little girl down the street selling cookies."

Something is definitely off. He's acting . . . weird. Not a novelty for my dad, but stranger than usual.

Dad crosses to the front door quickly, then glances back at me. There's a hesitation before he pulls it open. I can't see the woman on the other side, but her voice is loud and bubbly as she says, "Hi. I'm Ruby Madison. Are you Mike?"

There's something familiar about that cheery voice that has my mind spinning to place it.

"That's right." Dad extends a hand.

I take a step closer, and that's when I spot the bright-yellow backpack resting on the ground next to the woman. What are the odds that two people I've run into today have the same overstuffed, bright-yellow bag? My guess is not good. Confirmed when Dad steps back, opening his stance, and the woman from the airport walks past him. She comes to a stop in the middle of the entryway. A tentative smile curves her lips as she looks me over.

"You," she says, not exactly accusatory but not overly friendly either. You'd think I walked into her house unannounced instead of the other way around.

"You," I repeat, hands finding my hips. I look past her to my dad, who is carefully avoiding my gaze.

"You two have met?" he asks, still not looking at me but in my general direction. He comes to stand between us.

"Yes," she says at the same time I say, "No."

Her cheeks flush as she gives me a look that screams "go to hell" even as she somehow smiles politely.

"We had a run-in at the airport," she tells my dad. Then to me, "I'm Ruby. Sorry about that and the babbling. I realize joking about possible homicide with a stranger was probably awkward. More so when she shows up at your house. I'm not a serial killer, I promise. And I know I'm early. I thought it would take me longer to get my rental car and drive here."

Early?

"It's no problem at all," Dad says, recovering from her incessant babbling quicker than me. "I was just about to head down to the cabin and double-check that everything was ready."

"Oh. I can come back later if you prefer," she offers quickly.

Cabin? Come back later?

"No, no. It's fine, darling."

She grins, looking instantly relieved. "Thank you. I'm anxious to see it. It looks like an absolute dream in the pictures."

"What's going on?" I finally ask since it seems no one is going to tell me willingly and I can't make heads nor tails of their conversation. Why the hell is this woman in our house, and what does the cabin have to do with it?

Her brows knit together as she aims another annoyed look my way that I'm positive I'm mirroring back to her. Although in my case it isn't personal. Whereas I'm pretty sure it is for her.

"I'm Ruby Madison," she introduces herself again as if it should mean something to me.

My expression undoubtedly reads *"And that's supposed to mean something to me because?"* but I say nothing.

Ruby Madison has long red hair that hangs in soft waves around her face and past her shoulders. She's somewhere around my age, maybe a little younger. Blue eyes, fair skin, and a heart-shaped face. She's dressed in a top that only covers about four inches of her torso, cutting across the top of her generous tits and above her belly button.

Her full lips part as if she wants to say something, but no words come out. She glances at my dad like she hopes he can clear things up.

He does, but I'm not at all prepared for what he says. "Ruby is going to be staying in the cabin for a few weeks. She's an author from Arizona."

I feel both brows lift. What in the actual hell is happening? It's like every piece of information is more confusing instead of less.

I'm forgotten as he turns his attention back to Ruby.

"There's a separate driveway where you can park, that way you can come and go as you please, but we'll go out the back way so you can enjoy the lake view. It's gorgeous today. The water is sparkling just for your arrival." He gives her a friendly wink.

She beams back at him.

"Can I take your luggage?" He tips his head toward the yellow backpack.

Her gaze flits to me, and the blush on her face creeps down her neck as if she's embarrassed about our earlier run-in. I wonder which part she's reeling about. Nearly running me over? Narrowly avoiding dropping her backpack on my foot? Babbling on about dead bodies and true-crime plotlines?

"Oh, uh, no, I've got it," she says finally, gripping the strap of her backpack a little tighter. To be honest I'm impressed she's been carrying it around all day. The thing must weigh forty pounds.

"Okay. The steps off the back deck might be a little tricky. Nick, can you grab that roller bag and follow us down?"

It must be shock that has me acting as her bag boy instead of demanding he tell me what the hell is going on. He rented out the cabin? I gave it to him, so technically it's his to do whatever he wants with, but he knows I always intended it to be a place for him, not a goddamn Airbnb.

"This is gorgeous." Ruby lifts her chin, taking in the space around her as she follows my dad through the house to the back sliding glass doors. She glances back at me. "Do you live here too?"

"This is Nicky's house." Dad raises his voice but doesn't look back as he speaks. "He lets me freeload. Penance for all the late nights I stayed up worrying about him when he was a teenager."

I don't manage to hide the annoyance in my expression before Ruby catches it. She smiles. "You're his son?"

"Yes," I say, then mutter to myself, "Unfortunately."

Because whatever is going on here is undoubtedly going to be a huge pain in my ass. I don't want some stranger living in the cabin next door, especially one that seems so . . .

I'm still trying to put my finger on the right adjective to describe Ruby as I heft her roller bag down the steps. She walks slowly, taking in the view with a delighted squeal.

"Oh my gosh! It's even better than the pictures."

Dad stops and lets her soak it all in. A pleased smile dances on his face. It's almost enough to smooth my irritation at being blindsided. I want my dad to be happy, and if the cabin doesn't do that, then we'll just have to figure out something else. He's been through enough.

Ruby's hair lifts and falls around her shoulders as the wind blows off the lake. A delicate gold chain with a four-leaf clover charm hangs around her neck and catches the sunlight. She looks so carefree and happy, like life hasn't worn her down and put lines on her face yet.

Her obvious excitement has me taking in the view, wondering how she must see it. It's easy to take it for granted now, but I spent years working for this. Mountains in the distance, the lake stretched out for miles in either direction. The first thing I do every morning is walk out here. It never fails to center me.

The only house close enough to see is the cabin. It sits about a hundred yards to the right with pine trees that run along the property line, giving it some semblance of privacy. Privacy that I thought would be nice for my dad, but now realize will be paramount for me since we're renting it out to a complete stranger.

Once she's had her fill of the view, Ruby starts moving again. There's a pep in her step and an obvious glee the closer we get.

The cabin is fifteen hundred square feet. Two bedrooms, one bath, with an updated kitchen, and windows that look out toward the lake. My favorite feature is the wraparound porch. I pictured Dad sitting out here with his morning coffee and Aidan running over to see him after breakfast.

"It's perfect!" she exclaims as we walk up to the front door. Her irritation at me seems completely forgotten as she turns in a circle, grinning from ear to ear.

She hasn't even seen the inside, so her words feel at the very least premature and at the worst—wrong. Just . . . *so wrong.* Because absolutely nothing about this scenario is perfect. Not even close.

Chapter Four

RUBY

"Can I talk to you?" Nick asks his dad in a low voice that doesn't conceal his annoyance.

At me? His dad? The world?

He sets my suitcase down next to the front door but doesn't look at me. Which is fine because when he does, it makes strange things happen in my stomach. The man is intimidating even without all the jaw-clenching moodiness.

"Whatever it is, I'm sure it can wait." Mike ignores his son and smiles at me. "Let me give you a quick tour, darling."

He pats at his pockets. "As soon as I find my keys."

After another few seconds of searching, Mike glances to Nick with an "aww shucks" expression. "Would you mind running back to the house? I must have left the keys there with the cleaning supplies."

Nick looks like he wants to tell his father to go to hell, but instead he dips his head in a nod and leaves us. The tension in the air lets out like a balloon in his absence.

I take the opportunity to fix my stare back on the lake. It really is perfect. Breathtaking. It's colder here than I imagined, but surely I packed a sweatshirt somewhere in my giant suitcase. It was hard to decide what to bring for a six-week trip. The longest I've ever vacationed or traveled for work is two weeks, and when confronted with packing the things I couldn't live without—I was maybe a skosh too presumptuous.

"Don't mind my son. He's just cranky from traveling," Mike says in his son's absence.

"He was a perfect gentleman." Which is mostly true. Not friendly or polite, but he did help me with my bags, twice now. Aside from making me feel like an idiot, the only real issue I have with him is his general aloofness and the daggers he shot in my direction. Which might have been aimed at his father instead of me. It's hard to tell where his irritation lies, but suffice to say, I am not winning him over. "He doesn't seem thrilled about having me here though."

"Don't worry. You two will barely know the other exists." Mike reaches into his pocket again, and this time he pulls out a key. "Ah, there it is."

I glance back at Nick, expecting Mike to call out and let him know he doesn't need to retrieve the keys from the house, but his son is already halfway across the yard.

"How long have you lived here?" I ask, inhaling the scent of pine and lake as he works the key into the lock.

The porch is stunning and goes all the way around the house. Next to the front door, a white rocking chair is angled toward the lake. Resting on the seat is a throw pillow with the words *#1 Grandpa* crocheted on the front. It isn't the décor I was expecting, but I'm already picturing evenings out here with my laptop and a glass of iced tea.

"Almost two years now, I guess. Time moves in leaps and bounds when you get to my age."

"I have heard forty is a rough age for that."

His mouth pulls into a pleased grin. "You and I are going to get along just fine."

He rattles the doorknob as he gives the key a final twist and then pushes the door open. I follow Mike inside with one last glimpse over my shoulder.

The cabin is in a direct line from the main house. The landscaping gives it some semblance of privacy. The idea of staying so close to the man who clearly doesn't want me here has me feeling uneasy.

I would describe the general aesthetic of the place as masculine. Woods and dark colors, very little art or clutter. Still, it's clean and well-kept. The front room has a soft brown leather couch and a coffee table staring at a small fireplace with a TV mounted above. There's also a dining area next to the kitchen with a circular table set for two. The stove sparkles like it's brand-new.

I run a hand over the countertop as I explore. "This kitchen is a dream."

"Do you cook?"

"Only when I'm on deadline." Which means there are a lot of chocolate chip cookies and banana bread in my future.

"Well, it's all brand-new. Top of the line, if I know my son."

"Nick picked out the appliances?" I ask. "I thought this was your place."

"It is, but he picked out everything."

I must look confused because Mike adds, "He bought and renovated the place for me when I moved in with them, but it's too much space. I don't need the fuss. Plus, I can bug him better from the main house."

Words fail me as I process this new knowledge of Nick buying a house for his father. It's such a generous, loving thing to do, and I'm having a hard time reconciling it with Nick's overall indifferent demeanor.

"You'll be the first person to test out everything." He walks over to the front windows and pulls back the curtains to let in light. Another jaw-dropping view of the lake greets me.

Beyond the kitchen, Mike shows me a small room that's currently set up as an office with a table and chair, then a larger bedroom with a sliding glass door that faces the lake and a nice bathroom with a tub, shower, and double vanity.

"The pictures didn't do it justice," I say after he's shown me everything. Forgetting about Nick, who still hasn't reappeared, it really is perfect.

Mike tips his head back, scanning the place like he's seeing it again for the first time. "I'm glad you like it."

"I really do." There's something about the lake glimmering under the sunshine and the mountains in the distance that sparks a need to capture the feeling on paper.

"I'll leave you to get settled, but if you need anything, don't hesitate to text me or come up to the main house. If I'm not there, ask Nick."

Fat chance of that. I'm not asking Nick anything. In fact, I hope I don't see him for the rest of my time here. I, of course, can't tell Mike that.

"Thanks, but I don't want to bother either you or him." Not the entire truth, but still accurate.

All Mike says is, "You're no bother."

He opens the front door to go and smiles. "Ah, there he is now."

Nick comes to a stop on the entryway of the front door. The time apart did not make his heart grow fonder. I always hated that saying anyway.

"I see you found the key." His dry tone is breathless, jaw still shockingly tight. Looks painful. And kind of hot. He has a dimple in his chin, barely visible under a layer of dark facial hair. I always loved cleft chins, and he pulls it off better than most.

Surprise, surprise. I'm attracted to the jerk. My libido has no sense of self-preservation.

"Sorry about that, son. Thanks for checking." Mike glances to me. "We'll leave you to get settled. You have my cell number?"

I think for a moment, then nod. "Yes."

"Text me if you need anything, or feel free to ask Nick."

His son's eyes go comically wide for a fraction of a second, but Mike is watching me, and whatever he sees on my face makes him laugh.

"Don't let him fool you, he isn't so scary." Mike grins and leaves.

Scary isn't the word I'd use. Grumpy. Frustrating. Handsome.

Nick lingers in the doorway after his dad is gone.

"Don't worry. I don't plan on needing anything," I reassure him.

His jaw tightens again.

"Doesn't that hurt?"

"What?" he asks in such a sullen way that a small laugh escapes my lips.

"Grinding down on your molars like that? You're going to break a tooth."

I should have guessed my prodding him would only make him glare harder, but it still catches me off guard, and I giggle again.

"I'm glad you find this amusing."

"Look, I get it. You're not thrilled I'm here, but I really won't get in your way. My only plan is to work and sit out by the lake." I don't think he's prepared to hear my entire summer to-do list. He thinks I'm weird enough as is.

He nods, jaw relaxing a fraction. "Fine. Do you need anything?"

I fight a laugh. I bet that hurt him to ask.

"No," I say, then do think of something. "Actually, can you tell me how far it is to the hockey rink?"

"Fifteen minutes or so. Why?"

"I'm meeting my contact there tomorrow."

"At the rink?" The way he looks at me, you'd think I brought up smuggling body parts again.

"Yeah. I'm interviewing a hockey expert."

His brow furrows harder. I have the ridiculous urge to step forward and smooth out all the lines on his face. I wonder what he looks like without all that hot grumpiness. *Gasp.* Maybe he's only hot when he's scowling. Nah, this guy is hot in any scenario.

"I'm a romance author, and I'm editing a book . . ." I let my words trail off. "The hero of my book plays baseball, but my editor wants me to change it to hockey."

He continues to stare at me like he expects the words to make sense if he thinks about them hard enough. So I spell it out for him.

"I need help with some of the rules and terminology. I don't know sports puck stuff."

"Sports puck?" It comes out more like he's questioning the universe instead of me. Slowly, he tips his head back and looks up like he's praying to the gods or in deep concentration, then as if connecting the dots that I just very clearly laid out for him asks, "You're an author, and you came here to interview a *hockey expert* for your book?"

"Mhmm." He's literally just repeating my words.

"And you're meeting this *expert* at the hockey rink tomorrow?"

"Yes?" I say, but now it sounds like I'm the one questioning my plans. It's been a long day, and his grumpy aura is throwing me off.

"Who is your contact?"

"I can't remember. Your dad knows though. He set it up. You know what? Never mind. I can see you're very busy perfecting your resting grump face. I won't take up any more of your time."

He lowers his chin, fixing me with that weighty scowl, then does the most surprising thing yet—he laughs. It's not a happy sound, but a deep, rough chuckle that skates over my skin. He has dimples in both cheeks that are, in a word, disarming. "Good luck with that, Red."

Then he turns on his heel and marches back toward the house.

"Good luck with that?" I mumble, then louder, "Red? Seriously? How original!"

What an asshole. I slam the door, hopefully sealing out all the bad vibes. I'm determined to make this cabin my happy place for the next six weeks despite Nick, despite months of not writing, and every other thing stacked against me.

I can do this. I *have* to do this. This is my shot to prove to Doreen, Molly, myself, and everyone else that I have another great book in me.

I hold on to that hope as I sit on the couch and pull out my laptop. Once I navigate to my email, I find the one Molly sent over with the hockey expert's contact details and meeting information. Nick was no help, but who needs him?

My body flushes from head to toe, and I read the name twice, then a third time, hoping I'm seeing things.

"Nick Galaxy," I say in a whisper as I let my head fall back against the cool leather. The grumpy man I just promised not to bother is the one person I need to finish this book.

Chapter Five

NICK

"No. Stop. You're killing me." Travis leans on his hockey stick, head bowed, as he cackles so hard it shakes his entire body.

We've got the ice to ourselves and are hitting a few pucks before camp starts. He stands tall and bows his back, then throws his laughter into the air, noise echoing in the empty stands and rafters.

"I'm glad you find this funny."

"I can't believe you don't."

I grunt and fire another puck into the net. I have a hunch the burn of my muscles would be more satisfying if Trav wasn't getting so much enjoyment out of my misery.

"What'd he say when you told him you weren't going to let her interview you?" he asks when he gets himself under control.

"I didn't get a chance. He conveniently had Bingo last night and was gone before I got back from the cabin." He left a note on the counter: *Bingo. Don't wait up.* Like it was any other day, and he hadn't moved in some strange woman and offered up my time to help her, then left me to deal with it. And if there'd been any doubt that I was the contact she'd mentioned, he'd also scribbled, *Ruby is swinging by the rink at ten to ask you a few hockey questions.*

I left a note in response. One word. *No.*

"Ha!" He lets out one more bark of laughter. "Bingo. Mike kills me."

"He's killing me too," I mutter.

Travis trails off into quiet chuckles. "Is she at least our age?"

"We are not the same age," I say, firing another puck. Trav is five years younger, though admittedly, his life experiences make him feel like an old soul. A wild, old soul.

"You know what I mean."

"Yeah. Best I can tell. Mid to late twenties. Thirty, maybe."

"Married?"

I glower at him. "How the hell would I know that?"

"Nah. Mike wouldn't have moved her in if she were married."

My jaw drops, and my throat goes dry. "That's not what this is."

Trav lifts one brow.

Fuck. Is that what this is? My dad has made it his mission to play matchmaker in the past, but would he really go this far? It started about five years ago when Aidan was getting old enough that things felt more stable. Before then, I honestly could barely keep my head above water, so dating was the furthest thing from my mind. Slowly, my son started becoming more independent, we got into a routine, and about that time my dad started meddling. He turned every woman he met into a potential wife candidate for me.

"You sure?"

"No," I admit as my mind reels.

"Okay. Well, what does she look like?"

My skin pricks, and I shrug one shoulder. "I don't know."

He sighs. "Short? Tall? Cute? Nerdy?"

"She doesn't look like what you'd expect."

His gaze narrows. "Meaning?"

I know I've said too much when his lips part and he flashes a big, wolfish grin at me. I look away and line up another shot.

"She's hot," he says in a tone that mirrors Aidan's when he's really, truly, unabashedly excited about something. "Your dad moved in a hottie next door."

My grip on the stick tightens.

"Woooweee. Well, this changes everything." Travis circles around me.

"It changes nothing, and I didn't say she was hot. I only meant that she doesn't look like the stereotypical bookish nerdy type." Even as I say the words I know they aren't the complete truth. Ruby is gorgeous. Chaotic? Sure. Quirky? Absolutely. But she's also undoubtedly beautiful. The kind that takes your breath and makes you feel unsteady on your feet.

Which now that I think about it is exactly why Dad invited her here. The man is relentless.

"D-Low doesn't either, but he's the single nerdiest person I know," Travis says, pulling me from visions of Ruby and her long red hair and pouty lips.

True. Our teammate, Danny Marlowe, is covered in tattoos and loves trendy fashion labels. He also happens to have degrees in both aerospace engineering and math. People are always surprised that he's so smart, but you really can't judge a book by its cover. My lips twitch with a grin. Look at me making book jokes. Now I just have to turn the page and figure out how the hell to get rid of the woman.

"Is she your type or mine?" he asks.

"What?"

"You tend to go for the nice, wholesome girl-next-door type."

My brows lift, and my mouth curves in amusement. I didn't realize I had a type, but that doesn't sound so horrible.

"As opposed to the mean girls you date?"

"They're not *always* mean. Brittney was an outlier. I was blinded by the septum piercing. I freaking love a nose ring." He groans like he's picturing a woman with one right now. "My type is more free spirit, while you prefer someone less . . . complicated."

I will say one thing about Trav. He knows what he wants, and he isn't afraid to go after it. Maybe my type is as boring as he makes it sound, but if so that's because most of the time, dating feels like too much effort to me. It isn't like I never hook up, but I prefer to do it when traveling or while Aidan is with his mom. It keeps all that separate from my real life.

"So . . ." Trav leans on his stick with both hands. "Free spirit or girl next door?"

"I don't know. She's just . . ." *Chaos.*

"It's fine. I'll swing by and check her out myself. What kind of book is she writing anyway? Do you think D-Low's read any of her stuff?"

"No."

"No, he hasn't read her?"

"No, you cannot check her out." I carefully avoid telling him what she writes because Trav would never let me live that down. He'd see it as some sort of sign. My dad moved a romance author in next door. That's ripe for jokes. And we both have long contracts with no-trade clauses.

"Why not?" His voice climbs.

"She promised to stay out of my way, so I'm going to extend the same to her." If I don't see or talk to her, then perhaps I can pretend like she doesn't exist. I wonder what she did when she found out her contact is me. Hopefully my dad handled it and she's on her way back to wherever she came from.

"I mean, if you're not going to ask her out, then I might."

I glower at him, but he just laughs at my predicament. Fucker.

"Kidding."

He's not.

"She's not hot," I say because on the off chance she's still there, I cannot have him showing up at my place, and if I tell him that she is, he absolutely, one hundred percent, will. Tonight. Probably as soon as we finish here.

"Fine. Fine." With a shake of his head, he says, "But I'll happily trade places with you. Eventually one of the women your dad hooks you up with has to be hot."

The slam of a door, followed by voices, alerts us to the arrival of our first campers for the day. Trav and I are both working a kids' hockey camp that the team puts on every summer. For the week, we'll be teaching children ages five through twelve a variety of skills based on their age and levels.

It's the second year I've done the camp, and I enjoyed it more than I expected last time. When Aidan was born, I knew next to nothing about kids. And even after, I still wasn't really a kid person. I love *my* kid, but I never thought about having more or coaching them.

"Done," I say as I skate to the edge of the ice. Trav falls into stride next to me. "You can come live at my house for the next six weeks, and Aidan and I will move into yours."

"Mike and I would have a blast. I think I could get behind a meddling parent setting me up with hot women. I can assure you it's better than the absent kind."

A hint of guilt stabs me between the ribs. He doesn't talk about his family much, but he's said enough for me to know they aren't a part of his life. My dad drives me crazy, but he's always been there when I needed him.

"That's what everyone says until their dad is inviting your pediatrician to Thanksgiving dinner," I mutter, then crack a smile because as uncomfortable as it was at the time, it is funny to think about now. "I had to find Aidan a new doctor."

Trav's lips pull up on one side of his mouth. "Better than the time he ran a wanted ad in the newspaper."

I shudder at the memory of that one. It still isn't funny. In fact, embarrassment heats the back of my neck like it's happening to me all over again. Apparently, back in his day people did that kind of thing all the time. I'm not sure I believe that, but even if it's true, it's not something people do now. I had to change my phone number and outright lie to a sports journalist who questioned me about it. *"No, I am not the Nick Galaxy looking for love with a beautiful, kind woman who likes kids and hockey."*

"Besides, you've already dated all the women in Moonshot." I let my first true smile of the day loosen. "Who would he possibly set you up with?"

"Except one." He winks, not at all bothered by my ribbing him. Though, it's true. I don't date anyone, and he dates everyone. Maybe us swapping houses is the perfect scenario.

We step off to greet the first of the kids trickling in. Their excitement is written all over their faces. Warmth spreads through me when I spot one particular face in the crowd.

Aidan grins as he approaches me. He spent the past week with his mom while I was in Dallas, and I missed the hell out of him.

"Hey." I place a gloved hand on top of his head. "Did you get taller?"

"No," he says, ducking away from my hand.

"You sure?" I pull him into a quick hug. "Missed you. Did you have fun with your mom?"

"Yeah. I guess so." He shrugs one shoulder.

"Little G!" Trav greets my son. "What's up, my dude? Ready to play some hockey?"

"Yeah." Aidan nods his head with enthusiasm. I'm glad that hockey is still one thing we both love.

The first hour of camp is spent on introductions, expectations of the week, and grouping the kids off by age. Trav takes the oldest group, including Aidan; the Moonshot assistant coach Lori takes the middle; and I work with the youngest. We'll switch around today, and through the week, but I like the excitement and energy of the five- and six-year-olds. Their skating levels will vary, and that's often the biggest factor in the young group. Most have skated with their families during the winter a time or two, so they're at least a little comfortable, but I have one little girl who has already told me this will be her first time.

We start off the ice. I lead my kiddos to the strength and training room.

"Whoa," they all exclaim, little heads tipping back as they stare at the rows of equipment and framed pictures on the wall of players and coaches. There's a board of pictures taken by the staff here while we were traveling or hanging out, casual, behind-the-scenes moments. For other people, it's a cool glimpse of players outside of the uniform. For us, it's a reminder that this is a job. A fun, amazing job but outside of that we're friends, we're teammates, we're people with families and lives outside of the jersey.

"What's that?" one little girl asks as she points to a bulletin board on one wall. She's missing her front two teeth. I remember when Aidan lost his. There's nothing cuter than a kid without their teeth. Not so cute on grown men playing hockey. I've been fortunate in that area, and the team dentist helps.

"Those are quotes left behind by all the coaches that have ever worked here," I say, then tip my head. "You can go read them if you want."

The kids all run at once. I follow behind them, standing at the back of the group.

"What do they say?" another kid asks. He's the tallest of the kids, almost awkward with his lanky arms and legs.

Right. I forget that most of them can't read yet. I pick a couple of my favorites and read them, but they're bored quickly and on to the next thing.

For a lot of these kids, the ones that care less about hockey and more about the adventure of it all, the coolest part of this week is getting the behind-the-scenes look at the facilities. I realize for some of them it's like going to a theme park or a museum. I do my best to keep them corralled while they explore the room for a few minutes before rounding them back up to stretch and warm up before getting on the ice.

I learn their names and ask each of them to tell me one thing they want to do this week at camp. Their answers vary from meeting Conrad Shepard, one of our star defensemen, to learning a slap shot, to lunchtime. Their honesty, the purity and courage to say whatever is on their mind has me feeling more relaxed than I have in days, maybe weeks. Beth, Aidan's mom, and I split custody fifty-fifty. The time when Aidan is with his mom is important for him and her, but man does it suck.

Once the kids have stretched, I take them to the locker room where again they spend several minutes scoping out the space, finding all their favorite players' lockers, and admiring the giant Moonshot logo on the ceiling.

I go to my cubby where the equipment manager has laid out my gear for me. I show them my stick and pads, my helmet, all of which they pass around with awe-filled expressions.

"All right. You guys ready to get in your gear?" I ask them.

Their heads can't nod fast enough.

"Okay, but first, I think you need these." I open the flaps of a box sitting on the bench and pull out jerseys for each of them.

The gasps and eagerness as they lunge forward to take one makes me chuckle. It's a major difference between this group and the older kids. Aidan will be excited to get one, even though he has plenty of Moonshot merch, but he and his peers won't be nearly this unabashed in their excitement.

"I'm number eighty-eight like Travis Bennett," one boy proclaims proudly as he holds it up.

"I want number ninety-one. Danny Marlowe is so fast." Another kid rummages through to find his favorite player. There's nothing more heartwarming than seeing the kids so pumped about donning their hero's jersey.

As soon as they've each picked one, we head back out to the main rink. I lead the younger kids to the area where they left their gear and instruct them to suit up. I find Aidan on the ice, already suited up in his jersey. It's mine, which makes me smile, even though he probably just picked it because we share a name.

Travis is leading his group through a warm-up drill on one side of the ice. When he sees me, he yells out a few more directions to the kids, then skates over to me. "Ready to have a little fun, Galaxy?"

"Yeah." I chuckle, then notice one of the parents is approaching me. Generally, the younger kids' parents stick around the first day, or at least for the first few hours, to make sure their child is going to be okay. Most of them sit quietly in the reserved section of the stands we rope off for them to view camp, but there are always a couple that think they need to come down and help out, give their kid a pep talk or a snack.

I glance back at Trav. "Can you get them out on the ice?"

He gives me a sympathetic glance as he also notices the mom on her way with a water bottle in one hand and a baggie of orange crackers in the other. "Yeah. No prob."

I raise my voice so the kids can hear me over the noise. "Once you're all set, my friend Travis will lead you out onto the ice. If it's your first time or you're feeling uneasy, then grab one of the skating aids."

Once I've given them their instructions, I walk around them to the mom on her way over. She's at least hesitant enough to hang back.

"Hi," she says cheerily when I get within a few feet of her. "I forgot to give these to Annabelle. And I also wanted to make sure she got her skates laced up right. She still struggles to tie her shoes."

There's a clear nervousness about the woman that mirrors the cute little redhead. Annabelle already told me she hasn't skated before, so I understand where her mom is coming from, and I can tell her intentions are good. It can be hard to stand by helplessly and watch your kid do something new and out of their comfort zone.

"I'm Nick." I hold out a hand to her.

"Kelly." She sets the crackers on top of the water bottle and shakes my hand. "And gosh. I know who you are. We're big fans in my family. My parents have season tickets. It's just, Annabelle is my sweet, accident-prone child. She hasn't really done any sports. Except a short stint in gymnastics that ended with both her and her coach in tears."

I smile and let out a small laugh. "Learning a new sport can be hard and stressful, but I promise we'll check all their gear before they get on the ice and do our best to make sure she has a good time."

She nods but doesn't say anything, and I can tell my words haven't really eased her fears. It might just be that she needs to see Annabelle conquer hockey as much as her daughter does.

"And I can take that for her." I glance at the water and snack she's holding.

"Oh, okay." She gives them to me, then wrings her hands in front of her.

"She can do this," I say. Not every kid walks out of camp a superstar, but none have left without being able to skate marginally well or hit a puck into the goal (at least at close range).

She nods again, and I offer one more smile before I head back. Annabelle is at the back of the line. She has a look of fear on her face, but she holds her head high as the kids step forward one by one. Trav checks all of them over before giving them the okay to enter the ice. We have other coaches this week assisting, so there are plenty of bodies to make sure each camper has someone to help, if needed.

I put Annabelle's snack with the rest of the kids' stuff, then stop next to her at the back of the line. She glances over and attempts to smile.

"Nervous?" I ask.

She shakes her head adamantly. Her red hair is pulled back in a ponytail, but a few strands fall around her face.

"It's okay if you are. I was terrified the first time I went skating."

"You were?" she asks, disbelief rampant in her tone.

"Mhmm." I squat down so I'm at eye level with her. Checking her gear over and adjusting as needed, I say, "My dad told me the most important thing to remember was that everybody falls."

She giggles, a small, anxious sound.

"Don't be afraid of it. Try to relax and not worry about going down. The more you fall, the more you get up, and the faster you'll get the hang of it." They are words I've had to repeat to myself a lot over the years. Especially lately.

Ever since my shoulder surgery, stepping out onto the ice makes me uneasy. It wasn't the first and won't be the last time I get hurt playing hockey, but for some reason this one really messed with my head. It's not so bad when I'm shooting around or helping the kids, but it's going to be a long journey to gearing up and playing full contact without worrying that I'm one injury away from retirement.

"What if I get hurt?" Her voice is small, and my gut twists as her fears mirror my own.

"That's what all this padding is for." I tighten the strap of her helmet under her chin and then tap the top of it lightly. It's her turn, so I stand and hope I've made her less nervous instead of more. I've been a parent long enough to know my pep talks aren't always awesome.

"Ready to fall down?" I ask her, but maybe I'm talking to myself a little too.

She grins, flashing that gap in the front. I go ahead of her and then watch as she takes her first tentative step. She doesn't let go of the wall until I slide a skating aid in front of her. The sturdy plastic aid is about three feet tall and a couple feet wide with handles to grip on to. It's essentially a walker that glides over the ice, keeping the kids upright while they get their footing.

It's hard to remember what it's like to learn to skate. I've been doing it so long that it feels so natural, but I give her, and the rest of the kids, the same basic instructions I've heard time and again, "Start with small steps, alternate lifting one foot then the other, glide, push off with one skate, feel the shift of weight."

Slowly they each get comfortable. Even Annabelle. The first time she falls, she looks over at me. Tears well in her eyes, but she picks herself up quickly.

By the time we take our first break, nerves have turned to excitement and an eagerness for more. While they snack, they sit on the benches, the lights dim, and the Jumbotron plays a flashy, pump-up video they run at the beginning of every home game.

Travis and I stand off the ice, taking our own quick breather.

"Pretty good group this year," he says.

I nod, loving how good it feels to be here. When everything else in life has felt hard or uncertain, hockey has always been there. I want to give these kids that same feeling.

"Aidan has improved a lot since I last saw him."

"Yeah. He's been working hard since he moved up to play with the older kids."

"That's great. Is he going to . . ." Travis's words trail off, or at least I don't hear them, as a flash of red catches my eye.

The hairs on the back of my neck stand at attention, and my body tenses as Ruby Madison stands ten feet away in a yellow dress with little straps that are tied in bows at her shoulders. Her hair is in a braid that hangs down her back, and she has her backpack looped over one arm.

"No," I say, and I'm not sure what I'm answering. No, I am not noticing how hot she is—*thanks a lot, Trav*. No, I don't want her here. No, I am not going to walk over and repeat myself that I don't want to be interviewed. Surely, she's pieced it together by now that I'm her contact.

"Holy Hot Mom," Travis says when he catches sight of the object of my attention.

I glare, though not directly at him, because I don't want to look away from Ruby.

"She's not a mom," I say, "or at least not a mom of one of these kids."

I do finally look at him. His brow furrows, and then ever so slowly I watch understanding dawn on his face.

"Nicholas Michael Galaxy," he says, voice filled with humor. "You dirty fucking liar."

Chapter Six

RUBY

Nick Galaxy. Six feet, two inches tall. Thirty-one years old. Captain of the Montana Moonshot. Wears jersey number thirteen. Previously played for Chicago and then, most recently, the Wildcats. Last season he led the Moonshot in . . . some stats that I can't remember but sounded very impressive.

I spent the morning looking him up, arming myself with information and preparing to face him again. I was prepared, in theory, but my memory had dulled the sharp edges of his personality. You know how some people walk around like they don't have a care in the world? Nick is the opposite. It seems like everything bothers him. Mostly, me.

His dark hair is messy, like he's been running his fingers through it or perhaps playing hockey. Don't they usually wear helmets? And pads? Maybe they only wear those sometimes, like when they're going to fight it out, WrestleMania style.

He's in black athletic pants eerily similar to the ones he had on yesterday and a light purple Moonshot Hockey T-shirt.

I'm taking all this in as he skates toward me. He looks good, and he looks . . . irritated at my presence. He knew last night that *he* was my contact as I babbled on about meeting a hockey expert at the rink today. I was certain of that even before Mike came over this morning to apologize and tell me Nick needed a few days to come around to the idea.

As a fellow optimist, I appreciate his sunny outlook, but I can't afford to wait and see. So, here I am. I couldn't sit around and do nothing. I couldn't not try. I need him. I don't relish the idea of begging, but I'm not above it either.

I had not predicted the rink to be filled with children when I got in my lime-green MINI Cooper and drove over, but it's too late to go back now. Nick's already seen me.

"Hi." I lift a hand in a wave as he gets closer.

His mouth moves in what I think might be an attempted polite sort of smile before he says, "What are you doing here?"

"Okay, right to it." No *"Hello, Ruby. Good to see you. Sorry I was a jackass yesterday."*

Man, he's grumpy. It must be exhausting. All that stomping and jaw clenching.

"Didn't my dad give you the message?" A muscle in his cheek flexes, and one dimple appears. It's so disorienting that I don't respond quickly enough, and Nick adds, "I can't help you. I'm sorry."

He doesn't sound sorry.

I break out of my dimple-induced haze as it disappears. The one in his jaw remains, though less visible today since he still hasn't shaved.

"Oh no, he did," I say. I glance back at the kids on the ice. They look adorable out there, all padded up like Randy in *A Christmas Story*. They're only missing the long scarf covering their head and face.

What I wouldn't give for a scarf right about now. If I had realized how cold it was going to be (which I absolutely should have since ice tends to be, well, cold), I would have dressed warmer. I'm not sure I've been good and truly warm since I stepped onto the plane in Arizona.

"Then, why are you here?"

It's not a perfect opening to launch into my well-rehearsed speech that ended with me somehow convincing him to help me, but here goes nothing.

"I know that you said no to being interviewed, but I was wondering—"

"No." He doesn't say the word unkindly, but it's unyielding.

"At least let me finish asking the question before you shoot it down. What if I was going to offer to shine your skates or something?" I wave my hand toward his feet.

"You came here to ask me if you could shine my skates?" One dark brow rises in challenge.

"Well, no, but . . ." I feel eyes on us and glance over to see a group of women, moms of kids on the ice I'd bet, staring in our direction. I'm aware they're probably staring at him because—why wouldn't they? He's nice to look at . . . from far away where he can't glare directly at you.

"I need to get back to the kids," Nick says. "So if you want to ask me something else, do it fast."

"Are you coaching some kind of camp?"

He looks at me like he knows I'm stalling and finds it . . . yep, you guessed it, annoying. "Yeah. The team holds a couple of these every summer for local kids."

"That's really cool, and you seem like a good coach."

"You got that in the two seconds you saw me on the ice?"

I roll my eyes. "Fine. I have no idea, but you weren't glaring at them, so it was a definite improvement."

His lips twitch with amusement. "They were invited."

"Ooooh, burn," I mock, laughing lightly.

He crosses his arms over his chest, which—whoa—the pose really does something for his biceps.

"What do you want, Red?" His eyes are a dark green that really pops when he's grinning.

He's purposely goading me so I'll leave, but instead, it fires me up.

Focus, Ruby. You can think about how hot the grumpy hockey player is later.

I square my shoulders and stand taller. "I am sorry about yesterday. You weren't expecting me, and I'm sure it was a lot to take in."

Silence. He doesn't confirm or deny, but he also doesn't stop giving me his attention.

"I have just a few questions—"

"I don't do interviews," he clips.

He's said that twice now. I thought it was an offhand comment the first time, but now I suspect there's something there. "Why not?"

"I don't like people in my business."

A laugh bubbles in my chest and slips free. It's a mixture of exhaustion from the past two days and honestly the past two years, disbelief that this man is so insufferable, and anger because yet another thing in my career is teetering toward disaster, and I am sick of it. This is supposed to be my chance to turn things around. A summer to save my career and my life. And no one is getting in the way of it. Not even this hot, grumpy hockey player.

"I don't care about your business!" I say, exasperated and too loudly. "I just need to understand the basic rules of hockey so I can fix my book, reboot my career, and prove the whole world wrong."

My outburst catches him by surprise, judging by his lack of reply. I take a deep breath.

"It's not information about *you* that I would be looking for. Think of it as research not an interview."

He doesn't immediately say no, so I keep going.

"It shouldn't take long," I promise, which is more hope than truth. I've never tried to swap out details like this after the book was written, but how hard could it be? "I just need the basics."

"The basics of hockey?" he asks as if still trying to make sense of it all.

"Enough to convincingly write a story about a guy who plays hockey." Then with a hand wave. "His job is a minor part of the story."

I give him my biggest, best smile, hoping it silently communicates how easy and breezy this can go. I'll ask him a few questions, then we'll go our separate ways. No big deal.

"I'm sorry you came all this way for nothing." This time there is a hint of sincere apology in his voice.

"Please?" I said I wasn't above begging, but it still pains me to do it. "I came to Moonshot because I need help. I have six weeks to do the research I need and edit my book. If I don't . . ." I can't bring myself to finish that sentence. I'm not even sure what will happen if I fail. I guess I'll lose the contract with Doreen and have to repay the very large advance, and the likelihood that anyone else will want to buy a book from me in the future will drastically reduce. That is if I can ever bring myself to write another book. So much rides on this, but I can't put it all on him. This is my mess.

"It's important to me. I love my job, and I am . . . struggling." The truth hurts to admit. Especially to him.

His jaw works back and forth, and he stares at me as if considering the offer. Holy shit, is he really considering it?

My heart pounds, hopefulness swirling inside me. I almost add another please, for good measure, but I'm afraid it'll hurt my chances instead of helping.

"All I'm asking for is a day or two of your time. Then if you really want me gone, I'll find somewhere else to stay while I edit my book."

"Hey," a guy on the ice says to Nick then flashes me a smile. "Sorry to interrupt."

His gaze slides back to Nick. "Lori was asking if you could help on the two-on-two drills."

"I'll be right there," Nick says, letting his arms fall to his sides.

I give them both a closed-mouth smile as the hope I was just feeling vanishes. He's busy, and I shouldn't have come.

The guy nods, then glances from Nick to me again. "I could swap with you, if you want." He sends the next question to me. "Anything I can help you with?"

There's something in the guy's tone and smile that is teasing, though I can't figure out why.

"No thanks. I was just leaving." I need to call Molly, buy myself a coffee the size of my head, and binge the newest episode of *Hookup Island* while I figure out what to do next.

Nick's grumpy glare returns, this time aimed at his friend.

"Wow, so it's not just at me," I mutter, realizing too late I've said the words out loud. My face heats. "Sorry. That was supposed to be an inside thought."

The other guy laughs, freely and loudly. "I love inside thoughts, and trust me, he gives that look to everyone."

"Good to know."

"I'm Travis."

"Ruby."

"Nice to meet you, Ruby. I've heard a lot about you."

"You have?" I look at Nick. I cannot imagine what he might have said. *I met this girl at the airport who joked about transporting a dead body, and then she showed up at my house. Turns out my dad rented the cabin to her and promised her, without my knowledge, she could interview me.*

"I'm his best friend."

"Only friend?"

Travis lets out another loud laugh. "I like you."

"Ignore him," Nick says to me. "Everyone else does."

"I'm wounded," Travis fires back with a playfulness that even eases the lines on Nick's face.

I think I like him too.

"We should grab a drink sometime and commiserate over his moodiness," Travis says.

I have no idea how to respond, and can't tell if he's hitting on me or joking around. Something tells me both.

"Thanks, but I'm heading out of town today."

"Bummer," he says.

"Okay." Nick motions with his hand for Travis like he's shooing him away. "Don't you have a camp to run? Children to corrupt?"

Travis skates backward. "Nice to meet you, Ruby."

"Thanks. You too."

Before he turns, Travis says to his friend, "Much better than the wanted ad."

Nick sighs and says some things under his breath. I only catch the words "pain in my ass," and I genuinely have no idea if he means me or Travis.

"Wanted ad?" I ask.

His mouth falls in a straight line as his dark green eyes lock on me. "I appreciate that my dad put you in a weird position too, but I'm coaching this camp all week."

"Right." I stare out at the adorable kids, then up to where the parents are seated. And then it hits me. I am at a hockey camp. This is literally where kids come to learn hockey.

I have been so caught up in doing my research a certain way, but this could work. And bonus points for avoiding the grumpy hockey player. Or mostly avoiding him. He can't glare directly at me while teaching them, right?

"Well, thanks anyway," I say when what I really mean is thanks for nothing.

I tighten my hold on my backpack and start toward the stairs.

"Where are you going?" Nick calls after me.

"To learn hockey."

He's back to glowering. "I just said—"

"I know. You're busy. Got it. Don't worry. I won't ask you a thing. I'll just sit quietly and observe with the other spectators. Maybe I'll pick it up by osmosis. I mean, how hard could it be?"

Chapter Seven

RUBY

I do not learn hockey by osmosis. At least not in the first hour.

I *do* turn into an ice block. It is so freaking cold in here. My arms and legs are covered in goose bumps. It's not the first time I've suffered for my art, and certainly won't be the last.

I'm seated a few rows up, off to the side of a group of moms. I thought maybe they'd chat hockey things that might be helpful in my research. Instead, they've spent most of the sixty minutes or so I've been sitting here talking about their kids' many summer activities. Outside of hockey camp, there's swim team, dance class, soccer, piano, karate—these moms are navigating CEO-level schedules. I'm exhausted for them—the moms *and* the kids.

One woman sits by herself on my other side with a book in her lap. She glances up occasionally to watch her child, then goes right back to reading. Some dads are here too. They're more intent on the action down on the ice. They call out things like "Move your feet, Billy!" and "Two hands on the stick," and "Shoot!" and the most confusing of all "Where's the D?" I'm not sure who or what "D" is, but one particular man is very adamant that his kid, Henry, find it.

I've been scribbling things into a notebook, but most of it is nonsense. This was perhaps not my best laid plan. Maybe I should start with some basic edits, like changing the word baseball to hockey in all one hundred and seventy-three instances in the manuscript.

As I reach for my laptop, I glance down at the ice. Nick glides across the rink, smooth and almost graceful. He comes to a stop in front of a little girl with hair redder than mine sticking out around her helmet. She's standing next to the wall, inching around the perimeter, clutching on to a bright-yellow walker-looking device that some of the kids are using to keep them upright.

Nick skates backward slowly as she inches forward. He bends his knees as he speaks to her, moving his hands around to punctuate whatever he's saying.

She nods, then tries to mimic his actions. It's pretty cute, her not him, and makes me think about my niece Greer. She's about the same age as these kids, sassy and adorable, and one of my favorite humans ever. The only good thing about possibly heading back to Arizona sooner than planned is seeing her. It's easier to stay in touch with my sister and the rest of the family when I travel, but Greer tends to get distracted on video or phone calls, and the texts she sends from Olivia's phone are ninety percent emojis.

While I do a find-and-replace in my book, I continually catch myself glancing back at the ice. The kids are in two groups on either side of the rink. The little ones are still learning to skate with Nick while Travis and a blond woman are with the older ones leading them through complicated-looking drills. Right now, they're sprinting (is it still called sprinting when you're wearing skates?) around orange cones and shooting discs into a large basket. It's impressive, but my attention keeps moving back to the littlest group. Or more specifically to Nick.

He's back with the redheaded girl. She places her yellow walker next to the wall and slowly inches away from it. She's unsteady, waving her arms around for balance. Nick offers her his hand, and she lunges for him, taking it, then wrapping her little body around his right forearm. It's a miracle neither of them goes down.

Nick is patient as he allows her to regain her footing. Once she does, he skates back, continuing to hold her hands while she gets the hang of it. He lets go of one hand, then the other. She's still wobbly, but she's grinning now. At least until she falls. He doesn't help her get up, but stays there, encouraging her. I'd been trying to be nice when I told him he was a good coach, but it looks like I was right.

My phone pings loudly, and I give the woman with the book an apologetic glance as I switch it to vibrate and then open the text from Molly. This morning I filled her in on the situation—namely that our hockey expert was not expecting me. I left out a lot of details, including that he was a jerk. It would only make her feel worse.

Molly: Hi! Checking in. How are you? I'm so sorry about all this. I'm making some calls to see if there's anyone else available on short notice. It's the off-season so a lot of players and coaches are on vacation. Hang tight. I will figure this out.

Poor Molly. The hot, grumpy hockey player has ruined her day too.

I thank her, then put my phone away and settle back in with my laptop. I pull up my browser and do a search for hockey terms and rules. A knot forms in my chest, and I'm transported back to my college French class, helplessly deciphering words and phrases. I feel hopeless, and I *really* hate that feeling.

A whistle blows down on the ice, and the kids are ushered off to benches where they drink water and eat snacks while the coaches talk with them. Nick stands next to the younger group while Travis and the blond woman demonstrate something.

Travis is cute. He has dark brown hair like Nick, but his is longer and wavier, and he's continually pushing it out of his eyes. Everything about him is looser and more carefree. Even the way Nick stands, arms crossed over his chest, back rigid, screams grumpy and inaccessible.

The woman is tall and athletic. She's in black leggings that show off toned legs and a butt that I'd kill for. Her hair is pulled up into a high ponytail, ends curled, and she has on a headband that covers her ears. She's Sporty Spice. Gorgeous and athletic. I watch Nick to see how he interacts with her. I wonder if she's his type. Sporty people dig other sporty people, right? It makes sense. Book people tend to like other book people. My last two boyfriends had been involved in the publishing world. The first one was an editor for a young adult publisher that I met at a book signing. He was wonderful, but three months in, he accepted a job in Australia and the time difference became too hard. One of us was always sleeping, and a relationship can't be sustained on texts alone—or at least ours couldn't.

The second was a fellow author. Decidedly not wonderful. Biggest asshole in the world? Possibly. Now that I think about it, I might want to venture out of my usual type.

"Hi." The woman with the book speaks quietly. "I'm so sorry to bother you."

"It's no problem." I close my laptop to give her my attention. It's then that I notice she's closed her book as well. The front cover catches my eye, and all the air leaves my lungs in a whoosh. White cover, with red foil details highlighting the title: *Becoming Alaric.*

My stare bounces around the familiar book cover, then lingers on the name—one that's been prominent in news headlines across the globe for months. Matthew Rose.

His real name is Matthew Rosenthyme, but I'd known him as just Matt. Sometimes Matty.

We met at a writers conference. He'd just published his debut novel and was struggling to find his voice and his audience. He was hungry to be successful but also had this confidence about him that I found dazzling. Instead of ducking in corners and avoiding eye contact like most struggling authors, he had this unwavering belief in himself that he would get there. And I guess he was right.

I was coming off my biggest book yet and still felt like an imposter. My friend Lily had to miss the event, so I was alone and seriously regretting not opting for the virtual option where I could have been sitting at home in my pajamas. I'm not a strict introvert, but I hate initiating conversations with people I don't know in situations where it feels like everyone is already grouped off.

I noticed Matt within the first hour of arriving. Tall, fit, a little preppy. He was alone too but looked perfectly at ease about it, flashing smiles and hellos everywhere he went. On day two, our paths finally crossed. We were at the hotel bar after a long, boring talk on legal issues for authors—copyrights, nondisclosure agreements, and contracts. All very important things but not particularly compelling. Matt was funny and self-assured, and that made me feel a little bit less like an imposter.

One article said he had the appeal of a Grisham or a Patterson and the looks of a Hemsworth or an Affleck. Proof that you shouldn't trust a pretty face. That last part is mine, not the journalist's, but only because they don't know what an asshole he is in real life.

The woman with the book stares at me like she asked me a question. Shit. I blink away the memories and tamp down the uneasy feeling swirling in my gut as I force a smile back at her. "Sorry. What did you say?"

"I wondered if you know what time camp ends?"

I shake my head. "No, I don't."

I avert my gaze back to the ice and will myself to get it together. I feel her stare linger a moment before she turns back around and opens her book again. I'm sure she thinks I'm rude, but it's all I can do to breathe and not cry.

Nick picks this particular moment to look up, and we lock eyes. His expression instantly morphs into the glower. All the optimism and determination I walked in here with evaporates.

Fuck it. I don't need this. I can google hockey shit in Arizona far away from this prick.

I pack up my laptop and notebook and head down the stairs. I'm rounding a corner when Nick calls out to me.

"Red!"

I swivel around so quickly, my braid flips dramatically over my shoulder and into my face. I brush it back with one hand, seething. "My name is not Red. It's *Ruby*."

For one moment he looks stunned at my outburst, then his usual bored stare returns.

"Where are you going?"

"I'm leaving. You win." My voice wavers. Dammit. I really don't want to cry in front of this guy.

"Osmosis didn't work?" he asks dryly.

I glower back at him, then stomp forward. He's in his skates but standing on some sort of rubber mat just off the ice. I march right up to him, close enough that I could poke him in his stupid, broad chest. Warmth radiates off him, reminding me how cold I am.

"I get that your dad blindsided you with this whole thing, but I was blindsided too. At least you didn't travel thousands of miles only to find out the man holding your career in his hands is the world's biggest jerk. Would it really be so awful to answer a few stupid questions? Well, guess what? I don't need you. There are plenty of people out there who can help me and do it without being such an asshole."

My chest heaves as I get out the last part. Plenty might be a stretch, but there has to be at least one person willing to help me, right? If there is, I know Molly will find them.

His jaw works back and forth. It's my cue to leave, but the crash of adrenaline is washing over me, and I am exhausted.

"One hour," he says, crossing his arms over his chest. "Camp is over at five. As soon as the kids are gone, you can ask me your questions. Then, we're square."

My muddled brain works entirely too hard to process his words.

"Wait. *Now* you're going to help me?"

He turns, giving me his back as he steps back onto the ice. Then he pauses and looks at me.

"Why?" I ask.

His lips curve down. "Beats the hell out of me."

I'm so cold, I'm numb. My butt hurts from sitting on the bleachers, and my stomach is growling mercilessly.

I spend the time waiting for Nick sitting back in the stands with the parents. I alternate between watching Nick and the kids on the ice, editing my book, and going over my questions to ask him.

I thought I was going to have plenty of time to get everything I needed, so I whittle the list down to what I think are the most important things. While I work, I sneak glances at the woman next to me. She's nearly finished the book now. "A gripping page-turner," one headline boasted. "You won't be able to put it down," another said. I hate that they were right. And I really don't like the way hating someone this much makes me feel. I'm not cut out for it. I love people, and I like to think they're generally good. I might hate that he's made me question that more than anything else.

Three hours later, the kids are finally done. I can no longer feel my fingers and have taken to sitting on them.

Nick changes out of his skates into regular shoes and helps corral the children to their parents. He accepts handshakes from the men and smiles politely back at the women who thank him.

Once they're all gone, he makes his way to me. My pulse picks up speed as he takes the seat next to me. He smells like the ice and a hint of something woodsy and masculine.

"Hi." I reach for my laptop, open it, then tilt my screen down so he can't read it. It isn't personal. I have a hard time letting anyone read my words until I'm finished with a story. It's too messy. Too rough.

"I have exactly one hour." He rests his hands on his legs, drawing my attention to his thighs. They're big, straining the fabric in a way that makes my pulse pick up speed. Attracted to someone's muscular thighs . . . that's a new one for me.

I blink back my focus and angle myself so I'm facing him with my computer still on my lap. "Great. Should I jump into the questions?"

He nods.

"Okay." I read the first one. "Can you walk me through a typical hockey game?"

He blinks.

"Is that not what it's called?" I glance back at my notes. "Is it called a match or something?"

"No. It's a game, but . . ." He seems to struggle choosing his words. "There isn't really a typical way it goes. It varies based on so many factors."

"Okay, then let's just go through the last one you played."

"You want me to describe in detail an entire hockey game?"

I can feel the heat in my cheeks and the tightening of my chest as my blood pressure rises. Is he trying to make this more painful or does he just frustrate me that easily?

One hour, I remind myself.

"I'm trying to get a feel for what happens. I know there's a disc and you try to get it in the basket by whacking it with your stick, but I'm a little lost on everything else." My lips are so cold that even talking feels weird.

He stares at me, unspeaking, for several long moments, then opens his mouth as if to speak, but before he does, a shiver racks my entire body. I narrowly save my laptop from crashing to the floor.

"Are they going to turn the heat up in here now that the kids are done?" I ask.

He tilts his head to the side, then slowly his gaze moves over me. "You're cold."

Not a question. A statement.

"Freezing."

"It is an ice rink."

"Yes, well, I packed for summer."

He stands like he's going to leave, and I have a moment of panic that he's changed his mind about helping me.

"Come on." He tips his head to indicate I should follow.

I grab all my things and stand. My butt tingles, and my legs protest the movement. I am so cold I don't think I'll ever be warm again.

"Where are we going?"

"Somewhere you won't turn into an icicle."

Chapter Eight

RUBY

"Hey, Champ," a woman greets Nick as we enter the restaurant together. Her gaze goes to me, and I get a far less enthusiastic, "Welcome in."

We're at a place down the street from the rink. It felt so good to walk outside in the sunshine I almost didn't want to go inside another air-conditioned building, but it's not nearly as chilly in here as the rink.

"Why did she call you Champ?"

He shrugs.

"Some kind of nickname?"

"Something like that."

Is he embarrassed? It's hard to read any emotion on his face.

"I can think of a lot worse nicknames than Champ," I say, thinking of all the terrible things people called me over the years as we sit in a booth in the back corner.

He quirks a brow in a silent challenge. I sit forward and place my elbows on the table.

"Red, for starters."

His lips quirk with a smile, and one of his dimples peeks out.

"Then there's Big Red, Carrot Top, Ginger, Firecracker—"

"I like that one. Suits you."

I don't know if that's a compliment or an insult, and I don't stop to think about it.

"Why are redheads the only ones tormented for their hair color?" I ask.

"I'm not sure." His gaze flicks up to my hair, then slowly moves down as if truly examining my face for the first time.

Goose bumps dot my skin, and I shiver, but this time not because of the temperature.

"Still cold?" he asks, quirking that damn brow again like there might be something wrong with me.

I nod. "Since I arrived. Does it get warmer here later in the summer?"

He shrugs. "Sometimes."

There are no straight answers with this guy.

The same woman who greeted us when we walked in arrives at the end of our table with two drinks and menus tucked under one arm. Her nametag reads Annie.

"Iced tea, no sugar," she says as she sets one glass in front of Nick. Then she looks to me as she sets the other down. "Here's a water. Do you want anything else?"

"Water is fine." I'm afraid if I say yes, she might spit in it.

She nods and sets the menus down between us, looking back to Nick. I don't know if she intends to hit on him, but her body language is solely focused on him. Angled so she basically has her back to me, jutting out one hip, and smiling. "The usual for you?"

"I think we need a minute," he says as he picks up the top menu and hands it to me.

"Right." Annie lingers another second before turning on her heel with flair. Nick is either clueless or purposely avoiding watching her dramatics to get his attention.

"What all is good here?" I ask as I scan the menu.

"The only thing that's good here are the burgers."

"Good thing there are so many options." One entire side is dedicated to burgers—from double patties of beef to veggie.

"Stick with something simple."

"Why did you pick this place if the food is bad?" I ask, smiling despite it all—this bizarre day, the reminders of Matt everywhere I turn, and now sitting across from this grumpy man.

"We come here a lot."

"We?" I ask. "You and your girlfriend?"

He gives me a dry, apathetic look like the idea of him having a girlfriend is stupid. Maybe he's not into women. "My teammates. It's close to the rink, and the atmosphere is nice."

I glance around at the place. It has a real sports bar vibe. TVs are mounted along the walls and behind the bar. A variety of sports games are on. I smile when I see the Mustangs game on one. They're playing a Montana team in Arizona. I pull out my phone to snap a picture of the TV. Olivia will get a kick out of it.

Nick swivels around to see what I'm taking a picture of.

"That's my brother-in-law," I say.

"Where?"

"The guy pitching on the TV."

"Flynn Holland is your brother-in-law?" he asks with a hint of surprise and possibly interest.

Pride zips through me. "You know him?"

"Sure. Great pitcher."

"He is," I say proudly. "And great guy too."

I send the picture to my sister and then tuck my phone back into my purse.

When Annie returns, Nick orders a cheeseburger and fries.

"Same for me," I say.

He leans back in the booth when she's gone. "Are you a baseball fan then?"

"I'm not sure I can answer that, since we have a no personal questions rule in place."

The dry look he gives me is so on par for him that it pulls a laugh from me.

"My grandfather works for the Mustangs, and Flynn plays, so I sort of have to be, but otherwise, not really. I'm not very sporty."

His right dimple appears as he flashes a half smile at me. It is . . . dazzling. Good thing he doesn't smile more because, sweet baby rhinos, it's a good look for him.

"You're not sporty, and you don't know hockey. Why did you decide to write a book about hockey?"

At the mention of my job, I reach for my notebook and pen to jot down any notes because that's what I'm doing here, not being dazzled because the grumpy hockey player has the ability to smile. "I didn't. My publisher requested it."

"They can do that?"

"They can when the author is desperate to publish another book," I admit.

He gives me a pitying look, and I think I may have said too much.

"Anyway." I flip open my notebook. "You were going to walk me through a hockey game."

His face scrunches up, pained. "Yeah, I thought about that. I can do that, if you want, but it might be easier to cover the rules and objectives. Then I can go over a few of the standard plays we run."

"That would be great." I fight the blush heating my cheeks. He's being so amenable. Maybe he was just hangry. Though the food hasn't arrived yet, so I'm not sure that logic works.

For the next half hour, Nick talks hockey. I scribble furiously as I write down everything he says, nearly word for word. Half of it doesn't make sense to me, and his answers to my follow-up questions don't provide a lot of clarity.

Annie brought our food somewhere between his explanation of the different positions and rules of the game, but mine still sits untouched.

"Okay, let me see if I can summarize." I pop a fry in my mouth and chew as I review my notes. Once I'm finished chewing, I say, "The game starts with a face-off at half-court."

"Center ice," he corrects.

"Right. That's what I meant."

The corner of his mouth twitches, revealing one of his dimples again.

"The disc is called a puck, and players try to shoot it into the other team's goal." Not basket. He already corrected me on that.

"Simple, right?"

I stifle a laugh. If that's all there was to it, then sure. "I still don't understand the rules or job of each player, but I'm not sure I need that level of detail for my book."

"Well what position does he play?"

"He *was* a shortstop. Any chance you have one of those in hockey?"

Nick blanches. Guess not.

"What position are you?" I ask.

"I'm a forward. I've played wing, but I'm primarily a center."

"Which means?"

His body language has relaxed, and his expression doesn't seem to hold any annoyance at my complete stupidity on his profession. I think I've figured it out. It's hockey that makes him less grumpy. In Nick Galaxy's world, people are the worst. But hockey and children are okay.

"I play in the middle on a line."

"Like the lines on the ice? Blue, red . . ." I try to remember if there are other colors. I stared at the ice for hours today but still can't picture it.

"No." He shakes his head, a little of his usual scowl returning. "The three forwards make up a line. There are four lines, typically, and we rotate in and out, so no one is out on the ice for too long."

"How long is too long?"

"Depends on a lot of things."

"I'm sensing everything in hockey depends on a lot of things."

"That's not too different from everything else. One decision has cascading effects."

My mind automatically goes to Matt. If I had never met him, never let him into my life, never fallen in love with him, I could have avoided so many problems.

Most likely I wouldn't be here right now.

"Are you okay?" Nick asks, voice gentle in his question but somehow still taking on a slightly annoyed tone.

I shake my head to clear the thoughts. "Sorry. I was . . . I get it."

He looks like he wants to ask more but doesn't. "Forty seconds."

It takes me a beat to realize he's answering my question from earlier. "That's quick."

"Doesn't feel like it when you're out there."

"I'll take your word for it." I look down at my notes.

"Have you ever skated before?" he asks.

"Me?" I squeak. "No way. I can barely stay upright on solid ground."

"Ice is solid."

I huff a laugh, and we smile over our food. Nick glances away first, then picks up his burger to take another bite. For a few minutes we eat in silence while I try to figure out what else to ask him.

"What's the season like?" I ask. "When do practices start? When are games? Championships? How long is the off-season?"

I think I remember Flynn saying that the hockey season wasn't too different from baseball. Maybe all sports follow a schedule. A sports schedule? That could be a thing, right? Makes sense to me.

"We have training camp in mid-September. That kicks off practices, and regular season games begin in October."

"Oh." My brow furrows. That is not like baseball. There goes my sports schedule theory. "When is the season over?"

"June, if you're lucky. Playoffs start in April. Elimination style."

"Meaning?"

"Only the winning team from each series moves on. Loser starts vacation."

"Not such a bad consolation prize."

He lets out a hearty laugh that makes my stomach flip. "Nobody wants to start vacation before June."

"So, assuming you win, you have July and August off? Can you go wherever? Do you have to check in with the coaches or anything?"

"For the first month, everyone spreads out. Guys travel to see their families or go on vacation. But by August most are back to training full-time."

It tracks with what I know of Flynn's schedule. He took a little bit of time after the end of the season last fall but then got right back into his routine well before spring training began.

"That's a lot of hockey. Do you love it?"

He stares at me blankly, mouth slightly open.

"Is that a dumb question?" I give him a sheepish smile.

"No. It isn't that. I was trying to remember the last time someone asked me that."

I study him as he finishes off his burger with a contemplative look on his face. Freckles stretch across the bridge of his nose. There's a small scar just below his bottom lip. His face is covered in darker stubble than this morning. He's the kind of handsome I typically avoid. Too good-looking, too muscular, too everything. Maybe it's so high school to admit, but he's the jock, and I'm the nerd who looked forward to book reports. There is no other situation in which I can imagine sitting across from someone like Nick and sharing a meal. The closest to dating a jock I've ever come was a blind date with a guy who played intramural soccer. When he suggested I join for our second date, I knew I had to bow out.

When he speaks again, his tone is softer. "It's a job. For nine months out of the year, I see more of my teammates than I do my family. We play eighty-two games, half of them out of state. But the thing is, even saying all that, I still do. I think you have to love it. There's no other way anyone would be willing to sacrifice as much as we do."

His words hit me like a shovel to the head—or maybe the heart. I can tell he loves it by the look in his eye, the reverent tone. There was a time I loved writing that much.

My eyes go watery, and my throat tightens. I glance down, unable to hold his gaze. How humiliating. I just cried over hockey, or at least that's probably what it seems like to him.

Annie steps up to the table while I'm composing myself. "Hey, Champ, sorry to interrupt. Could you bring a keg out from the back for our bartender?"

"Yeah, of course." Nick slides out of the booth and gets to his feet.

Annie and Nick head toward the bar, then he disappears behind it with the bartender. I use the time to clear my thoughts. I can't believe I almost cried in front of him. The last few days have been an emotional rollercoaster.

Annie comes back to the table and clears some of the plates.

"Thanks," I say.

"You want anything else?" she asks me. She's not as warm with me as she is with Nick, but she's not ignoring me anymore.

"No. I'm good. Thanks."

She nods.

"Why do you call him Champ?"

She stares at me stone-faced. Okay, maybe she hasn't come around to me as much as I thought.

"He won the championship with the Wildcats before coming to Moonshot," she says.

"Right . . ." I wait for her to explain further.

"He was a big get for us. I still can't believe the Wildcats let him go. They had to juggle around a lot of players to fill his shoes. And between me and you, they still aren't as good as they were when Nick was with them. He brought them a championship, and he's going to bring us one too. I can feel it."

I don't totally understand the logistics of composing teams, and trade details are definitely out of my wheelhouse, but what she says makes sense. Why then did they trade him?

She leaves before I can think of anything else to ask her, and then Nick returns.

"Sorry about that," he says as he takes his seat.

"It's no problem."

"Do you have any other questions for me?" he asks after a beat of silence.

"There are probably a million more things I should ask, but I've reached the limit of sporty knowledge that my brain can hold."

He wears a guilty expression as he smiles awkwardly.

"Thank you for this. I appreciate it. Especially after the misunderstanding yesterday."

"You're welcome."

Nick won't let me pay even after I tell him I can write it off as a business expense, then we walk out to the parking lot.

"Well . . . in case I don't see you before I head out in the morning, it was nice meeting you."

"Yeah, you too. How long is the flight back?" His brow furrows. "I don't think I asked you where you're from."

"Lake City, but I'm not heading there."

"Why not?"

"Eh . . . it's a long, boring story." And depressing. "The lease on my apartment was about to end before I left so I'm sort of homeless right now. I mean, not that I don't have anywhere to go. Any of my family members would be happy to let me crash, but I need to finish this book in six weeks, and I can't do that with my mom hovering over me, asking me if I've showered or eaten today, you know?"

One side of his mouth pulls up, but he still looks embarrassed for me.

"Anyway, I'm waiting for my agent to find someone else I can interview so until then, I found a hotel not far from here. Hotel Thirteen, I think. They're holding a room for me through the weekend until I figure out what's next."

"Hotel Fourteen?"

"Yeah. That's it." My smile brightens. "I wonder why it's called that?"

"Urban legend says it's the number of times someone has been murdered there."

I laugh, but he doesn't join in.

"You're serious?" A bit of anxiety creeps in, but I bat it away. This entire town is gorgeous. Even if it's the worst hotel here, it can't be that bad. Right?

His mouth pulls into a thin line as he nods. "You can't stay there."

"I will be fine. Besides, it's the only thing for miles that has vacancy."

"It's tourist season. Everything books out months in advance." The way he says it like I should have prepared better rankles me. His jaw does that flex thing that makes me worry for his teeth.

"Well, I *thought* I had a place to stay," I fire back then take a deep breath. Arguing is pointless. I'm never going to see him again. He can go back to being grumpy in his beautiful lake house, and I'll go . . . anywhere else. I flash him a smile. "Goodbye, Nick."

Chapter Nine

NICK

"What were you thinking?" I ask, then have to repeat the question at a shout.

Aidan is learning to play the guitar, and he hits a particularly sour note that has me wincing.

I motion for Dad to follow me outside to the back patio. I glance over at the cabin. I can't see her, but I know she's there. I can feel her, which doesn't make any sense, I know, but it's true. I like my space. My privacy. I don't have time to sit around every day and teach her hockey.

"Tell me you've officially lost your mind. Something to explain why you invited some stranger to stay on my property and told her I'd be available for interviews." Over the past few years, I have very purposely avoided reporters and media, even my own team's marketing and publicity department as much as I can. I work hard to be the best leader and captain to my guys, but I let other people—much better suited and more well-spoken—speak on behalf of the team.

"Her agent called the house asking to speak to you. I was taking a message for you, but what she was asking didn't sound like much. A couple of interviews and a place to stay."

I wait for more of an explanation. None comes.

"You've gone too far this time, Pop. You had no right to do that without talking to me." I love him, but damn he tries my patience.

"What's she hurting?"

"I'm not a landlord."

"I can manage it. It's my cabin after all."

"Chalet Galaxy, really?"

His mouth hitches up on one side. "I thought it was clever."

I sigh. "If you want to Airbnb the cabin, fine, but you can't promise people I'm going to help them. I have a life."

He scoffs. "Hardly."

"Dad, don't start."

"You can't hide away in this big house. You're young. You should be going out and having fun. Aidan is old enough to understand his dad has needs."

I groan, letting my head fall back. "Please, for the love of God."

"It's only natural, son."

"What isn't natural is having this conversation with my dad."

"I hate to break it to you, but I'm aware that you've had sex before. Unless Aidan is a sperm donor situation."

Oh my god. Somehow the more he talks, the worse it gets.

"No more matchmaking or interfering. I don't want to date or get married. Especially not to her. I mean, really Pop, she lives thousands of miles away." Apparently, he's widened the search to the continental United States.

He's always talking me up—to women at the grocery store or at his doctor's office. I know because he does it even when I'm standing right next to him. It's humiliating. I'm a thirty-one-year-old man. If I wanted to date, I would.

"Well, hell, son, I wasn't expecting you to marry her. She needed help, and we could give it. You might lock yourself away in this house more than I'd like, but you've always been good at doing the right thing."

The words hit just like he intends—a compliment intermixed with a sucker punch. Yes, I generally try to help people when I can, but this is a stretch.

"But if you want to have a little summer fling, I don't think it'd be the worst thing for you."

"Oh my god." I rub my forehead with two fingers.

"What? Like I don't remember what it's like to be young." He huffs. "You're wound so tight. It's not healthy. You need to let off some steam, and she's a gorgeous woman. Even you must have noticed that."

I raise a hand, palm out, and close my eyes, effectively silencing him. I literally cannot take another word.

"Fine. Fine. Not interested. I got it."

It isn't a promise that he won't do it again, but I'd say this very painful conversation buys me a month or two.

I let out a long, tired breath. Next door, Ruby walks out of the cabin pulling her large roller bag down the gravel drive.

I look away from her, something like guilt twisting in my chest. Dad's brows lift in question.

"She got what she needed, and she's leaving."

"She came by the rink today?" he asks in a way that suggests he already knows the answer. "Determined little thing."

I grunt. That she is.

Dad's smile is all pride. He likes her. Maybe I would too under different circumstances.

"I answered all her damn questions, so you can stop yapping about doing the right thing." I sit in one of the patio chairs. Dad leans back against the deck railing.

"That's why you asked me to pick up Aidan."

"Yeah. We went to MVP."

"You could have at least taken her somewhere the food is edible."

"It wasn't a date," I remind him. "And I like MVP."

He makes a rumble of disapproval. "What made you change your mind about helping her?"

"It seemed like the quickest way to get rid of her."

Dad stares at me a beat, so intently I have to resist squirming with unease, then his lips curl into a grin that stretches across his face. "She got under your skin, didn't she?"

"No. She didn't," I protest too quickly. "I just felt bad. It isn't her fault you went behind my back like you did." It was guilt. Has to be. "And Travis threatened to help her if I wouldn't."

He would have done it too.

"Ha!" Dad's laughter gets lost in another loud, ear-piercing chord from Aidan. "He was busting your chops, wasn't he? I always liked that boy."

"Yeah, well, he's pretty fond of you too. Maybe you should focus your matchmaking skills on him."

"He doesn't need my help."

"But I do?"

He doesn't respond, which I guess is all the answer I need. I'm not interested in my dad meddling in my love life. I date when I want and how I want, and it's none of his damn business.

"She is more Travis's type than yours," Dad says, staring over toward the cabin.

Jesus, since when did everyone start categorizing women as my type or not?

He looks back to me. "One question."

"What's that?"

"If you weren't interested, why do you care if Travis helps her or not?"

"I don't."

Dad cocks his head to the side, silently calling my bluff. "Where's she heading now? Back home?"

I hesitate and consider lying outright, but that would be admitting some sort of blame, and it's not my fault she's headed to the roach-infested, sketchy-as-fuck hotel. I did warn her. "Hotel Fourteen."

Dad's brows rise and his mouth opens. Several seconds of silence stretch out between us before he pushes off the railing and steps forward. "She can't stay there."

"I told her it wasn't a good idea, but she wouldn't listen. She's stubborn," I grit out. "And it sounds like it's only for a night or two anyway."

"Why doesn't she just stay at the cabin until she's ready to leave town? She isn't hurting anything." He looks like he's two seconds from marching over there and insisting she unload her bags and stay.

"She's a grown woman, and this was her choice."

"Sure, after you made it very clear she isn't welcome here."

That guilt is back, prodding at my sternum. "She'll be fine. Like you said, she's a determined thing."

He gives me another disappointed grumble before lifting his noise-canceling headphones back in place and heading into the house.

"She'll be fine," I repeat to myself as I watch Ruby get into her car and back out of the driveway.

Chapter Ten

RUBY

"How did this happen?" Olivia asks, her voice is filled with indignation on my behalf. We're on a video call, and it's so good to see her face. "I thought Molly set everything up with the hot hockey player."

I'm checked into my hotel room, which is as bad as Nick warned me. There are fourteen rooms, hence the name and not the number of murders (at least I don't think that part is true). However, it looks like the kind of place that it might be true.

"She did. It wasn't her fault. Somehow the communication got crossed, and Nick's dad agreed for him without running it by his son. Molly had no idea either," I say, readjusting in a feeble attempt to get comfortable.

There's no chair in the room, and the multi-colored comforter on the bed is polyester and looks like it came from the 1970s. Not to mention it smells awful, like cigarette smoke and a hundred years of dust.

I pulled back the top covers, hoping the sheets would be less horrifying, but it only got worse. I'm not sure if it's blood or marker or some other red-tinged stain, but there's no way I'm sitting on the bed, let alone sleeping in it.

I've made myself at home on top of a small table. It's maybe three feet long and two feet wide, but if I curl up tight then I think I can sleep on it. It's only one night. Tomorrow I'm getting the hell out of here.

"Wow," Olivia says.

"I know. I can't believe Nick's dad thought he would be okay with me showing up randomly on his doorstep." I've known the guy for a day and could predict how well that'd go over.

There must be some reason Nick's dad rented out the cabin and signed him up to be interviewed, but I can't guess why. Does it have something to do with him not talking to the media?

"Is Molly going to find someone else?" she asks. "Or did you get what you needed already from the hot hockey player?"

"Will you stop calling him that," I say with a small chuckle.

"He's hot. I looked him up."

I make a noise of disagreement. "He answered some of my questions, but I was hoping to have more time while I was editing for anything that came up during the process."

"I'm sorry."

"It's fine. I will figure it out. And in the meantime, I'll be back in Lake City. Dinner tomorrow night?"

I can't stay in this place another night, so despite my reservations about heading home, it's a far better option than this.

In the corner of the room, movement catches my eye. A very large bug skitters across the floor and disappears behind the bed. *Oh god.* My skin itches, and my stomach churns. Maybe sleeping in my car is a better option.

"Ruby?" My sister calls my name.

"Sorry. I . . . thought I heard room service outside." I don't think my amazing, sweet sister can handle the horrors of this place. I'm very carefully angling the phone away from anything that would set her alarm bells off.

"I said the Mustangs are playing at home again tomorrow night. Flynn isn't pitching, but it's hat night. Free pink hats to the first thousand people in the park and all you can drink lemonade. You should come with us. Gigi is going. She misses you. So does Greer. So do I." She steps out onto the back patio of her house. The sun has set, but the last bit of light still streaks through the dark sky.

"I've been gone for forty-eight hours."

"Still true."

"I miss you too." And I do, but I'm also disappointed. I wanted this summer to be a clean start for me. And instead, it feels like a continuation of my year from hell.

"Did the Mustangs win tonight? The game was on at the restaurant earlier."

"They did." Her voice is filled with pride. "And now he's out here building a playset for Greer."

She talks louder now as she slides the door closed behind her. "Ugh. It's still so hot outside. Enjoy Montana while you're there. I'd kill for a few days anywhere that I wouldn't sweat through my clothes. I'm disgusting."

"You're gorgeous." Her husband comes into view.

"I'm talking to my sister," she says.

"Ruby!" Flynn lifts a hand. He's sweaty and shirtless and pulls his headphones down to rest around his neck. "How's Montana life?"

"Don't ask," Olivia tells him.

"Uh-oh. What happened?"

"I'll tell you all about it tomorrow. I'm heading back in the morning," I say.

He winces. "That bad, huh?"

"Worse."

"Bummer." He kisses my sister on the cheek and then dips his head lower. She smiles, and the phone tilts so I can see him rubbing her pregnant belly. He murmurs lovingly, and my heart swells.

Olivia giggles and then swats playfully at him. "Don't get the baby all excited. I don't want her to kick me all night again."

Flynn chuckles softly as he stands tall. He's a foot taller than my sister, but they're so cute together. If I hadn't witnessed their love story, I might be inclined to believe that happily-ever-afters only happen in books. Seeing them interact, hearing them talk about the other, watching how they can't stop kissing and touching, it's hard to deny that big love exists. Maybe not everyone is fortunate to find it, but it's out there.

"I'm going to finish up here and head in and shower," Flynn says to her, pulling his headphones back on.

"Okay." Olivia leans forward this time, and I can hear them kiss but can't see it. Several seconds pass with no indication that they're going to come up for air anytime soon.

"Don't mind me over here listening to you two make out," I say with a laugh.

"Oops. Sorry," Olivia says with a flush to her face. Her blond hair is pulled back into a messy ponytail. She has that glow that pregnant women sometimes get. She's due in two months. I can't wait to have another niece.

Flynn comes back into the frame. "Later, Rubes. Travel safe."

"Bye," I call as he walks off.

Olivia focuses back on me, but the happy and in love expression doesn't leave her face. "So . . . what's the plan? You're welcome to stay with us."

"And listen to you and Flynn make out all the time?"

"Not *all* the time."

"Thanks, but I can crash with Mom and Dad until I find a new place. And once I'm settled, I'll look for another hockey expert." Then I remember something about my wonderful brother-in-law: He has sporty brothers. Four of them. "Do any of Flynn's brothers play hockey?"

The Holland brothers are all professional athletes—motocross, football, baseball . . . I don't remember any of them playing hockey, and I'm certain Flynn would have mentioned it before I headed all the way to Montana, but it never hurts to ask. Maybe they played hockey as kids or something.

"No, sorry. But you know his agent, Everly?"

I nod, noncommittally. Flynn talks about his agent sometimes, but I've never met her.

"Her husband plays hockey. Do you want me to ask Flynn to put you in contact?"

Before I can answer, there's a loud bang next door.

"What was that?" Liv asks with a look of concern aimed at me.

My voice wavers slightly. "I think it was a car door."

"Are you on the first floor?" Her brows pinch together as she studies the area around me more carefully.

"Yes." There is only one floor. It's one of those roadside motels where the doors are accessed directly from the parking lot instead of through a lobby.

"I better go," I say.

"What about your hockey expert?"

"I'll find someone," I say with as much determination as I can muster. "But thank you. If it comes to that, I'll see if my awesome brother-in-law can pull a favor."

"Of course." She smiles at me in a way that reminds me she'd do anything for me. And by extension, so would Flynn.

"I'll see you tomorrow," I say.

"Okay. Text me when you get back."

"I will."

As soon as I hang up the phone, I ease off the table. My stare is locked on the floor, searching for any more giant bugs, while I walk over to my suitcase. I pull out a pair of pajamas as well as a few more articles of clothing. But instead of changing, I lay them down on top of the table to make a sort of pallet, then roll up the pajama bottoms to use as a pillow. At least it isn't cold in here, though it is somehow muggy.

My neighbors next door are moving around. There's a lot of thumping and other weird sounds I can't make out, but no talking. There isn't even a TV in the room to drown out the noise. I guess I could put in my AirPods, but then how would I hear the murderer when they arrive?

One night. I'll be out of here as soon as the sun comes up.

By some miracle, I manage to fall asleep. Or at least doze off. I wake up to more banging around next door. I shift, then wince as the hard table digs into my hip bone. I have no idea what time it is, but I feel like . . . well, I feel like I slept in the fetal position on top of a piece of wood.

The banging comes again, this time louder, and . . . I freeze, panic washing over me. The noise is at my door. I know because the cheap metal rattles on the hinges.

I stand and step in front of the door and grab the first thing within reach—a lamp. It's gold-plated with a dingy, what was once maybe white, shade. I'm clutching it in one hand as I stand poised a foot away from the door.

Do I open it? Am I more or less likely to get killed if I ignore whoever it is on the other side?

I'm still thinking when the person on the other side yells, "Red, open up."

Slowly the voice and the nickname needle their way through the adrenaline and fear haze. I fling open the door, and there he is. Nick Galaxy is standing outside my cheap motel room looking like he spent the night sleeping on a tiny wooden table too.

His hair is disheveled, and his beard is longer. He's in gray athletic pants and a black T-shirt—both slightly rumpled.

"What are you doing here?" I ask him.

He takes me in, stare dropping to the lamp I'm holding like a weapon, then walks past me into the room, glancing around and shaking his head.

"Hello? I didn't invite you in." I set the lamp back on the table.

Turning to face me again, Nick places both hands on his hips. My face heats, though I'm not sure why I'm embarrassed.

"How did you find me?" Surely, he didn't knock on every single door until "Red" answered. Actually, that sounds exactly like something he would do.

"I asked the guy at the front desk which room you were in."

"So much for privacy," I mutter.

Nick grabs my suitcase and rolls it toward the door. "Let's go."

"What?" I shake my head. "Go where?"

He gives me a droll look. "Chalet Galaxy."

I keep staring at him. Maybe it's the lack of sleep or the emotional rollercoaster I've been on today, but I can't seem to make sense of his words.

"You can't stay here. This place is . . ."

Awful. Disgusting. Straight out of a horror movie.

It finally hits me that he's attempting to swoop in and rescue me. No, no. He doesn't get to be the good guy now. Not when he's the reason I'm here in the first place.

"No, thank you. I'd rather stay here."

"Really?" He huffs, the sound a gruff low timbre that sends goose bumps up my arms.

"Yes, really. I'm not going anywhere with you."

"Why the hell not?"

"Because . . ." I throw my hands up in the air. There are so many reasons.

He waits, like he's expecting a detailed and thought-out list to accompany my outburst.

"You don't want me around. You made that very clear. And in a few hours, I'll head out and find somewhere else."

"A few hours?"

"Yeah, it has to be what two or three in the morning?"

"It's ten thirty."

Well, crap.

"It doesn't matter. I'm good here."

No sooner than the words leave my mouth, a high-pitched scream pierces through the night. All pretenses of bravery leave my body as I leap into Nick's arms. He catches me with one arm as I hide my face in his hard chest. He smells like fabric softener and that same woodsy scent I noticed earlier at the rink. Some sort of cologne maybe. My brain processes all this at the same time I realize I've just thrown myself at him.

"Sorry." I slide down him until my feet hit the ground and very ungracefully compose myself. I clear my throat.

"Ready to go now?" he asks, as a smug, satisfied smile curls his lips.

He pulls his truck into the driveway out front of his house and then walks over to the cabin as I'm getting my suitcase out.

"It's unlocked, and I left the key on the kitchen counter," he says like my coming back here was a foregone conclusion.

Damn him. And damn the tourists who planned ahead and left no vacancy in town.

"Thank you," I say, but it doesn't come out sounding very grateful, so I try again. "I appreciate it."

"You're welcome."

"I'll be out first thing in the morning."

His jaw works back and forth. "You can stay at the cabin this summer as planned."

Well, that's surprising.

"I'm coaching at the camp all week, so I don't have a lot of time, but if you have any more questions, I'll try to answer them."

"Who are you and what have you done with the grumpy man I met yesterday who couldn't wait to get rid of me?"

"Look, it wasn't personal."

"It felt personal."

"I'm sorry for that. I was frustrated with my dad, and I took it out on you."

This has officially been the strangest day of my life.

"Anyway, I can't have you writing a hockey book where you call the puck a disc."

My mouth curves up. "Hey, I came a long way in a single day, I think."

He huffs a quiet laugh.

"You're really okay with this?" The "this" being me staying in a cabin on his property and asking him more questions. Before he apologized, I was prepared to stay here regardless of how he felt about it, but now he's being nice, and my need for retribution is fading.

"Yeah." He dips his chin in a nod.

"Okay." A wave of relief floods through me. "That would be great. I will work around your schedule."

"The easiest thing would probably be to stop by the rink. I have about thirty minutes first thing before the campers arrive, and I can get away during breaks or lunch."

"What time?"

"Eight."

I know that eight o'clock isn't that early, but one of the perks of working for myself is setting my own schedule. And that schedule usually doesn't start until after nine. But I will take what I can get.

"Perfect," I say as I mentally calculate how many hours of sleep I'm going to get tonight.

"You can ride with us if you want."

"Us?"

"My son, Aidan, and me. He's part of the camp."

"Oh." My mouth drops open with the reply, and I tilt my head to the side. Having a kid is a perfectly normal thing for someone his age, but I was not prepared.

The hot hockey player has a son.

Chapter Eleven

RUBY

The next morning, I walk up the path to the house with my laptop and notebooks in tow. I slept incredibly. Nothing like a near-death experience to lull you to sleep.

And I woke up excited. I texted Molly to let her know the change in plans, as well as Olivia. Now it's time to get to work.

Nick is already in the driveway. A little boy with the same messy dark hair walks down the front steps with a large duffel bag over one shoulder.

The kid's steps slow when he sees me approaching.

"Who's the chick?" he asks.

Nick steps forward and takes his bag, tossing it into the bed of his truck. "Don't call girls chicks. And that's Ruby. She's coming with us to the rink today."

Nick tips his head to the kid while looking at me. "This is my son, Aidan."

"Hi, Aidan." I lift a hand in a small wave.

"Hello." He opens the rear right-side door of the truck and gets in. Not rude, just unfazed by my presence.

"Sorry about that," Nick says more quietly to me.

"It's fine. He looks just like you," I tell him. And acts like him. A little grumpy around the edges.

In reply I get a small huff. He's freshly shaved this morning. His chin dimple is prominent, and there are small wrinkles on either side of his mouth where the other two dimples would be if he smiled.

Nick's truck smells like coffee. As I buckle into the passenger seat, I glance longingly at the to-go mug in the console. Coffee is my favorite meal of the day. Hopefully I can get some at the rink.

The three of us ride in silence for several minutes. I gave a lot of thought to the whole Nick-has-a-son thing last night when he casually dropped it, but seeing Aidan has me thinking about it again.

"Are you married?" Something I probably should have considered sooner. Is there a Mrs. Grumpy Galaxy?

"What?" His brow furrows as he asks in a *are you stupid?* tone. "No."

"My parents aren't married," Aidan says from the back seat. "My mom lives in Bozeman."

Nick glances in the rearview mirror and frowns.

"Oh. Cool," I say when no other words come to my mind. "Girlfriend?"

Aidan snorts. "Pop wishes."

"All right. Pipe down back there."

I curl my lips between my teeth to keep from laughing. Maybe Aidan isn't so much like his dad after all.

"You aren't exactly reeling in the ladies either," Nick says to his son, and I think I detect a bit of an edge.

"I could have a girlfriend if I wanted one," is Aidan's reply.

"Me too," Nick says.

And I don't doubt it. There's no way he has a problem attracting women . . . at least until he glowers at them. No, not even then.

At the rink, Aidan runs ahead of us, duffel bag slung over his shoulder and looking like it weighs more than him, into the building.

Nick and I are slower. He waits for me at the front of the truck, coffee in hand. He hasn't so much as had a sip of it, and the smell is killing me.

The parking lot is filled with cars and trucks. Parents dropping off their kids, all with big bulky bags like Aidan's. Some of the smaller kids have someone walking them inside.

"Hey, Coach Nick," a little girl calls to him, blond braids bouncing as she passes us by.

"Morning, Aubrey."

She walks as fast as her little legs will carry her.

"There are more girls than I expected. Is hockey a coed sport in high school too?"

"No, but at this level it makes sense. I'm guessing you didn't play as a kid?"

"I wouldn't really be seeking expert advice if I had, now would I?"

"I did a summer of basketball, and I don't remember shit about that, so maybe." He holds the door open for me. As I step inside, the chill of the ice hits me. In all my preparations this morning, I forgot to dress in multiple layers. At least I'm in jeans, but a tube top was not the best choice.

I suck in a breath. "Wow. You'd think it would have created a core memory yesterday, considering I only got warm after taking a very hot shower."

He notices me rubbing my arms, and his jaw works back and forth, probably silently judging me for being so unprepared.

"I'll survive." I force out, not letting my teeth chatter. "Is there coffee around here somewhere?"

"No." His brow knits. "There's a small café, but it doesn't open until ten."

"Oh, okay." Ten o'clock. I can survive until then. Probably.

He looks down at his mug and then holds it out to me.

I stare at it like a poisoned apple.

"Take it," he says.

"Oh no, I couldn't. I'm fine." My mouth is salivating as the smell wafts closer to me. I wave both hands dramatically in front of me again. Nope. Not taking this man's coffee no matter how badly I want it. He's agreed to help me and let me stay at the cabin, but I'm still not certain he wouldn't also poison me.

He keeps it held out a moment longer, then nods and takes it back. He still doesn't drink it. What is he waiting for?! I swallow down all the saliva collecting in my mouth, then force a smile and head toward the parent section.

"Where are you going?" Nick calls after me.

I point, as if it isn't obvious.

He motions with his head for me to walk toward him. "Come with me."

He has me sit on a bench next to the ice, in front of the plexiglass. I'm so close to the ice it feels like the cold is radiating off it.

Nick changes into his skates and grabs his hockey stick. The kids are still filing into the rink, getting dressed and slowly entering the ice.

"Do you have more questions for me?" he asks. "I probably have five minutes before we start."

"Yeah," I answer then stifle a yawn. I stayed up late, showering to get warm (and because I felt disgusting after the motel), then reading over our notes from yesterday and brainstorming follow-up questions. I'm a weird mixture of cold and tired that has my brain moving slowly. I scan the list of questions. "Let me think where to start."

He nods. "I'll be right back."

I watch the kids when he's gone. They're cute. I recognize a few from yesterday and note they look more comfortable. When I spot Aidan, I'm astonished all over again by the resemblance. Even the way he skates is similar to his dad. Same athletic presence and easy movements, like they were born with skates on their feet.

Nick comes back a minute later with a sweatshirt in one hand and a coffee cup in the other. He holds them both out to me.

"Here," he says, voice gruff. "So you don't get hypothermia."

My heart does a funny little flutter thing in my chest. I stare at him, more than a little shocked.

"Concerned about me?" I ask as I take the sweatshirt. The material is soft and smells faintly of his laundry detergent. It's big and baggy, but as I pull it over my head, my body warms instantly, like I'm being wrapped in a big Nick hug. Or what I might imagine his hugs are like. Which to be honest, now that I really try to picture it, I struggle with the visual. He has a kid, so he must like hugging someone, at least occasionally.

His response is only a slight uptick of his lips—his version of a smile, I'm learning. I take the coffee next. I'm nearly giddy as I wrap my hands around the cup and take a tentative sip.

It's a little stronger than I usually take mine, but it tastes heavenly right now.

"Thank you." I don't know what to make of this nice, accommodating version of Nick. I've had glimpses of it before, but something seems to have shifted since last night.

"You're welcome." He gives me a curt nod, then looks away.

The ice fills as more kids arrive. Travis waves to me from the other side, then skates by.

"Ruby. You're back!" He's about the same height as Nick with similar dark brown hair, but everything else about them is different. Travis is unfiltered enthusiasm. He smiles with his entire face. His lips pull wide, and his eyes crinkle at the side. Even the way he faces me, angling his body to give me his full attention, is friendly and inviting.

"I am a glutton for punishment."

His easy grin moves from me to Nick.

"Interesting night?" he asks his friend.

Nick sighs heavily, then levels him with a glare that's not very convincing, thanks to the way he fights a smile.

Travis skates off as quickly as he came. Nick turns back to me.

"I thought we'd have more time this morning," he says.

"It's okay." I knew it would be a long shot that he'd answer all my questions, but I was hoping to get a few more in.

"Most evenings I'm busy with Aidan."

"I get it," I say, realizing he's letting me down easy. He might even feel bad about it.

"We could come to the rink earlier tomorrow. He'll never turn down some extra ice time."

Earlier. Yikes.

"Whatever works for you. As long as I have coffee, I'll be fine."

He chuckles. A deep, rich sound that I feel deep down in the pit of my stomach. His dimples are on full display, and dear lord, the man is doing the world a favor by being so grumpy all the time. Women would be lining up around the block if he flashed that smile around all day long.

"Does the cabin have a coffee pot?" he asks, then looks contemplative like he's trying to remember.

"I didn't see one, but I don't mind buying one. I need to get some groceries anyway."

He leans on a hockey stick, casually, staring at me with a hint of that killer smile still lingering on his face. I wonder how the heck he stays upright so easily out there on the ice. Then I remember I can ask.

"When did you start skating?"

His body language switches immediately, as if he just remembered this is an interview and I broke our rule of no personal questions. He really seems to have an issue with answering questions about himself, and I can't help but wonder why.

"This isn't for the book. I'm just curious. You look so comfortable out there."

"I was four," he says finally.

"Were you good at it right away?" I bet he was.

"I don't really remember, but I've been doing it so long it feels as easy as walking or riding a bike."

I don't point out that those things aren't easy for everyone.

"Morning, everyone." The woman coach from yesterday skates in the middle of the rink. "We're going to start in two minutes, so get your gear on. We're starting on the ice today."

Nick looks to me as if prompting me to ask whatever I can in the short time we have left.

"Okay." I look at my notebook. "Can you tell me what a week during the season looks like for you?"

"It varies by team and coaching preferences, but I get to the rink around nine and I'm here until one or two o'clock in the afternoon."

"And is it all . . ." I wave my hand around. "Skating around with a puck?"

His lips twitch with a smile. "No."

"Walk me through a day." I find I'm curious to know more about him and not strictly for the book.

"I eat breakfast, then meetings, work out, get on the ice for drills or scrimmaging, then recovery—ice bath, red light therapy, a massage, something like that, then I head home to pick up Aidan from school." While he speaks, he moves back and forth—pacing on the ice. His stick moves in front of him, guiding a puck effortlessly. It's kind of distracting and a lot hot. Who knew hockey players were so sexy. Maybe my publisher was onto something.

"Meetings?" I try and fail to picture him in a stuffy boardroom.

"We'll watch video from the last game or scope out the next team."

"Research."

"Exactly."

I scribble down his words as I ask a few more follow-up questions about his daily routine. His answers are short and concise, but I never feel like he's holding back—more that he takes for granted how ingrained he is in the sport. The more he talks, the more things I realize I don't know, and when camp starts, I fight back a tinge of disappointment.

I close my notebook and slide my pen into the spiral binding.

Nick looks to me as kids swarm around him. "Are you sticking around?"

"Will you have time to chat more?"

"Yeah. I'll make sure Travis can cover lunch."

"Okay." I stand quickly, making myself a little lightheaded in the process. I think I'm high on nice Nick vibes. "I guess I'll see you then. Good luck."

Good luck? I groan inwardly. I don't know what it is about this guy, but now that he's playing nice, I find myself reverting back to my teenage self, and she was one hundred percent awkward.

"Thanks." Nick offers me one last dimpled grin.

* * *

During lunch, he leads me down a hallway to a small office. Nick stands in the doorway and waves for me to enter.

I take a seat in front of the desk in one of two blue plastic chairs. Nick stands behind the desk, arms crossed over his chest and leaning against the wall.

"Okay. Should I . . ."

He nods. "Fire away."

Before I can, Travis appears with two food containers.

"Sandwiches?" he asks Nick, then glances at me and smiles. "Ruby-Doo!"

"Hi." I laugh at the nickname. "That's a new one."

Up close, he's even cuter. Big brown eyes and long lashes, and that smile is full of charm.

"Thanks," Nick says, stepping forward and taking both containers of food. He holds one out to me.

"Oh. Thanks." I hadn't considered food for the day, and my stomach is growling.

Travis walks farther into the room, ignoring the annoyed look Nick sends in his direction, and takes the seat next to me. He leans forward in his chair. The excitement splashed across his face has me reciprocating his smile.

"What kind of books do you write?"

"Romance. Mostly paranormal, but I'm branching out to contemporary."

"Like werewolves and dragons?"

"Vampires, actually."

Somehow his smile stretches wider. "What about historical? Dukes, viscounts, bodices, and long walks around gardens? I was obsessed with *Bridgerton* when it first came out. It was basically my entire personality."

"No. I haven't tried historical yet. Are you a big romance reader?"

"I'm more of a film guy." He glances at Nick. "I get it now."

"Trav," Nick says in a low, warning tone.

"Get what?" My brows pinch together in confusion.

"You're beautiful, and everyone knows Nick's dad loves to set him up." He tips his head toward Nick without looking at him. "His dad thinks a good woman will make him less grumpy."

I glance over at Nick in time to catch an eye roll.

"Yes, I definitely feel less grumpy every time he sets me up with someone against my will." Nick sits in the leather office chair on the other side of the desk. There's something I like about seeing him slightly off-kilter, a little exasperated. It makes me feel like less of a mess for not having it all together, like he appears most of the time.

"Mike means well." Travis waves it off.

"I don't think that's why Mike brought me here," I say, mulling over the idea and immediately dismissing it.

"Maybe not. It could just be a happy coincidence that you're beautiful."

I'm blushing, which is ridiculous. Travis seems like the kind of guy who throws out compliments like confetti.

"Dude." Nick winces then rubs his forehead with two fingers.

"What? She is." He looks to me. "You are."

"Thanks."

He stands quickly. "How long are you in town?"

"I'm not sure," I say because even though Nick has agreed to let me stay, it feels like he might still change his mind.

"We should grab dinner sometime."

"Trav," Nick says, sounding more exasperated. "She's here to work."

"Fine. Fine. Well, if you need any research help on the Victorian era, I'm your guy, but Nick is one of the smartest hockey players I know, so you're in good hands."

"I appreciate it."

He flashes me another giant smile, then slides his gaze to Nick. "Later, loser."

As quickly as he waltzed in, he's gone.

"Sorry about him," Nick says with a heavy sigh.

"Don't be. He's funny. Have you been friends a long time?"

"Since I joined the team."

"Two years ago," I say, realizing too late that I've just admitted too much. I give him a sheepish smile. "I looked you up."

Birthdate June twentieth. Drafted out of college. Played in Chicago, then Minnesota, and now here. And no social media as far as I could find.

"I looked you up too," he says.

"Really?" I don't even try to hide my surprise.

"You're not just an author, you're a *bestselling* author, translated in a bunch of different countries."

My face flushes with embarrassment. Are you still a bestselling author if your last book flopped? I know the answer is yes, but it doesn't feel that way.

I glance down as the heat continues to creep down my neck. I can't even let myself think about what he might have read about me online. I've seen more than a few headlines about "disappointing sales numbers."

He clears his throat and leans back in his chair as he pops open his lunch container, carefully avoiding my gaze.

I'm still wearing his sweatshirt. It's light purple with Moonshot Hockey written across the front in white letters. His number is on the right shoulder, but in my case, it hangs down at elbow-length. I push the sleeves up and open my lunch, but I'm too jittery to eat.

"What other questions do you have for me?" he asks as he pulls out a sandwich.

I set my food aside and glance down at my notes, happy to have the distraction from thinking about my career.

"I have a couple gameplay scenarios. One where the hero needs to do something amazing and another where he screws up."

"Something amazing?"

"The heroine is in the stands, and he wants to impress her," I say, setting the scene. "Does that happen? Do you invite women and then try to impress them with your hockey skills?"

"No," he says quickly as if the thought is absolutely ludicrous.

"Never?"

He pauses as if considering it, but only for a second. "Maybe in high school or early in my juniors' career."

I want to pick at that but keep myself in the professional zone. "Okay, well, what's the most impressive thing you've done during a game?"

He grins but doesn't answer immediately.

"Was it a hat trick or a slick deke move against a defender." I don't even know what I'm saying. I've read just enough hockey stuff over the past day to use a few terms, probably not the right way.

"Fans tend to be more impressed by goals than anything else, so I would go that route," he says.

"Okay. Great. What does that look like? Play-by-play."

He chuckles softly. "Usually people are critiquing my game, not asking for my interpretation of it."

I smile back at him, waiting. He takes a moment to collect himself, then gives me the play like he's a sportscaster. His face is more animated than I've seen it, and those dimples are continually on display.

I write it down word for word, pen moving fast over the paper. I feel giddy, like I was there for it. And I can't stop smiling at him.

"And no girls were impressed?" I ask, disbelieving. I'm impressed now, just hearing it. Sure, I don't really know that much about hockey, but I could feel the passion of it. There's no way the fans in the crowd didn't feel it too.

"Maybe, but I don't see a lot beyond what's happening on the ice. The fans and the lights, the music . . . it all becomes background noise."

"I guess that makes sense." I chew on the end of my pen as I think. "What about a time when you screwed up?"

"How badly are we talking?" he asks, then adds, "Mistakes happen all the time. Missed shots or passes, penalties at the wrong time that shift momentum. Most of the time, I push past it and keep going. Lingering on it can cause cascading effects."

I nod. "Something bad enough that you couldn't shake it off."

I want to know for the book, but I also want to know because it's him, and I find him fascinating.

"Last season during our final game, I had a breakaway in the first minute of play. Defenders were too far back to stop me. I flew down the ice. Just me and the goalie, this young kid, his first playoff appearance. I knew the pressure he was feeling. I remember what it was like—nothing really prepares you for it."

I nod along like I know. Maybe it's like publishing your first book—that all-consuming fear and excitement. Everything feels like unlimited possibilities . . . and countless ways things could go wrong.

"What happened?" I ask, literally and figuratively on the edge of my seat. Adrenaline courses through me as I wait for him to finish the story.

"I had him. He was freaking out, watching me so intently, but a second behind my every move. I faked left and then went right . . ." He pauses, leaving me hanging for several long seconds as a bashful look crosses his face. "A wide-open look and I rung the pipe."

"You missed?" I ask, genuinely surprised even though I knew this story was leading in that direction.

"Yep." He shakes his head. "I was so certain I had him. I took my eye off the goal and . . . missed."

I feel the embarrassment of the moment or at least the embarrassment I would feel. An entire stadium of fans watching you mess up. At least for me I can generally hide behind my keyboard. Every typo or poorly executed plot point is discovered miles away from me.

"How do you recover after something like that?" I ask because something tells me he doesn't follow my method of eating ice cream and binge-watching reality television.

"There isn't a lot of time to dwell on it in the moment. It's usually after the game when I rehash it and think about what could have been." He takes the last bite of his sandwich and then sits back in his chair. When he's finished chewing, he asks, "Anything else before I head back out there?"

I'm still lost in his story, imagining how I can tweak it for the character in my book. Originally, I told it from the heroine's point of view, but maybe I should do it from his. "No, I think this is good for now."

I gather up my stuff, and he throws away the trash.

"Can I read it when you're done?" he asks as we head for the door.

"The game scene?" I nod. "Yeah, in fact, that'd be great."

"The book."

"All of it?" I pause. Per usual, the idea of someone reading the words I'm writing (and yes, I know that's the point) makes me break out into a cool sweat.

"Yeah. I'm intrigued."

"You don't even know what it's about."

"I know it's about a hockey player."

"Are you a big reader?" I think of Flynn. He reads every single one of my books, but I think that's mostly because Olivia gets a kick out of it.

"Eh." He bobs his head. "I wouldn't say I'm a big reader, no, but I always have something on hand during the season while we're traveling a lot."

"What genres do you like?" I have a very nice visual of him in some reading glasses with a hardback in his hands. Maybe he's more my type than I originally gave him credit for.

"All sorts. Some nonfiction, sports biographies mostly, an occasional fiction book."

"What's the last fiction book you read?" I ask. I am fine-tuning my visual and . . . I like it. I like it a lot.

"I read that murder mystery about the guy who turns into a vampire after having bad sushi." He snaps his fingers as he smiles. "Becoming . . ."

The blood drains from my face, and I work to keep my expression schooled. My voice wavers slightly. "*Becoming Alaric*?"

"Yeah. You know it?"

"I've seen it." I look away and step out of the small room into the hallway. It isn't his fault that he read the most popular book published last year, but my visual is officially ruined.

"Are you sticking around this afternoon?" he asks as he catches up to me with his long strides.

"I think I have what I need to get started editing."

"Okay."

I want to flee before he sees something in my expression I'd rather he didn't, but instead I meet his gaze. "Thank you for helping me."

His mouth pulls into a half smile. "You're welcome."

"Oh." I remember I'm wearing his sweatshirt and pull it off.

"Do you need a ride back?"

"No, thanks. I think I'll catch a ride to a coffee shop. I saw a couple cute ones on our drive in."

"I could ask my dad to pick you up and take you back to the cabin."

"No, it's fine." I hand him his sweatshirt back.

"It doesn't bother you to write with people and noise?"

"I like to write with silence, but when I'm editing, the more noise the better. I usually blast music."

"My dad would get a kick out of that."

"I'll keep it down," I promise.

"We're used to it."

"Aidan?"

He seems a little young to blast music. I thought that was an angry teenager thing. Then again, I don't have a lot of experience with kids. Just Greer, and everything she does is adorable.

"He's learning to play the guitar." Nick winces as if just talking about it has him shuddering. He gives me a sheepish grin as he holds the door open for me, leading to the ice. I brush past him and then pause in the hallway.

"Thanks again. I guess I'll see you tomorrow?"

"Yeah. If you have more questions, we can plan on getting to the rink earlier." He pulls out his phone. "Let me give you my number."

My stomach flutters in that way it does when you're talking to someone and taking the next step to stay in touch.

"So we can coordinate," he adds.

"Right." Official business, not flirting with me. Fumbling, I pull out my phone. I add his number to my phone, then text him so he has mine.

Somewhere on the ice I can hear one of the coaches tell the kids lunchtime is over. Nick takes a step backward, flashing me those dimples. "If you need anything before tomorrow, just text me."

"You've given me plenty for now." I clutch my laptop to my chest.

He nods, turns on his heel, and jogs off.

Café Moon smells like dark-roast beans and sweet sugar. A rich, wood bar takes up half the counter space, and there are tables along the windows and spaced out around the room. It's cozy and warm, and to my surprise, filled with more people than I thought were in all of Moonshot. It's bustling with people hurrying in and out. Others sit with friends or dates, and a few have laptops in front of them, working like me.

After I settle into the booth by the window, I pull out my laptop and my notes. Excitement courses through me as I read through Nick's answers to all my questions. He's turning out to be different than I thought. I think he might be a genuinely nice guy underneath his jerk exterior. I like the way he lights up talking about hockey. He transforms. Even in reading his thoughts to things like his daily schedule, I find myself grinning at the screen as I remember the way he was so animated as he told it.

Unfortunately, his excitement, and mine, doesn't translate well. As soon as I switch over to my manuscript, the blinking cursor looms, and I'm frozen, fingers poised over the keyboard. I take a deep breath, sit back, and eat my scone, giving myself the mother of all pep talks.

You can do this. One word at a time. You've done it before. You can do it again. You have got this!

Except with my scone gone and coffee cup empty, I still haven't made a single edit.

I grab my phone and swipe to read a new text from my sister.

Olivia: How is it going with the hot hockey player?

Chuckling, I tap out a reply.

Me: You can't keep calling him that.

Olivia: Why not? He's hot. Flynn agrees.

Me: Because I'm working with him.

And because I don't need a reminder. Those dimples. Those eyes. Those muscles.

Olivia: Fine. How is it going with the hockey player (who is definitely hot)?

Me: Better than expected.

Olivia: That's great news!

I can feel her hopefulness. She has always been my biggest cheerleader, and I don't want to let her, or anyone else, down. I send a smiley face in reply and go back to staring at the cursor.

I can do this . . .

Chapter Twelve

RUBY

The next morning I am ready to go to the rink, appropriately dressed and prepared with new questions, fifteen minutes early. I head out to my rental car with plans to stop by Café Moon on my way. I want to be bright-eyed and bushy-tailed because I am capable. I am a talented writer. I have a fantastic work ethic. I've been given another chance. I am under deadline. And I can freaking do this.

I've been giving myself that same pep talk since yesterday afternoon when I closed my laptop for the day without writing a single word. I just need a little more information first. More hockey research, more time to let it all soak in.

"Morning." Nick's rough voice startles me.

He's on the front porch, duffel slung over one shoulder, and two coffees—one in each hand.

My heart speeds up at the sight of him. He's freshly shaved again this morning, and I take in those glorious dimples. His face has so much character. It isn't smooth and perfect. It's filled with a million interesting details like it was sculpted by an artist with an impeccable eye. Perhaps that's why his scowls feel so weighty. All those details spark to life with his emotions.

"Good morning," I reply, a little breathier than I'd like. I stop walking as he takes the steps and crosses the driveway toward me.

The wind brings his scent to me before he's close, something clean and woodsy like he showered in the great outdoors. Now there's a nice visual.

My face flushes as he holds out one of the coffees to me.

"For me?" I ask, a smile lifting the corners of my mouth.

His answer is a tiny nod.

"Thank you."

"The coffee at the rink is awful," he says as if that's the only reason for the nice gesture. I can't get a good read on him. He's nice, considerate even, good with kids, successful, has at least one normal friend. What the hell does he have to be so moody about?

I mean besides the whole his dad invited me here without him knowing, because admittedly that might make anyone grumpy. Still, that was days ago. We seem to have moved past it, and yet, he still walks around like he has the weight of the world resting on his shoulders.

The screen door slams as Aidan walks out the front door. Nick steps back, opening his stance to his son.

"Got everything?" Nick asks him.

"Yeah," Aidan replies with that distinct childish air of incredulity, like how dare you question my ability to pack a bag.

"Good." Nick looks to me. "Meet you at the rink?"

"Yeah."

We're the first ones to arrive. Nick unlocks the door to let us in, then disappears to turn on the lights in the building. Aidan wastes no time getting dressed and heading out onto the ice. I wander down to the same spot on the bench where I sat yesterday.

After setting my stuff down, I peer over the ledge at the ice. A shiver makes my whole body jump.

Aidan steps out from the other side, smoothly gliding across the surface with his hockey stick in one hand. He tosses a puck down and starts doing a very complicated-looking drill.

"How hard could it be?" I say to myself as I open the gate. I take one tentative step onto the ice. It feels solid enough. The cold seeps through the flimsy soles of my shoes as I step out with my other foot.

I feel wobbly, like a baby deer or a toddler attempting to stand. Greer was so stinking cute when she was at that stage.

Feeling a little more confident, I take another tentative step, this time farther from the gate.

"It's easier with skates." His deep voice startles me, and I swivel around, losing my balance in the process and going down hard on my butt.

It hurts. My pride hurts worse.

"Shit. Sorry." He hurries out onto the ice to help me up. His big hands wrap around each of my wrists, and he pulls me to my feet. He looks me over as the cold radiates through my clothing.

"Are you all right?" His fingers hold me in place as he continues to stare at me with concern. His eyes spark a darker shade of green, and up close that dimple in his chin is so tempting. I want to trace it with my finger . . . or maybe my tongue.

"Yes," I say, reeling my thoughts in. I'm filled with a sudden embarrassment for daydreaming about licking his face and the sting in my butt. "You all make it look so easy."

One side of his mouth lifts. "I could grab you a pair of skates from the back. What size are you?"

"Oh no." I shake my head. "I don't want to skate."

He lifts a brow, calling my bluff since he just found me walking onto the ice.

"I had a momentary lapse in judgment, but I remember now why I don't do sporty things." I summon the use of my wobbly legs and carefully make my way back to the safety of the bench.

"So," I say, composing myself in a professional way that hopefully wipes his memory of me flat on my ass. "Should we jump in?"

He hesitates a beat, perhaps surprised by my switch in topic, while I gingerly sit. Finally, he waves a hand, indicating I should continue.

My tailbone still aches, but I push it from my mind as I read the first question on my list. "What's game day like?"

"Home or away?"

"Are they different?" I ask. "Aside from location, of course."

"Not for everyone, maybe."

"But it is for you?"

His jaw works back and forth. It's not in the angry, annoyed way I've seen before, but in a more contemplative way as if he's rethinking his answer or choosing his words carefully.

"Maybe you want to just walk me through both?" I ask, hoping to make it easier for him to explain.

It's another few seconds of quiet, only Aidan's skates and the sound of him hitting the puck in the background, before Nick speaks again. "I do pretty much the same thing regardless of where I am once I get to the rink. I change clothes, set out my gear, then tape my stick. After that I have a protein shake and then chug some water so I'm hydrated. Then I stretch, get treatment, if needed, go to meetings."

"More research meetings?"

"Before the game we have a team meeting to talk about power plays or any last-minute lineup changes on either team that are going to impact our style of play."

"Strategy."

"Yeah." He bobs his head in agreement.

"How soon is that before the game?"

"About two hours before."

"And then what do you do?" I'm sitting forward, the pain in my butt completely forgotten. It's hard to pinpoint why I'm so intrigued—by him or the intricacies of hockey. My guess, based on a lifetime of disinterest in sports, it's the former.

"Then it's time to get loose and warmed up before we take the ice."

"More stretching?"

"Some of the guys do that."

"What do you do?"

A boyish grin lifts the corners of his mouth, and a swarm of butterflies takes flight in my stomach.

"I kick a soccer ball around with Travis."

"Soccer?"

"Yeah. It's a thing a lot of hockey guys do. It's a fun way to work out any nerves while getting the legs warm."

"Makes sense." I bring the pen to my lips as I think. I hadn't expected this much detail in his game-day routine, and I have a dozen more questions now. "It's just you and Travis?"

"Yeah. Some of the younger guys have a big game going in the hallway, but Trav and I go to the training room, where it's a little quieter."

"Was it different at your last team?" I ask.

"It was similar enough."

"Is switching teams hard?"

"Sometimes."

"Was it for you?"

"No. It was the best thing for me and Aidan." His tone leaves no room for debate, so I don't pry, but I am curious. I saw a few news articles and fan discussion boards questioning his trade. Some people think there was friction with his Wildcat teammates or coaches. Others speculate that he wanted more money.

"So you and Travis go off, just the two of you, and . . . kick a soccer ball back and forth?"

He rests two hands on his stick and leans slightly. "Mhmm."

"Is there music or conversation?"

"The guys in the hallway have music going, which filters in to us."

"And conversation?"

"Mostly Travis fills me in on his dating escapades."

A surprised laugh bubbles up in my chest. "He's that guy, huh?"

"Women love him."

My gaze narrows. I wonder if he thinks women don't like him. No. No way. That'd be crazy. There's absolutely no world in which he doesn't have women vying for his attention at every turn.

"What?" he asks.

I smooth out the questioning look on my face and smile. "Nothing."

The weighty scowl he returns tells me he knows I'm holding back.

"What about before you go to the rink on game days?"

"If we're out of town, then there's a team breakfast and a morning skate, then a nap in the hotel."

"And at home?" I prompt him.

"I still have breakfast and get to the rink for a skate, but the time at home varies on what else is going on."

I must have a confused expression as I stare at him because he continues without prompting.

"Aidan might have stuff he needs to do, or my dad might have plans that interfere with my schedule."

"Like inviting a stranger to stay on your property?" I ask, hoping we're at the joking phase of the situation now.

"Yeah." A rough, short laugh slips from his lips.

I smile back at him, and for a moment it feels like we're in on our own private joke. He looks away first, and when he glances back, the grumpy version of him is back in full force.

I guide the conversation back to more easy questions about game day, before and after, then during. What's it like being out on the ice? What are you thinking about? How do you decompress after the game?

"It depends" is his favorite answer. He never says it in a way that makes me think he's trying to put me off, but more that he can't seem to drill things down so simply. Maybe hockey really is that complex. It definitely feels that way as I try to make sense of the different penalties.

He's listing them out for me. "Tripping, high-sticking, hooking—"

"Hooking?" I ask, certain I heard him wrong.

He nods.

"It's really called that?"

Another small smile pulls at one side of his mouth. "Yep. It's a minor penalty."

"Which means the player spends two minutes in the box?"

"That's right."

I breathe a sigh of relief that I've managed to remember one tiny detail.

"Have you ever had a hooking penalty?" I still can't believe it's called that, though I can't seem to come up with a better name.

"Oh yeah."

I quirk a brow. "So they're common, then?"

He doesn't strike me as someone who makes a lot of mistakes.

"Yeah. Minor penalties are more common than major, but they all happen. Emotions and adrenaline run high during games. And sometimes, guys just piss you off."

"You get them on purpose?!"

His smile is even bigger, and those damn dimples are winking at me.

"Wow. I had no idea," I say at the same time Aidan's voice carries from the other side of the rink.

"Dammit," Aidan curses quietly again, head hanging low.

Nick looks from his son back to me.

"Is he okay?" I ask.

Everything in his body language screams his desire to check on Aidan, but his words are calm. "He's fine. Hockey can be frustrating."

"At least that makes sense to me."

"Writing is frustrating?"

"Sometimes." Lately it's more like always.

Nick glances back at his son. Even through the mask, I can tell Aidan is scowling like his father.

"Do you want to . . . ?" I let the question hang because I'm not sure what one does in this situation. When I'm frustrated over a bad writing day, I usually don't want to talk about it. I know that isn't everyone's preference though. While I prefer to stew and mull over my plot issues, I've sat on calls with Lily for hours helping her get unstuck.

"Yeah, maybe I should check on him. I'll be quick."

"It's okay." I check the time on my phone. The time has gone fast, as usual, and the campers will be arriving soon.

"You're leaving?"

"I think I have enough for now."

"What will you do with the rest of your day?"

If I didn't know better, I'd think he cared how I was going to spend my day.

"Write." Hopefully. "I have to turn in the new first chapter on Friday."

He skates slowly backward, still staring at me.

"Thanks for your time." I lift my cup. "And the coffee."

"You're welcome."

I lift a hand in a wave before turning to leave. I swear I feel his eyes on me, but when I turn around, he's on the other side of the rink with Aidan. Pausing at the door, I watch him. Aidan's head is bowed, his stare downcast as his dad talks to him. Eventually, he nods, and Nick places a reassuring hand on his son's shoulder.

I'm still watching when Nick looks up. His gaze goes to the bench where I was sitting, then scans the rink, almost as if looking for someone. Maybe me. I slip out of the door before he spots me.

Chapter Thirteen

NICK

"Why is that chick staying in the cabin?" Aidan asks after dinner. He's rinsing off his plate next to me, staring out the window. I follow his gaze to Ruby walking down by the lake. She's in a blue sleeveless top and jean shorts, her red hair whipping around her face.

"She needed a place to stay for the summer."

"Is it true she's writing a book about you?" He glances over at me, spaghetti sauce on his face.

"No." I wipe his mouth with a rag. "Where did you hear that?"

He shrugs. "Uncle Trav."

"What'd I tell you about believing Uncle Trav?"

He ducks away from the rag, grinning as he says, "That he's full of bull crap and I should think of everything he says as mostly exaggerated."

A chuckle scrapes up my throat. "Exactly."

The doorbell rings.

"Speaking of Uncle Trav."

Aidan's grin widens. He looks up to Travis and listens to him, much to my dismay, more than just about anyone else. Of all people it had to be Travis. Surprisingly, he's good with kids. All the reasons I worry about his influence on Aidan are the exact reasons kids adore him. He has no filter, he doesn't talk down to them, and he's got this funny, charismatic way about him that makes people want to be his friend, even kids.

"You get the door. I'll finish up in here," I tell him. He's taken off at a sprint before I finish the sentence.

I glance once more out the window at Ruby as I toss the rag onto the counter. Outside of our morning interviews at the rink, I've barely seen her. She's shown up every day this week, staying until the kids arrive for camp to ask me questions. So many questions and things no one has asked me before like, "Which team jersey was my favorite?" and

"What color tape would you use for your stick if you had your choice?" and "What does it feel like to step onto the ice each time?"

She's . . . interesting. Perhaps it's because I'm used to the people asking me questions having a deep love, or at least a baseline knowledge of the sport, but I find myself trying to anticipate what she'll ask me next, and I almost never get it right. But maybe most perplexing of all is that I've found myself dreading our time together a little less each day.

Outside of our time each morning, she's kept to herself. She's often walking down by the water or sitting out on the porch of the cabin (not that I'm looking), but otherwise, I could almost pretend she isn't here. Almost.

As I turn from the window, Aidan is running back to the kitchen. Travis is behind him, followed by our teammates Conrad Shepard and August Penn.

"Hey," I greet them all at once, but go to Shep first. I haven't seen him since he left after the season to visit his family in Washington. "You're back. Good to see you, man."

We slap hands, and I pull him in for a quick, side hug.

"You too." He offers a half smile with the quiet words. On the ice he's one of the fastest, toughest defenders I've ever played with, but off it, he's soft-spoken and happy to fade into the background. Which honestly is easy to do in our group.

I look to Penn next. Our goalie has been with Moonshot longer than any of us. Like Shep, he's on the quieter side, but from him it has more of an edge. Travis says the only one grumpier than me is Penn. Far be it for me to judge, but next to Trav we all probably seem like moody motherfuckers.

"How's it going? How's the knee?" I ask him. He had surgery after the end of the season, one of many since I've joined the team. The man is a beast.

"Good." He glances down at his right leg as his mouth pulls into a tight, straight line. "The doctors think I can get back on the ice this week. And your shoulder?"

"Good." I mimic his words.

Penn is one of the best netminders in the league and our team's not-so-secret weapon, but he's also a hell of a guy. There's no one else I'd want stopping pucks for us, and I know the team feels the same. I might wear the captain's "C," but that's only because he can't lead while stuck in the net. Plus, he has no interest in it. Either way, we all look up to him. He's been around long enough that he's seen it all. The ups and downs don't get to him the same way they do the young guys, and for the rest of us, we recognize the sacrifices he's made, body and mind, and the discipline needed to keep playing as long as he has. Realistically he has maybe another three or four seasons, and I want to bear witness to all of them. The man is a legend. His jersey will be hanging in the rafters for sure.

"Is D-Low coming?" I ask at the same time the doorbell rings in rapid succession like someone is repeatedly pressing it.

Shep laughs softly. "That'll be him."

"Grab a beer and head on down, if you want," I tell them as I move toward the front door.

Pulling it open, I smile at the man on the front stoop. His finger is poised on the doorbell like he was considering ringing it again.

"Don't even think about it," I tell him, using my dad voice.

Danny Marlowe, otherwise known on the team as D-Low, smirks. At twenty-three he still has a streak of youthful playfulness that sometimes reminds me of Aidan and his friends.

"Just wanted to make sure you heard me, old man." He steps forward and wraps me in a hug, slapping my back twice, hard, before brushing past me.

"And here I thought you might have grown up during the break. Isn't there a book on that?" I find myself ribbing him, some of his playfulness rubbing off on me.

"If there is, rest assured I've read it and dismissed it as crap."

A small chuckle leaves my lips. "I don't doubt it."

He's the best-read person I've ever met, and an honest-to-God rocket scientist. Most hockey players, especially the good ones, either skip college completely or spend those years focused on getting drafted but not D-Low. Sometimes I think he'd be just as happy if he'd ended up in a lab somewhere. I thought I was smart until I met him. He's always listening to a book or reading one, spouting facts like a one-man trivia genius.

Seeing him and thinking about books has my thoughts returning to Ruby. Travis must have really gotten in my head because I can't help but wonder if D-Low's more her type than me.

Sure, he doesn't look the part of book nerd with his tattoos and piercings and extrovert personality, but he's smart, and something tells me Ruby is into smart.

As we walk back through the house, voices drift from the kitchen. Aidan has disappeared, but my dad has joined Travis, Shep, and Penn at the back door. Their backs are to us.

"She's a looker," my dad says with a low whistle.

"I always did have a thing for redheads," Travis adds. He glances back, finds my gaze, and smirks.

I don't have to look myself to know exactly who they're watching or talking about.

"I think that's what they call a string bikini," Dad says.

"Seriously?" I ask, dryly.

No one moves, but Penn slides his gaze back to us.

"Hey, D-Low. Good to see you."

"Yeah, you too." D-Low steps closer to the group of guys and stares out the back door with them. "Who's the redhead?"

"She's an author," my dad says, then tips his head toward me. "She's here interviewing Nicky boy."

D-Low's brows lift as he turns his attention briefly back to me. "Are you writing a biography?"

"God no."

"She's a romance author," my dad says with a smile. "She's writing a book about a hockey player falling in love."

That's the tidbit that finally gets all of them to look at me.

"Don't worry, he didn't tell me either. I had to find out from her," Travis says to them.

"Yeah, and now I remember why," I say under my breath.

"Hold up." Shep's brows tug together in the center. "Why would someone interview you for a romance novel?"

Penn chuckles, and immediately Shep's cheeks take on a ruddy red flush.

"I just mean . . ." he starts, but I head him off by holding up a hand.

"Don't worry about it. I'm well aware that I'm about the worst possible candidate for the job." I tip my head toward my dad. "He invited her."

"Ah. Now that makes more sense," D-Low says.

"Yeah," I agree. My body hums with a desire to move the conversation along or maybe look out the window with the rest of them at the woman that's currently making my life chaos. Instead, I ask, "Are we ready to get started?"

There's a buzz of agreement, but no one makes a move to the basement.

"Dad, are you playing?"

"One hand," he says. It's always what he says, but he usually stays much longer than that.

"Maybe we should move our poker game to the back deck," Travis says. "Nice night and all."

I roll my eyes. "Everything is already set up downstairs."

"Fine. Fine," he says with a heavy sigh. He's trying to get under my skin. And it's working.

Still, no one moves.

"For the love of . . ." I step in front of them, at least partially blocking their view of Ruby, but not before catching a glimpse of her. Dad was right on several counts. She's stripped down to her bikini, and she is definitely a fucking looker. *Damn.*

Shep blinks as if he didn't realize he was staring for so long, then offers me a sheepish smile. D-Low still looks like he's piecing together the situation. Penn looks bored. Dad tries to look around me. Travis fights back a smile. Fucker.

"Someone's feeling protective," my dad notes as they finally shuffle away from the back door.

"What I'm feeling is annoyed," I say, mostly to myself.

"Don't worry, Nicky boy. We won't get in your way," Travis says.

"I thought she seemed like your type," my dad says to him.

"I'm on a dating cleanse."

"That doesn't sound healthy," Dad says, which makes Travis laugh.

"Probably not, sir. Probably not."

Downstairs, we take our usual seats around the poker table. We've been playing every Saturday night for the last two years. The group is slightly different depending on the time of year. Other guys pop in and out during the season, and often we're on the road, sitting around in someone's hotel room instead of my basement. During the off-season it's whoever is in town.

Dad winces as he carefully drops into the seat to my right. His leg is bothering him more and more. Not that he'd admit it. Another symptom of the heart issues he's been having. I need to make sure he's walking every day. The doctor said if he was consistent with that, it would make a big difference.

Travis picks up the cards and starts to shuffle. "It feels like my night to take your money."

He says that every week, despite his epic losing streak. The last time he won was eight months ago when D-Low was absent and I was getting over the flu.

As the cards are divvied up, somewhere upstairs Aidan begins playing his guitar.

"Damn," my dad says. "I forgot my earplugs upstairs."

Shep chuckles and Penn grimaces.

"Go easy on him," I say. "He's just learning."

Aidan picks that moment to hit a particularly rough chord, and I wince involuntarily.

"Is that an old Metallica song?" Travis asks, bopping his head and shuffling through the cards in his hand.

"Nah, nah. I think it's Pink Floyd," my dad says.

It's as likely to be "Twinkle, Twinkle, Little Star" for as much as I can make out of it. It's really not my son's fault; musical talent does not run in the family. My mom put me in piano as a kid, and it was torture.

"It's 'Knockin' On Heaven's Door,'" Penn says as he tosses in his ante.

We all pause and listen. Sure enough.

"I'll be damned." Dad grins.

"How in the hell did you know that?" I ask Penn.

He shrugs. "I tried to learn guitar one summer to impress a girl."

A surprised laugh escapes my lips. "You did?"

A small smirk lifts one side of his mouth.

"How'd that go?" I ask.

"Turns out she was more into jocks."

"And?" I wait for the end of the story.

"So I asked my mom to sign me up for hockey camp."

Penn taking up hockey for a girl is as surprising as anything I've heard. As long as I've known him, he's dated almost as infrequently as me. A few hookups, but even those felt more like the girl fell in his lap than him making any effort. Lucky for him, he doesn't have a meddling father who refuses to keep his nose out of his business.

"God bless women." Travis lifts his beer.

"Here, here." Dad lifts his as well.

Shep does, too, absently without a word. D-Low and I exchange a look but join in.

"Speaking of women," Dad starts.

"Here we go," I mutter.

"I mean, she's out there all on her own. Would it kill you to invite her to play?"

"What makes you think she wants to play poker with us?"

"Better than sitting out there by herself," he fires back.

"Debatable."

For a few moments, the table is quiet as we look at our cards and start playing. Shep is the first one to break the silence.

He puts in his ante and says, "What kind of questions are you answering for a romance author?"

"Hockey stuff. The character in her book was a baseball player, and her publisher asked her to change it to hockey."

"Interesting," he says in a way that makes me believe he really does find it fascinating.

"Hockey romance is big," D-Low says.

We all look to him.

"What? I follow BookTok." He shrugs it off.

"Of course you do," Penn says.

"What's her name?" D-Low asks.

"Ruby Madison." I shift uncomfortably.

"I haven't heard of her."

"She's a big deal," Dad pipes in. "A *New York Times* bestseller."

"Impressive," Travis says.

"Mhmmm." My dad purrs his agreement.

"Maybe she is more your type," Travis says to me, a frown tugging the corners of his lips down.

I don't ask why he thinks that, but I do question the relief I feel at his statement.

Chapter Fourteen

RUBY

Nick's house is quiet as I pad up the back steps. I try to walk softly but not like I'm creeping up on them. If at all possible, I'd also love to come and go unannounced.

Several extra vehicles are in the driveway like maybe they're having a party. Except all I can hear is Aidan's guitar.

I step into the kitchen, relieved to find it empty. The song ends and I freeze, but there's no movement. He's probably switching between songs. Quickly, I go to the sink and check under the counter, which is where I keep my cleaning supplies, but come up empty. I try the cabinet to the right of it and then the next. Pretty soon I've opened and closed every single cabinet, and I'm getting more frustrated and perplexed with each one.

"How is a girl supposed to stress clean?" I ask to the empty kitchen.

"Dad keeps all that stuff up high, so I don't accidentally drink it."

I whirl around to find Aidan standing across the kitchen staring at me. I'm not sure how long he's been there.

"Hi," I say breathlessly. I angle my body and point to the upper cabinets.

"That one." He motions to the one on the far left.

As promised, the cleaning supplies are here. Bottles of all kinds, lined up with their labels facing out. I pull down the multipurpose bottle and turn back to Aidan. "Do you often try to drink cleaner?"

A shy smile tips up the corners of his mouth. He looks so much like his dad, but this smile is one I have not seen from his father. "He worries."

"Good. Parents are supposed to worry." I hold up the bottle. "Is it okay if I borrow this?"

He shrugs one shoulder. "I guess so."

"Thanks." I huff a small laugh, then note the guitar hanging off his shoulder. "How long have you been playing?"

"Not long." He glances down at his feet and shuffles. "I'm not very good. My dad and grandpa wear earplugs. They think I don't notice, but they aren't very good at hiding it."

"Being good at things takes practice."

"I guess so, but I don't want to annoy them all the time while I practice."

I get that. I used to make my family read everything I wrote. Poems, short stories, plays, eulogies—those didn't always go over very well, oops. I was so passionate about writing. I lived for the laughs, the smiles, the joy I could see on their faces. When I could get a real, genuine laugh out of my dad, I would buzz with excitement the rest of the day. Tears from my mom? A rush of adrenaline that lasted hours. And anything Olivia reread or asked to keep meant I had struck gold.

I learned a lot during that phase of writing, including that you can't force anyone else to feel the way you do about art. Something that brought me immense pleasure didn't always do the same for them. If my parents were busy or my sister was in a bad mood, then I was almost guaranteed to be disappointed by their response to reading something I'd written.

I never learned an instrument, so at least my practice could always be done in silence.

"If your dad is okay with it, you can come practice at the cabin anytime you like," I say to him.

His eyes widen, and a dimple appears in his cheek as he smiles. "Really?"

"Yeah." I find myself smiling back at him as I nod.

He tips his head to the side as if considering my offer. "And you won't wear earplugs?"

I let out a small laugh. "Of course not."

He gives me a strange look like he doesn't believe me.

"Were you always good at hockey?" I ask him.

He thinks for a moment. Those green eyes lift, and his mouth twists in concentration. "No, I guess not. My slap shot used to be pretty bad."

I have no idea what that means, but I think I'm still making my point. "And now?"

"Much better."

"Because you practiced?"

"Every day for months."

"See? You just need to keep practicing."

"Even if it forces them to wear earplugs?" His cheeks tinge red.

"Even then."

He doesn't look convinced. And I don't blame him. Other people's opinions can be loud and hard to ignore—even the ones offered with the best of intentions. We have a deep understanding of the people closest to us, which means we can tell when they don't love something. But the only way to get better is to push through the crap. It's a good reminder for myself.

"You'll get the hang of it, and I love to listen to music while I work."

"Even really bad guitar?"

"Especially that." I smile at him, and his grin returns.

"Okay. I'll ask him."

Laughter from downstairs draws our attention.

"I should get back. I didn't mean to interrupt your party," I say.

"It's their weekly poker game."

"Sounds fun."

"I'm sure they'd let you join if you want."

I hadn't really meant that it sounded fun, more that it was nice that they had a weekly thing. It's only been six days, but I miss my family, our dinners, and hanging out. I miss socializing.

"They were talking about you earlier," Aidan says with a sheepish grin.

Well, that's ominous. Nothing good, I'm sure.

"I have things to do, but thanks."

He eyes the bottle in my hands as if calling my bluff.

I backpedal. "I don't want to intrude."

"You're not." He steps forward and takes my hand, then pulls me with him.

I barely have time to do anything except glance down at myself. I'm still wearing my swimsuit from sitting out by the lake earlier, but I managed to put on a tube top and shorts with flip-flops before I walked over for cleaning supplies. Which I realize I'm still holding in one hand as Aidan hurries down the stairs, tugging me along by the other.

Six men are seated around a circle table in the middle of the room, and all eyes turn to me. Aidan drops my hand and runs to his dad's side. Nick scoots back to let his son on his lap while not taking his gaze off me.

"Hi!" I lift a hand in a wave. The rag whips through the air with my fingers. "I came by for cleaning supplies. Thought I'd do a deep clean of the cabin."

No one says anything, and I shift awkwardly.

"Cleaning on a Saturday night?" Mike asks finally, then scoffs. "Take a seat, darling. We're not much company, but we're better than what you have planned. You like poker?"

"I'm not sure. I've never played." I don't move because Nick is shooting red lasers out of his eyeballs. They seem to be directed at the inches of bare skin at my midsection, like he's never seen a belly button ring before.

"Grab a chair and pull it up. I'll show you." Travis motions at me, then picks up his cards.

"The only thing he can show you is how to lose," another guy mutters, then gives me a sly smile. His arms are covered in tattoos, including his hands.

"That's Danny," Travis tells me. "But everybody calls him D-Low. You can't trust anything he says while sitting around the poker table."

"All's fair in poker and hockey." Danny grins at me.

"I don't think that's how the saying goes," the guy to his right says. He looks at me with a shy smile. Holy mother of . . . hotness. "I'm Conrad. Nice to meet you."

Conrad is possibly the most attractive man I've ever seen in real life. Like stunningly so. Very pretty boy type, which isn't really something I'd normally be into, but it's really hard to tear my gaze away from him. And his face just gets redder the longer I stare. For his sake, I force myself to look away but OMG.

"And that's August Penn, but we just call him Penn," Travis says, tipping his head to the only man at the table not staring in my direction.

At his name he briefly glances up. He wears a polite, if not bored expression. "Hey."

"Hi."

He's broad and sits taller than the others. A black baseball cap is pulled down low on his face. Light-brown hair sticks out on the sides and in the back. He's wearing a faded Moonshot hockey T-shirt that pulls at his arm muscles. He and Nick are competing for grumpiest man alive, and I can't tell who's winning.

They are a lot to take in. I scan the circle of hockey players and Mike before my gaze lands back on Nick. I'm not sure what it says that among this group of extremely hot men, he's the one I feel most drawn to.

"Does the rest of your team look like this?" I ask.

"Like what?" Danny asks.

I open my mouth but then close it when I can't figure out how to politely ask them to rate the hot factor of the rest of their teammates.

"Never mind," I mumble.

They all look to me expectantly.

Mike finally breaks the silence. "What do you say, darling? Want to be my good luck charm? I haven't won a hand all night."

"Dad," Nick says in a pained tone. "I seriously doubt she wants to spend her Saturday night playing cards with us."

Mike scoffs. "Why not? I'm great company."

"Same," Travis agrees, grinning.

"Does that mean you don't want me to play?" I ask him. I can't read him, and frankly, I'm tired of guessing.

"Of course he does," Aidan says. "Right, Dad?"

Nick's jaw ticks as he nods slowly. He lifts Aidan and stands, then walks over to the corner to grab another chair. He sets it between him and Penn. He grunts what might be an invitation.

Part of me would like to tell him to shove that chair up his grumpy ass, but then I think how much fun it'll be to annoy him all night.

I set the cleaner and rag down on a side table next to a giant sectional that looks as if it could easily seat twelve. Interesting choice for a man who seems to only like a handful of people. The whole downstairs space has a real man-cave vibe. Big-screen TV, leather furniture, framed memorabilia on the wall, plus the poker table in the center.

Aidan moves to the couch with his guitar as I take my seat. I smile at the giant named Penn to my left.

"I'm Ruby," I say to him, realizing I hadn't introduced myself.

He tips his chin at me. I can't decide whether he's shy or antisocial. "I know."

I wince. "Uh-oh. What'd you hear?"

A smile tips up both sides of his mouth. "Nothing bad. Just that you're interviewing Nick for a book you're writing."

"I am," I confirm.

"Are you a hockey player too?" I ask, even though he's wearing a shirt that suggests so.

He nods.

"Penn is our goalie," Nick tells me, then adds, "You can play with me."

"Oh, interesting," I say to the less grumpy man beside me. It's a real standoff between these two, but with Penn, at least I don't feel like it's aimed at me. "I love your gear."

Everyone goes quiet, then Mike breaks the silence with a chuckle. "Now that's a compliment he doesn't hear every day."

The tips of my ears get hot as the rest of the guys join in laughing.

I glance at Penn, realizing I may have just insulted him or inadvertently hit on him. "Sorry. I'm still learning the sport."

"Nah." Penn gives me another smile. "The gear is cool, right?"

I nod with relief that he doesn't seem bothered by my lack of hockey knowledge. "Accessories were always my favorite part of sports."

Mike shuffles the cards and deals them. Nick nods for me to pick his up, so I do.

"Oooh." I smile at the two aces. I don't know much about poker, but I think I remember aces being good.

"First rule of poker," Nick says, reaching over and dragging my chair closer to him. My skin prickles at the heat of him beside me. "Learning how to keep a poker face."

His arm brushes mine, and I move my leg, so our knees don't knock under the table.

"Right." I force my lips into a neutral line. "Better?"

Nick's gaze drops to my mouth, lingering a beat before he looks away. "Yep," he says in his usual gruff, annoyed tone.

Around the table, the men glance at their cards, then place them on the table facedown. I do the same.

On my left, Penn tosses in a chip.

"Should I do that too?" I ask Nick.

"No. We already did. He's the big blind."

I raise a brow in question.

"The big blind is two seats to the left of the dealer. The small blind is one seat to the left. They have to put in forced bets before seeing their cards. We don't."

"Got it," I say with confidence, filing away the information. Maybe it's my inherent personality or maybe it's something about wanting to prove myself to Nick, but I am determined to be an A-plus student. "What kind of hand would I fold?"

It seems like the most logical question, but the way Nick's shoulders lift and fall in a sigh, you'd think I asked why the sky is blue.

"Let me guess." I grin at him. "It depends?"

He lets out a surprised chuckle that transforms his face. "Exactly."

We play several rounds. I learn terms like bet, raise, call, and fold—all fairly self-explanatory. And ones that make less sense like "river" and "boat." Once we get going, Nick is more patient with me than I expect, sort of like he is with the kids at camp.

It's hard to be stealthy and talk out our hand without the others overhearing. I lean in close enough that his scent wraps around me. Fabric softener and sandalwood. It's nice.

It's our deal. Nick hands me the cards. I grin as I take them. I've shuffled cards before, but it has been a long time, and I've never done it the way they are.

"Place your hands like this." He sets his over mine and adjusts until I'm in the right position. The size of his big hands next to mine is striking.

"Everything is so secretive in poker," I say as I attempt to shuffle so that no one can see the cards.

His lips quirk up higher on one side. "That's what makes it fun. You have to read the players."

"Can you read me?" I ask the group as I deal.

Mike grins. "You're a wildcard, sweetheart."

"What does that mean?" I ask, expecting another poker phrase that I'll need to add to my overflowing dictionary of terms. This game has a lot of rules.

"Some players, especially new ones, are easy to read, but they don't tend to act in the way a more seasoned player would," Danny says.

"Easy to read their cards, but hard as hell to play against," Travis adds with a frown. He tosses his cards onto the table. "I fold. Ruby-Doo was grinning too big when she looked at her cards."

Oops. I school my expression back into serious mode, then think back to seeing a poker tournament on TV once. I glance up at the hat on Nick's head.

I lean closer to him. His brows inch higher as my shoulder brushes his chest.

"Give me your hat," I whisper, though not quietly enough that the others don't hear.

Mike and Travis chuckle. Nick rears back like I asked him for the password to his bank account.

"I'm giving us away," I say and wave my hand toward the guys, each of them folding as they take their turns.

Reluctantly, and frowning like it's his job, Nick takes off his hat and places it onto my head. It's too big and falls over my eyes.

I tip my chin up so I can meet his gaze. "Better? Do I look like you now?"

I smash my lips together and try to look as grumpy and broody as him.

His lips split into a smile, and he gives his head a shake as he huffs a small laugh. The reaction lights me up. There's something very satisfying about making the grumpy hockey player laugh.

"Spot-on impression," Conrad says.

"Nick could never pull off a midriff shirt," Travis adds.

"Better than you could," Nick fights back.

"Keep your clothes on, Galaxy." Penn smirks.

I look between them and beam. "Oh my god. You're both smiling!"

Everyone else except Nick and Penn laugh. Penn's lips twitch with amusement, and when I glance back at Nick, he's shaking his head at me again. He reaches out and lifts the brim of his hat so it sits higher on my forehead. Absently, his pinky brushes my hair out of my eyes. His hand lingers there a moment, and electricity zips through me.

"Whose deal is it?" Mike asks.

Nick's hand drops, and his body tenses as if he's suddenly become aware of his actions.

It takes a few more hands until I finally feel like I'm getting the hang of it, and they deal me in my own cards. I'm terrible at calculating odds and all the other things that Nick instructed me as being important when considering your hand, but I've had decent luck flying by the seat of my pants. I spend my time trying to read everyone, like they claimed to be able to do with me. Unsurprisingly, Nick and Penn are the hardest to read.

I'm staring at the now hatless man to my right when it's his turn. He's stoic and almost robotic in his movements. If he has a tell, I haven't figured it out yet.

Nick raises on his turn and relaxes back in his chair. He must feel my stare because he slides his gaze to me. "What?"

I narrow my gaze. "Nothing."

His dark brow lifts in challenge as I continue to burn a hole through his face. Is he bluffing?

I take one more glimpse at my cards then decide to fold.

"Me too," Penn says as he slides his cards to the center of the table. Only then does Nick smirk. It's small, and it's gone nearly as quickly as it happened, but my jaw drops in surprise. He was totally bluffing!

"I should get home before you all cheat me out of the rest of my money," Travis says.

"The way you're playing tonight, you're practically giving it away," Danny retorts.

"I should go too," Conrad says.

"Is that the time?" Mike asks, holding his phone out and tipping his head back as if getting a good look. He stands. "It's way past my bedtime. Thanks for the game, boys."

Travis and Conrad stand, then Danny.

Nick reaches for the cards. "Penn?"

"I'm going to head out too." The big guy pushes back from his chair and stands. He's taller than I originally thought. He adjusts his hat on his head, lifting it, running his fingers through his light-brown hair, then placing the hat back on. "Are we still on for running around the lake tomorrow morning?"

"Yeah." Nick dips his head with a nod. "I'll meet you at mile marker one at five."

Penn nods—two nodding, stoic, grumpy men. I think they probably have entire conversations without using more than a dozen words.

"Nice to meet you, Ruby," Penn says.

"You too."

The men all say their goodbyes. Conrad and Danny wave to me as they start for the stairs. Travis pulls me into a hug that makes my bones creak.

"Later, Ruby-Doo." He shoots a smirk at Nick on his way out. Mike trails after him, leaving me with Nick.

I help him put the poker chips away. The room is quiet with only our movements proving noise. Aidan's asleep on the couch, cuddling with his guitar.

"Thanks for letting me join in," I say. "It was fun."

"You say that like you didn't expect it to be."

"I expected you to glower at me all night for invading your guys' night."

He lifts that brow. The man has expressive eyebrows that make up for his mouth rarely moving.

"I don't glower at you," he says in a grumpy tone accompanied by said glower.

A laugh bubbles up in my chest. I pull my phone out of my pocket and hold it up to snap a photo.

"What are you doing?" he asks, after blinking several times.

"Proving that you glower at me." I walk over and show him the screen of my phone. He studies it for a few moments, and then his gaze slowly flicks to me.

"No comment?" I ask as I pocket my phone again with smug satisfaction.

"That's just my face," he mumbles. "I was trying to save you from hanging out with a bunch of dudes who want to ogle you."

"They were not ogling me. If anything, they felt sorry for me."

He huffs a sound that I think is his disagreement. I glance down at my outfit. "I'm wearing an old tube top that belonged to my mother when she was my age, and these shorts are from a second-hand store."

They were already worn in and soft, but there's an ink stain on the crotch that has always perplexed me. It's only visible to me so it's not a big deal, but how does one get ink in that particular spot?

He continues to look at me like he's unable to comprehend my words. I lift my brows in silent question.

He sighs like I'm the most annoying person he's ever met. I've never had someone dislike me so much. In fact, I'd say people generally like me very much. I spent most of my twenties saying or doing little to make waves. I was too busy writing and working toward my dreams to be controversial. No one knew me. If they didn't like me, it was based on what they thought they knew and not the person I was.

But with Nick, I have been unapologetically myself. I'm not sure why. Perhaps I'm too tired to put on any pretense or maybe there's something about him that makes me want to push back.

Whatever it is, I like this version of me.

"You're beautiful." He says it so dispassionately that I wonder if I heard him correctly.

"Excuse me?"

"They don't care about your clothes. You're a beautiful woman, and they were drooling all over you."

My cheeks flush despite the way he seems to not care that I am, as he put it, beautiful. Like, oh Ruby? She's beautiful, but meh, I'm not into beautiful girls. Which only makes me wonder what kind of woman is Nick into?

"No, they weren't," I insist once I've recovered.

I get another gruff noise of disagreement.

"They weren't," I say again.

He shakes his head. "If I'd begged off with an excuse that I was going to clean, no one would have tried to change *my* mind."

"Well, I'm nicer than you."

Oops. Did I say that out loud? My face flames warmer as I give him a shy, slightly apologetic smile.

Almost in slow motion, his lips pull up on either side. "No doubt about that."

His grin makes my pulse race more than the compliment had. We keep staring and smiling at each other, and my body lights up everywhere. The front door closes upstairs, effectively snapping us out of our stare-off.

He looks away first, and then we fall back into picking up and putting away the cards and chips. Once everything is in place, we look at each other again.

I'm surprised by my reluctance to leave. Maybe if I stick around, he'll accidentally compliment me again. This is what my life has come to, hoping this grumpy man will compliment me in the most unaffected way possible. Big sigh.

"I'm going to head back to my side of the property." I hitch a thumb over my shoulder. "Where no one can ogle me."

He huffs another one of those small laughs. I can't get enough of that noise from him.

"Thanks for the poker lessons."

"You're a quick learner."

Another compliment. I'm practically floating.

I take a step backward, still watching him, then remember I'm still wearing his hat. I take it off and slowly walk toward him. "If only I were writing a book about poker instead of hockey."

His brows pinch together like maybe he wishes that too. Hockey has not come quite as easy to me. "Yeah."

"Okay then." Seriously, I need to get out of here. The room doesn't have enough oxygen for the both of us. I lift up on my toes and place the hat on his head, then turn it to the side. Even like this he's hot.

He adjusts the hat, watching me as I step back to the stairs. "Don't forget your cleaning supplies."

"Right." I grab the spray and rag, then we continue to face each other, lingering. If I didn't know better, I'd think this grumpy man wants me to stay as much as I do. What a strange development.

A warm, fuzzy feeling bubbles under my skin. "I'll bring it back tomorrow. Promise."

His chin lifts in acknowledgment but doesn't offer me any quippy remark to give me a reason to keep bantering with him. Pity.

I finally turn to leave. I don't look back, but I swear I can feel his gaze on me as I go.

Chapter Fifteen

RUBY

On Sunday morning I wake up with the sun. In only a week my body has attuned to the early morning shift in my schedule. I wander out of my cabin with a cup of hot tea (I still need to get a coffee pot) and smile at the view. A girl could get used to this.

The water laps quietly, and the birds chirp. It's so nature-y. I take a short video and send it to Olivia. Her response is immediate.

Olivia: It sounds like you're living in a forest. Is there a flock of birds directly over your head? Have you taken up bird watching? Do they eat out of your palm? Did you buy one of those feeders that takes video? Should I send help?

A small laugh leaves my lips because a week ago I would have been as horrified as she sounds, but now, it's kind of nice.

Me: No, but it is stunning here.

Olivia: Here too.

She's attached a picture of Flynn working out in their backyard. He's shirtless and holding dumbbells that make his arm muscles strain. Shaking my head and smiling, I click off the image. Flynn is a handsome guy, for sure, but the way I feel about him is too brotherly to enjoy checking him out.

A pang of something else hits me, though. A restlessness to have that type of relationship. They're still so in love, but they also have a deep trust and connection that I've never had with a man. I can see how it's changed my sister. She's more secure somehow, less guarded. Let me be clear, I don't think a man is going to make me less of a hot mess. It'd still be nice to have someone that brought out the good in me instead of the usual insecurity, fear, and lastly, rage.

I'm downloading an app that says it can identify birds by their sounds and appearance when something catches my eye down by the water. Or rather, someones.

Two men are running side by side. I pick out Nick first. His dark hair flops with every step. He's too far for me to make out his facial expression, but his jaw is set in its usual hard line. When I'm finally able to pull my gaze off him, I recognize the bulkier man next to him as Penn. Their words from last night about meeting up to run around the lake resurface. Jesus, did they literally run around the whole damn lake?

I'm still wondering about it, and staring, when Nick stops jogging. He lifts a hand in a wave to Penn, who keeps going, and then starts toward the house.

The closer he gets, the better able I am to see him. I have the sudden desire to snap a picture and send it to Olivia because my view just got a lot better. He's tall and broad, but lean. His waist tapers in, and his muscles are well-defined.

Nick's gaze drifts to me when he's halfway up to the house. He adjusts his path, heading toward the cabin instead of his place. My heart beats rapidly. I take a sip of tea, hoping to appear completely unfazed, but the heat of it mixed with the warmth fluttering through me with the hot, grumpy man coming my way has sweat beading up on my forehead.

"Morning," he says, a little gruff and a little breathless, when he's ten feet away.

This close I can make out the sweat dripping down his temples and chest and abs. Good god. I swallow hard.

"Morning," I chirp back, so high-pitched it doesn't even sound like me. I glance down into my tea and take another small sip. I am on fire, inside and out.

He rests both hands on his hips, and his chest moves as he works to catch his breath. "You're up early."

"Not as early as you, apparently."

"Trying to beat the heat. It finally feels like summer."

I glance down to the lake, so I won't be tempted to check him out again. Who am I kidding? I'm tempted. Fuck, am I tempted.

"Maybe I'll take a swim today." I glance back at him and am hit with that buzzy, warm feeling in another wave.

"I wouldn't suggest it unless you're looking to do a polar plunge. It'll be another couple of weeks before the water is warm enough to brave swimming."

Momentarily I think of the pool at my old apartment building. The hot concrete that burns your feet and the lounge chairs with blue and white striped umbrellas overhead. Hard as I try, I can't imagine being back there. Though a dip in the non-frigid water does sound nice.

"No writing today?" he asks.

"No, I try to take Sundays off. Though now that swimming is off the table, I'll have to find something else to do."

"I might have a solution."

My brows lift. "You do?"

"Meet me out front in twenty minutes?"

"Ominous." A grin pulls at my lips. "Where are we going?"

"You'll see."

I tamp down the giddy sensation rising in my chest. "I need more information. What should I wear? Do I need to fix my hair? Do I need a hat? Sunscreen? Wait. You're not going to make me run around the lake, are you?"

A small huff of a laugh leaves him, and his hands fall to his sides. "No running. And wear whatever you want. Where we're going, it won't matter."

Even more ominous. But I'm still grinning as he starts for the house. A few steps away, he glances back over his shoulder. "Wear socks."

"Socks?!" He doesn't care what else I wear, but socks are necessary?

Of course, he doesn't bother responding, and I'm too excited to let it stop me from springing into action. I should probably question the excitement of going somewhere with Nick, but I shove all that away. And I pull on socks.

Of all the places I imagined Nick taking me, this wasn't in the top one hundred. And it absolutely should have been.

"The hockey rink?" I ask as his truck comes to a stop in the parking lot.

Disappointment must be splashed across my face because his mouth pulls up on one side. "Come on, Red. I promise it isn't what you think."

What I think is he's going to make me work on a perfectly good Sunday afternoon. Which honestly, I should. The notes from Molly on my first chapter were encouraging, but I also got the feeling she was being very cautious not to scare me off with any tough changes right out of the gate.

"I didn't bring my laptop."

"You won't need it." He opens his door and hops out. There's a pep in his step that I haven't noticed before. He's excited, and that makes me all the more curious. He comes around the front of the truck to my side as I'm getting out.

"You're surprisingly less grumpy-looking."

"Am I?" His lips pull wider.

My stomach flutters.

"You're kind of freaking me out." I take two steps to each of his long strides. My heart pumps fast with anticipation, and I find myself admiring his profile.

Grumpy Nick is hot, but this happy, excited version is downright irresistible.

We step into the rink, and the cool air blasts me immediately. My pink summer dress with sneakers was a cute idea when I thought we were going anywhere else.

My feet move in the usual path, down to the ice, but Nick touches my elbow and tips his head to the left. "This way."

I don't ask the millions of questions that pop into my head as he leads me down a dark hallway. Dim lighting casts an eerie glow, and our footsteps echo around us.

He finally stops a few paces from a doorway. I lean forward to see inside, but he crowds me.

"What are we doing?" I ask, feeling my heartbeat pick up speed in my chest.

The door behind him opens, and a man in a T-shirt and gray slacks steps out, then stops when he sees us.

Slowly his mouth curves into a smile. "Galaxy. What are you doing here?"

"Hey, Ron." Nick opens his stance. The two men shake hands. "We're going out on the ice for a bit."

Ron's eyes twinkle with a friendly playfulness. "Missing it, huh? Season will be here soon."

"Not soon enough." Nick reciprocates the smile.

"Well, if you need anything, holler. I'm working in the equipment closet. Gotta make room for the new gear."

"Thanks," Nick says. "We could use an extra pair of skates."

"Sure. I've got a bunch of your extras I can sharpen up."

"Not for me." Nick shakes his head.

And then both men are looking at me.

Wait, what? Cue the record scratch. Everything finally locks into place and . . . no. No freaking way.

My eyes widen. "Nuh-uh."

I back away, waving my hands in front of me. My shoulder blades collide into the wall when I run out of room to flee.

"I'll set out some options," Ron says.

Nick tips his head to him. "Thanks."

Rubbing the spot on my back that will probably be a bruise, I continue to shake my head as Nick approaches me.

"I know you said that you're not athletic," he says gently.

Is he for real? Not athletic? That's like saying he's not a bad hockey player. True, but wildly underselling it.

"I fell walking on ice," I say dryly. My heart is racing at the idea of going out there. No, not just going out there, going out there with *him*. It'd be one thing if I were learning with someone less . . . professional. And less hot.

"You didn't have on the right gear," he says, and bless him, he sounds like he genuinely believes that all I need is the appropriate footwear. "Learning about hockey and experiencing hockey are two different things. Look how fast you picked up poker last night."

That didn't require me to wear blades as shoes.

His expression is earnest as he says, "Think of it as more research for the book. And if I'm wrong, then we'll go back to doing it your way."

A logical and practical argument, but I'm feeling far from levelheaded right now.

"No. I . . . can't." It's a bad idea. Terrible, in fact. "No," I say again, this time determined.

There is absolutely no way I'm going out there.

Chapter Sixteen

NICK

I'm trying really, really hard not to laugh.

Ruby glares at me as she stands on the ice, clutching the wall so hard her knuckles are white.

"No," she says for maybe the millionth time since I suggested she learn to skate. "I want to go back."

"You can do it." I'm standing two feet away—close enough that I can catch her if she falls but far enough away that she can't punch me—which feels likely right now.

"You can do it," she mocks back to me.

I can't help the rough chuckle that slips free. She glares harder.

"Are you sure you don't want me to grab a skate aid?"

"My pride is already taking a real hit here, and you want me to use a walker in front of a professional hockey player?!"

"We all start somewhere," I assure her as I move closer and hold out a hand.

She eyes it, blue eyes on fire with a mixture of annoyance and determination. She's sexy as hell. Not that I should be noticing.

Slowly, she lets go of the wall with one hand and then flings it at me, now gripping my forearm like a lifeline.

"I've got you. Now let go with the other hand."

She shakes her head as the tip of her mouth pulls down at the corners. It's a real role reversal, her glowering at me like she's always accusing me of doing. I doubt she finds it as hot as I do.

"This is the most humiliating moment of my life."

"Really?"

"No." She sighs, staring down at her feet. "But it's top five, for sure."

"No reason to be embarrassed. You're doing great."

"I'm barely moving and only upright because you're a brick wall of muscle keeping me that way." Her tone is full of exasperation, so I fight another laugh. "And I'm a fashion disaster."

I told her to wear socks, but the little, flimsy things she had were going to give her blisters, so Ron pulled out a pair of socks for her too. They're way too big and come up over her knees. Maybe it isn't fashionable, but it's doing something for me. Really, *really* doing something for me.

"Also, this dress was the worst possible option in my suitcase. If I go down, you're going to see my underwear."

I press my lips together to keep from smiling. "I promise not to look."

"Joke's on you because they're my full-coverage, comfy undies. Not cute, like at all."

A disbelieving huff leaves my lips. "I doubt that very much."

Her blue eyes finally lift to mine. "Seriously. Picture the ugliest undergarments you can imagine."

Instead, an image of her in that red bikini last night flits into my mind. I skate backward while she's focused on me instead of falling. "I'm struggling to believe anything looks that bad on you."

"Because you think I'm beautiful?" One brow quirks up as she repeats my words.

Oops. I hadn't meant to say it last night, but I was proving a point. I can't tell if the look she gives me now is because she thinks I'm full of shit or if she thinks I'm a creep.

"Don't worry, I'm not going to hit on you."

Now she laughs. Probably at my expense, but it doesn't matter because the truth is no matter how beautiful she is, getting involved with her is a terrible idea. She's here for a short time and staying next door. No matter how attractive or fun she is, I'm not looking for anything messy or complicated.

Not that she even wants to. She's more likely to hook up with Travis or D-Low. My jaw tightens at the thought.

"Why are you back to glowering at me?" she asks, breaking me from my thoughts.

"Was I?"

She nods.

I force the unease away. What the hell do I care who she hooks up with? This is a business arrangement, plain and simple. Her being the sexiest woman I've ever seen is irrelevant.

It's my turn to look away from her. "I didn't want you to feel left out, with all the glaring you've been doing at me."

"I have not!" She squeaks out the denial, then laughs. "Okay, fine, maybe I was."

I flick my gaze back to her. "Maybe?"

She smiles at me, that big, sunshine smile that feels much more natural for her. "I guess we swapped places today. You're less grumpy in skates."

That's probably true. On the ice everything feels a lot simpler.

"Grumpy doesn't suit you, Red. Besides, you did it."

Her grip on me has loosened, but when I come to a stop, her fingers tighten on my arm. She glances around as if to verify that we've gone around the rink. Her lips part and then slowly pull into a huge grin.

I like her spunk and determination and how quickly she slips back into her happy and carefree demeanor. When was the last time I felt like that?

"Oh my gosh! I did it. I skated around the rink!" She bounces in place, which has her feet sliding on the ice. Her legs go out from under her, and she careens backward, arms flailing.

My arm slides around her waist, catching her before she bounces off the ice. Her fingers find purchase on my forearm again, and she holds on with a death grip.

My heart hammers in my chest at the thought of her hitting her head. I should have insisted she wear a helmet. She'd scowled when I suggested it, but now I'm thinking I should have made her anyway.

"You good?" My voice comes out hoarse.

Her eyes are squeezed tight like she was bracing for impact, but at my question she squints them both to look at me. "Am I dead?"

The tightness in my chest eases. "No, not dead."

I pull her back upright, but because she's holding on so tightly, we're standing close. She tips her head back to look at me.

"Good." The word is breathless. "I'd never live down the shame of dying in rented shoes."

I chuckle.

"Why is ice so cold?!" She shivers.

"Necessity, I suppose. Want to go for another lap?"

She nods, and this time she looks a little more at ease.

I tell her to start with small steps, alternate lifting one foot then the other, glide, push off with one skate.

One side of her mouth tugs up. "That's what you told the kids."

"Is it?"

"And to feel the shift of weight."

"That was my next instruction."

We fall quiet as we skate. I take both of her hands in one of mine. There's a momentary look of panic on her face until I say, "I got you."

I'd dive under her before letting her land face-first on the ice. Although my hard head may not be any softer of a landing.

"Somehow, I believe you." Another smile loosens on her lips. "You're a good coach. Is that what you want to do after hockey?"

"I'm not sure. I haven't given it a lot of thought, but I am looking forward to teaching you." I stop near the gate and grab my stick.

"I can barely stay upright. I don't think I'm ready for that."

"Just take it."

She does, and I send up a silent prayer that she doesn't go off-balance and take us both down.

"It's heavier than I expected."

I adjust it in her hands so she's holding it correctly. I amend my earlier fantasy to this. Ruby Madison in a dress and skates holding my hockey stick. Fuck me.

"Sometimes focusing on something else helps."

"And I can lean on it for support." She tests this, and I put a hand out just in case. She seems determined to fall.

I take it back after she appears more stable and less focused on standing upright. The next time we skate around the ice, she's gliding on her own. It isn't graceful but she stays on her feet.

I stick close, letting her use me for balance as needed, but with every lap she needs less support.

"Am I ready for the team yet?" she asks once she's gone around twice without assistance.

"Definitely," I answer. "We just need to speed you up a bit."

"Like how much?"

"Fast enough that you can beat the defenders to the other end."

"I think I could take you," she says with so much confidence that I laugh. Thirty minutes ago, she was terrified. I might have liked that version better. She reaches for the stick in my hands, and I let her have it, admiring again how good she looks with it.

"Maybe we should get you a helmet."

"Give me a puck."

"You're not ready for that."

"I want a puck," she all but demands.

"Feisty thing," I mutter and skate over to the bench without taking my eyes off her. "Don't move."

"I'm feeling more confident," she says, then wobbles. Thankfully, she rights herself without falling and shoots me a sheepish smile. She has a knack for making my blood pressure rise.

I come back with gloves, a few pucks, and a helmet.

She pouts adorably as I toss the pucks onto the ice and move toward her with the helmet.

"I really don't look good in hats."

I know that's a lie. She looked hot in my old baseball cap. Come to think of it, I can't remember a single time she hasn't looked gorgeous. "Better than you will with a concussion."

She rolls her eyes. See? Fucking adorable.

While she holds still, I put the helmet on her. It's one of mine, so it's a little big, but it should do the trick. I slide the visor down, then take the gloves from under my arm.

She holds out her right hand and lets me put it on, then the left. I've helped a lot of kids put on gear, but this is . . . different.

"These are very uncomfortable," she announces, moving one around like it's a robot arm.

"You get used to it," I say. "And they'll keep you warm."

"I haven't been warm since I left Arizona."

My lips twist into a smile. She's all geared up now and ready to go.

"All right, Madison. Let's see what you got."

She quirks a brow with an amused grin. "Look out, Galaxy. I'm coming for your job."

And then she falls on her ass.

Things I learn about Ruby over the next hour.

She is stubborn. Maybe more than anyone I know. She hits so many pucks at the net, determined to get one in the goal. Any other person would have given up long before she finally manages to get one on target.

When she's excited and happy, she bounces in place, which almost always ends with her on her ass.

As such, I learn she lied about her underwear (as I suspected) and that they're pink. I tried not to look, promise.

And lastly, she is by far the clumsiest person I've ever met.

"My entire body hurts," she groans as we take a seat on the bench.

"I have no doubt."

She gives me a side-glare but can't manage to keep it up for long. Her lips curve, and as she laughs, she rubs one hip.

"There's an ice bath in the therapy room."

"More cold?" She shakes her head vehemently.

"It might help."

"All I need is a hot shower and to not move for twelve hours."

"All right." I chuckle.

She lets out a groan as she attempts to bend down to untie her skates.

"Never mind. I'm never leaving this bench. Got any pillows around here?"

"I have some sweaty pads that might do the trick."

She wrinkles up her nose.

I reach down and wrap my fingers around her ankle. "May I?"

She nods, and I lift her leg up onto my thigh to take off her skates. I've done this dozens of times for Aidan and the kids at camp, but the intimacy of it hits me too late.

"How's the book coming?" I ask as my fingers work at the laces, untying and then loosening them.

"I finished the first chapter," she says in a cheery tone but grimacing.

"Isn't that good?"

"I was hoping to be further along by now."

"Ah."

"I will figure it out," she announces with a sigh. "I have to."

"Anything I can help with?"

"No. Well, actually, this helped, I think. Getting out of my head, experiencing a little of what it's like for you—minus all the falling of course."

"Of course." I smile back at her. "And I'm glad it helped."

"What's the equivalent of writer's block for a hockey player?"

"I'm not sure. Maybe a scoring slump?"

"What do you do when that happens?"

"Take more shots, try not to let it get in my head too much."

"More shots, huh?"

"What do you usually do?"

"Binge-watch reality TV and eat ice cream." Her lips twist into a shy smile.

"That works?"

She thinks for a moment, gaze flicking up. I take the time to study her. Her blue eyes framed with long, black lashes, and the cold of the rink has her cheeks a bright pink. The gold four-leaf clover necklace she's always wearing catches the lights.

"No, I guess it doesn't really work except for eventually I get so disgusted with myself I finally force the words."

"So writing gets you unstuck."

"Take more shots," she mutters as she repeats my words.

"We're more alike than I thought."

She lets out a soft laugh.

"What's the deal with your necklace?"

"The deal?" She lifts a hand to it and smirks.

"You know what I mean. You always wear it. It must be important to you."

"My sister gave it to me a long time ago, and I found it while packing up my apartment. Four-leaf clovers are lucky, and I need all the luck I can get right now." She scrunches up her nose. "That probably sounds silly. I'm not usually so superstitious."

"Nah, everyone can use a little luck, now and again. I know guys who wear the same socks during the playoffs or follow the exact pregame routine down to the smallest detail."

"Do you have a lucky charm?"

"I have a routine, but no one thing I rely on like your necklace."

"Maybe you need one," she says playfully. "Though I'm not sure yet mine is working."

"Maybe." I pull the skate off and set it on the ground.

"Oh, god, that feels good." She moans and scrunches up her socked toes. My thumb slides into the arch and rubs softly. She lets out another contented sigh that has my blood warming.

"I changed my mind. Keep doing that, and I'll sleep on the sweaty pads."

My chest feels tight as I give her foot one last squeeze. Our gazes lock, and the air feels thicker around us. She pulls her leg off my thigh.

I glance to her other skate, a silent question, but she flushes and looks away. "I got it."

I nod, then stand and head back onto the ice to pick up the pucks. I need to get a hold of myself. Jesus. I'm blaming the pink panties for my brain and body being on high alert over touching her foot. What. The. Fuck?

Chapter Seventeen

RUBY

I am a badass hockey player. I eat professional hockey players for breakfast. I am a mean, lean, puck-scoring machine.

I tilt my head back to see out of the helmet. It's fallen down into my eyes again. Nick smirks back, almost like he can read the internal pep talk I'm giving myself.

We're back at the rink today. Camp is over, and Aidan is visiting his mom this week, so I've got the grumpy hockey player to myself this morning. I couldn't wait to get back and try again, despite the ache of my body . . . everywhere.

I stand in front of him in skates and pads (and the most unflattering helmet ever). I probably look ridiculous, but I don't care.

"Show me the deke again," I say, voice echoing in the rafters.

He backs up (why is skating backward so hot?!), grinning in a way that has my heart fluttering. There's not even a hint of the grumpy man I first met.

"I'm not usually faking out people using a skating aid."

I stick my tongue out at him. My butt cannot take another fall. Neither can my pride.

"Don't get cocky, Galaxy. I'm going to stop this one."

He doesn't even bother smack-talking back. We both know the only way I'm stopping the puck from going into the goal behind me is if he lets me.

With the stick in his right hand, he pushes off his left skate. Leaning forward, his other hand wraps around the stick, and he moves toward me with the puck. He shifts his weight from side to side. I'm enthralled, and my pulse speeds up as he gets closer. I know it's coming, but when he fakes left and snaps the puck to the right and easily shoots it past me, I'm still impressed.

"I almost had it," I say, turning to the goal. With one hand on the skating aid, I use the other to fish the puck out with my stick. "Don't defenders know it's coming?"

"Players have tells, and we all have our go-to moves, but at any given moment a guy might go left or right or take a shot. A good hockey player reads the defense and adjusts."

"And a good defender?" I ask since that is my current role—however ineffective.

"Is always one step ahead," he says, swiping the puck back from me and skating away before I can do anything about it.

"Cute," I mutter.

He circles around the goal and heads back in front of me. "Do you want to give it a try?"

I shake my head. All morning he's been showing me different things. From slap shots to backhands, all the different penalties, he even humored me by showing me how fast he can skate from one end to the other. The answer: very fast.

"All right. What else do you need for Act One?"

The butterflies in my stomach flutter and then drop. The reminder of my book and how much work I still need to do feels overwhelming. Today we've been focusing on all the hockey scenes in the first ten chapters or Act One. It's cute he remembered. I force a smile. He's been so helpful and so concentrated on doing whatever it is that I need. Above and beyond what I ever imagined from anyone, let alone the grump I thought he was.

"Galaxy!"

Nick and I turn as Danny skates onto the ice. He's dressed casually like Nick in athletic pants and a T-shirt.

My eyes go to the tattoos on his forearms as he gets closer. They're beautiful, colorful and intricate. I'm drawn to the red and white cartoon rocket, but before I can make out any of the other individual artwork pieces, Conrad appears as well, followed by Travis.

The men are all geared up with their sticks. Conrad has on his helmet, and the other two carry theirs.

"What are you guys doing here?" Nick asks, moving closer to me.

"Trav said you'd be here," Danny says. "Thought we could get in a little friendly scrimmage."

I feel Nick's body tense beside me. His arm brushes against mine as he says, "Sorry. I promised Ruby I'd help her with her book today."

"It's okay." We've been at it for a few hours, and I'm well aware I'm taking up a lot of his time. "I think I got what I need."

"Are you sure?"

I nod. "Yeah. Plus, my fingers hurt from holding on to the skating aid so tightly."

"All right." He turns to me and lowers his voice. "I'll give you a lift back."

"No. Stay with your friends. I'm going to grab an Uber to MVP."

"Craving a bad burger?"

"It's all about the atmosphere," I tell him, skating as coolly as one can with a colorful walker. "Thanks for the lesson, Galaxy."

I flick my gaze to his friends. "Watch out for his deke. He really favors the right side."

Travis busts out laughing first, the rest joining in. Nick's mouth falls open.

"I was teaching. That wasn't my best stuff!" he yells after me.

I smush my lips together to keep from laughing, inevitably failing. "Whatever you say, Galaxy."

I'm floating when I walk into MVP. Not even the hostess's heavy sigh or annoyance as she sets down the menu in front of me gets me down. When the server walks up, I shut the menu and look up. I trust Nick that the burger is the only safe option.

"Hey, darling, what can I get you to drink?" the guy asks as he pulls a pen out of his pocket and poises it over a pad of paper.

Recognition flickers as I look from his face to the nametag, which reads "Lonnie."

"Bobby?" Otherwise known as Curtis at the rental car place.

"MINI Cooper girl."

"Ruby," I remind him.

"How's Moonshot treating you?" He lets both hands fall to his sides as he smiles at me.

"It's been good." My brow furrows. "You work here too?"

"One of many jobs. I like to keep busy and try out a bunch of different careers, you know?"

I nod. I kind of do get that. One of my favorite things about writing characters is putting myself in different mindsets and situations, kind of like trying on different jobs.

"Anywho . . ." He twirls his pen in one hand.

"Can I get a water, and do you have any coffee back there?"

He makes a face. "Yes."

"That bad, huh?" I laugh. "Just the water is fine."

"Good choice. Back in a minute." He turns on his heel and heads off, returning not long after with my drink. I order the burger and then settle in with my laptop, notes, and a buzz of information in my head from being on the ice with Nick the past two days.

I start by typing out everything I can remember. From the way the skates felt tight on my feet—something Nick assured me was important, the difficulty of holding the stick in gloved hands, to the nip of the air as we circled the rink, and the exhilaration of finally hitting the puck into the goal. I can see why he loves it so much. It's hard, like writing the first draft of a book, but once you conquer it, there's no better feeling.

My eyes are bleary, and my half-eaten burger is cold when I finally stop typing. I glance down at the bottom left of the screen. Eight pages of notes. It's more than I've written in . . . as long as I can remember.

Sure, it's not a book, yet, but it's something.

I pick up my phone to text Olivia and tell her I've broken through my slump, but a text from Lily is already waiting for me.

I smile as I tap on her name. Between the time difference and her touring schedule, we've barely had a chance to talk since I've been here.

Lily: Have you seen this?

I type back a reply before clicking the link she sent.

Me: Hi! I miss you. How are you? How's the tour?

I can't wait to hear all about her week. Her publisher sent her to independent bookstores around the country to celebrate her latest book. I'm so happy for her and excited for her to fill me in on all the usual things: the joy of reader interactions and signing until her wrist hurts, and the less than glamorous travel delays and bags under her eyes from lack of sleep. I'm not even feeling any jealousy or sadness wondering if I'll ever publish a book and go on tour again.

And I guess that's why I'm not prepared when I click the link. I assumed she sent me a news article or interview she'd done while I've been in Moonshot with my grumpy hockey player and not keeping up with the world. Instead, I'm greeted with a headshot of Matt in a shirt I bought him before I knew he was a lying, manipulative, book-stealing asshole.

Gradient Pictures to Develop Matthew Rose's Bestselling Novel Becoming Alaric

My stomach drops, and an acidic taste fills my mouth. I should have seen this coming. It's the biggest book of the year, maybe of the decade. Of course someone was going to adapt it for television. With my luck there'll be merchandise and kids dressing up as the characters for Halloween.

I skim the article and then close out and go back to my messages with Lily.

She sent another text.

Lily: Proof that good things happen to bad people. Are you okay?

Me: Fine.

Lily: Is that a real fine or an 'I'm currently plotting a novel where he gets decapitated' fine?

Me: The second.

Definitely the second.

Chapter Eighteen

NICK

"Where've you been?" Dad asks as I come through the door.

"At the rink with Ruby and the guys."

"Oh yeah?" He's standing in the kitchen next to the stove. The smell of fake cheese and starchy noodles wafts in the air.

The corners of my lips twitch with amusement as I spot the macaroni and cheese box on the counter.

"Aidan is with Beth tonight."

"I know," he says, then looks away with a hint of embarrassment playing on his face.

My mouth curves as I lose the battle with a smile.

"It's fucking delicious," he finally admits, flashing his own grin at me.

"You never let me eat that shit when I was a kid."

"Yeah, yeah." He turns back to the stove to stir the cheese into the cooked noodles.

I grab the milk from the fridge for him and then lean against the counter.

"I thought I saw Ruby down by the lake earlier. How's the book research going?"

"Good, I think. I'm teaching her how to skate and some hockey basics."

He grins in a way that tells me he thinks teaching her to skate is code for dating.

"She left to work on her book once the guys showed up for a pick-up game."

He stops stirring. "How'd that go?"

We haven't outright talked about it, but he knows I've been reluctant to get back out there and play since I was cleared by the doctors.

My skin feels tight under his scrutiny. "We were just messing around mostly."

"That's great. First time since the surgery, right?"

"Yeah." I push off the counter. "Do you want me to grill some burgers or chicken to go with that?"

"Nah, nah. I'm going to eat this and then head into town for Bunco night at the Y." Absently he massages a spot on his chest.

Just like that a seed of panic works its way through me.

"Are you feeling okay?" I ask him.

He glances down at his hand and then lets it drop. "Oh yeah. Fine."

I must not look convinced because he adds, "I'm good. Don't go worrying about me. I'm healthy as can be."

"I think your cholesterol numbers would disagree with that assessment." I try to joke it off, but the tightness remains.

He hums his dismissal at that, but the reminder of everything that happened has me walking to the fridge and pulling out an apple. I peel and cut it, then give him half.

The look he gives me is akin to Aidan's expression when I put green beans on his plate. He grumbles some more but takes the apple slices.

I take my share of the apple outside to the back patio. It's my favorite place of the house. The view, the quiet, all of it. Without realizing I'm looking for her, I scan the lake and over by the cabin for Ruby. She's nowhere in sight, but the front windows are open.

I was having fun with her today. More than I've had in a long time. And it carried over through the afternoon. That hit messed with me in ways that go far beyond the physical. I don't know if I'll ever be able to step onto the ice for a game and not wonder if the next injury is the end. We played no-contact today, but just messing around together and remembering the good instead of dwelling on all the bad was nice.

It's small but it's a start.

Sometime after midnight I give up on sleep and head downstairs. Dad's snores are the only noise in the house. I close his door on my way to the kitchen, so the light won't wake him, and then I pull out a mug from the cabinet to make some tea.

Maybe it was too optimistic to think that because I had a breakthrough on the ice my sleep would improve as well. I'm restless, plagued with nervous energy about hockey, my dad, Aidan, and every other possible thing in my life that could go bad.

Tea in hand, I step out onto the back deck. The night air is cool against my bare chest. The moon is full tonight, shining bright down on the lake.

The cabin lights are still on, but there's no sign of Ruby. Most likely she left them on when she went to bed, but I still find myself picturing her inside, maybe lying awake, unable to sleep like me.

I settle into the couch on the deck and pull the throw blanket around my shoulders. Sleep doesn't feel any closer, but there's a peace out here that never fails to calm the voices in my head. The ones that have me questioning if I'll ever get another good night's sleep again. Or if I'll ever be able to play hockey again, if my dad's going to be okay, and if someday not that far away, Aidan will be in my same position.

I let my head fall back and stare up into the sky. The warmth of the mug feels nice in my hands, and I focus only on breathing and clearing my mind.

I'm not sure if it's the sound or the movement that finally catches my attention, but the hairs on the back of my neck stand as I sit up, gaze darting to the cabin and then scanning until I spot a figure down by the lake.

Something or someone is moving around down there. Too big to be a raccoon. A kid maybe? We get an occasional teenager, or group of them, that wander onto the property occasionally.

Then the figure moves and her hair blows in the wind. Ruby.

My heart rate settles down, but my gut swirls with unease. I stand, set my tea on the table in front of me, and head for the lake without thinking. My bare feet pad quickly down the steps and through the grass. My pulse picks up speed again as I get closer.

Ruby has her back to me. A long T-shirt hangs down mid-thigh on her. Her hair is pulled up in a high ponytail that swings around as she . . . what the hell *is* she doing?

She's tossing something into the lake. Rocks, I think. More noises greet me as I approach her. Grunts and little screams. She leans down to gather more pebbles, and I get a look at her profile. Her mouth is pulled into a tight line, and there's a stubborn, frustrated set to her jaw. She rears back and throws, slingshotting her arm and squealing as the rock soars ten or twenty feet and drops into the lake.

She does it again and again, finally stomping one foot.

"Why isn't this more satisfying?" she asks . . . herself? The lake? The rock? I haven't a clue, but the fire in her tone and fight in her body language has a smile tugging at the corners of my lips.

"What the hell are you doing?"

My voice startles her, and she spins around, rock held up like she's going to launch it at my face.

"Whoa." I hold my hands up in front of me. "Don't fire."

Her body goes slack, and she drops her arm back to her side. "Nick. You scared me."

"Sorry. I was on the back deck and saw someone down here."

"Right." She glances toward my house and then back to me. "I didn't mean to wake you."

"You didn't."

"It's late. I thought you'd be sleeping," she says, facing the lake again.

"I rarely sleep," I admit.

Her gaze shifts to me, and I can see the question there, but she doesn't ask.

"Why are you up?" I ask, then offer the first answer that comes to mind. "Are you still stuck on the book?"

It's been fun teaching her to skate and play hockey, but it hits me that maybe it's not really helping her like I thought it would.

"I . . ." Her lips twist like she's working out what to tell me. I find it intriguing that she's being so secretive. Ruby always seems like she says whatever is on her mind. I like that about her. "It's just publishing drama."

I feel one brow arch. "There's drama in book publishing?"

"Always." A hint of a smile appears but just as quickly disappears. "Why don't you sleep?"

I shrug.

She tosses another rock into the lake, this time with less oomph.

Without thinking, I move behind her to show her how to do it correctly. She's using only her arm to throw instead of stepping and getting her body into it.

"Angle your body and step back with one foot," I say as the wind whips her hair into my face. It smells nice, like coconut and strawberries.

She does as I say, and I lift her right arm over her head and back. My fingers wrap completely around her delicate wrist.

"Now, step forward, and when your arm comes back up to this position . . ." I move her arm to show her, pausing by her ear. "Let go, but throw *through* the movement."

I step back, and she does it again, this time sending the rock farther into the water. That ghost of a smile returns and falls.

"Better," I say.

"Thanks." She smooths her hair out of her face, holding the long strands to one side. She doesn't make any move to throw another.

"Still not satisfying?"

"I think the lake is too peaceful or something. Not enough noise or destruction."

I quirk a brow. Sunshine Ruby wanting to destroy something is maybe more surprising than anything else.

"Do you want to talk about it?" I ask. "I don't know publishing, but I'm a good listener, and I have tea up on the porch."

Her mouth pulls up on one side as she glances in that direction. She shakes her head. "No. I should get to bed."

She lets her hair free and brushes off her hands. "Thanks for the lesson."

I nod, then watch her head to the cabin. I stay down by the lake until she's inside and the lights go out, then I pick up a rock and fire it as hard as I can across the lake.

She's right. Not nearly as satisfying as you'd think.

I don't hear from Ruby for a few days, except to say that she's writing and doesn't have any more questions for me yet. Then Friday I get a text from her.

> **Ruby:** Good morning. Do you have time today to answer a few more questions for me? I can be available any time that's convenient for you. Thanks.

It's such a damn polite message that I stare at it for a good five minutes before replying.

Fifteen minutes later, she's outside waiting for me in front of my truck. She's in another dress, this one a light yellow. It's the only thing sunshiny about her though.

I wondered if she'd recovered from whatever was bothering her earlier in the week. Now I know.

I hand her a coffee, which softens her scowl slightly.

"Thank you."

"Welcome."

We drive to the rink in silence. She sips her coffee, and I steal glances at her, trying to wrap my head around this version of Ruby.

Once we arrive, I lead her inside but bypass our usual route. She brightens slightly, like she's shifted into work-mode. Maybe like hockey makes me less grumpy, writing makes her happier.

"Aren't we going down to the ice?" she asks.

"Yeah, but I want to show you something first."

She nods, expression shifting back to . . . grumpy. The idea that Ruby Madison could be genuinely grumpy is mind-boggling.

I don't like it. Not one bit.

I pick up my pace, taking her through the building until we reach the rec area. It's a big, open space that's most often used for stretching and soccer before games.

In the corner a hockey net is set up. I grab two sticks, and I find a few pucks waiting in the goal.

Ruby gives me a questioning gaze as I hand her one of the sticks but doesn't ask what we're doing. She's frowning, and she's silent. Yep, something is definitely wrong. I've racked my brain the past few days for what publishing drama could mean, but . . . I have no idea.

I drop a puck in front of her. She eyes it but still doesn't ask or say anything.

"Do you remember how to hit a slap shot?"

She gives me a very uninspired nod, and I step back to give her room.

Pride zips through me as she adjusts her grip and stance, then fires the puck into the net. The sound of it hitting the wall echoes in the space. Ruby's eyes light up.

Silently, I toss another puck in front of her. She hits this one with a little more fire than the last.

I keep going, and so does she. Toss, shoot, toss, shoot. The only noise is the puck hitting the floor and then the back of the wall. Over and Over. I don't stop until she does.

The smile she aims my way makes my chest tighten.

"Better than throwing rocks into the lake?"

"So much better." Her shoulders sag as she breathes heavily. "I think it's the sound that was missing. I might need to get a setup like this in my next apartment."

She waves the stick around, nearly hitting herself in the head with it in the process. I take it from her and lean it against the wall, then pull out a couple chairs from nearby.

She grabs her coffee and laptop then takes a seat across from me, still catching her breath. "I think I understand now why you're obsessed with hockey."

"Obsessed?"

"Aren't you?"

I think about that for a second and then shrug. "Maybe. No more than the average person is with their career probably."

"I'm not sure most people would do their job even if they weren't getting paid."

"Fair." I smile at her. "Would you?"

"I would still write, for sure, but I wouldn't publish it."

"Why not?"

"There's something special about the words just being for me. My favorite part of the process is the time between when I finish the book and send it off to the editor. Before anyone else has read it or offered up their feedback. That moment feels perfect and . . . hopeful."

All the frustration and tension she's been carrying slides away as she speaks, and she stares off like she's remembering it and telling herself instead of talking to me. A second later she looks back to me and offers a sheepish smile.

"Anyway."

I can tell she's about to jump into asking me questions, but I want to know more, so I cut in before she has the chance.

"Is that how you felt before you found out you had to change your book from baseball to hockey?"

"No." Her brows scrunch together. "I wrote this book a couple years ago, and my agent has been shopping it around. No one wanted it at first, so I did some other things."

"The writing slump isn't because of hockey, then?"

"Were you worried I was hating on your favorite sport?"

My mouth lifts on one side. "Maybe."

She grins back, shaking her head. "No, it isn't because I had to switch the book to hockey."

I think that's all she's going to say about it, but to my surprise, she adds, "I went through a messy breakup, and then my next book didn't perform like I hoped. It was a rough year."

"Ah." I hadn't expected that answer, but I should have. She's beautiful and smart, successful. She must have guys falling down to get her attention. Something a lot like jealousy swirls around in my stomach and then lodges itself at the base of my sternum.

"What about you?" she asks.

"You want to know about my scoring slump?"

She shrugs both shoulders. "Was it because of a woman?"

"No." I shake my head definitively.

"But you do date."

It isn't a question, but I nod. "A little. Nothing serious."

"What about Aidan's mom?"

"We were together while I was playing in the minor league. She was in medical school, and I was traveling a lot, so it wasn't serious at first. We hung out a few times a month when it worked for our schedules. Then when Beth found out she was pregnant, we tried to make it work." I can still remember everything about that day she told me. I had never given a lot of thought to having kids, but as soon as I found out, I couldn't wait to be a dad.

"Aidan's great, so you've obviously got the co-parenting thing down regardless of it not working out between you two, and who knows . . ."

"She got married two years ago."

"Oh." Her mouth holds the "O" shape and then twists into a smile. "Sorry."

"Don't be. She and I are better as friends, and Cory, her husband, is great to Aidan."

"They live in Bozeman, right? I think that's what Aidan said."

"Yeah."

"That's convenient."

Another unspoken question.

"She's from here originally and moved back when a position opened up at the hospital."

"And you just happened to get traded here too?"

I run my palms down my thighs. "I asked to be traded here when my last contract was up."

Her brows shoot up in surprise.

"You know, I read about the trade when I first got here, and the server at MVP said something about it being a big deal that you were here, but at the time I didn't really understand it. You led the Wildcats in goals during the playoffs the year you won the championship. No one thought you should be traded based on your performance, so they speculated that it had to have been intrapersonal friction or contract disputes."

Plenty of people weighed in on the Wildcats' decision to let me go. There were rumors that I was mad about playing time or not getting along well with my teammates, even some that said I wanted more money, but that was all bullshit. The truth is I did it for Aidan, but I don't want that out there. Sure, people would understand me wanting to move closer to family, and they'd probably even spin it to make me a hero, but it's none of their business, and I don't need their approval.

"It's all bullshit. My contract was up, and I wanted to be here. It was the best thing for Aidan. He's thriving and happy. And the team is great. The organization has gone through a lot of changes the past five years, but the GM and coaches are some of the best I've worked with. The players too."

She stares at me a beat. I can't read her expression, but the intensity of it makes me squirm.

"Please don't tell anyone. Most of my old and current teammates know the real reason, but I don't want it to get twisted or for Aidan to overhear and get the wrong idea. I made a decision, and I stand by it."

I don't ever want Aidan to feel the weight of the sacrifices I've made for him. It's my job to make hard choices that make his life better.

"Of course. I would never."

I think I already knew that, but I smile at her with my appreciation.

"You have a knack for getting me to talk," I say, feeling like I've overshared. "Here I am blabbering on."

She laughs. "This is you chatty?"

I hold her smile until she looks away. She tucks her hair behind her ear and looks down at her notes.

"What about you?" I ask because I'm not ready to answer more questions and because I want to know more about her. "Why'd you and your ex break up?"

"Oh . . . it's not a very interesting story." She shifts uncomfortably in her seat.

"Neither is mine, but you've been making me answer questions about it for weeks."

"It's only been two weeks." A little of her spunk returns.

I lean back and cross my arms at my waist, waiting for her to go on.

She does after a few beats. "He's an author, like me. I met him at an event."

I'm quiet, giving her room to keep talking, which she does, thankfully.

"He was just getting started in his career and so full of excitement and energy. It was . . ." She pauses, choosing her words carefully. "Inspiring. I got wrapped up in him and his enthusiasm. We dated for about six months. We were both in the middle of writing a book, so we spent those months mostly holed up in coffee shops or one of our apartments, typing and sharing smiles over our laptops."

A pang of jealousy twists in my gut. I don't know why the idea bothers me so much. I guess sometime over the past two weeks, she's gotten under my skin. I like her. She's gorgeous, of course, but it's more than that. I think she might be the most fascinating person I've ever met.

"What happened?"

"He finished his book and sold it to a publisher. It did well and then he pitched another book idea, this one slightly different than his previous two, but he sold it quickly."

"I meant what happened between the two of you."

Her gaze drops to her lap. "When I saw the publisher's deal announcement, I thought it was a mistake. And then I thought maybe I was legitimately losing my mind."

"I don't understand. You broke up because he got a book deal?"

Her head moves side to side slowly. "I have this notebook filled with story ideas. Most of them are silly—one-liners or an interesting character or piece of dialogue. Sometimes they're more fleshed out and I'll pull them for my next book."

My chest tightens as I get a good idea where this is going.

"I had this one story that had been percolating in my mind forever. It was so silly I kept dismissing it, but I couldn't stop thinking about it either. I would jot down scene ideas as they came to me and little bits of dialogue or scene description. I had ten pages of an outline and rough chapters." She pauses and lets out a breath as if letting it sink in all over again. "Anyway, I guess it wasn't as silly as I thought because he received a very nice seven-figure advance to write it."

"He stole your book?"

She shrugs.

"That's awful. What happened when the publisher found out?" That twisting sensation in my gut intensifies.

Her expression alone gives me my answer, or at least that the answer is nothing good.

"They didn't believe you or you didn't tell them?"

"How was I going to prove it?" she asks, voice wavering. "I had no way to verify when I'd written the pages or even that they were my ideas."

I run a hand through my hair. "Fuck. That's . . . awful. I'm sorry."

"Thanks."

I can't believe someone would do that. Let alone to her. What a fucking prick. God, no wonder she's had writer's block. That would mess with anyone's head. I suddenly feel a thousand times worse about my reaction when she showed up. She was coming off something awful, and I acted like an asshole.

I stand and walk over to her. She looks up, confusion marring her brow.

I take the laptop and set it on the ground, then pull her to her feet and hug her. She squeaks her surprise and then slowly wraps her arms around my middle. The way she fits there is nice, my chin resting on the top of her head, and I inhale that coconut and strawberry scent. Fuck, I really like her.

"Nick?" Her voice is small.

"Yeah?"

"Are you trying to squeeze all the air out of my lungs?"

I loosen my grip. Shit. "Sorry."

There's a distinct possibility that I just channeled all my rage into that hug.

She laughs. "Don't be. Actually . . ."

Her grip tightens around my waist for a few seconds, then releases. "That's not a bad way to work out my frustration either."

A laugh slips from my lips. "I'm at your service, Red."

Chapter Nineteen

RUBY

A knock on the cabin door pulls me from my edits. I put my laptop on the coffee table and stand.

Nick is on the other side of the door wearing jeans and a white T-shirt. His dark hair is wet like he might have showered recently. I just saw him yesterday morning, but wow, every time it's like a shock to my system.

"Hi," I say, happy to see him but surprised all the same. "Did I forget about something we had planned?"

"No." His rough laughter skates over my skin.

My body relaxes, and I step back to let him inside. "I just finished writing the first hockey game scene."

"Yeah?" His expression morphs to something full of excitement and maybe pride. "Can I read it?"

"Soon," I promise. "I need to triple-check all my hockey facts, so you don't think all this research has been for nothing."

His grin widens. "In that case, I know just what you need to celebrate."

"What?"

"To watch a hockey game," he says simply, walking over to my couch and making himself at home. "Wear something warm. The rink gets cold."

A small huff leaves my lips. "I . . ." A dozen excuses are on the tip of my tongue.

Nick arches a brow like he's silently daring me to come up with a single good one.

"I'm a mess." I glance down at my cut-off shorts and then bring a hand up to smooth over my ponytail.

"I'll wait." He kicks his feet up on the table next to my laptop.

* * *

Twenty very rushed minutes later, we're in the truck. The music is on but turned down low.

"Who's playing?" I ask when I realize I didn't get a lot of details beyond him taking me to a hockey game.

"Aidan."

"Wait. Really?"

"Yeah, his club team is playing."

He pulls up to a rink smaller than the one in Moonshot, but inside it's filled with people. Nick walks with purpose, and I lengthen my stride to keep up with him. As we're going up the bleachers to our seats, I spot Travis, then Conrad, Danny, and Penn.

"Do they all have kids that play too?"

Nick chuckles. "Nah, they come for Aidan."

Somehow it doesn't surprise me. The limited time I've spent with them, I can see how close and supportive they are of each other. "That's so nice."

Travis stands as we get close.

"Ruby-Doo!" He holds his arms out to his sides, and I step into a hug.

"Hey," I say with a laugh. I'm still not used to his easy charm and affection, but he's sort of impossible not to like.

"Nick didn't tell me you were coming. I would have dressed up, brought flowers." He tosses a grin at his friend.

Impossible not to like and an incorrigible flirt.

I sniff the air, the scent of popcorn wafting from a concession stand somewhere. "Popcorn is the way to my heart."

"Noted." Travis releases me, then hugs Nick.

I move over, smiling and waving at the rest of the guys.

"Hey." Danny is the only one that speaks, but the other two men acknowledge me with smiles, and Penn lifts a hand.

Conrad scoots over, and I take a seat next to him. Down on the ice, I look for Aidan.

"Number nine," Conrad says, pointing to the right side. It's possible those are the most words I've heard him say.

I find Aidan, then grin. He looks so much like Nick.

"Thanks."

He nods.

"Do you all go to all of Aidan's games?" I ask him, but then glance to the others.

"We make it when we can," Danny says.

"That's really nice."

"Ruby," Nick calls my name. He's still standing with Travis a few feet away.

When I meet his gaze, he says, "I'll be right back. You good?"

I give him a thumbs-up, and he and Travis head down the same stairs we just came up.

"So, how's the book coming?" Danny asks, leaning over from the other side of Conrad.

"Slow," I admit. "The more I learn about hockey, the more I realize how little I know."

His chest lifts and rises with a silent laugh. "I'm sure it's great. You're a fantastic writer."

My face heats and my eyes widen. "You've read my books?"

It didn't even occur to me, probably because ninety-eight percent of my readers are women, but I'm instantly self-conscious.

"I binged you this week."

I open my mouth, then close it. I don't quite know what to say to that.

"Dude. You made it weird," Conrad says to him.

"No," I say quickly. "I'm just surprised."

"Danny's a huge book nerd." Conrad has this low, quiet voice and timid expression that I can't quite get over. He's ridiculously good-looking and doesn't seem to realize it.

"Me too," I say to him then to Danny, "You really read all of them? Like *all*?!"

He nods and grins wide. He has a small gap between his front teeth that's hot and adorable at the same time.

"Thank you." I don't know how else to respond.

"I'm excited to read more. Are you going to write a sequel to *Love Bites*?"

"I hadn't planned on it," I say, thinking. No one has ever asked me that before.

"I loved Xander. I bet you could write a hell of a story for him."

"He dies," I say.

"But did he really?"

I laugh. I didn't explicitly show it on the page, so I guess he's right.

"When is the one you're writing now coming out?" Danny asks.

"Early next year."

"Cool. I look forward to it."

"I'll send you a copy if you want."

"Hell yeah." His body rocks back and forth with his excitement.

I sit back in my seat, grinning as I stare down at the ice. Molly will be so happy to know I'm garnering more male readers while I'm here.

The kids on both teams clear off the ice to their respective benches. When I spot Aidan again, he's heading for the center. Instinctively, I look for Nick. He and Travis are at the bottom of the stairs, staring out at the ice for the puck drop. Nick's mouth moves, but I can't make out the words he sends his son.

"He's such a good dad." The words, which I absolutely did not intend to say out loud, not only are spoken but also come out dreamily. I've seen how hard it is being a single parent. My sister juggled being a single mom for years before she met Flynn. I respect him a lot for his dedication, especially knowing what Nick gave up so Aidan could have both parents in the same place.

My cheeks flush, and I wince as I glance at Conrad to confirm . . . yep, he heard me. His brows lift, and then a slow smile curves his lips. He has these bright blue eyes and dirty-blond hair. He's one of those guys that gets cuter the longer you look at him to the point I'm wondering if maybe he ever did modeling as a kid.

"That was an inside thought."

He huffs a laugh. "It's cool. And yeah, he is. Nick's a good guy all around."

I can only nod. All signs do point that way, which is great because I still need to finish my book, and there'll be more questions for sure. It has nothing to do with the fluttery feelings I get when he's nearby. Or when I talk to him. Or he looks at me.

I focus hard on the puck drop. Aidan wins the face-off, and the guys around me cheer. I get lost in the action. These kids are seriously fast and skilled.

Travis comes to sit next to me. He's holding a drink in one hand and nachos in the other. I eye the food, stomach grumbling.

"I wanted to get you popcorn," he says, then side-eyes the man walking up behind him. Nick stops in front of us, rolls his eyes dramatically, and then holds out a bag of popcorn to me. My mouth waters. For more than one reason. There are those fluttery feelings again. Probably hunger pangs.

* * *

After the game, I'm more amped up than Aidan.

"That was incredible. You're so fast!" I tell him.

He grins, looking shy and proud all at once.

"What'd you say?" Nick prompts him.

A hint of annoyance creeps into his expression but he says, "Thanks, Ruby."

"You're welcome."

A couple approaches us slowly. I know instantly she's Nick's ex, Beth. She's every woman's nightmare ex-girlfriend. Tall and beautiful. She has an effortlessly chic look about her. Simple clothes, hair pulled back in a low ponytail, minimalistic makeup. And still stunning.

Nick spots her, smiles, then ruffles Aidan's hair. "See you tomorrow."

"All right." Aidan nods and hefts the giant duffel bag onto his shoulder. The amount of gear these kids carry around is impressive.

Beth and the man I assume is her husband hang back, giving Aidan time to say goodbye to his dad. Nick waves when Aidan turns to go to them.

I'm still staring at her when Nick says, "Ready?"

I tear my gaze from her to him. He's wearing a cheeky smile.

"For what?"

He tips his head. "The guys want to hang out with you."

I glance over at where Travis, Conrad, and Danny are standing waiting for us. Penn must have left.

"If you don't want to go, I'll make some excuse," he says.

"No," I say quickly. "I do. Are you sure you don't mind me tagging along?"

His mouth pulls up on one side. "I'm sure."

We go back to Moonshot and to a bar that has a view of the lake and an outdoor patio. It's packed. I stick close to Nick as we navigate through the place. Nick glances back to make sure I'm still with him. I shuffle closer and loop a finger through the belt loop of his jeans.

He grins as he glances down to see me holding on to him, then continues guiding us to the bar. Once we're there, he places an arm around my back, placing me in front of him and boxed into the space.

"What do you want to drink?" he asks, leaning next to my ear and sending a shiver down my spine.

I open my mouth to order a vodka tonic. Sometime over the past few years it became my very boring, go-to order. I want to try something new.

"What's your usual order?" I ask Nick.

"Corona."

I wrinkle up my nose.

"Get whatever you want, Red."

"That's the problem. I don't know what I want."

He thinks for a second. "Anything you don't like?"

The bartender is getting antsy in front of us. I flash her an apologetic smile.

"Scotch. Red wine. Beer. Ooh, no tequila." I shiver at the memory of the last time I had it. It was post-Matt. Olivia invited me out with her and Flynn and a bunch of his teammates. The night got blurry after the third round of tequila shots.

Nick nods, patient and warm, not at all bothered by holding up the line. "How do you feel about rum?"

I shrug. "I'm not sure."

He finally looks to the bartender. "Can we get a cable car and a mai tai?"

She bobs her head once and gets to work. I turn to face Nick, putting my back to the bar. His gaze drops to my lips and then slowly roams over my face. I'm ninety-nine percent sure he's as attracted to me as I am him, but I'm not confident enough to make the first move. I'm not even sure if I want to make a move. Okay, that's a lie. I do, but I'm a smidge worried it'll make things awkward for the rest of the summer.

"What's in a cable car?" I ask him.

"Rum."

"I figured that," I say with all the sass I'm feeling.

He grins, unfazed.

"Thanks for inviting me out tonight."

"Don't thank me yet. The guys are playing it cool, but they're about to bombard you. Travis is probably planning out how to get you to go home with him."

A laugh slips from my lips. "He's not really my type."

"Really?" Nick cocks a brow.

"That surprises you?"

"Pretty much everyone has said the opposite since you arrived."

"Who?" The idea of anyone talking about me . . . let alone me and Travis together boggles my mind.

"Trav, for one."

"I should have guessed." Another laugh bubbles up in my chest and spills out.

Nick leans forward until his chest brushes mine. He reaches past me and then holds out a drink to me. It's a yellowish orange color in a coupe glass with what smells like sugar and maybe cinnamon around the rim.

He watches as I bring it to my lips and take a sip.

"Ooh." The taste surprises me. "I was expecting it to be sweet."

"Little sweet. Little sour."

I take another sip. "It's good."

He leans forward again to get the other drink. This one is in a short glass. The pinkish hue and pineapple wedge give it a fun, fruity feel. I'm certain at some point in my life I've had one before, but it's been too long to remember what it tastes like.

We switch off. Nick holds the cable car as I take the mai tai. The same way I had the last glass, I slowly bring it to my mouth. The coconut and pineapple scent is strong, and it tastes exactly like I imagined. Sweet and fruity and fun.

"Do we have a winner?" Nick asks.

I nod. "It tastes like summer."

"It smells like you."

"I smell like summer?"

"Coconut," he says.

I take another sip. "I'm not sure I could drink more than one of these."

"What else do you want to try?"

"Are you going to make that poor bartender make every drink they have?"

"No," he says, then grins. "Just the ones without scotch, red wine, beer, and tequila."

I laugh, mostly because I think he might be serious. "What's *your* typical type?"

He takes the mai tai from me and sips it. "I'm partial to coconut, but it's a little sweet."

"I meant in women."

He absolutely knew what I meant, judging by the cocky smirk he aims at me.

"Let me guess. Tall, graceful, willowy, gorgeous."

"According to Travis, my type is the nice and wholesome girl next door."

"Really? I did not get that vibe from your ex. I mean, I'm sure she's nice, but she's far too beautiful to be the girl next door."

"You're beautiful and literally live next door."

"You know what I mean."

He laughs again. I let the quiet fall between us, hoping he'll tell me more. I don't want him to tell me just because I'm asking. I want him to share because maybe this could be more than a business arrangement.

"Is convenient a type?" he asks, looking sheepish or maybe regretful. He shrugs those big shoulders. "Since Aidan was born, I've kept things casual."

"Like hookups?"

He gives a reluctant nod.

"It isn't that I set out to be a guy whose sex life revolves around one-night stands and hooks up with women on the road, but it's simpler."

"No judgment here. I get it."

"What about you?"

"I went through a phase in my early twenties where I kissed a lot of guys at bars or clubs, parties. Olivia called me the make-out queen. I really like making out."

Amusement creeps into his features, and his smile is crooked. His gaze drops again to my mouth. I'd like to make out with him. I bet he'd be great at it.

"Sex with strangers always feels too scary. And with no guarantee that he'll be able to get me off." I shake my head. "Too risky."

"Fair," he says.

"I did have a one-night stand once."

He moves beside me, standing close as he rests one hip against the bar. I have his full attention and it's heady.

"It was a cousin of a friend, so I wasn't worried about him murdering me."

"And did he get you off?"

"Yes. Although I wish he hadn't."

Nick's brows lift.

"He lived with his parents."

He laughs, the movement bringing his chest closer to mine. My skin buzzes with the contact.

"A tidbit he failed to tell me. The next morning, I got up to leave and stumbled right into his parents, who were excited to talk to me about my relationship with their son." They must have assumed that if he was bringing me home, we were serious, and I guess I was too embarrassed to correct them. "I went along with it, smiling and trying to find my shoes so I could leave."

Nick laughs harder.

"I was mortified. Especially when his mom said how happy she was to know her son was pleasing me so well in the bedroom."

The man in front of me full on cackles. It's such a good look for him, I continue, despite my humiliation.

"That's when I swore off one-night stands forever and ever. I'm too much of a hazard risk to put myself in potentially dangerous or embarrassing situations. The pancakes were good though."

"You had breakfast with them?" He barks out another laugh before I've defended myself.

"His dad asked me, and I didn't want to be rude!"

I join in, laughing at the memory and the happiness bubbling up in my chest now.

"You're something, Red." The taunting nickname sounds more like an endearment from him now.

"Galaxy! Ruby-Doo!"

Nick's gaze lifts slowly from me, and then he opens up his stance. Travis stands on a chair across the bar.

Nick tips his chin up and then looks back at me.

"You good? Want anything else from the bar?"

I hold up both hands, a drink in each. "I think I'm set."

Nick leads me over to the guys. Travis jumps down from the chair, grinning.

"Double-fisting it. See?" he asks Nick. "My type."

Nick looks at me as if to say, *See, told you everyone thinks you're Trav's type.*

"I might be your type, but you're not mine," I say, taking a sip of the mai tai.

His smile falls. The other guys go quiet. It feels like the entire bar is one big record scratch. The usual smirking, happy Travis looks downright crestfallen. Oops.

"Oh my god. I'm sorry. I didn't mean . . ." I get flustered as the guys all explode with laughter. Danny is doubled over, and Conrad's whole body shakes with silent laughter.

Travis hangs his head, a small grin finally pulling at his mouth. "I thought we had something special, Ruby."

"You're super hot and very charming."

"So you're into ugly, boring guys?" He nods definitively. "Got it. You're up, Nicky boy."

My face is on fire.

"Oh man. That made my entire night," Danny says, wiping tears from the corners of his eyes. "Thanks, Ruby."

I sneak a glance at Nick as the heat continues to bloom in my cheeks.

Still laughing, Conrad and Danny move to a tabletop shuffleboard game on the patio. Travis follows them.

"Did I crush his ego?" I ask when they're gone.

"Travis?!" He shakes his head. "Not possible."

"I feel bad," I admit.

"Don't even sweat it. He's just busting my chops. Since the minute you showed up, he's been taking every opportunity to give me shit."

We spend two hours talking and laughing, playing shuffleboard (them), and drinking (me). Travis forgives me after making me tell him again how hot and charming he is, then he and Danny spot some girls they know and disappear. Conrad sits across from me and Nick as the three of us drink and chat. Though it's mostly been me and Nick holding the conversation.

Conrad's been staring at the same girl for thirty minutes. It's so obvious he's into her, but when I suggested he go talk to her, he shook his head adamantly and said he was good.

"Does he know he's the most attractive man in this bar?" I ask Nick, tipping my head toward his friend.

"He's shy around women."

"Yeah, I'm getting that, but why? Has he looked in the mirror lately?"

Nick smirks. "We've tried telling him that, but he says it doesn't matter because as soon as he opens his mouth, he says something dumb."

"I'm familiar with that," I mumble, then finish off the last of my second mai tai. The cable car was good, but I decided tonight needed a happy, celebratory drink.

"Another?" Nick asks, eyeing the empty glass.

"God no." I giggle. I'm in that happy, tipsy state. I like to linger there. I'm clumsy enough without adding inebriation. Then I cover a sleepy yawn.

Chuckling, Nick stands then offers me his hand. It isn't that late, so I'm afraid to ask what we're doing. I'm not sure I have it in me to do anything but sit here like a lump.

"It's been a long day. You must be tired."

"I am." I get to my feet eagerly, but I guess the last drink hit me harder than I thought because I wobble and then catch myself by placing both hands on his very nice, very hard, muscular chest.

Nick's hands settle on either hip in a firm, steadying grip.

"Thanks," I say, staring up at him, maybe leaning into him a bit more. "You're so strong. I bet you could throw me over your shoulder without a lot of effort."

One side of his mouth quirks up.

"Inside thought," I whisper.

"I think I'm going to head out too." Conrad's voice reminds me we aren't alone.

I step away from Nick and smile at his friend. If Conrad heard my ramblings, I can't tell.

"It was nice to see you again," I say. I really like Nick's friends, but since our interview sessions are almost over, I'm not sure how much more I'll see them.

"You too." He smiles then gives Nick a salute as he heads out.

Nick and I stare at each other again. The air buzzes around us, and my face flushes, possibly from the alcohol, probably from the thoughts of him running through my mind. I can't get the idea of him hoisting me up with those big hands out of my head. Is it weird that I want him to manhandle me? Maybe. Probably. Oh well.

I wasn't lying earlier. Travis isn't my type. Matt was more like him than Nick, but he was an outlier. I had lots of guy friends in college that were fun, life of the party types, but I always fell hardest for the quiet, brooding types.

"I should probably say goodbye to Travis and Danny too in case I don't see them again," I say to Nick, looking around the bar for them. I spot Danny first. He's got a girl in his lap, and they're kissing so intensely it makes my body light up.

"Or not," I say, a little breathy. Note to self: No more going out and drinking without a quality masturbation session first. My pheromones are standing at attention, waving green flags in every direction.

"Don't worry, Red. You'll see them again. Travis will want to hear you tell him he's hot again at least a dozen more times." He places his hand on my back, and I melt into the contact.

Outside the bar, it's quiet as Nick leads me to his truck. Correction: I'm quiet. I can't think of a single thing to say that isn't something that should be kept as an inside thought. Maybe I should tell him?

No. Too much room for error. The ride home will be torture if I've misread the signs.

He steps ahead of me to open the passenger side door for me. Very date-like behavior. Or maybe he's just being nice?

His brow furrows when I hesitate to get in. "Everything okay?"

"Mhmm." I squeak and then avert my gaze as I try to brush past him.

He cuts me off, moving in front of me. "What's wrong?"

"Nothing," I insist and flash him my most convincing smile.

He doesn't budge.

I fake a yawn. "Oh man, I'm so tired."

He crosses his arms over his chest. Okay, not buying it, and I guess he's prepared to wait me out.

I sigh. "Inside thoughts, Galaxy."

His brows lift, and an amused smirk dances across his face. "I like your inside thoughts."

"I'm not so sure you'd like these," I murmur.

"Try me."

"I . . ." Ugh. I feel so junior high right now. Exasperated, I say, "I like you."

His smile lifts higher. "I like you too."

"No, I *like* you."

"I like you too, Ruby."

"Yeah, but do you like me in a 'she's not as annoying as I originally thought' sort of way, or are you also wondering . . ."

Instead of letting me finish the question, he steps to me, places a hand at the nape of my neck and drops his lips to mine.

Sparks crackle between us. I lean up on my toes and wrap my arms around his neck. The movement closes the last stretch of distance between us. My body shivers as his warmth envelops me.

"Sorry." His voice is gruff as he speaks against my lips and the word rumbles from his chest. "I didn't mean to cut you off mid-sentence."

"It wasn't important. They were inside thoughts."

He leans back to meet my eyes. "I want to know every one of your thoughts, Red. Haven't you figured that out yet?"

My answer is to slam my mouth back to his. He doesn't miss a beat. His mouth slants over mine, and we're one big, tangled heap as our hands roam and bodies press together. His tongue sweeps into my mouth, and he lets out a groan.

Nick leans down, strong arms drop to my upper thighs, and he lifts me into his arms.

"That answers one question," I say, breathless and giddy.

"What's that?"

"Whether or not you can toss me over your shoulder."

Another soft chuckle whispers across my lips. "Definitely. I'll prove it later."

He kisses me as he places me in the passenger seat of his truck. He stands between my legs, and I wrap myself around him.

The man is a very good kisser, and his hands are magic. They roam up and down my back, tangle in my hair, then around the sides of my neck, to my face, a thumb brushing across my bottom lip and his fingertips gliding across my cheeks.

I'm putty in his big, sporty hands. They drop back to my sides, and one holds my hip in place as his mouth travels down my neck to nip at my collarbone.

I'm vaguely aware of the seat belt moving around me and clicking into place, but it isn't until Nick steps away and the air cools around me that my foggy brain makes sense of it.

My eyes open and my lips tingle. "What's happening?"

"Taking you home, Red, before we end up naked in a bar parking lot."

"Doesn't sound so bad." In fact, it sounds near perfect. The cab of the truck is a little small and confining for any sexual gymnastics, but I'm so amped up on him it will take very little to do the job tonight.

He grins, winks, then shuts the door, closing me inside his truck.

Chapter Twenty

NICK

The ride back takes an eternity. Neither of us says much, but I can read the thought bubbles over Ruby's head, and they're in line with every dirty thing I want to do with her.

Any hesitations I had were lost the moment she admitted to thinking about me throwing her over my shoulder. I can't stop picturing it, and now I fully intend to show her.

The house is dark when I pull into the drive. I hop out of the truck and round the front. She's already got her door open and seat belt off when I reach her.

"You sure you want to do this, Red?" I ask.

Her answer is to launch herself at me.

Chuckling, I wrap an arm around her to hold her in place while I shut the truck door. My steps are quick as I carry her to the cabin. Once we're inside, I shift her up and toss her over my shoulder the way she wanted.

She squeals with delight. Navigating through the cabin takes some effort with only the moonlight streaming in through the windows as my guide. I've only been in here a handful of times since it was finished.

The bedroom smells like her. Everywhere I walk lately she haunts me. I have a feeling she will long after she's gone too. I'm not about to let those thoughts in tonight though.

I bring her back down to stand in front of me. Her cheeks are flushed and her eyes big and expressive.

"This hair." I push it back over her shoulders and place my hands along the column of her neck on either side. "I like it."

She glances up, then blows a few stray locks out of her face. A giggle works free, but as soon as my hands glide down her shoulders to her waist, she quiets, and her pupils widen.

"Give me those inside thoughts."

"Kissing you might be my new favorite sport."

A laugh breaks free. I always think I'm prepared for what she's going to say, but she keeps surprising me.

"I'm not sure that's an official sport, kissing."

"It should be. You're really good at it."

I spin her around. She wobbles, but I steady her with a hand at the back of her neck and another at her thigh.

She giggles again. The sound worms its way through my chest, and warmth spreads through me. My fingers slip under the hem of her dress. She arches into me, pushing her perfect ass into my crotch and driving me out of my fucking mind.

"I'm good at a lot of things, Red. Spread those legs for me and let me show you."

She does, flashing a smile over her shoulder at me. Fuck, she's sexy. Sunshine and happiness, sass and wit. I didn't think I had a type, but I just hadn't met her yet.

My palms glide over smooth skin as they travel up her thighs. "These little dresses and skirts you're always wearing make me insane."

"Good. I should have some retribution for freezing my ass off all the time."

"This ass?" I slide my hand up and squeeze one lace-covered globe.

She nods frantically, letting out a little whimper.

"Let's see what we can do about that." I spin her around again so we're chest to chest, then crash my mouth down onto hers. This woman. This goddamn woman.

Both of my palms cover that gorgeous ass as I walk her back to the edge of the bed and ease her onto it. I stand in front of her.

"So many inside thoughts." Her lips curve up, taunting, as she sits on the mattress.

"You better get ready to scream them, Red."

"That right?" She gets to her feet and slowly fingers the hem of her dress. I'm frozen, captivated. My gut swirls and a deep ache slices my chest as she slowly lifts the fabric up, exposing her panties, then her stomach, and then the dress is lifted over her head.

She holds the material in one hand as she stands before me in nothing but lingerie. Black and lacy. The definition of temptation if I've ever seen it.

"Goddamn beautiful," I mutter.

"Was that an inside thought?" she asks as she drops the dress to the floor.

"No, Red. I don't plan on holding back a single thought tonight either." I hook my finger in the front of her bra and tug her to me. "But the only thing I'm thinking is how badly I need to be inside you."

"What a coincidence." All her earlier sass is gone, and her voice quivers, and her chest rises and falls with quick breaths. She reaches around behind her with one hand and unhooks her bra.

Her breasts are as perfect as the rest of her. Light pink nipples almost as pale as her skin are peaked tight, begging me to glide my tongue over them. Something I have every intention of doing.

"Get on the bed, baby."

She steps backward and sits slowly, all the while eyeing me.

With one arm, I reach back and pull my T-shirt over my head. Ruby's gaze is locked on my every movement.

Several seconds stretch out with silence as she openly checks me out with appreciation.

"Fuck me," she mumbles under her breath as her stare continues to roam over my bare chest. The tip of her tongue darts out to wet her lips.

"That's the plan." Since the moment she showed up, I've been fighting this, but right now I can't remember any of the reasons why.

I toss my shirt, and then, as I toe off my shoes, I unbutton my jeans. My dick throbs against the rigid denim.

"Need some help?" she asks when I don't immediately push my pants to the floor.

Smirking, I shake my head slowly. From my wallet, I grab a condom, then toss it on the nightstand. When I step in front of her, she lights up with a smile.

"This mouth." I swipe my thumb over her lips.

"What about it?" she asks in barely a whisper.

"It's as perfect as the rest of you."

The corners of her lips pull up higher. I love being the one responsible for that smile.

Bending down, I kiss her, smile and all. With one knee on the mattress, I guide her back until I'm hovering over her. Her tits press against my chest, and she lifts her hips to grind against the front of my jeans.

"Impatient little minx." I nip at her lip, then kiss a trail down her chest, stopping briefly to suck on each nipple.

She arches up into me, hands finding purchase in my hair. Her nails scrape lightly against my scalp and down my shoulders and back. I hook one finger into the waistband of her panties as I drop my head lower. She sucks in a breath as my lips ghost over her stomach and continue down.

I guide the lacy material over her hips and down to her knees, then lean back so I can pull them off the rest of the way. While I roll the black panties down her calves and ankles and drop them to the floor, I look at her.

Beautiful doesn't feel like a strong enough word to describe how gorgeous she is or the feelings swirling in my gut as I stare at her. I can tell her cheeks are flushed even in the moonlight. It's a pink that trails down her neck and chest. Her hair tumbles over her shoulders. The four-leaf clover necklace she always wears sits between her perky, full tits.

"You okay?" Ruby asks.

"Give me a second, Red. I'm committing this to memory."

She laughs, the movement jiggling her breasts. She's too damn tempting to resist. I'm back on top of her, kissing her smile with my own. I could kiss her all night, but the need to taste her has me moving back down her body. I spend a little extra time nipping and gently tugging on her belly button ring.

"I like this too," I say.

"Maybe you should get one."

I chuckle as she gives me a haughty, taunting look. I hook an arm under one of her legs, lifting her to me. Eyes glued to hers, I place a chaste kiss just above her clit. That sassy look is replaced with one full of need.

"Nick." Her head falls back, pushing her tits up to the ceiling.

I bite her inner thigh to get her attention. Her gaze snaps back to me.

"You want me to watch?"

I flash a grin at her. I want to see every reaction play out on her face. She sits up on her elbows and her gaze locks on my mouth as I bring it back down to cover her pussy. I hum against the sensitive flesh.

"You're soaked." I flick my tongue over her slit as I glance up at her. Her dark lashes lower, and she sighs. My plan was to take my time, but the taste of her has me losing my goddamn mind.

Ruby whimpers and gasps. She even laughs at times, though it's more of a manic sound than humorous, as I lick, taste, and start to fuck her with my tongue.

Goddamn. The noises she makes have my dick rock solid.

She calls out my name again, a warning, before her body tenses. I watch as the pleasure rolls through her. She isn't shy about chasing it, even holding my head in place like she's afraid I'll stop. No fucking way. I'll die here if necessary.

Like she does everything else, Ruby comes with a smile on her face. One that's going to be etched into my brain for a very long time.

Only when her grip on me loosens do I ease up. She falls back onto the bed with a contented sigh and a light laugh.

"Wow. Just . . . wow."

Yeah, that's about the extent of my thoughts right now too. I swipe the condom off the nightstand and finally push my jeans and boxers to the floor. That gets her attention. Ruby sits up, taking me in, then moves to kneel on the bed. She's smiling but doesn't say anything. She's thinking something, but I can't guess what.

I arch a brow in question.

"Just committing you to memory." She hooks an arm around my neck. "You are impressive, Galaxy."

A low chuckle vibrates in my chest, and I slant my mouth over hers as I push her back onto the bed. Our kisses turn from playful to frantic quick. All my best laid plans of going slow are quickly tossed out.

The head of my cock nudges against her entrance. Pleasure jolts through me, and I fight back the urge to push too fast.

"You good?" I ask as I move another inch.

"Never better."

Fucking same.

I rock my hips slowly, going deeper with every thrust. Ruby glides her nails down my arms and then my stomach.

"Maybe you can teach me how to get one of these," she says.

"A dick?"

She bursts into laughter. "A six-pack."

I join in, laughing with her. I'm not sure I've ever laughed during sex before. I should have expected it with Ruby.

"You're perfect, Red."

She leans up and kisses me as I finally bury myself to the hilt. Her tongue tangles with mine, encouraging me with moans and gasps and saying my name, as I fuck her harder and harder.

There are no words, no thoughts, except yes, more, and mine.

"I'm going to come." Another gasp as her head tips back against the pillow.

I wrap one hand around the side of her neck. "Eyes on me, Red."

Her lashes flutter open as her orgasm hits. Her lips part and her nails dig deeper into my biceps and it's the final push to send me over the edge with her. I've never come harder or longer.

I roll off her and sag to the bed as I catch my breath. Instead of exhaustion, I feel peace but in the most energizing kind of way. What the fuck even was that? I can't remember the last time sex felt like that. Has it ever felt like that? I'm spent, but all I can think about is doing it again.

"You were right," she says, turning on her side to face me. Her eyes close, and she gives me a sleepy smile as I bring my arm around her to pull her against me.

"About what?"

"You're good at lots of things."

"Like giving you orgasms?" I ask, brushing her hair away from her face so I can see the smile on her lips as she nuzzles against my chest.

"Like cuddling." Then she falls asleep.

Chapter Twenty-One

RUBY

The smell of coffee wakes me. I open my eyes and immediately look for Nick, trying not to feel disappointed when the bed is empty next to me. Then I hear him moving around the kitchen.

The sun is up, and the birds are chirping happily outside the window. I swing my legs over the side of the bed. My clothes from last night are scattered around the room, evidence that it all really happened. The sting of muscles I haven't used in a while is another clear indication that I wasn't dreaming. I pull the blanket off the bed and around me before padding out of the room and down the hall.

I come up short at the view in front of me. Nick stands in the kitchen with his back to me. He's changed clothes, and the ends of his hair are wet like he showered recently.

"Morning."

He turns and smiles at me. "Morning, Red."

He's shaved too this morning. A flash of shyness hits me as I think about how I must look by comparison. Hair messy, last night's makeup most likely smeared around my eyes. I passed out hard last night after the two best orgasms of my life.

"I got bagels and muffins and some fruit. I wasn't sure what you liked for breakfast."

And just like that warmth spreads through me.

"Coffee. Coffee is what I like for breakfast."

"Got that too." He steps to the side, revealing a fancy-looking machine.

I gasp as I step forward. "What is that?"

He chuckles. "I thought the cabin might need its own coffee pot."

"The cabin or me?" I ask, inhaling the smell of sweet, roasted bean goodness.

"Both."

"Thank you." I pull the blanket tighter around me.

"Welcome." He leans down slowly, holding my gaze as he brushes his lips over mine.

As far as waking me up, it does a better job than my usual coffee.

He stands tall and moves to take the food out. When he said he'd gotten things, I assumed he'd brought it down from his house, but there are takeout bags from at least four different places.

"Exactly what time did you get up?"

"Early." He sets the food in a row, buffet style, then grabs a mug from the cabinet and fills it with coffee, adding cream and sugar before handing it to me.

"Did you sleep at all?"

"Yeah, I did. More than I have in months."

I take a sip, staring over the rim at him.

"Sorry if I was snoring or thrashing around in my sleep." It's been a long time since I've slept with someone, and I was out so fast last night I didn't even have time to overthink it.

"You were perfect." He gets himself a cup of coffee while I watch him move around the kitchen and imagine what it'd be like to do this every day. He's going to make some woman very lucky one day.

"Why can't you sleep?"

He takes a sip then sets the mug down. He leans his back against the counter and grips the edge on either side of him. "My mind spins."

"About work?"

His chin dips. "Work, life, the gorgeous, naked redhead beside me."

My face flushes.

He stands tall and walks toward me. "When you're around, I have a hard time thinking of anything else."

"Guess it's a good thing I'm leaving in a few weeks then or you'd never sleep well again."

His body shakes with silent laughter.

I set my coffee down and cross the kitchen to him. He doesn't move except to smile as I lean up to press my lips to his.

"But until then," I murmur softly against his mouth.

"Until then," he agrees, then leans down and scoops me up, kissing me as he turns and sets me on the counter.

I wasn't sure where we'd stand on things this morning, but it seems like we both want this to be more than a one-time hookup.

"You make me feel graceful," I say as he steps between my legs. His lips trail aimlessly, softly and unhurried, down my neck and over to the other side.

"Graceful enough that you want to come with me to the rink today?"

"Really?"

"Yeah." He chuckles softly, places another kiss on my lips, and leans back to look at me. "Aidan's coming back tonight, but I thought we could hang today. I need to get in a workout, and you can write."

I have a feeling I'll be too distracted to be productive, but I can work tonight.

"Yes. I'd love that. I just need a few minutes to shower and get ready."

He nods, then tugs the blanket around me until it falls open. The cool air hits my skin, and my nipples pebble.

"It sounds like you're in a hurry."

"Nope." I shake my head adamantly. "Definitely not."

"Good. You need to eat something first."

I'm so surprised, I burst out into laughter. I'm naked on the counter, and the man is talking about food. He reaches over and plucks a strawberry out of the container, then brings it up to my mouth.

I bite into it, and the sweet juices fill my mouth. I guess he's not that patient either because he leans forward and presses his lips to mine. Our kisses are sweet and sticky, and it isn't long before the air crackles around us again. If I had any concerns that last night was a fever dream and the chemistry between us was a fluke, they're gone now.

My body hums with pleasure even before his head dips and spreads my legs wider.

"Fuck, Red. You're dripping." He brushes two fingers along my slit, dipping inside slowly as my cunt squeezes around him.

I should probably be embarrassed at how wet I am this quickly, but it's all his fault. Everything he does turns me on. Even his grumpy jaw clenching—though he's done a lot less of that lately.

"Are you sore?" he asks.

"I'm fine," I say, already breathless and needy for more.

Almost as if reading my thoughts, he adds another finger. My cunt twinges, protesting slightly at the intrusion. It's too much and not enough.

"Holy shit. How are you so good at this, Galaxy?" I ask, then mutter, "Never mind. Don't tell me."

With a laugh, he eases out, going back to two, but bringing his mouth to my clit. Every nerve ending lights up as he teases me with soft, gentle flicks of his tongue. "It's not ever been like this, Red. I can tell you that."

It's reassuring, in a way, to know that I'm not the only one way out of my depth here. Sex with other people has been good, but this is next-level. If sexual soulmates are a thing, I think I just met mine.

My attempts to lift my hips to get more friction are met with a quiet chuckle against my skin and a tighter grip on my legs. As soon as I relax, giving over control to him, Nick gives me the pressure I was searching for. His fingers fuck me at a steady pace as he lavishes my clit with licks and sucks that have me soaring so quickly.

He nips my inner thigh, a gentle reminder that has me smiling as I look at him.

"Always needing an audience," I quip, but my sass lasts only as long as it takes him to find my clit again.

I grip the counter with my left hand and tangle the fingers of my right in his hair. It's thick and soft, the ends still damp. Last night his beard scraped against my skin in the most delicious way, but his smooth cheek gives me a great view of his dimples as he grins up at me like a man who knows he's about to give me another top three orgasm.

The only problem is him smiling at me means he isn't using that gorgeous mouth for other things.

"Oh, god, don't stop," I beg and tug his head back exactly where I want it.

He hums what might be agreement before he grazes his teeth over me and pumps his fingers faster. I'm almost frantic in my need for him. Him eating me out on the kitchen counter might be the hottest moment of my life, and the way he groans like he's enjoying it as much as I am is too much. The next low hum vibrates against my sensitive flesh and sends me over the edge.

My legs are shaky as he releases them and stretches tall with a wide, pleased smile.

He swipes the back of his hand across his mouth, but the cocky grin remains. "Ready?"

"For what?"

"Breakfast." He winks. "I ate. Now it's your turn."

My gaze drops to his crotch and the obvious bulge.

Laughing, he moves to the buffet of food. "Food, Red. You're going to need your energy for the ice."

* * *

After breakfast, which included going down on him and a lot more sticky kisses, we shower and then head to the rink.

Nick has already gone for a run this morning (seriously, what time did he wake up?!), but he leads me to a weight room where I sit, legs crossed with my laptop, while I watch him and attempt to write.

Travis and Conrad joined him about twenty minutes ago, which put an end to our kissing between sets, but it was probably for the best. He was never going to finish at that rate.

The three of them are in a corner of the gym working out their legs. Conrad has two very heavy looking dumbbells, one in each hand, as he walks and lunges back and forth. Travis is taking a break—he does a lot of that—between calf raises. And Nick is doing squats. With the barbell across the back of his shoulders, he sits back slowly, holding the weight in place. His mouth is in a thin, concentrated line, and sweat makes his shirt stick to his back. Don't even get me started on his thighs. I'm having some real dirty thoughts about those big, tree trunk thighs.

The clang of metal against metal breaks me out of my trance. Nick meets my gaze in the mirror in front of him as he reracks the barbell.

My face flushes with heat. I'm not sure I've ever been this attracted to anyone before. Even his little grunts of exertion are turning me on.

"One more set, and then I'll be done," he says over the music.

"Sure. Take your time."

He smirks, and I drop my gaze to my laptop. Molly sent notes on the first half of the book. She likes the tweaks I've made, so far, and had a few additions that I think are good. I have a lot to do still, but it doesn't feel quite as daunting as it did.

Nick was right about getting out on the ice. It has helped. And maybe kissing him has helped too. Whatever the reason, I'm writing again, and it feels great.

I know the ending is rough, and I'm dreading the rewrites when I reach that point, but I'm making progress. A hundred pages to go. Totally doable, I hope.

I manage to focus for a short time while Nick finishes up his workout. When he's done, he takes a seat on the bench behind me and wraps me up in his arms.

"You're sweaty," I say, leaning into his embrace.

"Am I? I didn't notice."

I swat at him playfully and turn to face him. I want to kiss him, but I don't know what the rules are. We are at his place of employment, even if there have been very few people popping in, outside of his friends. He erases my hesitation by capturing my chin between his thumb and finger and dropping his mouth to mine.

"Yowza! Get it, Galaxy!" Travis calls from somewhere in the room.

I laugh against Nick's mouth, but neither of us pulls back. I'm pretty sure Nick flips him off, because I feel his right arm lift into the air.

When we break apart, he's grinning at me in a way that makes my stomach flip. He's wearing a T-shirt with the sleeves cut off, and a scar on his right shoulder catches my attention.

"What's this from?" I run my finger underneath the red mark.

"I had surgery earlier this year."

"The injury that ended your season?" I read about it, of course, and watched the video. He collided with another player during a game. He got up on his own, but immediately skated off and didn't return. The details on his injuries were vague, but they did say he should return this season, which I'd already pieced together seeing him in person.

"Yeah, I broke my collarbone and dislocated my shoulder."

I wince. "Sounds painful."

"Nick and Ruby sitting in a tree. K-I-S-S-I-N-G," Travis sings in a playful voice.

"It was. Not as painful as listening to him though."

"Does that happen a lot?" I ask.

"Getting hurt or Trav being obnoxious?"

I laugh. "The first thing."

"Right, because you already know he makes being obnoxious a full-time job." Nick's smile pulls higher on one side, then falters slightly. "Yeah. Injuries are a part of the job, for sure."

"The worst I have to deal with is eye strain from staring at the screen too long or the occasional hand pain from typing too much."

"And no annoying teammates."

"You love them."

He sighs, still grinning. "I do, unfortunately."

After the guys are done, we gear up. I'm more nervous with Travis and Conrad around to witness my skills, or lack thereof, but Nick is so damn comforting.

"You got it, Red. Nice and easy. Grab on to me if you need."

I'm not sure if I need to or not, but I take the opportunity to touch him. He skates backward in front of me. So smooth, so confident, so damn hot.

He's in practice gear—padding, jersey, helmet, the works. He's a big guy, and I always feel small next to him but now more than ever.

"If I punched you in the stomach, would you even feel it?"

He quirks a brow. "I don't know, but you'd probably throw off your momentum and fall."

I open my mouth to protest, but he's got a point.

"Are you looking forward to the season starting?" I ask. I overheard Travis talking about how he was excited to get back to it in a few weeks.

"Yeah." He bobs his head as he answers, not sounding all that convincing.

"But?"

"I get to spend more time with Aidan during the summer, and being gone so much is hard on him."

"On him or you?"

He gives me a sheepish smile. "A little of both, probably."

"Is your schedule and juggling time with Aidan why you haven't tried to date?" I ask. He told me last night that he's kept things casual out of convenience, but the more I've thought about it, the more it feels like a poor excuse.

"Yeah."

"I'm sure there are plenty of women who would be happy to work around hockey and everything else. You're a catch."

He keeps smiling, but he isn't quite selling it.

I stop skating, and so does he. With one hand on his forearm, I steady myself. "What's the real story behind why you and Aidan's mom didn't work out?"

Immediately, his expression shifts, and he looks like he'd rather face-plant into the ice than tell me.

"Sorry. It's none of my business." I flash him an apologetic smile. "I've gotten so used to interviewing you."

I drop my hand and start skating again, moving past him. He catches up, staying beside me.

"There really isn't much else to say. We were both busy, and neither of us made enough of an effort to keep things going."

"That surprises me."

He raises both brows in silent question.

"You don't seem like the type to do anything halfway."

A small smile lifts one side of his mouth.

"I think you'd be a good boyfriend, though, for the record. Who knew beyond all that grump you were such a nice, considerate guy?"

He lets out a hearty guffaw that lightens the mood between us.

"Ruby-Doo!" Travis calls, voice booming around the tall, echo-y ceilings.

I glance at him as he skates up. He smirks as he comes to a hard stop that sprays ice in front of me. I startle, which makes me wobble. Nick's hands are lightning fast, gripping my waist and steadying me.

"Dude. She's still learning. Take it easy," Nick admonishes him without any real bite in his tone.

"Sorry, Rube."

"Can you teach me to do that?"

"Absolutely," Travis says at the same time as Nick says, "No."

I am a safety hazard, but that looked fun. I side-eye Nick and then turn my attention to Travis. "What's up?"

"Question for you."

"Sure."

His smirk should be the indication that he's about to ask me something ludicrous, but I'm too distracted by Nick's hands still circling my waist and my pulse racing for the same reason.

"When you said I was the most handsome hockey player you knew, were you trying to ease the pain after breaking my heart, or do you really think I'm a ten?"

"Fucking hell," Nick mutters, then chuckles softly under his breath.

"I said you were hot and charming," I correct him.

"*Suuuuper* hot." He beams and then winks at the guy next to me.

"And you wonder why we're all single," Nick says to me.

"You are hot and charming," I assure Travis. "I didn't say you were the hottest or most charming."

"Fine. Fine. But if Nick fucks this up, then I might have a chance?"

I'm ninety-nine percent sure he's fucking with Nick and not at all interested in me that way, but I'm not going to lie, my ego still appreciates him shooting his shot.

"All right. Back to your side of the rink." Nick shoos him, then pulls me after him as he skates away.

* * *

For the rest of the afternoon, I alternate between trying not to fall on the ice and trying not to be distracted by Nick while I write. I fail on both accounts.

When we get back to the house, I'm hoping to lure him into the cabin for more making out, but Aidan comes running out the front door as soon as we arrive.

"Hey, there he is." Nick hops out of the truck and walks quickly to his son, pulling him into a hug.

I get out of the vehicle but hang back, watching them and thinking about how good of a dad Nick is and how fortunate Aidan is to have him, and missing Olivia and Greer and the rest of my family terribly.

"Thanks for your help today," I call to Nick as I take a step toward the cabin. I lift a hand to Aidan. "Hi."

Aidan waves back. "I learned a new song while I was gone!"

"Really?" I ask.

He nods. "Sort of. I'm working on it."

"That's great. I can't wait to hear it."

He looks adorably pleased at my interest.

"I'm going to head back and do some writing." I hitch a thumb over my shoulder.

"Can I come play you the song later?" Aidan asks, surprising me, and I think his dad too.

"Yeah, of course." I look to Nick. He has one hand protectively on his son's shoulders. "As long as your dad says it's okay."

"Fine by me." Nick gives me a half smile.

"Cool. I'm going to grab my guitar and come right over." Aidan runs into the house, leaving me and Nick alone outside again.

Nick comes back down the steps, and we meet halfway. I'm glad. I don't want to be away from him just yet.

"Sorry about that," he says. "I can hold him off for a few hours if you want time to write."

"No. I like the noise."

"All right."

Neither of us moves.

"See you tomorrow morning?" he asks. One hand reaches forward, and his fingers brush against mine.

"Yeah. I'm sure I'll have a few more hockey questions as I go through the last half of the book."

"And then it's just editing?"

"And hopefully coming up with another idea I can pitch my agent."

"You will."

The sound of Aidan's guitar has Nick stepping away. He continues to face me, smiling in a way that makes me wonder if he's remembering the last time we stood here and how differently it ended.

"Later, Red."

"Later, Galaxy. Thanks for last night."

Chapter Twenty-Two

NICK

"You're in a hurry this morning," Dad says as he sits at the table in the dining room, sipping his coffee and keeping one eye on the TV in the living room.

"Busy day." I pour two to-go cups with coffee.

"Heading to the rink with Ruby?" He smirks in a way that makes me feel like a teen who doesn't want to admit he has a crush. "You two have been spending a lot of time together."

"Yeah." It's been almost two weeks since we started hooking up. Every day, we go to the rink. She asks me whatever new questions she's come up with and then spends the rest of the day writing while I try not to distract her too much.

"You're welcome."

I roll my eyes. I should thank him, but it'd only encourage him to do it again. Which let's be honest, I'm sure he will. In fact, I'm probably giving him ammunition for what a good idea it was to bring her here.

"Aidan wanted to get in some practice time, and she's tagging along to finish up her book."

"How's that coming?" he asks, thankfully letting the inquisition on my time with Ruby drop.

"Good. She's almost done. Today might be our last session together."

"That's too bad."

Aidan's footsteps sound above on the second floor.

"The whole point of her being here was to finish the book, so I'd say that's a good thing." I grab a banana for the drive and head to the bottom of the stairway to meet Aidan.

"Did you already eat?" I ask him, even though I saw evidence of his cereal bowl in the dishwasher. Actually, it might have been Dad eating the Froot Loops.

"Yep." His dark hair falls into his eyes.

"You need a haircut."

"Mom will take me this weekend."

"Shit. Right. Her birthday." Every year Aidan stays over on her birthday. It's the only thing she ever asks for.

"We need to get her a present still," Aidan reminds me.

"We'll do it tonight." I hold open the door and step out behind him. Ruby sits on the front porch. Her laptop rests across her thighs as she stares at it, a divot between her brows.

At the sound of the screen door, she glances up.

"Hey." She beams as she closes her computer and stands. "Morning."

"Morning," I reply as my chest tightens. Maybe it's because Dad and I were just talking about it, but the reminder that she's leaving soon is hitting me. I went from wishing she'd leave to enjoying seeing her every morning.

To be honest, I've tried my hardest not to overthink the connection I feel to her. I knew it wouldn't be a one and done kind of thing from the second I kissed her, but I don't know how to navigate whatever it is we're doing while knowing she's only here a short time.

At the rink, the three of us get on the ice together. Ruby's come a long way. She still manages to find creative ways to fall or nearly injure herself (and sometimes me), but when Aidan tries to teach her a backhand shot, she picks it up fast.

"Coming for my job yet?" I say as I circle around her.

"Maybe I should start teaching you mine. A backup option for you." All sass and tease.

"I promise you that no one wants to read anything I write."

"A hockey memoir, perhaps?"

"Not even that."

"You can do anything you want, Galaxy. Don't let the world crush your dreams."

I come to a stop in front of her, spraying ice to the side like Travis had done to impress her. "I think I'll stick to what I'm good at."

Grinning, she closes the distance between us. I flick my gaze to Aidan, but he's not paying us any attention. I wrap an arm around her and drop my lips to hers. Her mouth is warm and inviting. I pull back way before I want.

"A hockey Kama Sutra?" She arches a brow in question.

I'm still thinking about the feel and taste of her, so the words take a moment to register. When they do, I chuckle.

"It's a good idea. If you're not into it, maybe Travis wants to work with me on it."

"The fuck he does." He would absolutely be on board, which is why I'll have to kill my best friend if she goes through with it.

She laughs as I tug her tighter to me.

"I meant as a work project only." She drapes her arms around my shoulder. "You already know he isn't my type."

My jaw tightens as I hold her to me. Being jealous and protective isn't my usual mode, but the thought of her hooking up with anyone else makes me want to set the world on fire.

A puck hits the goal post, the distinct clang echoing around us. I loosen my grip, and we break apart.

"I should check the time. I have a call with Molly at ten."

"There are some empty conference rooms down the hall to the right, just past the locker room."

"Thanks."

"That's it, huh? You have everything you need to make edits and finish the book?" I ask.

"I think so. All that's left are rewrites."

"You're going to kill it."

"I hope so." She bites the corner of her lip, and her expression shifts to one of worry.

I know how much it means to her and how hard she's worked. I wish I could fill her with my confidence. There's no doubt in my mind.

"You will."

"Thanks for the hockey lessons."

"Any time, Red." She lingers, stealing a glance down the ice at Aidan.

I don't look to see if he's watching before tugging her back to me and kissing her the way I've wanted to all morning.

When I pull back, I'm already thinking about when I'll see her again.

"What are you doing tomorrow?"

"Not sick of me yet?"

I don't answer aloud, but fuck no. Not even close.

"Writing, most likely."

"On a Saturday?" I ask like I'm not usually at the rink every single day, even most holidays.

"I have to finish this book. There is no time for weekends."

"Well, if you need a break, the guys and I are going out on the lake tomorrow."

Her eyes light up, and I know I have her. She's mentioned, a few times, that she's wanted to swim when the lake warmed up. I should have taken her sooner.

"It might be a nice chance to take a break and rest before you dive into edits."

"What time?"

"Be at the dock at nine."

"We'll see," she says, but I'm not even sweating if she'll show up.

She skates off the ice and steps carefully onto the rubber mat. She shoots me one more smile over her shoulder before she treks off with her backpack over her shoulder.

Once she's out of sight, I pull out my phone from my pocket.

The Boys

Me: Taking the boat out tomorrow if anyone's interested.

Trav: Hell yeah. Finally.

D-Low: I'm in.

Shep: Can I bring anything?

Me: Nah. I got it covered. Penn?

Penn: Sure. I don't have anything else going on.

Trav: Wow, tamp down the excitement Penn.

Penn:

Chapter Twenty-Three

RUBY

"All this time you had a boat?" I ask, lifting onto my toes to kiss him.

Today I'm finally going out on the lake. Nick grins as I give him my best put-out expression. I mean seriously, I could have been sunning on this gorgeous boat for the past four weeks. I probably would have frozen my ass off, but it would have been worth it.

He huffs a laugh, scruff scraping against my skin. "I've been busy. There's this girl who keeps dragging me to the rink and making me teach her sports puck stuff."

"You could have taught me . . . on the boat." A very big, very expensive-looking boat. I don't know boat things any better than I knew hockey things when I arrived, but this one is nice. There's a lower deck with a small living area and a bathroom.

He glances down at me, lingering on my cleavage for a beat. "Yeah. I fucked up."

My head tips back with laughter, and he uses his thumb and forefinger to hold my chin in place as he drops another kiss on my lips.

My entire body lights up. Even the most tender touch has me ready to strip down. He looks fantastic in red trunks and a white T-shirt. He has on a matching white hat that comes down low on his eyes and sunglasses hanging from his shirt. I'm looking forward to him taking his shirt off later. I'm also looking forward to talking and chilling. My brain and body are in a real situation, fighting over getting to know him and getting down with him. I want to do both on a continuous cycle.

I'm snapped out of my thoughts as Travis and Danny drop the cooler filled with beer and water onto the boat. Conrad is slathering sunscreen on his arms and chest. Even Penn looks relaxed and happy with a backward hat and sunglasses, beer already in hand. Today is going to be a good day.

"Grab a life jacket, Red," Nick says as he pulls back.

"I know how to swim," I tell him.

"Safety first." He winks. "I can't concentrate on driving if I'm worried you're going to fall overboard."

I mean, honestly, it's a fair concern. If anyone is going to find a way to fall out of the boat, it would be me.

"Aye, aye, Captain." I step back and give him a salute, definitely pushing my boobs out in the process.

He gives them an appropriate ogle, then shakes his head at me.

Nick drives, and I sit in the seat across from him, enjoying the view and the water whipping through my hair. The sun is still ascending in the sky, and goose bumps dot my skin.

The guys in the back are quiet, all seemingly taking it in as well.

I lose track of where we are or which direction we've gone from the cabin as the water stretches out in all directions. There are a lot of people out already. Couples and families, groups of people of all ages.

Instead of houses dotting the landscape, we're in a stretch where it's bars and restaurants. Boats dock to eat or drink. It's not even noon, but party music already pumps from the venues. I think I could get used to the lake life.

"Quick food stop," Nick tells me as he heads toward the shore. "Shep gets hangry."

"I heard that," the quiet man calls over the roar of the engine.

Travis's distinct laugh follows. "It's so true though."

As Nick guides us closer to the dock, Conrad stands and helps tie up the boat. Travis and Danny are the next off, followed by Penn.

"Are you guys coming?" Danny asks Nick.

"Nah."

"We'll grab some extra subs and chips," Penn says.

"Thanks."

When they're gone, Nick turns to me. I'm windblown, and the life jacket is not a great look, but the grin he gives me makes me feel sexy anyway. He reaches over and grabs hold of the front of the jacket and uses it to pull me to him. Very ungracefully, I fall into his lap. He settles me there, sitting sideways across his thighs with his arm wrapped around my waist.

I barely recognize the girl smiling at him in the reflection in his sunglasses. When was the last time I was this happy?

"How will we entertain ourselves while they're gone?"

"Hmm . . ." His finger dips into the front of the jacket and between my breasts.

"I could ask you some hockey questions."

He dips his head down and looks at me over the top of his glasses. "Kidding. If making out had been on the list of possibilities when I first showed up, I'd still have a shortstop with a disc throwing touchdowns."

A hearty laugh shakes his body and mine. I bring one hand up to his cheek and glide my thumb over one of his dimples.

"These are very cute."

"So are these." He uses both his hands to cover my boobs over the jacket.

I'm grinning at him like a fool, and the way I feel is so overwhelming but in the best way. I'm not sure I've ever felt this much anything—happy, excited, turned on, hopeful. I'm buzzing with it.

Kissing him seems like the only option. I pour everything I'm feeling into the press of my mouth against his and hooking my arms around his neck. He hums against my lips before deepening the kiss and taking over. My body sighs with pleasure and relief. There's something soothing about giving myself over to his very capable hands.

I tangle my fingers into the hair at the nape of his neck. His mouth travels away from mine and down my neck to my collarbone. Deft fingers unbuckle me from the life jacket, and his head lowers.

"What about safety, Captain?" I ask, pushing my breasts into his face.

"If you go overboard, I'll save you."

I was teasing, but I know that he would. I have full confidence in that. Nick is the kind of guy who is always looking out for other people. His son, his dad, his teammates, me.

The scrape of his beard over my flesh sends a shiver through me. His movements are unhurried and his touch a mixture of tender and confident. His thumb brushes back and forth over my nipple as he drops kisses and bites all around the bare skin not covered by my bikini top.

My pulse is a steady thrum, and an ache forms between my legs. There isn't time or privacy for all the things I want to do with this man.

The wind continues to blow my hair around us, creating a shield of our faces. Not that anyone couldn't tell what we're doing as I grind onto his lap.

The few kisses and lingering touches we've shared this week at the rink haven't been enough. And judging by the impressive erection under me, I think he feels the same.

His voice is deep and rumbly as he says, "I should have invited you somewhere more private for the day."

"Who says I would have said yes?"

He nips at my bottom lip as I slide my hands under his T-shirt. His stomach muscles flex as I run my fingers along the ridges and lines. When my hand drops lower, he groans.

"I don't think we have time for that," he says without making any move to stop me.

"Time for what?" I bat my lashes innocently as I slide one hand into his trunks. He shifts to give me better access, and I close my fingers around his thick cock.

"Can you stay the night later?" I ask as I pump him slowly, teasing him just a little.

Aidan told me he was staying at his mom's for the night, and I'm hoping that means Nick and I can have a sleepover. I'm leaving in two weeks and already wondering how I'm going to kiss him out of my system before then.

His lids are heavy and voice gruff as he responds, "Whatever you want, Red."

"I might want to stay on this boat."

"Done." His fingers tangle in my hair, and he deepens the kiss as I keep stroking him. The long stretch of hours between now and then has anticipation and impatience warring inside me.

He makes another rough sound deep in his throat as he pulls back. "Incoming."

"Ruby-Doo!" Travis calls as the slap of his flip-flops on the deck of the boat comes closer.

I discreetly move my hand out of Nick's trunks and let out a deep breath. It's going to be a very long day.

"Who's your favorite hockey player?" Travis asks.

"Umm . . ." I look from him to Nick and back. "Is that a trick question?"

His best friend grins at me as he holds up a bag of popcorn. He lifts it higher, like he intends to throw it my way. I put my hands up but then duck at the last second when he tosses it.

"What was that?" Travis asks with a laugh.

I sit up. "Sorry. I panicked. Did it go in the water?"

I look over the side, but then Nick hands me the bag.

"Nice catch." I lean forward and kiss him.

"Always stealing my thunder," Travis mutters behind us.

* * *

For the next few hours, we ride all around the lake, stopping to swim in one area and then hooking up with a line of other boats at party cove. More people hop on with us, friends of the guys, and girls looking to have fun with a boat of hot guys. I can hardly blame them.

I'm sitting on Nick's lap. My back rests against his chest, and he has one hand resting on my thigh. Penn is in control of the music. Conrad is stretched out on a bench. I thought he was sleeping at first, but his fingers tap to the music. Travis is mixing drinks on the lower deck for a trio of girls. Danny has been kissing a very pretty brunette for the better part of an hour.

"Oh, there goes her top," I say as Danny tugs the strings of the girl's bikini. They're in a corner of the boat but easily in sight for anyone that walks by.

"That's your warning to look away before he starts fucking her."

"Really? Right out here? I didn't realize that was an option. I'm not sure I'll be able to look your friends in the eye ever again, but okay. Let's do this." I motion to his crotch.

"No way, Red."

I'm surprised by his hesitation. "Why not? You like it when I watch you, what's a few more people?"

"I want to watch *your* reaction as you come. He wants everyone to watch as he makes her come."

My stomach flips and core tightens. There are too many hours between now and getting naked with him. "Acceptable, I suppose."

His chest rises and falls with a short, quiet chuckle.

I peek over at Danny again. They really don't seem to care who watches.

"Come on, Red." He sits up, taking me with him.

"Are we going to show them our moves?"

He laughs and tugs me to him. "Let's take a swim."

He dives in, and I, much more carefully, lower myself into the lake. I wrap myself around him and he treads water and kisses me until my lips hurt. I could make out with him forever.

When we climb back onto the boat, there are even more people on board. There's a small dance party happening. I take Nick's hand with the intention of dragging him in the middle of it, but I come up short when I spot Conrad.

He's still lying on one of the benches by himself, but he's pulled out a paperback. The image makes my book nerd heart smile until my brain catches up to the cover that has me freezing in my tracks.

I swivel around, nearly colliding into Nick's hard chest.

"Whoa." He steadies me with a laugh. I think I smile up at him, but whatever he sees on my face has his expression instantly tensing.

"What's wrong?" he asks, voice harsh but tender all at once.

"Nothing."

I turn back around so I won't have to look at him. He steps in front of me, blocking me from everyone else with his big body. "Ruby."

Hesitantly, I look up at him. Tears well in my eyes, and I fight to keep them at bay. Today has been amazing, and I cannot believe I'm still letting that asshole get to me like this.

"Really," I say. "I'm fine."

"Don't lie to me. You were laughing and smiling thirty seconds ago, and now you look really upset."

I force my mouth into a smile that does not convince him at all. He stares, unwavering, at me for an explanation.

"My ex."

His brows furrow. "Your ex is here?"

I shake my head, then point.

Nick turns, looks around like he's trying to make sense of my words. When his gaze drops to Conrad and the book in his hand, his body goes rigid.

"Your ex is Matthew Rose?"

I nod. God this is so embarrassing. A few of the guys shoot concerned glances in our direction. I do my best to look like everything is fine.

His jaw flexes, and I'm transported back to the grumpy Nick version.

"It's okay. Honest. That book is everywhere, but sometimes it catches me off guard."

I'm not even sure he's hearing me. He's still glaring hard. I reach out and take his hand. He glances down at the contact, and his shoulders relax slightly before he pulls me into him. He smells like sunscreen and sunshine, and I breathe him in as he cradles me against his chest.

I would be content to stay here the rest of the day, but Nick pulls back a moment later, drops a kiss to my forehead, and then stalks over to Conrad.

I hurry after him, but I'm no match for his long, angry steps. He snatches the book from his friend's hands and tosses it into the lake in one swift motion. My mouth drops open in surprise.

"What the hell?" Conrad asks, sitting up and looking over the side of the boat to the water.

The song that was playing ends, and the silence between tracks is just enough that everyone looks our way.

My body heats with embarrassment. I ignore their stares by peering over the side of the boat. I'm not usually a fan of destroying books, but I'm not ashamed to admit it brings me a great bit of joy to watch my ex's book sink to the bottom.

"That book is trash. If you want to read that shit, do it somewhere else."

Conrad opens his mouth to protest, but the look on Nick's face stops him.

"Yeah. All right. You got it, Cap. Do you want to approve my playlists and podcasts next?" Conrad shakes his head, disbelief and confusion still etched into his features.

"It wasn't that good anyway. Totally overwritten. Weak character development. Good concept though." Danny shifts his sunglasses to the top of his head as he watches the scene unfold from the bench seat adjacent to Conrad. He has his arm around the brunette from earlier and a beer in one hand.

My stomach dips and tears prick the back of my eyes. At Nick's protectiveness, Conrad's ruined book, and Danny's review that I'm embarrassed to admit makes me feel better, and at freaking Matt for invading this perfect day. I swallow the lump in my throat and hurry down to the lower deck before I cry in front of them.

Travis gives me a worried look from behind the bar where he's mixing drinks.

I duck into the bathroom and shut the door, then rest my back against it.

"Ruby?" Nick's voice comes from the other side not three seconds later. I knew it was too much to think he wouldn't follow me.

"I'll be right out," I say, trying to sound calm and happy and completely unaffected.

"Open up, Red."

I bite down on my bottom lip to keep it from trembling.

"Don't think I won't break down my own door."

A small laugh slips out, and I turn and open the door a crack.

"I'm fine," I tell him. And I am. Or I want to be.

"Uh huh." He places a palm on the door above my head and pushes his way in.

It's a small room, and he's a big guy. There's nowhere for me to go. I glance up into his eyes. The green is dark, and his brow is furrowed.

"You didn't need to do that," I say quietly.

"Of course I did. The guy is a prick and a total phony."

"Yeah, but no one knows that."

"You could tell them."

The idea sends a rush of panic coursing through me. The media frenzy that would unfold is unfathomable.

Nick's hands come up to rest on my upper arms, thumbs swiping slowly over my skin. "I don't mean everyone, but at least the guys. They'll believe you."

I consider it for a moment then shake my head. "I don't need anyone to know. It won't change anything. The book is out there, and I just have to deal with it."

"Not while I'm around, you don't."

"You can't toss every copy you come across." But I already know the image of him tossing Conrad's book will be one I replay over and over again.

His lips twist into a smirk. "Watch me, Red."

Chapter Twenty-Four

NICK

"Can I get another Coke and a piña colada?"

The bartender looks like he wants to murder my ass for ordering a complicated drink while it's packed, but I set a fifty on the bar, and he begrudgingly nods.

"Thanks."

He gets the soda first and sets it in front of me. Taking it, I turn and rest my back against the bar as I take in the scene of the busy lakeside hotspot.

A live band is playing "Save a Horse (Ride a Cowboy)," and people are dancing around, singing the lyrics at the top of their lungs.

My gaze goes to one person in particular.

Ruby.

Her red hair sways and bounces as she jumps around to the beat. She has my teammates out on the dance floor. Trav and D-Low are singing and dancing with her while Shep and Penn sort of shuffle and sip at their drinks.

Travis glances around until he spots me at the bar, then he leans in and says something to Ruby before walking my way.

He's grinning from ear to ear when he reaches me. I scootch over to make room for him.

"Your girl is a riot." He chuckles and shakes his head, then orders another beer.

Ruby isn't technically my girl, but I don't mind the label. At least it means he might stop hitting on her.

Once he has his beer in hand, he turns to stand with me. The band has moved on to another classic cover song.

"Can you believe she has Penn out there?" he asks me.

The big goalie looks like he's seconds from running away when Ruby takes his hands and raises them in the air, except she's so much shorter than him, they're only about shoulder height.

"After seeing his dance moves, I think I understand why he avoids it at every turn."

"No doubt," Travis quips, then lets out a happy sigh. "Today was a blast. Perfect way to end the summer."

"It's not over yet. A couple more weeks."

"And then it's hockey season, baby." He holds his beer out and we cheers.

As much as the time off is needed to rest and recoup, and spend time with Aidan, I love the start of the season. It's a fresh beginning. I'm still worried about playing, or rather getting injured again, but I've had less time to worry about it since I've been spending so much time with Ruby.

We stand together, watching our friends and leaning against the bar. I feel a contentment that's been missing since my injury. A day on the lake, soaking up the sun with good friends and a gorgeous girl. I've never been big on the bar scene, but even I don't want this night to end.

"What the hell happened today?" Trav asks, breaking the short silence. "Shep said you threw his book into the lake, and Ruby looked like she was about to burst into tears."

My jaw tightens at the reminder. For Ruby's sake I've done my best to put it out of my mind, but I'd like to burn every copy in a thousand-mile radius of that damn asshole's book.

"It's not my story to tell," I say through gritted teeth.

Travis's gaze narrows as he nods. "Got it."

We've known each other long enough that he can read between the lines. I also trust him more than just about anyone. He might come across as a guy who jokes all the time and cares about little, but that's not really who he is at all. He's the first guy to call when shit goes down, always has a smile or a joke, but will absolutely throw down—on the ice and off—at the first sign that someone he cares about is in trouble. I don't think his happy façade is a cover so much as his innate instinct to put other people's feelings before his own.

"Suffice it to say, I don't like the guy."

"So he's like the Victor Aven of the book world?"

Victor is a mouthy forward who plays for Houston. Nobody in the league likes him, not even his own teammates.

"Yeah, something like that."

"That sucks."

I can't even fathom how shitty it felt to be betrayed like that by someone she trusted or what it's like to see evidence of it out in the world daily. That fucking book is everywhere.

"It must be hard for you to think about her leaving," Trav adds.

"No," I say quickly. "She was always leaving. She's got a life in Arizona, family."

"Right, but now you two are all cozy and cute."

"It isn't like that."

"You don't want to keep seeing her?"

"It isn't that I don't want to, but come on, how would that even work?"

He shrugs one shoulder. "I don't know, but you're an idiot if you fuck this up."

A hearty guffaw breaks free. "I thought you were standing by, waiting for me to screw up so you could swoop in and have her for yourself."

"Nah, man. If you fuck up, I'm going to kick your ass."

I arch a brow when he doesn't smile or laugh. "You're serious?"

"Hell yeah."

"Some friend you are." I chuckle and take another sip of my Coke.

He angles his body to face me. "I'm your best friend, and that's exactly why I'd do it. I've never seen you happier. Kicking your ass would be for your own good. You don't let a girl like that walk away."

He's serious. Maybe more serious than I've ever seen him.

"Says the guy who's had even fewer serious relationships than me." Sure, the only one I had was eleven years ago, but it counts. Trav has never committed to someone for more than a few dates.

"You're right, and I give you permission to do the same if I'm ever in this situation."

"I see you cozied up to girls all the time. I'd be kicking your ass *repeatedly*." I lift my chin up as I emphasize the last word. Is he serious right now? He's always dating someone but never for long.

He shakes his head. "No. This is different."

I let out a soft chuckle. "If you say so."

"You might be too stubborn to see it, but it's true."

My stare is back on Ruby. She must feel my gaze because she looks over, movements slowing as she aims a smile at me across the bar.

I stand tall, grab the piña colada from behind me, and thank the bartender again. Travis eyes the drink with a smirk but says nothing.

"Can you guys catch a ride back tonight?" If I know my friends, and I do, they'll close the place down. I have a much better way I'd like to spend the early morning hours.

"Yeah. Go. We're cool."

"Thanks." I only get two steps away before he calls out to me.

"Hey, Galaxy."

I pause and glance over my shoulder.

His eyes shine with a playful taunt. "Happy is a good look on you, brother."

"Today was perfect," Ruby says as I cut the engine. Her head rests back, and she stares up at the sky, and her arms are wrapped around herself. She pulled on a dress over her suit before we went to the bar, but she's still cold. She's always cold.

I stand, taking her hand and pulling her to the front of the boat.

"Oh no," she says as she realizes where I'm taking her. All day she's avoided going up here. "I'm going to fall into the water."

"No, you won't."

"Okay, but don't blame me when I take you in with me."

"The walkway is perfectly safe." It's a narrow path that leads to the seating area up front, and to my knowledge no one has ever fallen in while walking it.

She squeals as I lead the way, tugging her behind me. Once we're there, she looks around. "This is stunning."

I chuckle as she spins in a circle, then takes a seat, leaning to resume her position from earlier, sky gazing, with her hands intertwined together at her waist.

"Do you think Danny had sex in this spot?" she asks me as I sit next to her.

"Probably."

Her nose scrunches. "Oh well. The sun and water probably disinfected it."

"One can hope."

I wrap an arm around her and rub my hands up and down her chilled skin.

She lets her head fall to the side to stare at me. "I like your boat."

I let out another small laugh.

"And your friends. And you."

I lean forward and kiss her, then because it's not enough (it's never enough), I lift her onto my lap.

She shivers against me.

"Want to go inside?" I ask.

Her mouth presses to mine as she shakes her head to the side softly.

I wrap her up in my arms instead as my tongue sweeps out to taste her. Coconut and rum and something that's uniquely her.

Ruby leans away from me with a sexy grin, then shifts and wiggles as she tries to pull her dress up, so she isn't sitting on it.

"What are you doing, Red?"

"I'm trying to have sex on a boat."

My chest loosens with a laugh, but as soon as she stands and shoves her bikini bottoms to the boat floor, I'm one hundred percent ready to go.

She has a mischievous grin as she steps back between my spread legs. Her palms rest on my thighs but instead of climbing back into my lap, she gets on her knees.

I don't move a muscle as she reaches for the ties on my trunks except to lift slightly so she can push them down far enough to free my dick.

Her tongue darts out to wet her lips before she leans in and presses a kiss to the head. My body is already strung tight, aching for release. She hums, then parts her gorgeous lips and slowly takes me in until I'm damn near hitting the back of her throat.

"Fuck, baby. I'm never going to last like that."

She bobs over my length twice more, driving me absolutely out of my mind, before she pops off to say, "Good. Otherwise, I'd doubt my skills."

I push back her hair with a hand on either side of her face. "Your skills are top-notch, Red, but I thought you wanted to have sex on a boat."

She hesitates just long enough that I know that's exactly what she wants.

"Fuck, I don't have any condoms."

"I'm on birth control," she says. "And I've been tested since the last time I was with anyone else."

"Same."

Her lips curve up in approval.

"Thank fuck. I need to be inside you, Red."

I wrap one arm around her waist and pull her down onto my lap. Our mouths collide in a hungry, eager search for more. I can't seem to get enough, not even of her lips.

One of her hands wraps around my dick as she lines me up. I'm about to check to see if she's ready for me, but the way she takes me gives me my answer.

"You're soaked, baby."

She slides down slowly, taking me inch by inch. "Boats really do it for me."

I nip her bottom lip.

She sits, letting me fill her completely. Her eyes lock on mine as she whispers, "You really do it for me."

"Is that right?" I push into her as much as I can from the bottom.

Her lashes flutter closed as she lets out a tiny moan. She's already close, and I don't stand a chance with her squeezing me so tight. My skin is hot and tight as my muscles strain to fight off my orgasm.

"Keep those pretty eyes on me, Red. Let me see how good you look as you ride my dick."

Her stare locks back on me as she starts to move again. My heart squeezes in my chest. Travis's words from earlier flash in my mind, and I wonder just for a moment if maybe he's onto something.

I haven't been able to picture myself dating in a long time, but if every night were just like this, I think I'd be the luckiest man alive.

"Nick." She pants my name as she takes my cock.

"That's it. Take what you need, baby."

She's right there. Fuck, it's a sight to behold. Lips parted, pupils blown wide, tits bouncing. Her dark lashes lower, and then a cry rips from her throat.

I thrust harder. I'm out of my mind with the need to come. Her pussy clenches like a vise as the orgasm continues on and on. Goddamn. I never want this to end. I bury my head in the nape of her neck as I lose the battle, coming hard and letting out a roar.

"Oh, god." Ruby comes a second time, whimpering as she tightens around me, a shiver rolling down my spine as we ride out the orgasm together. It feels like minutes pass as white noise fills my head and dots blur my vision.

We cling to each other, breaths ragged. Little shockwaves zap through me, and a deep, contented sensation lodges into my chest.

She stills, forehead resting on my chest as she catches her breath. Slowly, she lifts her head and locks her gaze on me. A lazy smile pulls at her lips.

I brush my mouth over hers as I lift her gently off me. She stands in front of me, dress bunched up around her thighs. The evidence that I came inside her drips down her thigh. I don't question the pleasure it gives me thinking about her filled up with my cum.

"I can now check off boat sex," she says with a shy grin. "Thanks, Galaxy."

I chuckle, the atmosphere turning light again. "Happy to help, Red."

I find a towel to clean us up, and once we're dressed again, she settles back in my lap.

"It's beautiful here." She glances out at the water.

"It is," I confirm.

"Will you stay here after hockey is over?"

"Yeah, I think so. What about you?"

"I thought about moving away from Lake City since I can work anywhere, but I really love being near my family. When I'm home, I see my sister and niece almost daily, and my parents and grandparents at least once a week."

"I get that. Family is important." It's why I wanted to be here. Aidan should have all his family in one spot so he can grow up with a lot of important influences in his life. And Ruby should have that too.

"Thank you for what you did today," she says, fingers curling in the hair at the nape of my neck. "Tossing Matt's book in the lake."

The reminder has me wishing I could go get it and do it all over again. Maybe set it on fire. "It was my pleasure."

"And for letting me hang with your friends and intrude on your life. For everything, I guess."

"You don't need to thank me for any of it. I'm glad you're here."

"Me too."

I wake up, as I usually do, a few hours after passing out. My arm searches for Ruby next to me, but the bed is empty. I open my eyes and find her sitting at the end of the mattress, legs crossed, with her laptop open.

"What are you doing?" I ask, voice rough with sleep.

She looks up and back at me, grinning. She fell asleep in my T-shirt. The material bunches around her hips. "Sorry. Did I wake you?"

"No, I don't think so." I glance at the screen of her laptop, recognizing the document as her book. "Are you working?"

"I had an idea, and I didn't want to forget it," she says with a sheepish grin, then goes back to typing. "It will just take me a minute. Promise."

"It's fine. Take your time." I sit up and look over her shoulder. Her fingers fly over the keyboard. She looks sexy in my shirt, red hair falling over her shoulders, working on her book. It's an image I've grown accustomed to, her hunched over her laptop.

My gaze falls to the words appearing on the screen. It takes my brain a second to follow along as I read, but when I do, I smile.

"You're writing a sex scene."

"Oh my god!" Both her hands shoot up to cover the screen. "You can't read it yet."

I look away to her startled face.

"Why not?"

"It isn't done."

"I know. He was still thrusting."

Her mouth drops open, and her expression turns shy.

"How can you possibly be embarrassed after the things we've done together?"

"That was different." Her hands drop, but she still looks hesitant. She bites the corner of her lip. "Okay, if I let you read it, can you pretend it isn't rough and filled with typos?"

"I doubt very much that I will find any typos. I think I stopped retaining grammar and writing rules in elementary school."

Hesitantly, she lifts the computer off her lap and hands it to me.

"It's a locker room scene. I had this dream . . ." She trails off, looking embarrassed, then waves a hand as if indicating I should just read it.

It shouldn't be possible to get hard reading the words, but that's exactly what happens. She's written a very thorough, very hot locker room scene that has me wondering a whole lot about this dream.

"Is the hockey stuff accurate?" she asks when I look up.

"I have no idea. I blacked out. Fuck, Ruby. This is good."

"Really?"

I nod, and then take the laptop with me as I settle back against the headboard. She comes to sit next to me, worrying her lip.

I scroll back up and read another scene. This one isn't sexy, but a hockey game scene. I remember her asking me questions for this one.

For the next hour, I read, and she cuddles up beside me. Her nerves fall away after the tenth or eleventh time I assure her it's really good.

"You're so talented." I already knew it, even before reading this. "I have a confession."

"What?" she asks, a slight edge in her tone.

"I read *Love Bites*."

Her eyes widen. "When?"

"About a week ago."

"Why didn't you say anything?" Her expression falls. "Wait. Did you not like it?"

"No." I chuckle. "It was great. But I had a hunch you'd be embarrassed if I mentioned it."

"Yeah, that's fair. I know it doesn't make any sense, but it's weird thinking about the people who know me in real life reading my work. I don't go to their jobs and judge them, you know?"

"People judge me at work all the time."

She tilts her head to the side. "Yeah, I guess so. We have another thing in common."

"One more confession."

"I like this game."

"I also read the rest of your books."

She huffs a quiet laugh. "All of them?"

I shrug one shoulder. "What can I say? You have me hooked."

In more ways than one.

Chapter Twenty-Five

RUBY

For the next five days I don't leave the cabin except to walk down by the lake each morning or sit on the porch with my laptop when I feel like I need a change of scenery. I write and delete and rewrite and sometimes want to scream at the screen, but I don't stop.

Aidan comes by every afternoon. He sits in the living room with his guitar and practices while I edit. I'm going to miss listening to him play when I leave.

Nick stops by in the mornings before he heads to the rink. I'm not always awake, depending on how late I stayed up writing the night before, but I know he's been here because of the freshly brewed coffee waiting for me.

On Thursday, Olivia calls for the third time in two days.

"Hi!" I answer, stepping out onto the porch and shielding my eyes from the bright sun. The mid-afternoon heat is sticky, and the air is thick.

"Hi? Really? That's all you have to say for yourself?" My sister shrieks on the other end.

"I'm sorry I haven't checked in sooner." A smile tugs at my lips as I take a seat in the rocking chair. "The words are finally flowing, and I didn't want to stop."

She's quiet for a beat.

"Liv?"

"I'm here. Sorry I yelled at you." She's so bad at being mean it makes me laugh.

"It's fine. I need someone to remind me the world is still moving around me. Sorry I didn't answer. How are you? I miss you."

"I miss you too."

It feels odd to have gone this long without seeing her. We've lived with or near each other for our entire lives.

"Is the writing really flowing, or were you just saying that to make me feel bad for yelling at you?" she asks with a laugh.

"It's really flowing. Finally. I wasn't sure it ever would again."

"You're too talented to retire before your thirtieth birthday."

"Thanks." I pull my legs up and hug them to my chest. "How's the bookstore? How's my niece?"

"Store is good. We have a new summertime reads table featuring our very own Ruby Madison."

My sister runs a family bookstore, started by my grandparents, and her passion for creating new book displays is up there with her love of her daughter and husband.

"I'm sure it's gorgeous."

"And Greer's good. She's why I'm calling. Her softball team made it to the championships."

"Really?"

"Mhmmm."

"That's amazing!"

Since I've been gone, Olivia's kept me up to date with pictures and videos and an occasional chaotic voice message from my favorite little girl. She's done a variety of activities over the years, from dance to tennis to Lego club, but since she started softball, it's become her obsession.

"I'm so sad I've missed all her games this summer."

"Trust me. There will be plenty more."

"Still. The championships? That's . . . wow." A pang of longing and homesickness stirs inside me.

"Yeah, she's really excited. She wanted me to invite you to the game. I know you're not supposed to be back until the end of the month, but I promised her I'd tell you anyway. She said you would want to know."

"She is correct. I'm so proud of her. Where'd she get all this athleticism from?"

"Beats me. The game is Saturday evening. Mom is planning to record the entire thing, so if you can't make it, then I'm sure you can catch the replay from her."

"Tell her I'll send the team jet to get her if she wants to come," Flynn yells in the background.

"Is he serious?" I ask, brows lifting at the idea. I mean, is that even a thing?

"Sadly, he is one hundred percent serious. He's flying so many people in you'd think she was playing in the Little League World Series instead of a local championship game."

"It's a big deal!" Flynn shouts, still far away.

"I love that he's so good to her."

"Yeah, me too. It's why I let him knock me up."

I chuckle.

"Is she in?" he asks. "Is she coming?"

"I'm definitely in," I say with a laugh.

"Really?" Olivia asks with a hopefulness that confirms it's the right thing to do.

"Of course. I can't wait to see you guys." I *am* excited to see them, but the thought of leaving has an uneasy feeling swirling in my stomach too. God. I'm one big ball of emotions lately.

"Ahh. I'm so excited. Flynn made shirts. Be prepared."

"Ask her if she wants hers to say Aunt Ruby or The Cool Aunt," Flynn says in the background.

"Dealer's choice," I say. That man truly loves my niece as if she were his own.

She relays back what I said to him, and he promises to send me all the details later tonight. Then Olivia and I spend a few more minutes talking while she fills me in on everything happening back home—from Dad's new pickleball hobby to Grandma's knee surgery. All things I already heard via text, but getting the full update is so much better.

My well is full by the time we hang up. I sit on the porch, smiling out at the lake with my chin resting on my knees and the wind blowing through my hair. This might be my favorite place in the entire world, but I miss my family. If I could plop them here it'd be perfect.

I wonder if I can work out an ongoing summer rental agreement with Nick. Spending a few months here every year to write sounds lovely. We could continue our fling every summer. Walks by the lake, boat rides, skating, writing, listening to Aidan play guitar, and hanging out with Nick every possible moment. I know it isn't a realistic fantasy, but I indulge in it for a few minutes anyway.

My attention is broken only when I hear the slam of a door. Aidan has his guitar slung over his shoulder, and it bounces against his little body as he jogs down the steps and then toward the cabin.

I stand to greet him as he approaches. "Hey."

He's carrying a glass container in one hand and stretches it out toward me when he's close. "From my dad. He said you probably haven't eaten all day since you're on deadline."

I take it but laugh. I guess he forgot that he brought breakfast and coffee by this morning.

"Thanks."

Inside the cabin, I take the food to the kitchen.

"Did you eat yet?" I ask him as I pry off the lid. The smell of chicken and cheese and some sort of spices or sauces that I can't place makes my stomach growl and my mouth water.

"Yeah. It's not bad." The way he says it has me second-guessing. I could DoorDash tacos for the third time this week.

"He's been trying new recipes, swapping out foods to make them healthier for Grandpa. He has a bad heart."

"Your grandpa does?"

Aidan nods.

Nick never mentioned it. Not that he should, but it hits me how little of our lives we've shared. Somehow, I still feel like I know him better than just about anyone.

"That's nice of him," I say of Nick making special foods for his dad.

"Yeah, I guess so, but it's not really working."

"No?"

Aidan's mouth turns down at the corners, but he still somehow smiles. "Last night I saw Grandpa eat an entire bag of chips and then hide the evidence before Dad got home."

And that sounds just like Mike.

"Well, some healthy food is probably better than none."

"Yeah, I guess so." Aidan shrugs one lanky shoulder.

He goes back to strumming the guitar, and I take a chance on the food. It's actually pretty good. Nick Galaxy can cook. Who knew?

After I eat, I get back to work. One of the many things I love about writing is that I can do it anywhere. Especially when I get stuck. I move from standing at the kitchen, to sitting on the living room floor, to the front porch, back to the kitchen. I keep hoping that the change of scenery will unlock the missing pieces to finish this book.

I'm about to run a bath and see if soaking in the tub will help when Aidan hits a chord that makes my eyes cross.

He grunts in frustration. "I suck at this shit!"

As soon as the outburst is out of his lips, he looks over at me like he's expecting me to admonish him.

"Sorry." Aidan's face scrunches up in apology as he lets his hand fall away from the strings.

"You don't need to apologize." I lean back from my computer screen. "I just deleted an entire page that was almost entirely describing the smell of hockey pads."

I scrunch up my face in the same way he had, and a laugh erupts out of him. I join in.

"Some days are hard. It makes us appreciate the good ones more."

He looks unconvinced.

"My mom says that. I have no idea if it's true," I admit.

"I'm never going to get this song right."

"Of course you will. You just need a break. You know what else my mom says?"

He grins in that half-smile way his dad does, showing off the same dimple.

"When all else fails, bake something."

I move to the fridge to inspect the ingredients on hand. It's not much, but I can work with it.

I preheat the oven and pull out everything we're going to need. Aidan hasn't moved from the couch, but he watches me.

"Are you going to help or what?" I ask him.

He sets his guitar down and gets up, walking slowly to stand on the other side of the counter.

"I don't know how to bake."

"It's easy. Do you have any allergies?"

He shakes his head.

"Okay." I nod my head toward the sink. "Wash your hands, and then I'll show you how to make one of my favorite cookies."

He's hesitant at first, cracking eggs and measuring out the flour, but by the time we're scooping the dough onto a cookie sheet, Aidan is all smiles.

"What's your favorite dessert?" I ask him after I set a timer.

"Ice cream," he says quickly.

"That's my niece's favorite too. Chocolate or vanilla?"

"Cookies and cream."

"Ooh. Good answer. I like that one too. My favorite is butter pecan."

"My dad likes that one too."

"Does he?"

Aidan nods. "And peach pie."

"Really?"

"He tried to make it once."

"Tried?"

"It looked weird and tasted awful. Even Grandpa wouldn't touch it."

Poor Nick.

"Pies can be tricky."

As I start to clean up our mess, Aidan surprises me by jumping in to help. I load the dishwasher while he puts away everything else. When the timer goes off, we share a smile.

The smell of sugar, butter, and chocolate wafts out when I open the oven. Aidan hangs back, but peers down to watch as I pull the pan out.

"Whoa. Those look like the ones at the store." His eyes are wide with excitement.

"Hopefully they'll taste better." There's nothing like homemade treats.

I smile over at him as I set the pan down to cool. "Now we wait for them to cool."

"How long?" His eagerness has me feeling impatient too.

"Five minutes."

He frowns, looking like a mini grumpy Nick.

"Want to play the song for me while we wait?" I ask.

"It's probably still going to suck."

"So what? We have to do things badly in order to do them great."

He mulls that over for long enough that I'm prepared for him to say no, then trudges over to the couch. He picks up the guitar and then looks up at me with a resolved but hesitant expression. "Here goes nothing."

I take a seat on one of the barstools in front of the kitchen counter and give him my undivided attention. For all the times he's practiced here, I haven't had the opportunity to unabashedly watch him. I knew he didn't want that any more than I want someone peering over my shoulder while I write.

He takes his time getting situated, guitar resting on one leg, hands in place on the strings. His dark hair falls onto his forehead and into his eyes, and his mouth pulls into a line of concentration.

The first strum has goose bumps dotting my arms. Not because it's the best thing I've ever heard but because I feel like I'm witnessing someone push through the suck. The greatest lesson I've learned with writing and in life is to keep going. I haven't always taken my own advice, but I believe it with my whole chest. For a few people, maybe they're great at something the first time they do it, but for the rest of us, it's determination mixed with a healthy dose of optimism. It's awful now, but it won't be if I just keep going.

When he hits a wrong chord, he looks up with a bashful grimace, but he doesn't stop. The song moves slower than it should as he picks out each part, but I can see him getting more comfortable with each passing second.

The back of my eyes sting as I sit there and listen to him fumble his way through the entire song. When he's finished, quiet rings out in the cabin for a beat. He stares down at his guitar like he's lost in the moment of completion. My chest swells with pride.

As soon as he meets my gaze, I break out into a smile and start clapping. His shy grin appears, and it eggs me on. I stand, jump up and down and cheer like I'm at a sold-out concert venue. Maybe someday I will be.

"You finished it!" I take his hand and raise it, making him get silly with me.

"I messed up a bunch still."

"Celebrate the small wins."

The timer goes off on my phone.

"Speaking of celebrating."

We rush to the kitchen together. I hand him a cookie, then take one for myself. At the same time, we take a bite.

"Oh wow," I say with my mouth still full.

Aidan takes another huge bite and nods. Only when the cookie is gone does he say, "I can't believe we made that. It's the best cookie I've ever had."

"You know, it might be the best one I've ever had too."

A knock at the cabin door makes us both look in that direction.

"Come in!" I call as I take another cookie from the pan. Aidan does the same.

Slowly, the door swings open and Nick steps inside.

"Dad!" Aidan runs to him. "We made cookies."

"I see that." He uses the pad of his thumb to wipe a smudge of chocolate from the corner of Aidan's mouth. His son ducks away and then comes back to the kitchen.

"I'm going to take one to Grandpa!" Aidan says, taking a stack, then grabbing his guitar off the couch.

"Don't eat yourself sick," Nick tells his retreating son's back.

"I won't!" Aidan yells over his shoulder.

Nick and I grin at each other.

"Ruby." Aidan doubles back as he calls my name. He has that adorable chocolate smile aimed right at me as he stands in the doorway.

"Yeah?"

"I hope you write a really bad chapter." His grin widens, then he rushes off.

A laugh bubbles up in my chest and spills out.

Nick arches a brow. "I'm hoping that's an inside joke."

"Yeah. We're suffering for our art."

"Another reason I'll never be an author or a musician." He steps closer and then brings his hand up to wipe the corner of my mouth too. I'd be embarrassed if these cookies weren't so freaking good.

"How was your day?" he asks.

"Good. Yours?"

"Good." He leans down and presses his lips to mine.

"Better now," I admit.

I feel his mouth curve into a smile.

"Thanks for dinner," I say when he pulls back.

"You're welcome." He stands next to me with his back against the counter. "How'd writing go?"

"Still stuck, but I'll get there."

"Any chance you want to take a night off tomorrow?" he asks. "Aidan and my dad are planning a *Rocky* movie night."

"That's adorable."

"It's my dad's sly way of getting junk food into the house." He raises his hands into the air and does air quotes as he says, "For Aidan."

"That sounds fun, but I'm leaving tomorrow."

"Oh." His body stiffens.

"Not *leaving* leaving. Just for the weekend. My niece is in a softball championship. I'll be back Sunday or Monday."

He nods with a thoughtful expression on his face.

I've made it weird somehow, or maybe it's only awkward because it's the first time we've talked about me leaving since we started hooking up.

"Maybe we can hang out next week sometime?" I ask.

"Sure. Of course." He smiles, but it feels all wrong. "If you have time. I know you need to finish the book. That's the whole reason you came, right?"

The pit in my stomach grows. "Right."

Because it is the reason I came. But it isn't the only reason I want to be here anymore.

The next morning, I leave early for the airport and stop by the rink. Nick is exactly where I expect to find him. He looks up from the ice, brows pinched together, when he spots me. He skates over to me, a smile forming as he gets close.

"What are you doing here? I thought you were leaving this morning."

"I am. I'm on the way to the airport now." I hold up two coffees, one in each hand. "Time for a quick break?"

"Yeah. Of course." He steps off the ice, and we sit on the bench. His leg presses against mine as he asks, "Excited to see your family?"

"I am. I've missed them."

"I'll bet."

"What are you going to do this weekend? You know, besides hockey."

He smirks. "My dad has a doctor's appointment in Bozeman this afternoon. I'm going to drive him and make sure he stays out of trouble."

"For his heart?" I ask, then admit, "Aidan mentioned something about it."

"Yeah." Nick's chin dips as he looks away. "He had a heart attack at the beginning of the year."

"I'm sorry. That's scary."

He bobs his head again.

"He's okay now, though. Right?"

"The doctors say everything looks good for now. I guess I'll know more today."

I hadn't meant for this visit to turn into an interrogation, but now that we're on the topic of parents, there's one thing that I've been wondering about.

"You never mention your mom. Is she in the picture at all?"

His mouth falls into a straight line. "She died when I was in college. About a year before Aidan was born."

A pit forms in my stomach. "Oh, god, Nick. I am so sorry. I had no idea."

"I know." He shakes his head. "It's okay. You couldn't have."

With my free hand, I squeeze his arm. He attempts a smile.

"I should talk about her more, I suppose. I think about her a lot. It's weird passing by big life moments without her. Having a kid, getting drafted, moving around, buying a house . . ."

"You were close, then?"

"We were. She was the best." He clears his throat and then turns his head to look at me. "What time is your flight?"

I tell him and then we chat about all the things my family has planned for the short time I'm in Arizona. Greer's baseball game, family dinner, a trip to the bookstore where my grandma and sister work to sign their stock of my books, and my dad really wants me to play pickleball with him now that I'm "into sports." I didn't have the heart to tell him no, so that should be interesting (aka, a disaster).

When it's time for me to go, I stand and wrap my arms around Nick. I am excited to see my family, but I think I'm going to miss him.

"See you in a few days," I say as I pull back. "Don't have any fun without me."

A real grin finally pulls up the corners of his mouth. "See ya, Red."

Chapter Twenty-Six

NICK

On Sunday I head to the rink after I drop off Aidan at his mom's house. Camp is less than a month away, but most of the guys that left for the summer are already trickling back into town. We'll start working out together and getting ready for the season. I like to stay in shape year-round, but some of the younger guys need that time before camp to sharpen their skills and conditioning.

The building is quiet as I walk back to the locker room. The only light streams out of our recovery room. I slow and peer inside as I come to it. Dr. Scott sits at his desk in the front corner. He looks up when he notices me.

"Nick!" He leans back in his chair. "I should have guessed I'd run into you here."

"Hey, Adam," I say as I step into the room. "What are you doing here?"

There's a stack of boxes filled with things, and my gut twists.

"Moving to a new office," he says with a reassuring smile. He joined the team of doctors on staff last year, right after his residency, but despite being new he has quickly become everyone's favorite. "Finally getting out of this closet."

"That's great."

He comes around his desk to move a box out of one of the chairs, then motions for me to sit. "How's the shoulder and collarbone?"

"Really good. No pain at all."

"That's great. Did you have a nice summer?"

"I did." My mind drifts to Ruby. It's only been a day since she left, but things have felt weird without her around. "You?"

"It was great." He pulls out his phone and then turns the screen to show me a picture of a baby wrapped in a pink and white striped blanket. "Meet Daphne."

"She's beautiful, man. Congrats. I had no idea."

He waves off my concern. "Thanks. It's been a blast. I'm going on zero sleep but all totally worth it, right?"

"Yeah, it is."

"I swear I'm a doctor, but I had no idea what it'd be like. Reagan, my wife, shooed me out of the house today because I was hovering too much."

I laugh as I try to remember those days. Aidan was a good sleeper, or at least that's what people told me, but there were plenty of long nights worrying and taking care of him.

"Anyway." He smiles at me. "Everything's good? Ready for the season to start?"

"Definitely."

When I don't say more, he nods. "Well, if you need anything, I'll be . . . actually I don't know where I'll be yet, but you've got my number."

I nod to confirm that I do.

"Thanks, and congrats again. It gets easier."

"I appreciate that."

I start to leave, then pause and turn back. "Can I ask you something?"

"Anything."

I mull over the right way to ask then decide there is no easy way to talk about it. It's why I haven't. Only with Travis and my dad.

"My dad had a heart attack earlier this year."

"Oh Nick, I'm sorry. How's he doing?"

"Better. He had an angioplasty and has been gaining his strength back."

"That's good news."

"His doctor told me heart disease is often hereditary."

"It can be, but you get screened every year, and nothing has come up, right?"

"Right. Totally fine. I saw a cardiologist earlier this year."

"Did he have any concerns?"

"No," I admit. "But my mom passed away young, and then after everything that happened at the end of the season, I don't know, I guess it's been weighing on me heavier."

He nods slowly like he's finally understanding. "It's definitely something to keep an eye on, but you're young and take great care of yourself, so even with any predisposed genetics, I would put your risk at low."

I know what he's saying is the odds are in my favor, but it doesn't make me feel better like I think he intends.

"Have you talked to Dr. Ariak?"

"I did my sessions with her after the surgery." Our team psychologist is great, but I guess I wasn't ready to talk about it at the time.

"It might not be a bad idea to keep seeing her. Taking care of an aging parent can be hard. Especially when you add in your own health anxiety."

"Health anxiety?"

"It's common. Especially in your line of work where injuries are inevitable. If you aren't comfortable with Dr. Ariak then I can make a referral outside of the team too."

"Thank you. I appreciate it."

"Of course."

I shift my weight to leave, and Adam moves back behind his desk.

Standing in the doorway, I linger. "Congrats again on the baby. Best thing I ever did."

Once I step on the rink, I mull over everything Adam said. The only other time I had anxiety was right after my mom died, but it makes sense that it would show back up now.

Surprisingly, it's Ruby that I find myself wanting to talk to about it. I haven't shared much about my injury or my dad's health with her, but she's become someone I trust. My friends are great, and I know they'd listen, but I like the way Ruby sees the world with her rose-colored glasses and endless optimism.

I pull out my phone to text her, hovering over her contact. The last I heard from her was a picture of her with her niece after the game last night. They won, and she looked so happy and proud, pure sunshine. I know what her family means to her, and I'm happy she could be there, but it's a reminder that this isn't home for her. In another week, she'll be gone for real.

I'm not the only one that's going to miss her when she leaves either. Aidan has gotten attached to her too. Every day when we get home from the rink, he's practically giddy to grab his guitar and head over to the cabin. He talked about the cookies they made all day yesterday.

I type out a text asking her when she's coming back, then delete it. Fuck. I'm really not good at . . . this, whatever it is we've been doing the past few weeks. Calling it a fling feels disingenuous, but a relationship with an expiration isn't much of one at all.

I toss my phone onto my bag, sitting on the bench, and push my legs faster to warm up. I'm on my third lap when I hear music playing from somewhere. I recognize the catchy upbeat Sabrina Carpenter song, but as I scan the empty seats, I can't figure out where it's coming from.

Finally, the music gets louder, and I locate its direction. Out of the darkness steps Jack fucking Wyld.

He holds up the phone and bops his head in rhythm. I skate over to him, happy to see my old teammate but confused too. I'm not even sure how he got in the building.

"What the hell are you doing here, Wyld?"

He presses stop on the music and flashes a grin at me. "Miss me?"

Chapter Twenty-Seven

RUBY

This weekend was incredible. I loved visiting my family, seeing Greer's team win the championship, and soaking up the sunshine.

But, it also sucked. I missed Nick and Aidan and the lake view. And I might have even missed hockey.

The people in front of me groan as they step out of the airport into the parking garage.

"Oh, it's so hot," one of them says.

I fight a laugh. I'm still wearing a sweatshirt because the plane was so cold I haven't warmed up yet. My Arizona blood is still not accustomed to Montana, but my heart is happy to be back.

I get in the MINI Cooper and head straight for the rink. I don't even need to text Nick to know that's where he is. Aidan is at his mom's house this week, so Nick will be filling his time with hockey.

I pull into the lot and smile when I spot his truck. I park next to him and am stepping out of the car when he walks out of the building with his bag on one shoulder. His head is down, so he doesn't see me until I'm only a few feet away.

He stares at me a beat as if he's sure he's seeing things, then a slow grin tugs at the corners of his mouth.

I pick up my pace, closing the distance between us and flinging my arms around his neck. I missed him too damn much to play it cool.

"You're back," he says, wrapping his strong arms around my back and squeezing. He lifts my feet off the ground, and I burrow closer into him.

"Yep, and . . ." I pull back so I can look up at him. "I finished the book!"

"When?" His lips are pulled wide as he searches my face for understanding.

"I got on the plane, and I don't know . . . it just all came together. I wrote the entire ride to Arizona and then stayed up last night after

Greer's game, and I sent it to Molly this morning." I don't know if it's any good or if anyone will want to read it, but I'm so damn proud of it.

He sets me down but keeps his hold on me. "You finished, but you still came back."

He seems to think there was some question in that. Silly boy.

"Of course. I have one week left on my rental and a hot hockey player that I'd love to show my appreciation for all he's done to help me."

He grins.

"I meant sex," I whisper, not so quietly. "Like right now. Immediately. I've been thinking about all the fantastic things you can do with that glorious dick for the past forty-eight hours. Minus a few hours where I was around other people because that would be weird."

"Loud and clear, Red, but, uh—" He gives me a bashful smile that doesn't register until a soft laugh sounds behind us.

"I *love* her," a woman I did not notice says with a smirk. A guy steps up beside her with a shake of his head.

"Sorry. Inside thought." I pull away from Nick and then pray the ground swallows me up.

My attempts to hide behind him are thwarted when he pulls me into his side with an arm around my hip. "Ruby this is Jack Wyld, an old teammate, and his wife, Ev—"

"Everly Wyld," I say, piecing it together. "I know who you are. You work with my brother-in-law, Flynn Holland. He says so many great things about you."

She's his agent. His very fierce, beautiful, downright terrifying sports agent.

"Right." Nick laughs. "I forgot about that. Have you two met?"

"No, but I'm gagging," Everly says, smiling so big at me. "You're Olivia's sister, the romance novelist." She turns her gaze to Nick and hisses, "How could you not tell me that you were dating Ruby Madison?!"

"My apologies," Nick says dryly. "I didn't realize I needed to run these things by you."

"Yeah, well, now you know." She looks back to me. I can't tell if she's serious or not.

"I have heard so much about you," she says. "I thought you lived in Arizona."

"I do."

"How did you end up here?" Her brows pull together as she glances between me and Nick.

"It's a long story," I say.

"Well, I have to hear it. Are you coming to dinner with us?" she asks.

"I didn't know you were back. We were planning to go to MVP and watch the baseball game," Nick explains.

Embarrassment heats my cheeks.

"No, you guys go. I'll see you later tonight."

"You should come," Jack says. And he is . . . wow. Tall, hair so dark it's nearly black, and a face that's handsome and friendly yet reserved. His wife is terrifying, but he's pretty intimidating too.

"Sports ball isn't really my thing." Unless Greer is playing. Or Flynn. Or Nick. Hmm. The list is getting longer. Maybe I'm a sports fan after all.

Everly nods. "I'm meeting up with a client that just moved here. You can hang with us."

"Oh, I don't want to intrude while you're working."

"It's not even like that. She's become a friend and when I told her I was going to be in town, she insisted we have a girls' night. Besides, I am obsessed with you and need to know everything. Starting with how you ended up here with Galaxy." She leans in and does a bad job of whispering, "I also need to hear more about his glorious dick."

"Ev," Jack says with a sigh that turns to a chuckle.

"You can't tell me you aren't curious now," she says to her husband.

"The only glorious dick you're allowed to talk about is mine."

"In that case we can share our stories," Ev says to me with a wink.

I decide I absolutely must go to dinner with her and maybe befriend her forever.

At MVP, the four of us prepare to go our separate ways.

"You good?" Nick asks. He and Jack are heading to the bar while I'm going to the restaurant side with Everly.

"Yeah. I'm good."

"All right." He looks past me to Ev. "Best behavior."

"Yeah right, Galaxy," she says, linking her arm through mine.

He shakes his head, gives me one more long look, then turns to follow Jack to the bar. I stick with Everly as she leads me to a table across the restaurant. A woman with long blond hair waves and stands as we approach.

She's shorter than I am, but she gives off a confidence and friendliness that has me liking her immediately.

"Hannah." Everly hugs her. "It's so good to see you."

"You too," Hannah says as they pull back. Her light-brown eyes flick to me. "Hi."

"This is Ruby," Everly says.

"Hannah," she says, reaching her hand out to me. "Are you one of Everly's clients too?"

"Oh god no," I blurt out as I shake her hand.

Everly's brows rise, and a humored smirk dances across her lips.

"I'm not sporty," I clarify. "At all."

"She's dating Nick. Jack's former teammate that I was telling you about." Everly slides into the booth, and Hannah takes the seat across from her.

"Dating might be the wrong word." I sit next to Everly.

"I've known the man for something like five years, and I've never seen him so much as talk to a woman, let alone grope her in public. You're dating." Everly's words leave no room for debate, so I keep any further arguments to myself. And honestly, I like it.

"So, Hannah, what do you do?" I ask to take the questioning off me.

"I'm a gymnast."

Everly looks at me as she says, "She's the best gymnast in the world."

"Okay, that's a stretch, but I don't hate it." Hannah sits back in the booth across from us as the server approaches.

We order food and drinks, then Everly and Hannah talk a little about work stuff. I learn that Hannah recently moved here to train at a top gym and that she's originally from Iowa but spent the past five years training in Colorado. She talks fast and animated, and when she rests her elbows on the table, I'm distracted by her arms. She might be little, but every inch of her is lean muscle.

"What brought you to Moonshot?" Everly asks me as our drinks come.

"Nick, sort of," I say, then explain how his dad invited me here and volunteered Nick to help me with my book edits with his son having no idea about any of it.

Everly is in a fit of giggles as I finish.

"Oh my gosh. I can picture his face when he found out." She does a surprisingly accurate impression of grumpy Nick's face, down to the jaw flexing.

"He's been great, though. I couldn't have done it without him."

"So the book is done?" Hannah asks.

"Yeah. In fact, I just sent it to my editor today."

"No way. We have to celebrate properly then," Everly says, and I already know there will be no dissuading her.

A smile pulls at my lips. "What do you have in mind?"

What she has in mind is shots, followed by karaoke. After we finish our dinner, we move over to the bar side. The three of us down a round of lemon drop shots and then sing a poor rendition of "Livin' on a Prayer."

My face flushes as Nick watches from the bar. I sing right at him anyway, and he mouths the "whoa-oh" back to me each time. I stop by to say hi on the way back to our table.

"You have a nice voice," he says, grinning.

"Can we never speak of this again?"

"Why? It was good."

He's being generous.

"Having fun?" I ask him.

"Yeah," he says in a way that suggests he might not be telling the truth.

I lift my brows in question.

"I'd rather be somewhere alone with you, but Jack is only in town for the one night."

"We can still hang out *alone* later." I step closer to him, resting my hands on his chest. "I have a present for you."

His fingers brush against the side of my waist and rest against my lower back. His head lowers and his mouth hovers above mine. "You are the present."

I press up on my toes and kiss him. My insides sigh with happiness as he pulls me flush against him and sweeps his tongue into my mouth, making out with me like there isn't a bar full of people watching.

"No, no, no. She's mine tonight, Galaxy." Everly interrupts by tugging my arm and prying me away from Nick. He holds my hand, not resisting but touching me as long as possible.

"Later, Red." He winks at me.

Back at our table, Everly has another round of drinks waiting for us.

"I waited as long as I could, but I need to know . . ." She trails off as if the question is obvious. If it is, then I'm clueless.

"Need to know what?"

"Nick. You. What is happening? He just kissed you like the world was ending."

I roll my bottom lip behind my teeth as I remember the feel of his mouth on mine. Hannah and Everly sit forward, waiting for more.

"We're just . . . hanging out."

"Boo," Everly says loudly, shaking her head. "No. I refuse to believe that."

"I'm leaving in a week, and anyway, he doesn't do anything but casual."

"Not before you, maybe, but that was not a casual kiss."

Hannah nods as she gives me a rueful smile. "I'm with her."

I fight the hope their words build. The past five weeks have been the best, but maybe it was only supposed to be a summer fling. I glance over to the bar. He stands sideways, talking to Jack, but looks up and at me as I'm staring. One side of his mouth pulls up.

"Ugh." Hannah's groan draws my attention back to her.

"What?" Everly asks.

"This guy I've been talking to just asked if he could bring his sister on our date tomorrow."

"Because?" Ev asks with a chortle.

Hannah reads from her phone, "Is it cool if my sister comes to dinner? She's been dying to eat at that restaurant."

"Sweet and odd all at once," Everly says.

Hannah types something back to him and then sets her phone down on the table.

"What'd you tell him?" I ask her.

"That he should just take her, and we can go out another time."

"So polite and considerate," Everly says.

"And then I blocked him," Hannah adds. "I don't have time for guys who can't even make me the priority on date one."

"Fair." Everly takes another sip of her drink. "I thought you were dating that podcaster guy."

"No. We broke up a while ago. We hook up occasionally when neither of us is seeing someone, but we're better as friends."

"Friends with benefits, apparently," Ev says.

Hannah shrugs. "It's hard to date right now. And every guy I talk to lately feels like the type to not notice if I went missing."

Ev snickers, then leans forward. "You know what we should do?"

She pulls out her phone and uses voice text, "Text Jackson."

Hannah and I share a grin then listen as Everly continues, "If I went missing, what would you do?"

After she's done, she puts the phone down and looks to me. "Now you text Nick."

"And ask him what he would do if I went missing?"

She nods then looks to Hannah. "Unblock your potential date and ask him."

"He's going to think I'm an insane person."

"Fine. Text your ex then."

Everly's phone pings. I glance over at Jack and Nick. Nick's staring at the baseball game on the TV, but Jack is looking at Everly.

"What'd he say?"

"I'm not looking until they all respond."

I pull out my phone and text the same thing to Nick. I can't watch as I press send.

"Done," Hannah says.

Her phone pings next. Then mine.

"Okay. Hannah, go." Everly juts her chin toward Hannah's phone.

"He says, 'Everything okay?'"

The three of us laugh.

"It's a hypothetical," she says and types back.

We wait for his reply, staring at the phone.

When it pings again, she reads it to us, "I'd call the cops and then check all the places I could think where you might be."

"Practical," I say.

"Boring," Hannah adds. "But he is a very practical guy, so it tracks."

"What did Jack say?" I ask Everly.

She grins as she picks up her phone and it widens as she reads, "That would never happen because I know where you are at all times."

Everly rolls her eyes and replies to him, "Pretend someone snatched me up while you were traveling with the team."

When he responds this time, she sets the phone down and covers her mouth with a laugh. Hannah and I lean in to see the screen. He sent a gif of Liam Neeson saying, "I will find you."

"That's perfect," I say.

"Your turn," Ev says, still grinning. She texts back to Jack without reading what she writes.

I'm nervous to see what Nick said. In a few days I will go missing, at least from his life.

My stomach flutters nervously as I tap on the message. "I'm looking at you right now, Red, so if you're missing then I'm hallucinating the most beautiful girl in the world."

"Aww," Everly and Hannah croon together.

"Who knew Nick had it in him," Everly says to me, then shouts louder across the bar, "Well done, Galaxy!"

I finally peek over at him. His stare is playful and intense all at once and my body lights up in response.

Well done, indeed.

Chapter Twenty-Eight

NICK

I should have known letting Ruby hang out with Everly was going to end in trouble. The two of them are at the bar, and Everly is ordering another round of shots. Everly holds up one of the glasses, says something I can't make out that has Ruby laughing, and then they clink their glasses together.

Jack slaps me on the chest. "I'd apologize for my wife, but we both know she does whatever the hell she wants no matter what I say or do."

The night is winding down. There isn't much of a crowd on a Monday night. Everly's client, Hannah, took off not too long ago, and I don't think Ruby is going to last much longer.

"What are you going to do about that?" Jack asks me.

"What?"

"What?" he mocks back to me. "Your girl. Ruby. You said she's leaving in a week."

There's no question, but I know what he's asking.

"I don't know. I guess that'll be it."

"Come on, really? *That's* your plan?"

I know it's weak. It isn't like I haven't thought about it, but what am I supposed to do? "I don't have a plan. She lives in Arizona, and I live here."

"Have you talked to her about it?"

I shake my head in response.

"Maybe she'd be open to moving here."

"I can't ask her to do that. She has family and friends, a life there. And we've been . . ." I struggle for the right word to describe whatever it is we're doing. "It's only been a few weeks."

"I'm ready to go home," Everly says, appearing at Jack's side and intertwining her fingers with his.

I find Ruby behind her.

"Yeah. Me too," Jack tells her, then looks to me. We shift so we're paired off and Ruby's back at my side.

"I'm glad I came," Jack says. "It was good to see you."

"Yeah. It's been too long. Tell the guys I said hey when you get back."

"Will do. We'll see you in October." He holds out his hand, and we shake, then he pulls me into a hug.

"Can't wait," I say when we pull apart.

Jack turns to Ruby. "Pleasure to meet you. I hope I'll be seeing you again."

He smiles at her, then turns his gaze to me and winks. Arrogant fucker.

"You too," Ruby says to him.

Everly hugs Ruby, rocking side to side. "I'm going to text you when I'm in Arizona next month. Let's grab a drink or dinner."

"Definitely," Ruby says.

Everly comes in to hug me next.

"Good to see you, Ev," I say.

"Don't fuck this up, Galaxy," she says loud enough that it's likely Ruby heard. Good ol' Everly.

I chuckle, but the expression on her face when she steps back tells me she isn't joking.

Everly and Jack head out, leaving me and Ruby alone with the last of the people at the bar.

"Hi." She wraps her arms around my neck.

"Have fun?" I slide a hand around her waist.

"Everly is a blast."

"That she is."

"I do have one problem."

"What's that?"

"I need a ride home."

"I think I can help with that." I expected as much, which is why I stayed sober.

She beams. "Hey, I have a hypothetical question for you."

"O-kay." One corner of my mouth lifts as she gives me a playful smirk. Damn, I missed her this weekend. Even tonight, being near her but not touching her or catching every word she said.

"What would you say if I suggested we spend the next week hanging out every possible second?"

"I'd say, 'Prepare to be sick of me, Red. I'm not letting you leave my sight for the next six days.'"

On the way back home, Ruby sings along to the radio. The windows in the truck are down, and the night air is crisp and fragrant. I drive slowly, soaking it all in.

When I finally pull into the driveway and park, I kill the engine and roll up the windows. The radio keeps going. It's some old nineties ballad, and when Ruby belts out, "Is this love, or am I dreaming?" it accurately sums up the thoughts running through my head.

She grins at me as she unbuckles but keeps serenading me. There isn't a whole lot of room, but she successfully maneuvers from the passenger seat to straddle me on the driver's side.

"I love summertime," she says.

"Yeah, me too." My hands rest at her hips.

"Oh, I can finally give you your present."

"Is this not it?" It feels like a damn good one to me.

"You were already getting that." She reaches behind her neck and unclasps the necklace, then holds it up. The shamrock dangles in the moonlight. As she moves to put it on me, confusion mars my brow.

"I can't take this. Your sister gave it to you."

She ignores me, clasping it around my neck and then pressing her fingers to the charm. "It brought me the luck I needed. Now it's yours."

"I already feel pretty lucky, Red."

"Then it's something to remember me."

There's no way I'm ever going to forget her, but instead of saying that, I glide one hand to the back of her neck and pull her mouth to mine.

Her hair falls around my face, enveloping me in her coconut scent.

Ruby grinds over my dick, and we both groan.

"Fuck, Red. I missed you." I missed her and I missed this. I didn't know it was possible for someone to work their way into my life so quickly. Days and nights are just better when she's here.

"I missed you too." Her hands rest on my chest, and she drags them down, lightly scraping her nails over my pecs and abs.

A knock at the window makes both of us jump. Through the foggy glass, my dad stands on the other side.

"Oh my god," Ruby mutters as she tries to scramble out of my lap. Only all she manages to do is knee me in the balls.

I wince, and a look of horror etches into her features at the scene playing out before her.

"I'm good," I assure her through gritted teeth. I hit the button to roll down the window.

"Dad." I clear my throat. "Uh, hey."

"Son. Ruby."

"Hi, Mike," Ruby squeaks out.

"Nice night," Dad says, looking out toward the road.

"Yeah," I agree. Does he really want to talk about the weather right now?

"Might want to take it inside, kids. Unless you're planning on giving the neighbors a show."

I glance over at our nearest neighbor. A nice older woman lives there. She brings cookies and fudge over every year at Christmastime. All the lights are out, so I doubt very much she's awake. Still, it's a fair point.

"Be right in," I assure him.

"Good." Dad nods. The corners of his mouth twitch but he keeps his smile contained. "Excuse me. I'm going to see if I can find my earplugs before I turn in."

"Night," I call after him, then roll the window back up.

Ruby bursts out laughing when we're closed into the truck cab again. She collapses into me, burying her head in my chest. I join in, and it's several seconds before either of us stops. Ruby looks at me, and we start in again. Despite it all, my chest is light and my face hurts from smiling.

"I can't believe your dad just caught us making out. I kept waiting for him to send you to your room and threaten to call my parents."

"Not his style."

She chuckles again, and then her expression goes serious. "Wait. Did your dad just go to find earplugs so he wouldn't hear us having sex?"

"Yeah." I cringe inwardly.

She covers her face with both hands. "Oh, god. I'm never going to be able to face him again."

I pry her fingers away. "You don't need to be embarrassed. He's thrilled. This is exactly what he wanted when you showed up."

Ruby slowly lets me uncover her face. "I am a catch."

She is. No denying that.

"Are you okay?" She glances down at my crotch. "I am so sorry."

"I'll survive." I think. I hold back a groan as I shift again. The music finally cuts out, leaving the cab in silence. "Want to stay at my place tonight, Red?"

Chapter Twenty-Nine

RUBY

"Yes! Eat ice, Galaxy!" With my hands raised over my head, I yell as the puck hits the back of the net.

Nick smirks as he watches me do my victory pose.

"Hell yeah, Ruby-Doo!" Travis skates over to me, wrapping me in a big bear hug. I'm in full padding but I still wince as he squeezes me. This is the third time we've celebrated this way, and I'm starting to feel like his personal rag doll.

"We're unstoppable." He shakes me a few times, rattling my bones, as Nick comes to a stop in front of us.

We're playing two on two, me and Travis versus Nick and Conrad.

"Okay. Okay. My turn," Nick says.

Travis continues to hold on to me but shifts so he can look at his friend. "Go hug your teammate."

Nick gives Travis a dry, unyielding scowl.

"Fine, but only because I feel bad. We're killing you." Trav squeezes me around the shoulders one last time before releasing me.

I wobble and sway until Nick skates forward to steady me.

"He's freakishly strong," I say as my bones settle back into place.

Nick chuckles as he wraps his arm around me looser than his friend had but much more possessively. I think his hands are on my butt, though it's hard to tell through all the layers.

"Congrats on your goal, Red. It's hard to get past Penn."

I glance over at the big goalie. I'm certain he let me score on him, but I still feel proud. He blocks so much of the goal just by standing in it; it's no small feat to get the puck around him.

"I'd kiss you, but someone insisted I wear this gaudy helmet." It's one with a cage like kids wear.

His lips twitch with the promise of a smile, and he buries his head in the crook of my neck, kissing me on the sliver of skin not covered by padding. A thrill rushes through me.

We have done a lot of kissing and groping over the past week. We've alternated between staying at the cabin and his house. I wake up every morning to coffee and kisses—the perfect combination. During the days, I go with him to the rink where he works out and skates, and I brainstorm new book ideas, stealing more kisses during his breaks—also a great combination. Nights, we take the boat out or walk along the lake. And yes, there are more kisses, and it is also . . . yep, perfect.

This entire week has been a dream. The kind that can only happen under the pressure of a ticking time clock. I'm leaving Sunday, and every day the anticipation and impending heartbreak increase tenfold. We haven't talked about it, but there's an unspoken agreement to enjoy every second before it ends.

"Okay. That's enough, you two. Have some sympathy for the single folks," Travis says.

Nick's mouth pulls away from my neck, but he keeps his arms around me.

"Are we that annoying couple who makes everyone else uncomfortable?" I ask Nick.

"Hopefully. Fuck knows he's made out with enough people in front of me."

"I heard that," Travis says. "And I don't do that. You're confusing me with D-Low."

"Where is Danny?" I ask.

"He went to visit his family this week. He'll be back tomorrow," Conrad says.

"He'll be at your going-away party," Travis adds.

Nick's body tenses.

"My what?"

"Trav!" Conrad and Penn say at the same time.

Trav's smile twists into a remorseful sort of smirk. "Oops."

"The guys want to have a little thing tomorrow night," Nick explains. His voice is quiet and clipped.

"You don't have to do that," I say, feeling at once a little closer to heartbreak and touched by their thoughtfulness.

"Of course we do," Travis says.

"He just wants an excuse to party." Penn's goalie mask is lifted, and he squeezes water into his mouth from a purple bottle.

"But it's poker night," is all I manage to get out as my throat tightens.

"So, we'll play some cards too," Travis says, then points. "You're on my team this time."

Nick growls, which has the tightness in my chest loosening.

Once we're finished with the game, we say goodbye to the guys, and then Nick and I take a few laps around the rink.

"I'm going to miss this," I say to him.

He squeezes my hand. "I'm sure there are rinks in Arizona."

"Yeah, but who will keep me upright?"

"You don't need it anymore." He lifts our hands and kisses my knuckles.

"Debatable." I haven't fallen the last couple days, but I'm not exactly graceful yet.

I breathe in the cool air and force myself to catalog it all. The chill on my face, the sound of our skates moving across the ice, and Nick's warm hand engulfing mine.

Nick's phone pings as we're skating by the bench.

"Do you need to get that?" I ask him.

"Nah." He pulls me along, and we do another lap, but as we're coming around again, his mouth is pulled into a tight line.

"It's okay," I tell him. "I want to do one on my own, and then we can go."

"All right." His lips curve up, and he stops, letting me skate forward without him. Our hands stretch out, holding on until the last moment.

Once I've made the slow circle without him, he's waiting for me next to the gate.

"Everything okay?" I ask.

"Yeah," he says in a way that tells me maybe it's okay but less than good. "My dad can't find his blood pressure meds."

"Oh. Sounds important."

"I don't know how he could have possibly lost them. They've been in the same spot for seven months."

"I'm ready if you want to go save him."

He nods with a sigh. "After I get him situated, then maybe we can take the boat out or grab dinner, whatever you want."

"Yeah, that sounds great."

* * *

I'm doing my makeup in the bathroom when there's a knock on the front door.

"Come in!" I yell, assuming it's Nick, but after a few seconds, there's no movement.

I wait another moment, then hurry to the door only . . . no one is there. I step out and then look left and right.

"That's odd," I say to myself, turning in a circle. As I'm about to walk back inside, I spy the note taped to the door.

Meet me at the dock.

I glance down to the water, but there's no sign of Nick. Rushing back inside, I finish my makeup and hair and take one last look at myself before heading out to meet him.

Nick stands at the end of the dock. The boat behind him is lit up with hundreds of twinkle lights that sparkle dimly in the sunset.

"Wow. This looks like a dream," I say as I reach him.

"So do you." His gaze roams over me from head to toe before he leans in to brush a kiss over my lips.

When he pulls back, I glance to the boat again. It's the most romantic scene. "When did you find the time to do this?"

His brows tug together in the center. "I didn't do this. I thought you did."

"No. I was getting ready." I wave a hand down the length of me. Picking a dress alone took most of the thirty minutes since we've been back from the rink.

We stare at each other a beat, then laugh. Nick glances at the house.

"Your dad," I say, piecing it together. "Of course."

"He just can't help himself." Nick chuckles softly, running a hand over his jaw. "Needed his meds. Jesus. I can't believe I fell for it."

"Wow. I'm not sure if I'm impressed by his setup skills or worried." As in I won't be here the next time he decides to send his son on a romantic sunset boat ride.

"Probably both, but tonight we can both just be glad." He holds out his hand to me.

"It would be a pity to waste all his efforts," I admit as I slip my fingers into his.

Nick steps onto the boat and helps me up.

"He really went all out." I lift a bottle of chilled champagne from a bucket of ice. There are blankets and trays of covered food. "I might have picked the wrong Galaxy."

Nick does that playful, jealous growl and wraps me up in his arms.

The moment feels heavy with unspoken truths. Inside thoughts that neither of us want to say out loud.

"It's starting to hit me that this is our last night together like this." Aidan comes back tomorrow, and while I'm ecstatic to say goodbye and spend time with him before I leave, I know that it will be different. Nick has kept our relationship separate, and I get it, but it makes tonight all that more bittersweet.

His green eyes search my face, almost like he's trying to etch me into his memory the same way I've been trying to do all week.

"We could ditch the guys tomorrow night, but I have a feeling they'd track us down. I think if they had to pick, they'd send me packing in exchange for you."

I know it isn't true. They like me, but Nick is the glue that holds them all together. He has a quiet presence, but they all respect him fiercely.

"I could get used to this view and this boat." And to waking up to him. "I'm sure my parents wouldn't mind if you crashed on their couch. My dad always wanted a son."

Nick huffs a quiet snort of a laugh.

"I'm going to miss you."

"You too, Red."

There are so many more things I want to say, but it all feels too soon. Too complicated. Too uncertain. I know Nick likes me. I even think he'd eventually be open to dating more seriously if I lived here. But there's a big jump between that and planning a life with someone who lives a thousand miles away.

Forcing down all the worry and impending heartbreak, I smile at him. "One last boat ride?"

"Anything you want, Red."

"Have you heard back from the editor on your book?" Nick asks as we lie on a blanket in the front of the boat. We've been out here so long the night sky is pitch-black and the twinkle lights have dimmed.

"Not yet." A new kind of nerves swirls in my stomach.

"She's going to love it."

"I hope so."

"When do I get to read the ending?"

I hadn't planned on letting him read anything but the hockey scenes, but he keeps stealing my laptop. And I guess I like seeing his reactions. If no one else but him likes the book, that'll be good enough by me.

"Soon," I promise, then roll over so I'm partially lying on him. He lifts one hand to push my hair behind my ear.

"Should we go in?" I ask, begrudgingly. It's late, and even the combination of him and the blankets aren't keeping me warm enough.

"Yeah. You need your rest for tomorrow."

"I thought the party was at night?"

"Knowing Travis, he'll be here before noon."

Nick pulls me to my feet.

"Will you sleep?"

"Yeah."

I give him my best unconvinced face. Every morning when I wake up, he's already gone from bed. I have no idea how much he sleeps, but I don't think it's much.

"Believe it or not, Red, I sleep better with you."

"Was that supposed to be reassuring?"

I get another one of his soft huffs.

"Have you talked to someone about it?"

"Kind of," he says, then falls quiet. A few seconds later, he adds, "The team doctor thinks I have health anxiety. After my injury last year and the stuff with my dad . . ."

I wrap myself around him. "Of course. That makes perfect sense."

"I thought it was an age thing." One side of his mouth lifts. "As I'm getting older, realizing my own mortality or something. My mom died young—in her forties—and I guess it's just hit me recently."

"You've dealt with a lot. I think it's perfectly normal to have a heightened fear after all that."

"It's not just about me. I want to be around a long time, don't get me wrong, but the thought of leaving Aidan." His throat works with a swallow.

"You're a good father."

He's quiet again, and I let the silence stretch out, making room for his thoughts and feelings, but he seems lost in his own head.

"What are you going to do?"

He blinks and then settles his stare back on me. "For starters, I'm going to carry you back up to the house to my bed."

I swat at his chest lightly. "That is not what I meant."

One corner of his mouth lifts in a small smirk. "I have an appointment with the psychologist next week."

"Have you considered talking to your dad?"

Nick's brow furrows.

"He's been through a lot too. It might give you some perspective."

He lifts his head off the blanket and presses his mouth to mine, and any further conversation dies off as he kisses me like it's the only thing he wants in the whole world. Maybe it is, but I'm too chicken to ask.

Later, when I wake up alone in his bed, I check the time and then head downstairs to find him. He's exactly where I expected, on the back porch, lying on the wicker couch with his eyes closed. He looks asleep, but I doubt he is.

"It's better since you got here." Mike talks softly, but he still startles me. He's in his robe standing in the kitchen with a mug in one hand.

Instead of walking outside, I step into the kitchen with him. He gets down a second mug, and I nod.

"I'm worried about him," I admit as he pours the coffee.

"He'll be all right. That incident in the spring was really hard on him." He tilts his head to one side. "I don't know how he does it, but he's tough. Tougher than I ever was. Hockey is a brutal sport."

"Did you play?" I ask.

"Oh no." Mike hands over the mug to me. "I grew up on a farm. From an early age I had to help anytime I wasn't at school. Didn't leave a lot of room for sports. His mom was the one that got him into skates at a young age. She grew up in northern Michigan, playing hockey with her three brothers."

"I didn't know that," I say, then think about all the other tidbits I haven't learned yet. And I guess now I never will.

Mike reaches out and squeezes my forearm. "You've been good for him in more ways than one."

"I hope so."

"Will I be seeing more of you?" I know exactly what he's asking, even though he doesn't outright ask if Nick and I will be continuing our relationship.

"I don't think so."

He nods slowly. "Pity."

"From everything Nick's told me, I thought you'd be excited to play matchmaker again."

A small laugh slips from his lips. "No, I think I'm retired from that."

We fall quiet, perhaps neither of us knowing what else to say.

"I'm going to check on him," I say, lifting the mug. "Thanks."

"Welcome."

I start for the back door.

"And, Ruby," Mike says.

I pause.

His mouth opens then closes as if he's second-guessing his words. He gives me a smile instead. "If I don't get a chance to say it before you go, good luck with the book."

"Thanks, Mike," I say, then slip outside.

Chapter Thirty

NICK

"Nick said you're going to some sort of book convention after this," Shep says to Ruby.

"That's right." Her smile widens. She's been nothing but big, happy smiles all night long as the guys pepper her with questions about what comes next for her.

The poker game was abandoned long ago, and we moved outside to the back patio. Ruby's on my lap, and the rest of the group is sitting around us in a circle.

"Sucks that we have camp." D-Low tips his beer up and takes a drink before adding, "I'd love to go to that."

"I'll get you tickets to another one," she says. "If you want."

"Definitely," D-Low and Trav say at the same time.

She rests her back against my chest, and I soak it all in. It's been the perfect night, but it's coming to an end, and I'm not ready.

"Did you figure out what you're going to write next?" D-Low asks.

She lets her head fall to the side and stares up at me. We share a smile before she glances back at him. "I did."

"What's that look? I don't like these secret looks," Travis says, waggling a finger between us.

I flip him off behind her back and pull her farther onto my lap.

"I took your advice," she says to D-Low.

He thinks for a second, and then his face lights up. "You're writing a sequel to *Love Bites*?"

"Yep."

"Badass." He leans forward and rests his elbows on his knees, giving Ruby all his attention. "Tell me everything."

"Well . . ." she starts, grinning back at him. "I kept thinking about what you said. It's so obvious. I don't know why I didn't think of it."

D-Low waves it off but he's smiling. "You'd have come up with it eventually. Xander's alive then?"

"I'm going to grab you another drink," I say softly, pressing my lips to her temple.

"Okay." She turns to kiss me proper before moving off my lap. I stand with her empty glass. She settles back in my spot, and I head inside and fill her flute with champagne.

On the way back out, I pause in the doorway and take in the scene.

My closest friends are all here tonight: Trav, Shep, D-Low, and Penn. All of them wanted to say goodbye to Ruby, and they've given her a hell of a send-off. They went in together and bought her a pair of skates, complete with sparkly laces.

Travis also brought her a jersey—his, of course. D-Low brought his copy of *Love Bites* for her to sign, Penn showed up with Dom Perignon in a blinged-out, diamond encrusted bottle that made Ruby smile bigger than I've ever seen, and Shep pulled her into a bear hug that had them both blushing.

Earlier, Aidan sat outside with us and played guitar for us. He was even taking requests, although my friends were nice enough to ask him to play songs they knew he could do. He's come a long way this summer. Dad has even stopped wearing his headphones while he practices.

I'm not sure I've ever been happier. Or sadder.

Travis stands from the rest of the group and walks over to me. "You good?"

"Yeah," I say, unconvincing even to my own ears. My body is wound tight with too many warring emotions. I'm so glad for the time we had, and I wouldn't change a thing, but it sucks that she's going. Every minute, every conversation is leading toward it, and I can't stop it.

"She's really leaving, huh?"

"Of course she is." As much as I hate it.

"I really thought . . ."

"What?"

He hesitates a beat, head bobbing to either side. "Look, I know. It's crazy. You barely know each other, blah, blah, blah. But I really thought you two were endgame."

"I thought *you* were determined to be her endgame."

"I decided to let you have this one."

I bark out a laugh, and a smirk appears on his face.

"How nice of you," I say with a shake of my head, but despite the joking nature of our conversation, I'm filled with a sinking sensation of dread throughout my body.

"It is. Very nice. So don't make me regret it." He backhands me square in the chest and then leaves me standing by myself. He makes a beeline to Ruby, draping an arm around her shoulders.

I think my friends are as in love with her as I am.

Fuck. *I'm in love with her.* Of course I am. How could I not have fallen for her? I drag two fingers over my chest to loosen the tightness that's worked its way there.

Is there really a chance she might stay if I asked? It feels like too much to ask someone to give up. Especially her. She deserves it all. I can't leave my family and career, so how could I think she'd do that for me?

Laughter fills the air as they all guffaw at something Ruby said. She looks up and scans the deck until she finds me.

I move toward her. She shifts to let me sit behind her, and I hand her the champagne flute before taking my seat and gathering her back into my lap.

She stares at me for a beat like she's analyzing my expression. I can't guess what she sees.

"Thank you for this," she says quietly then presses her lips to mine.

"You're welcome." I glide one hand around the side of her neck, fingers combing through a section of her hair. My gaze drops to her chest and up.

Her lips lift and twist with amusement. "Your eye twitches every time you look at Travis's jersey."

"You just had to put it on, didn't you?"

"It would have been rude not to," she insists, but she has a devilish glint in her eyes.

I close the distance between our faces until my lips cover hers. "I think you're full of shit, Red. I think you like pushing my buttons."

"Is that what I'm doing?"

I nip at her bottom lip, then, because I can't fucking resist her, even in Trav's jersey, slant my mouth over hers and kiss her hard. She leans into me, resting a hand on my chest, as she kisses me back with the same fierceness. All week it's been like this. Every kiss feels more frantic than the last.

"I think I'm going to head out," Penn says. He stands slowly, aiming a smile at Ruby. "Good luck with everything."

"Thank you."

"You're coming back next summer, right?" Trav asks, voice almost a whine.

She laughs. "I just might."

"I hope so," he says.

"Me too," Penn adds.

She gets up to hug the big goalie, and that sets off a chain reaction. Shep and D-Low say their goodbyes next, then Trav.

"I'm going to text you the next time I'm in Arizona," he says, rocking side to side as he hugs her way longer than necessary.

"You better," she replies.

When he pulls back, my best friend looks almost as heartbroken as I feel. He looks over to where Aidan has wandered back outside and is trying to catch lightning bugs between his hands. "A-bomb. You want to stay at my place tonight? I got a new video game, and I need someone to teach me how to play it."

"Really?" Aidan's eyes widen, and he looks hopefully toward me before flinging himself across the deck to stand in front of me.

"Yeah, it's okay with me. Behave yourself."

"I will," he says.

"I was talking to Trav." I rustle his hair. "Say bye to Ruby. She's leaving in the morning."

Aidan's smile drops, and he moves over in front of Ruby.

She squats down to his level. "Thanks for being my writing soundtrack all summer. I couldn't have finished the book without you."

His smile lifts back in place. "Thanks for teaching me how to make cookies and being so funny on the ice."

I fight a laugh, but one slips free from Ruby's lips. "You're welcome."

He steps forward until his body is nuzzled against hers, and she hugs him around the waist. My throat closes up, and I swallow thickly.

As Aidan and Trav head out, Ruby turns to me. "Did he just burn me or was that just honesty?"

"The latter, I think. You brought us all a lot of joy this summer."

"By falling on my ass?"

"Among other things."

She drapes her arms over my shoulders, and I bend down to swipe my lips across hers.

"How do you want to spend your last night?"

"Just like this." She rests her head on my chest.

"Do you still need to pack?"

She groans. I guess that's my answer.

"You pack, and I'll clean up over here," I suggest.

"Okay."

Neither of us moves.

"Meet you in ten?"

She nods and with a reluctant sigh, steps back from my embrace.

"Better take off that jersey too, Red."

"Why? I think I look cute."

"Fine. Don't, but be prepared to crawl on your hands and knees later when you're begging me to fuck you."

"Ooh. I pick option two."

Fucking hell.

She tosses a sassy smirk at me as she swivels around, practically prancing toward the cabin.

I head back inside, cleaning up quickly and finally feeling like I can see a path forward. I want more of this, whatever she wants that to look like and for as long as she wants. We'll figure it out.

I doubt it's even been five minutes when I'm jogging down the back steps and cutting across the yard to the cabin. I haven't worked out how I'm going to ask her, but I know what I want. I hope she feels the same.

She's still packing when I get there. Her suitcase is overflowing, and she's shoving more inside. "How did I end up with more stuff than when I came?"

"Maybe you should leave the jersey here then."

"Oh no. I'm wearing this home." She pulls on the hem of it.

I go to her, stopping a foot away and tugging her the rest of the way to me. "Maybe don't go at all. Problem solved."

"I wish."

"Me too."

The smile she aims at me makes me think maybe this could work.

My pulse quickens and my heart hammers in my chest as I lace my fingers through hers. Can I really ask her to stay? Does she even want that? Living this life during the summer is one thing, but once the season starts, I'll be gone more than I'm home, and Aidan's schedule will pick up too.

"I was thinking . . ." I stop and clear my throat.

Her phone pings before I can finish the thought.

"Go ahead," I say because I need another minute to figure out what to say.

She pulls it out of her front pocket and then pauses. "It's from Molly. Probably just confirming my travel."

Her gaze roams over the screen, and her thumb scrolls. A tiny divot forms between her brows.

"Is everything okay?"

"Yeah," she says, unconvincingly.

"What is it?"

Ruby's expression is dazed and her tone hard to read as she says, "They've increased the print run, and two bookstores have asked to do a special edition."

"I don't know what any of that means, but I'm guessing that's a good thing?" I seriously can't tell by the shocked look on her face.

Slowly it morphs into a huge smile. "Better than I could have imagined."

"I told you they'd love the book." I've seen how hard she's worked this summer, and I know how good the book is—at least what she let me read. I binge-read damn near the whole thing in one sitting. Would have finished it too if the rest had been ready. She left me on a cliff-hanger. It feels sort of fitting. Not knowing the ending until after ours. Poetic even. Or maybe that's my current sappy mood coming through.

"They want to add a tour, possibly including international stops." She's still smiling but looks genuinely baffled by it all.

"That's fantastic, Red. You deserve it."

"I think I'm in shock."

I watch as the excitement finally hits her full force. "I can't believe it. I'll be traveling nonstop. I'll have to make sure none of it interferes with Olivia's due date. I can't miss that. And my grandma's seventy-fifth birthday is coming up, and we're throwing a big party for her."

She prattles on as if she's thinking through her schedule for the next six months and reimagining it.

"I've never been to Italy though. That would be fun. Pasta and wine and . . ." She stops and shakes her head. "I'm sorry. This is all stuff I can figure out later."

"No, Red. It's great news. I'm really happy for you." And I am, but it hits me again how big of an ask it is to suggest she stay. Maybe after she's done all these incredible things, she'll come back. But it needs to be on her terms. I'm not going to be the guy to hold her back.

"I couldn't have done it without you."

"Sure, you could have, but I'm happy I got to be a part of it."

"What were you going to say before?"

"More sappy musings about not wanting you to go."

"About that . . ." She lifts one shoulder and grins. "I was thinking about what Travis said."

"Which thing? Because he talks a lot."

She lets out a quiet chuckle. There's a pause before she continues, and my heart is hammering in my chest.

"Maybe I could come back next summer or even visit some weekend and catch a hockey game."

"I'd love that."

"Really?" She seems surprised by my answer.

"Hell yeah."

"And you have an open invitation to Arizona too. It's gorgeous in the fall and winter. You could meet my family. They'll love you. My sister refers to you as the 'hot hockey player' though, be forewarned." She talks fast and animated.

"I'm sure I'll love them too," I say, and what I mean is I'll love them because I love you. Is saying the words before she leaves cruel or romantic? I can't decide.

"Let's make a plan right now." Her eyes flash with that determined optimism I recognize from the day she showed up at the rink to ask me to help her. "That way we'll know we're going to see each other again."

"All right." I like this game. "We have several home game weekends in October and November, but the first long break I'll have is December."

A little of that optimism drains from her expression. "December?"

It's a kick to the gut to admit it'll be that long. "Yeah, and I'll have Aidan, so I probably can't come to you."

"I don't mind coming back here."

"It'll be cold," I warn her with a grin, but the logistics of it all are making my gut swirl with unease. "Real cold."

"Then you better make it worth my while." She closes the distance between us and tips her head back, an open invitation to kiss her, which I do.

"December, then?"

"December," I agree. Four months away. But I'd wait longer, if it meant holding on to her.

"If for some reason you change your mind and this doesn't work, this was the best summer of my life."

"Yeah, me too." I brush her hair back from one side of her face and kiss her again. It's smart to leave an out for either of us, but I can't help but wonder if she's the one that needs it.

Who knows what she'll want once she gets back home. She has her entire family there and this incredible opportunity at work. I'm not going to put it all on her shoulders because I can't go anywhere. That isn't fair to her. It reinforces to me how selfish it would be of me to ask her to stay.

She nods, and we fall quiet, perhaps both realizing this isn't likely going to work no matter how much we want it to. After a few seconds of silently staring at each other, she asks, "What should we do now?"

I take a breath, releasing thoughts of the future for later. I want to be here with her. For as long as I have her.

"For starters, take off this fucking jersey." I fist the material in one hand.

With a playful smirk, she lays a hand on my chest and pushes me back. It catches me off guard, and I fall back onto the chair. My grip on her jersey loosens, and she steps back a foot, then two more.

There's a glint in her eye that tells me she's up to something, but before I can ask, she lowers herself to the floor on her hands and knees.

Fuck me.

Slow and deliberate, she crawls to me. My dick presses against my zipper, eager as he's ever been. When she reaches me, she sits back between my spread legs. "Now what?"

I grip her chin between my thumb and finger. "Take my cock out and wrap that gorgeous mouth around it."

She doesn't waste any time obeying me. I'm already leaking for her. When her tongue flicks across the head, I guide her down over my length.

"Eyes on me, baby."

Her gaze flicks to mine and holds as she sucks me. Up and down, torturing me in the best fucking way. Trav's number on the side of her arm catches my attention, and I let out a low growl, then gently pull her off me. I lift her onto my lap and then pull his jersey over her head.

"I didn't even have to beg," she says, looking all too pleased with herself.

"You'll beg, all right." I take the jersey and tie her wrists, one at a time, so she's effectively bound with it. Ruby's face flushes and pupils widen.

Standing with her in my arms, I walk her over to the bed and lay her down on the mattress. I move her suitcase onto the floor and then strip. She shifts onto one elbow and stares intently as I take my time removing my shoes, socks, shirt, pants, and finally boxers.

"So many inside thoughts," she says, gaze locked on my dick.

"What'd I tell you about those?" I pull off her shoes, then her shorts and panties.

"Sometimes I can't believe you're real."

"I'm real, and I'm about to fuck you so hard you can't look at this jersey without thinking about me." I move onto the bed over her.

She falls back, grinning up at me. I raise her arms over her head. The movement has her tits straining and spilling over the top of her black bra. I hook one finger in the lacy material and pull until one nipple peeks out the top. I cover it with my mouth, nipping and sucking. I do the same on the other side.

I had plans to drag this out all night, but the sweet little moans coming from her tell me she's already as needy for me as I am for her.

I peel her out of her bra and toss it with the rest of our clothes.

"Nick." She says my name on a ragged breath as I trail kisses over her chest and stomach, then lower.

"Hmm?" I hook one arm around her right leg and push her legs farther apart.

"Please fuck me."

My dick twitches in response, but instead, I flatten my tongue over her center. She gasps, and her body jolts, then she pushes her pussy against me for more friction. I keep going until she's grinding all over my face. When I pull back, she mewls in frustration.

"Please?"

"I don't think you're ready yet," I tease.

Her expression is predictably annoyed. "I'm so ready I could come just looking at you."

"Now there's an interesting challenge."

She gives me another haughty, exasperated glare.

"But not tonight." I crawl back over her, inadvertently the head of my cock nudges her entrance, and we both still.

Her expression pleads even before she does. "I'm begging you, Nick."

I push into her tight pussy, just the tip. Holding back is probably torturing me more than her. I keep it up, giving her just enough to have her climbing toward an orgasm but not enough to get there.

"Nicholas Galaxy!" She screams my name more like a threat than a beg, but it gets my attention.

"There you go, Red." I drive into her.

"Really? Your name was the magic word?" She starts to laugh, but when I push fully inside her, the sound is lost to a whimper.

"Needed to make sure you knew which hockey player you were fucking."

I find her mouth and communicate all the things I want to say but don't through kisses that feel soul deep. She keeps begging. "More." "Harder." And again, "Nicholas Galaxy."

I never want to stop. My heart is in my throat, and my pulse pounds in my ears. We come together in a scream of words and moans that make little sense.

She clings on to me as we catch our breath. I bury my head in the nape of her neck, and I breathe her in, promising myself I'll remember all of it.

By the time we pull apart, I'm wrung out physically and emotionally. And judging by Ruby's heavy lids, I'd say she is too.

I get up and go to the bathroom, then come back with a washcloth to clean her up. When I'm done, I untie her hands and throw Trav's jersey in the direction of her suitcase. I probably just guaranteed she'll wear it again, if only to get a reaction. That's fine. I'd gladly fuck her wearing every single one of my teammates' jerseys to get the message across. She belongs with me.

I leave her once more, this time to grab something I left in the kitchen. When I reenter the room, she's sitting up. Her cheeks are flushed and lips puffy. I toss it into her lap, and she holds up the jersey I brought with me in front of her. Mine.

"Maybe next time I should tie you up." She tries for a smirk, but the sadness in her expression doesn't quite allow for it.

If there's a next time, she can have whatever she wants.

Chapter Thirty-One

RUBY

"What a mess," I mutter under my breath.

The room. Me. *Everything.*

My sister is on her way over to our parents' house to help me pack before the convention, and it looks like my closet exploded. I could make some parallel to my heart having also exploded, but I think shredded is a better description for the way I've felt since leaving Moonshot.

"Aunt Ruby!" Greer yells as she runs through the living room to my open bedroom door. She has a brownie in one hand that she holds out to me.

"For me?"

She nods. "Gigi made them."

"Thank you." I hug her to me as I take a bite and groan. My parents might be the chefs in the family, but my grandma Gloria makes the best brownies.

Greer giggles as I take another giant bite, moaning and throwing myself back onto the bed with great exaggeration. It really is that good.

Olivia walks in and her eyes widen. "Wow. It's worse than I thought."

I sit up and look around me. My sister is glowing with her cute baby bump, even through the distressed expression currently on her face as she takes in the state of my room. Then, she looks to the TV.

"Are you watching SportsCenter?!"

I search around for the remote, which is likely buried somewhere under my clothes. "I turned on the TV, and that's what was on."

She cocks one brow, silently calling me on my bullshit.

"Shut up." I toss the first thing I grab, a bra.

She catches it, then holds the lacy red material up in front of her. "Pretty. Sadly, this won't fit me."

She tosses it back on the bed and then looks at the mess again. Her cheeks puff, and she lets out a slow breath. "Are you planning to take every piece of clothing you own?"

"No." I laugh lightly. "I did laundry when I got back, and I haven't put it away yet."

She reaches for Nick's jersey. That article of clothing hasn't been washed. I may or may not have been sleeping in it nonstop. I know it's not possible after days of being home, but I swear I can still smell him on it.

"I think you should wear this. Pair it with some cute sneakers, and then you're good to go. You're the new sporty Ruby Madison."

I swipe it back from her and hold it protectively to my chest.

"Have you heard from him?" she asks, clearing a spot on the bed and sitting.

"Can I go help Grandma and Grandpa in the garden?" Greer asks before I can answer Olivia.

"Yeah. Go ahead," Liv tells her. "But no more brownies."

Her little face is crestfallen for only a moment before she shrugs and rushes off.

When she's gone, Olivia starts to fold and organize the clothes around her.

I move the suitcase over and sit on the other side. My sister looks up, as I say, "Yeah. We've been texting."

Her mouth quirks up at the corners. "And?"

"And . . . that's it." It's hard to look her in the eyes. I resist squirming as discomfort vibrates through my body. I have felt every emotion possible this week. Sad. Grateful. Happy. Nervous. Excited. Scared.

So many things are happening. Molly has emailed no less than a dozen times with more meeting invites and schedule updates for the convention. The pitch I wrote for my new book hasn't even gone out on submission officially, and we have two publishers interested in making an offer. It's all the things I was so eager for just months ago, and now . . . it feels hollow. Like maybe for the first time, I'm realizing that it's not enough. The job, the career, all of it. I want it, but it's no longer the only thing I want.

"December is so far away." It's only been a few days. How am I going to make it that long without seeing him?

"Any chance you can see him before then?"

"Maybe. Once the tour dates are confirmed, we're going to compare schedules."

She looks hopeful, and I want to feel that too, but I get the feeling he's purposely holding back. Maybe he's just being realistic about the possibility of a future between us. As in, it isn't much of one if we only see each other twice a year.

It sucks. I miss him so much.

"Can I tell you something and you won't think I'm dumb or naïve?" I ask her, finally glancing up.

"I would never," she says, sounding personally affronted at the insinuation.

My heart squeezes. She's right. Not once has she been unsupportive of even my wildest dreams. Even as kids, she would act so excited every time I let her read something I'd written. I don't know if it was genuine or not, but it didn't matter—it inspired me to keep going.

"I thought he might ask me to stay. I know it's new and logistically it's messy. We live in different states, and he's got a lot with his job and his kid, plus caring for his dad . . . He can't change the fabric of his life for me."

"You'd have to be the one to make the jump?" she asks, nodding like she already knows that's true. "Would you have stayed if he asked?"

"I don't know." It's a question I've asked myself at least a thousand times. It would be a lot to give up. I like living close to my family. I love that I'm able to watch Greer grow up and be part of her daily life. I'm close with my grandparents, who I know won't be around forever. If I were ever to get married and have my own kids, I'd want them to have my family around too.

"You still wish he would have asked though, right?"

"Yeah." I feel bad even admitting it. "Is that selfish?"

"No, it's human."

"Sometimes being human really sucks."

She laughs, shoulders shaking with the boisterous noise that loosens something in my chest. Admitting it out loud and having her reassurance does make me feel better.

"Ooh." She winces and presses a hand to the middle of her stomach.

"What?" I ask, concern taking hold of me. "Is everything okay?"

"Yeah. The baby either loves or hates it when I laugh. She's kicking the crap out of me."

A smile spreads across my face. "Can I feel?"

She nods and moves closer. When I stretch out my hand to her bump, she guides it to the correct spot, and then we wait in silence until the baby kicks again.

"That's so weird and cool at the same time," I tell my sister.

"It really is."

"Hi, baby girl," I croon to my niece. "I'm your aunt Ruby, and I can't wait to meet you so I can spoil the shit out of you."

Olivia laughs lightly, and the baby kicks a little harder.

"You're right. Loves or hates it," I say.

When I finally move my hand away, I look up at my sister filled with awe. "You're remarkable."

"Me?" She laughs then winces and rubs her belly again.

"Yeah. You've created this beautiful family. You're badass at your job, and you still have time to show up for me and help me organize my life." I wave a hand around the messy bed. "I'm supposed to be the older, wiser sister, but you are continually showing me the kind of person I want to be."

Her eyes widen, then fill with tears, then she smiles and another small laugh escapes. "Oh my god, stop it. You're making me cry."

She wipes at the tears falling from her lashes.

"Sorry." I smile back.

She waves a hand in front of her face. "Stupid pregnancy hormones."

I pick up a dress from the clean laundry pile. I wore it the last night Nick and I went out on the boat. I wonder what he's doing right now. Probably at home, listening to Aidan practice guitar and pretending to be annoyed with his dad.

"Okay." Olivia swipes at a few more tears and then looks back at the suitcase with determination etched into her features. "Let's tackle this mess before I run out of energy. I swear by eight o'clock every night I'm so tired I can't function."

For the next thirty minutes we work in companionable silence. Olivia folds everything and puts them into piles, and I pick out what I want to take to the convention and put the rest away in the dresser I'm using while crashing at my parents' house.

"Last item." Olivia hands me Nick's jersey.

"Wow. You're good."

"We're a great team. I'm organization and purpose. You're chaos and creativity."

I snicker.

"What time do you leave tomorrow?"

"My flight is at eight."

"Oof."

"Yeah. Molly has a full day of meetings scheduled for us."

"I wish I could be there to watch you be a rock star."

"Me too."

"Are you nervous about seeing *Matthew*?" Ever since we broke up, she's refused to call him Matt like she had before.

"Not nervous as much as dreading it."

"I'd love to have a few words with him." Her gaze narrows and she glares as if picturing him. My sister is sweet as can be ninety-nine percent of the time, but she is not afraid to throw down for the people she loves.

"Will Lily be there?"

"No."

"I hate that you'll be alone when you face him. I could send Flynn."

A real honest laugh bubbles up in my chest and spills out. "I would love to see Flynn take out Matt."

"No contest, right? Flynn would destroy him." Her eyes light up.

"I appreciate you offering up your tall, muscular husband, but I'll have to face him on my own eventually."

"We've always got your back."

"I know."

"That goes for everything," she says, nodding toward the jersey still in my hands. "No matter where you live or how fucking much I'd miss you if I couldn't see you every day, I'll always be there for you."

"I know."

"Do you?"

"I do." I nod. But that just makes it all that much harder to think about leaving.

"We'd all come visit you, and we could video chat every morning. Maybe we could take up letter writing like the old days."

I huff another quiet laugh.

"My point is you should follow your heart. Wherever that leads you."

What if my heart is in two places?

"Okay." She stands and holds her arms out. "Give me a hug. The next time you see me, I might be too big for you to wrap your arms around me."

I toss Nick's jersey back on the bed with every intention of sleeping in it again tonight.

"I love you," I say as I hug her tight. "Thank you for being the best sister ever."

"Right back at you."

When my flight arrives in Denver, Molly is waiting for me at baggage claim.

"Hi!" She hugs me then takes my backpack from me. "Ooh. What do you have in here?"

I almost tell her a dismembered head.

"I couldn't decide which shoes to bring," I admit instead.

"Comfortable ones." She hikes the bag to her shoulder. "I've booked three more meetings for you since you got on the plane. Anna Vohn with Lawrence Publishing and . . ."

My eye catches on a TV screen inside one of the many airport restaurants as we walk the corridor to exit. I've watched more sports news in the past week than my entire life, so I instantly recognize the sports news channel and the three men sitting around a large, curved desk. At the top of the screen are headshots of several Moonshot hockey players. My gaze locks on Nick immediately. His dark hair and the scowl that I used to think was his default expression.

I pause long enough that Molly power walks ahead, still talking a mile a minute. She finally realizes I'm no longer beside her when she reaches the sliding doors to the exit. She hurries back to me, gaze flicking to the screen.

"Ah, the hockey player," she says. "Did he convert you into a sports fan?"

"Maybe not a fan, but an appreciator."

"And of him?"

"Definitely a fan."

She grins. "Can't blame you. He is cuuute. Nice?"

"Yeah."

"Single?"

My cheeks heat. "Yes."

Unfortunately, and as much as I wish I could tell her he isn't single because he's mine, he isn't. I don't know if he ever was, technically speaking, but I know I wanted him to be. I still do.

"Maybe for your next book we can send you to Paris or Italy. How do you feel about soccer?"

"Clueless."

"Which is why you'll need to interview an expert. Say the word, and I'll make a few calls."

I have no doubt she would. "I don't think I can handle learning another sport yet."

I want to live in my hockey era a bit longer. And my Nick era. I wonder what he'd say if I suggested stopping by for a quick visit after the convention. It's been less than a week, but if he misses me even a fraction as much as I miss him, then I think he'll be on board. And if he isn't, then I guess that's my answer on whether or not this will truly work.

His photo flicks off the screen, and Molly and I begin walking again. I'm excited to look for flights later and text him to make sure it's okay. My lips curve. Kick ass at this convention, and then I can go see him.

Almost like he knew I was thinking about him, my phone pings with a text from him. It's a picture taken on the ice, and he follows it up with another message.

Nick: Wish you were here.

Me: Just landed in Denver. Wish I were there too. X

"Everything good?" Molly asks.

"Yeah. Sorry." I pocket my phone, feeling more certain about making a little detour after the convention. I didn't imagine it this summer. I know it. He felt it too.

I let out a breath. "So who am I meeting with today?"

Her smile widens. "You're booked solid, girl. Everyone wants to talk to you, and they are so excited about the book."

I nod, feeling the first strums of genuine excitement. "All right. Tell me when, where, and what to say."

She laughs again. "I'm one step ahead of you. Check your email."

No doubt, I already have one waiting from her with a detailed agenda.

"You're good," I tell her.

"I know." She purses her lips and lifts one shoulder. "Now, let's go. We've got to haul ass to get back to the hotel for your dinner meeting."

* * *

For the next twelve hours, I do nothing but eat, sleep, and talk about the book. Molly whisks me off to meeting after meeting, keeping me fueled with caffeine and sugar.

The excitement for the book is more than I ever could have dreamed. When I'm at my best I soak up their praise and allow myself to feel proud and happy. At my worst, it all makes me think of Nick and miss him so much it hurts. None of this would have happened without him, and I know he'd get such a kick out of it all.

On Thursday night, one of the event sponsors hosts a cocktail party. As I'm walking through the lobby, readers are starting to arrive. The convention kicks off tomorrow and goes through the weekend. The hotel staff are putting up the banners and signage for the event.

Tomorrow, thousands of people will be here. Book lovers from all over the world. The first time I came to one of these conventions, I was blown away. Ten-year-old me who loved books and writing and had very few friends who shared my hobby couldn't have dreamed up this life.

The hotel is massive with so many different areas that it's easy to get turned around. Luckily there's plenty of signage pointing toward the conference area. Event posters, balloons, and publisher marketing banners cover the windows and walls. Seeing the cover of my book on the elevator doors is surreal in the best way. I snap a picture and text it to Olivia.

The noise of the party travels from the large banquet room to the bottom of the escalator. My nerves kick up a notch with every step closer.

As soon as I'm inside, I scan the room searching for Molly. I find her in what looks like a deep conversation with an editor from Lawrence Publishing.

I make my way to the bar and order a Corona because it reminds me of Nick. Once I have my drink in hand, I circle slowly around the room. I smile at industry people I recognize and say hello to other authors that I haven't seen since the last event I attended.

I'm only starting to relax when I spot him. Matt stands in a circle of at least ten people. He has that air about him, charming arrogance that comes off as magnetic until you get to know him. He's personable and well-spoken. And in a room filled with introverts, he carries conversations and enjoys being the center of attention.

Our gazes meet briefly. I have no intention of stopping to say hello, but another author calls out to me.

Leah Amaretti writes gothic romance. We shared an editor at my first publisher, and she is always lovely when I see her at events.

"Hi," I say, stepping closer to her but still avoiding Matt.

"I heard you were coming, but I didn't want to believe it." She's tall and fit, and when she hugs me it reminds me of Travis's bone-crushing squeezes. "I missed you last year. Where've you been?"

"Writing," I say with a smile as she pulls back.

"I heard you wrote a sports romance?" Kenna, another author I've met a handful of times, asks with a smile that is filled with surprise.

Slowly the whole circle opens and readjusts to let me in.

"I did. Yeah." I take a sip of my drink. My cheeks feel hot as I feel Matt's gaze on me. Looking at him feels like giving him the satisfaction of feeling important, but ignoring him also feels like I'm allowing him too much power over me.

"I love hockey," Kenna says. "I had no idea you were sporty."

"Me either," Matt says. "New hobby?"

I flick my stare slowly to his. To everyone else I'm sure that his smile looks friendly, but I know better.

"Something like that."

"I overheard Molly say you spent the summer interviewing a professional hockey player?" The statement comes out like a question as Leah's eyes light up awaiting my answer.

"That's right."

"Which one?" she asks at the same time Matt snorts and says, "Those guys barely have enough brain cells left after a career of being knocked around all the time."

I happen to know that Matt has a sore spot when it comes to athletes. He was cut from his high school football team, and he's been holding a grudge against jocks ever since. I open my mouth to defend Nick and every other player I met this summer, but before I can, a server steps up beside me.

"Cookie?" She holds out a tray filled with a variety of options. Chocolate chip, sugar, and one M&M cookie.

I take it, smiling so hard that I lose track of the conversation, and the anger I was feeling dissipates.

"Ruby?" Matt says my name.

"Sorry." I blink a few times and refocus on him.

His expression is smug masked as polite amusement. "I asked if you heard the news about *Becoming Alaric* getting picked up by Gradient Pictures?"

"Yeah, I think I saw that somewhere. Congratulations."

The smile on his face falters, almost like he hoped I wouldn't be so generous in my praise. He wants me to be pissed off or sad, anything other than detached. That way, he's won. Not only did he steal my book idea, but he did so with wild success. I can't change that, but I don't have to stand here and let him see how it broke me. Past tense. I'm all put together now. Or ninety-nine percent anyway. Maybe that kind of break never fully heals, but it's no longer keeping me from moving forward.

"Excuse me," I say to the rest of the circle. "I'm going to mingle."

I only get two steps away when I pull out my phone and snap a picture of the cookie and send it to Nick. Our communication has become a series of pictures, cataloging our days, and a hundred unique variations that all say how much we miss each other.

He calls as I'm heading back up to my room.

"Hi!" I answer, already smiling before I hear his voice.

"Hey, Red."

My eyes close, and my grin widens.

"You there?"

"Yeah. Sorry. How are you?"

"Good. Just sitting on the back deck enjoying the sunset."

I can picture him, feet kicked up, leaning back, and staring out at the water.

"That sounds nice. How was Aidan's first day of school?"

"Good. He likes his teacher, and Abigail is in his class."

"Who's Abigail?"

"She's the Ruby Madison of fifth grade."

"Is that a compliment?" I ask with a laugh.

"You know what I mean. She's cute and cool and way out of his league—according to him."

"You think I'm out of your league?"

"I know it."

It isn't true, but I soak up his words anyway. "At the risk of sounding like a broken record, I really miss you."

"I know. I keep looking over at the cabin expecting to see you sitting on the porch or walking down by the lake. How's the convention?"

"It hasn't really started yet. Today was filled with meetings and then a cocktail party."

"Ooh fancy. What are you wearing?"

I glance down at my dress. "Your jersey and a pair of heels."

He groans. "I know you're fucking with me, but I don't even care."

"I'll send you a picture later to prove it."

"I look forward to that."

In the background, Aidan says something I can't quite make out, and Nick says quietly, away from the phone, "I'll be right there."

When he speaks to me again, he says, "I gotta go learn fifth grade math."

"Ewww."

"Yeah." He chuckles.

"Okay, well, I'll text you tomorrow. You have the team barbeque?"

"Yeah. What time does the convention start?"

"Molly has me scheduled first thing in the morning for coffee with one of the editors interested in the new book."

"That's great. We're all rooting for you. Not that you need it, but good luck."

"Thank you."

"All right. Well . . ." He pauses like he doesn't want to hang up or there's more he wants to say.

"Yeah," I say because I know the feeling.

"Talk to you tomorrow."

"Okay."

"K. Forcing myself to hang up now, but don't forget to send me that picture, Red."

Chapter Thirty-Two

NICK

"Galaxy!" Eli Briggs holds both of his big, beefy arms out to his side when I walk into our general manager's house for our annual team kick-off barbeque.

"Hey." A smile tugs at my lips as I approach him. I hold out a hand, and he takes it in his, then pulls me into him and slaps me on the back with his free hand.

"How was your summer?" he asks.

"Good," I say, then realize I mean it. My brows pinch together.

"That bad, huh?" He mistakes my surprised expression and grins, then gives his head a shake. "I figured you were dying to get back out there. Did you take any time at all for yourself this summer?"

"I did, actually."

"Yeah?" he asks, seemingly surprised. "Good for you."

"How about you?"

"Ah, man, it was great. We took the kids on a little RV road trip through Yellowstone National Park and then headed west to visit my family in Washington." The smile he wears is so happy and genuine. He's one of the more senior guys on the team. Came in as a rookie and has now spent his entire career here. He has a little girl a year younger than Aidan and a boy that just turned four.

"Sounds fun."

"It was, for sure. How's Aidan? Is he in fifth grade this year?"

"Yeah. Somehow."

"Goes fast." Briggs gives me a reassuring grin. "Mary is in fourth, and EJ started preschool. They're so damn cute at that age. His back-pack is bigger than him."

My chest lifts with a laugh as I picture Aidan at that age. Damn. It feels like just yesterday.

When our laughter dies off, his expression takes a serious edge. "How's your dad?"

"Good. He's doing good. Thanks."

"I'm glad to hear it." Briggs's dad had a scary bout with cancer last year, and he's made it a point to check in with me a lot ever since my dad's heart attack. He knows what it's like to care for a parent, maybe better than any of my other friends.

"Yeah, thanks, I appreciate you being there for me."

"Of course. If there's anything you need, let me know."

As appreciative as I am of the offer, the reminder of my dad's health has anxious energy strumming through me. He does seem better, but no matter how good he's doing, I can't help but worry about the future. Picturing a world without him plain sucks.

"Did you and Trav get out on the ice a lot?" Briggs asks, and I'm happy for the change of topic.

"Did I hear my name?" Trav steps up to join us. He hands me a beer, then grins at Briggs. "How've you been, Briggsy? I missed you this summer. And your wife. Is she here?"

"She's home with *our* kids."

Trav's smile doesn't falter. "So you're saying there's still a chance for me?"

"I see you haven't changed a bit," Briggs says to him.

"Never." Trav smiles with all his teeth bared. "But you know who has had a *transformative* summer?"

Slowly his gaze slides to me with his smirk firmly in place.

"Oh yeah?" Briggs looks at me with renewed interest. "I feel like you left out some important details in our catch-up."

Before I can answer, Trav does it for me. "He met a girl."

Briggs's brows shoot up.

I pop open the beer and take a sip. "I'm going to pretend not to be insulted by the shocked look on your face."

"I'm sorry." He schools his expression. "But you haven't dated anyone seriously the entire time I've known you."

"Ruby's different," Trav adds in an almost taunting voice.

"Okay. Enough out of you," I tell him.

"Ruby, huh?" Briggs doesn't miss a beat.

Looks like I'm having this conversation. I shoot a glare at my best friend, then nod. "Yeah."

"Is she here? I'd love to meet her."

"No, she lives in Arizona. She was only here for the summer."

"Ah, bummer. Maybe I can meet her the next time she's in town."

I'm grateful that Travis doesn't pepper in more fun facts because the few words I've said already have me feeling unsettled. Look, I'd love to shout about her from the rooftops, tell everyone about her and how fucking great she is, let them and her know how goddamn in love with her I am. But I can't tell them before I tell her.

"Yeah, maybe," I say.

For the rest of the day, I catch up with my teammates that were gone for the summer, chat with the coaches. It's a bittersweet feeling this year that I haven't felt before. Usually this get-together signals the start of the season and with it an anticipation. I feel all that, but it's dulled by something else.

Ruby's gone. Six days. Six really fucking awful days. How the hell did she become so crucial to my happiness in that time?

A quiet voice in my head reminds me that maybe I wasn't all that happy before she came. Ruby brought disruption to my carefully scheduled life. Disruption, chaos, and sunshine. And instead of going back to that guy I was before she came, I want to hold on to it.

I notice, more than once, Travis staring at me throughout the day like he's waiting for some sort of reaction out of me.

By the time I get home, I'm exhausted and ready to sit in my own Ruby-centered thoughts. I grab a beer from the fridge and flip through today's mail on the kitchen counter. It's mostly junk, but at the bottom of the pile is a large manila envelope addressed to me.

I push everything else aside and pick it up. I recognize Ruby's handwriting even before I see her name in the left-hand corner.

My pulse picks up as I flip it over and rip it open. I pull out a heavy stack of papers. A yellow Post-it note is stuck to the first page.

Nick,

Thanks for being my inspiration and my muse. If you hate the ending, then just tell me the package must have gotten lost in the mail.

xo,

Ruby

Smiling, I flip the page. *To my favorite grumpy hockey player.* I can already hear Trav giving me so much shit, but I can't stop smiling.

With the book and my beer in hand, I head out to the back patio to read it. Instead of skipping to the end, I start over. It's just as good as I remember. Her wit and personality is woven into the story so much that I can almost hear her telling it like she was next to me, eyes lit up and smile wide, hands waving around.

My fingers go to the clover charm around my neck. I've grown accustomed to the weight of it against my chest, like a tactile reminder that she was here.

Eventually Aidan comes outside with his guitar and sits on the other side of the deck, playing as I keep reading. Dad peeks out on us as the sun sets, then flips on the outdoor lights. I thank him, then go right back to reading.

I can't turn the pages fast enough. And when I do finally come to the place I'd left off before, I'm amazed all over that anyone can come up with a story out of nothing like this.

After I read the last line, I sit there in stunned awe. All the sadness I've been keeping at bay this past week hits me hard. She's fucking gone, and I should have told her I loved her or asked her to stay an extra day or a week or forever.

"Did you finish?" Aidan asks.

I blink away the haze and look over at him. "Yeah."

I set the pages down on the table in front of me, gaze catching on her handwritten note again.

"Was it good?"

"Yeah, it was really good." I nod.

"Figured," he says.

I huff a small laugh. "You did, huh?"

He shrugs. "Ruby's smart."

"That she is," I agree.

"You miss her, don't you?" he asks.

The question knocks the wind out of me. I've tried my best to show up for him the best I could this week despite the way I was feeling, but I guess that tells me how well I pulled it off.

I nod.

"Me too." He looks down at his guitar.

Fuck. All this time I was wallowing alone, not thinking about how he might be feeling. I cross over to him and pull him into a hug as I sit next to him.

"I'm sorry. Of course you do. I know she misses you too."

"She's coming back though, right?"

"I'm not sure," I tell him honestly. A lot could happen between now and December. "Maybe."

His brows pinch together. "But if she's your girlfriend, shouldn't you guys live in the same place or at least visit regularly?"

"My girlfriend?"

The look he gives me is a mixture of annoyance and mistrust. "Come on, Dad, I saw you kissing at the ice rink and at her going-away party. Plus, you were always making googly eyes at her."

"Googly eyes?" I bark out a laugh.

His smile lifts on one side as he nods. "*All* the time."

I ruffle his hair. "Googly eyes." I laugh again. "I probably was."

A tinge of guilt seeps in as I think about how long he knew without me talking to him.

"I'm sorry I didn't tell you. You should have heard that from me instead of finding out the way you did. I haven't dated in a long time. I wasn't sure how you'd feel, and you're my number one. No matter what. You know that, right?"

He nods.

"Okay. Good." I settle my arm around the back of his shoulders.

"It's cool if you date or whatever. Grandpa has already talked to me about the birds and the bees." He groans and makes a face that tells me how much he disliked that conversation.

"Oh god, not the birds and the bees. Did he actually call it that?"

Aidan's wide-eyed, disgusted face remains.

"I got the same talk when I was your age," I tell him. "You'd think he would have come up with something better by now."

"Heading in early?" Dad asks as I come downstairs the next morning. He's standing in the kitchen with a coffee mug in his hand. "I figured you'd be sleeping in today."

"I'm meeting with the team psychologist before camp."

His carefree expression shifts quickly. "Everything all right?"

"Yeah," I say immediately, then hesitate before admitting, "I've been struggling a little to get my head right, and I want to make sure I'm set before the season starts."

Dad sits at the dining room table, an open invitation for me to do the same. "This about your shoulder? Are you worried about going back out there and getting hurt again?"

"I am, a little," I admit. "But no. That isn't all of it."

His puzzled expression remains. "What's been on your mind?"

"You, Pop."

"Me?" His brows lift as he flashes me what appears to be a genuinely shocked look. Slowly, though, he seems to unlock the puzzle of my worries. "I'm okay. The doctor cleared the blockage, and my last test results looked great."

"I know, but . . ."

He's patient as I figure out how to get my head around my own feelings. "I think it brought up a lot of old wounds. Mom died so young, and as I get closer to her age, I can't help but think about things."

"Think about what?"

I let out a breath. "What would happen if you weren't around to meddle in my business all the time." I go for lighthearted, but my throat is thick with emotion anyway.

A sympathetic smile spreads across his face. "I'm fine, son. Truly. I want to be around too."

"I know. That's the thing. *I know.* I shouldn't be spending so much time worrying about the future instead of living now, but I can't help it. It's like my brain won't switch off from panic mode."

"You've been through a lot and seen more tragedy than most your age. I hadn't thought about what that might be like for you."

"When Mom died it was awful, but I was too young to fully understand what the rest of my life without her was going to look like. I know exactly how fucking awful it would be to lose you."

"I'm stubborn." Dad reaches across the table and squeezes my hand. "I'm not going anywhere."

"Good."

Admitting it to him eases a little of the tension I've been carrying. "You drive me to the brink of insanity sometimes, but I like having you around."

"At some point we all realize we aren't immortal, and neither are the people around us. I remember realizing that too."

"You do?"

"Yeah. When I turned forty and pulled a muscle sneezing."

"Something to look forward to," I joke.

"I'm glad you're talking to someone. You're right, you shouldn't spend all your time worrying about things you can't control."

"How do you do it?" I ask him. He lost a wife, and he's dealing with his health stuff too.

"I don't know. Maybe it's the wisdom that comes with age or maybe you just accept things easier as you get older. If I've learned anything, it's that you can't make a game plan for every scenario. There are too many twists and turns to track. You want assurances that everything is going to be okay, but it doesn't work that way, and how heartbreaking would it be if you could see it play out anyway? I don't regret a day I got to spend with your mother. Do I wish we'd had thirty years more? Of course. I bet you feel the same way."

"I wish she could see Aidan and that he had gotten to know her."

"Me too. She would have spoiled him rotten," Dad says.

"Kind of like you do?"

"Someone has to." He grins, then his mouth falls into a serious expression. "You're a good man. A good dad. A good son. I'm sorry you've been struggling. We all do from time to time. You're doing the right thing by reaching out to someone who can help. And I'm here if you ever need anything too. I don't pretend to have it all figured out, but I can listen."

"Thanks."

"And for what it's worth, I've done my share of projecting my feelings and fears in maybe less than productive ways."

I run his cryptic words through twice, but still can't make sense of them. "What do you mean?"

"Over the past few years, I've thought about it too—what it'll be like for you when I'm gone. I want you to have someone in your life. You deserve that."

"The constant matchmaking," I say as I finally understand his meaning.

He nods. "Losing your mom was tough, but I felt some solace knowing I was here to help you navigate hockey and school, then becoming a dad. I'm so proud of the man you are, but the things you've been through made you put up a wall too. You've let few people in outside of your family and teammates. And I guess I selfishly thought if you had someone like I had your mother, then life would be easier when that time comes for me."

It's a simple answer to his behavior that I never considered.

"I don't think anything is going to make that easier, but I get it. I don't like it, but I see your point."

His grin pulls up on one side. "They weren't all bad."

I hum my reluctant agreement. No, they certainly weren't.

"Have you talked to her?"

I don't have to guess who he's talking about.

"Yeah, we've been texting."

"But?"

"There's no but."

"Of course there is. If there weren't, you wouldn't be moping around here without her."

He's not wrong.

"You're scared that you'll let her all the way in and then she'll leave anyway."

As soon as he says the words, I know they're true, so I don't bother denying it. I'm not sure if I'm more afraid of asking her to be mine, and her saying no or her saying yes, and then it ultimately not working out.

"You can't predict the future, but you can fight like hell to make the here and now everything you want. And I think what you want is in Arizona."

Technically, she's in Colorado for the convention, but I get his point.

Aidan comes down the stairs with his dark hair sticking in every direction and smelling like body spray—a new development this year.

Dad's face tells me he smells it too.

"Morning," I say as he comes into the kitchen area. He goes straight to the fridge for the milk. Then pulls out a bowl and a box of Frosted Flakes. He makes a massive serving of the sugary cereal before bringing it over to the table.

The smell is almost enough to knock me out of my chair.

"New scent?" I ask him. He went shopping with his mom before school started, but I don't think she expected him to wear the entire bottle.

He bobs his head as he spoons a huge bite into his mouth.

"Well, I better get ready. I'm taking you to practice this morning," Dad tells Aidan.

"Okay," he replies.

"Thanks," I say to my dad.

"It's a nice morning. We'll put the windows down and enjoy a little fresh air."

I hold back a laugh. "Good idea. I'll open a few windows in here too."

Chapter Thirty-Three

RUBY

By the second day of the convention, I'm exhausted but in the best way. Yesterday I signed books until my hand ached and my face hurt from smiling. There is truly nothing better than chatting with readers. I love fangirling with them over our shared favorites. After all, I was a reader before I was an author.

As soon as I leave my room, I'm plucked back into the chaos. People are already out with their carts and wagons filled with books they brought from home to be signed. They're armed with iced beverages and water bottles and wear comfortable shoes and shirts that proudly proclaim their love of books and devotion to particular fandoms.

Molly greets me at the elevator with a coffee.

"Good morning," she chirps with a cheery smile as she extends the cup toward me. "How'd you sleep?"

"Not great," I say as I eagerly take the coffee. My voice is slightly hoarse from all the talking I did yesterday. "Thanks for this."

"Everything okay?" Molly asks, always ready to problem-solve.

"The girls in the room next to me were laughing and talking until late into the night. And maybe jumping on the bed? It was hard to tell, but they were having a great time."

"I'll talk to the front desk about switching your room. There's a cheerleading camp here this week too. You must be next to one of their groups."

"No. I'm fine." I stop her before she pencils in her to-do list to demand a new room in this sold-out hotel. I'd say it's impossible, but nothing is with Molly. "I haven't been sleeping that great lately anyway, and I have earplugs if it comes to that."

Molly doesn't look convinced, but she must decide we have bigger things to discuss. "Okay, well, keep me posted. I need you rested."

"One more day. I'll survive." Today is the last day of the convention. Tomorrow I'm having breakfast with Molly and Doreen to talk about promotional details for my upcoming release, but after that it'll all be over. And I'll be free to do whatever I want, which in this case is to go see Nick. I found a few flights, but I can't decide if it's better to run it by him or show up unannounced.

"Panels this morning, right?" I ask after taking another sip of coffee. I already feel better.

"Yes." A hint of unease flickers in her expression.

"What's that look?"

"They made a last-minute adjustment to the author lineup on your panel."

It takes no time at all for me to read between the lines. There's only one person at this entire event that I'd be unhappy about sitting next to. "Matt?"

I successfully avoided him all day yesterday, and it was glorious.

Her mouth falls into a sympathetic smile. She doesn't know that *Becoming Alaric* was my idea, but she does know that we dated, and that it didn't end well. "We could pull you. I can tell them you are feeling under the weather or had a conflict in your schedule."

"No." I'm touched by the lengths she's willing to go to protect me. "Thank you, but no. I'll be all right."

After a small hesitation, as if she's giving me time to reconsider, she nods. "Okay."

We walk through the massive hotel to the conference area and down another long hallway to find the room for the panel.

I peek inside. The chairs are already filled with readers, and several of the authors are seated on the stage up front. Including Matt. He stands, instead of sitting, almost like he just can't help himself and needs everyone to have a view of his perfectly polished, fake as hell, smile.

"Ready?" Molly asks.

I let out a slow, steadying breath. "As I'll ever be."

I look around for a trashcan to toss my coffee. Molly takes it and then hands me a mint and ChapStick.

"What would I do without you?" I take both items, slip the mint in my mouth, and pocket the ChapStick for later.

"Have dry lips and coffee breath." She beams. "Good luck."

"Do I need luck?" I ask, too late. She's already hurrying off, probably to add more meetings to my schedule.

I make my way along the side of the room to the front and then up the steps to join the other authors. Kenna is at the end of the table.

"Hey, Ruby," she says.

"Morning." I take the seat beside her, putting several people between me and Matt. I can't avoid him completely, but at least I don't have to sit next to him.

A few minutes later, the event coordinator gives the panel moderator the thumbs-up to begin. There are five authors across different genres. We start off by introducing ourselves and then answering a few preplanned questions. Once it's opened to the audience, the questions are directed more at individual authors than the group.

To no one's surprise, Matt is in the spotlight. Women love him, but men too. He has a mass appeal that I used to admire. Now I realize it's all a show.

I get a few questions too. One reader wants to know if a side character from my first book is getting a story, and another reader asks me if I've ever considered writing a rugby romance. Molly sits in the back, smiling at me and silently encouraging me to speak more than five words to answer each question. The spotlight is not where I shine, but hopefully my appreciation and love for my readers and this community comes through.

"This one is for Matthew." A woman holds the microphone up to her mouth, hiding a shy smile. "How did you come up with the idea for *Becoming Alaric*? It's such a unique concept."

For the first time since I sat down, I look right at Matt. There's absolutely no trace of discomfort or guilt on his face as he leans forward to speak into the mic in front of him.

"That's a great question," he says, grinning back at her.

What a fucking asshole.

"To be honest, I don't remember exactly how it came to me."

Like hell he doesn't remember because I sure do. I can see him so vividly, sitting across from me and picking up my notebook.

"What's this?" he asked as he flipped through the pages.

I'd been embarrassed to let him read it at the time. We'd only been dating a short time, and my idea notebook was sacred to me. I felt vulnerable sharing it with anyone. What if he thought my concepts were dumb or silly?

He'd said nothing when he'd finished reading it. Not a single thing. We never spoke about it again, and I'd all but forgotten about it until

I saw his book deal announcement for a "vampire rom-com." Still, I thought it must be a coincidence until I read the blurb. He didn't even bother changing the names of the characters.

A cold sweat forms at the back of my neck, and my foot bounces under the table.

"Ideas come to me from lots of places. Conversations with friends, things I overhear as I'm traveling, dreams, and news headlines."

The woman who asked the question looks disappointed by his answer but nods politely as she hands off the microphone to one of the event assistants.

"I can tell you that the inspiration for Autumn is based on an ex-girlfriend." He holds a finger up to his lips like it's a secret, and the audience giggles. Autumn is the hero's girlfriend at the beginning of the book. She was his addition, and though I haven't read it, I already knew, based on reviews and everything Lily had told me, that he was taking another jab at me. Autumn is a redhead who is so clumsy she falls down a manhole and is killed off in chapter three before the hero meets the heroine of the story.

My cheeks burn.

"Okay, I think that's all the time we have," the moderator announces.

I'm already getting to my feet when a familiar deep voice booms from somewhere in the back of the room.

"I have a question," he says.

People swivel to look from him to the moderator to see if she's going to allow it, but Nick doesn't wait for her go-ahead.

"This one is for Ruby Madison." The way he says my name makes my stomach flutter.

My legs wobble as I take my seat again.

"In your upcoming novel, you dedicate it to your favorite grumpy hockey player."

"Is that your question?" I ask him, smiling so hard I think my face might crack.

"It's a little vague. One might be confused on who you meant. Any chance you want to tell us who it is?"

"Sorry. I promised to protect his identity."

Nick's mouth pulls up on one side.

"All right, everyone." The moderator speaks more forcefully this time. "Thank you all for coming."

I hurry off the stage, but there's no getting through the mass of people between me and Nick. I push up on my toes and crane my neck to find him. I can't spot him anywhere, but then a hand wraps around my wrist, and I'm being pulled to the side.

Nick smiles as I stumble toward him. He reaches out to steady me.

I stare at him, a little stunned, before throwing myself into his arms. It's only when his arms wrap around my back and crush me to him that I truly believe he's here.

"It's really you," I say into the crook of his neck.

"Hey, Red." His voice rumbles in his chest.

I pull back only to look at him some more.

"You're a hard woman to get to," he says.

We're still in the middle of a packed room, and people are looking at him with curiosity and interest. Even if they don't follow hockey, he looks the part of a professional athlete in his black athletic pants and fitted T-shirt.

"I feel like I'm dreaming. What are you doing here?"

He frames my face with both hands, then gazes at me like he's refamiliarizing himself with it. "I'm so proud of you. All the people carrying your books around, dying to meet you. I took an elevator with your face on it."

A laugh slips from my lips as he brings his mouth down on mine. His beard is back, and the feel is scratchy against my face.

All the panels are letting out now, and the hallways are filled with people moving to the next event. Which means I don't have a lot of time.

"How did you get in here?" I ask him.

"I bought a ticket."

"They sold out months ago."

"Fine." His lips curve up. "I bribed a nice woman in the lobby to borrow her badge. He flips the tag attached to his neck lanyard around. It says Debbie. "I had to give her my ID in exchange so she knew I wouldn't take off with it. And I thought hockey fans were intense."

"Speaking of hockey, shouldn't you be at camp?"

"We have today off, but I have to get back tonight for a meeting."

"You came all this way for the day?" My heart squeezes.

"Hello!" Molly chirps as she pops up next to us. "You must be Nick Galaxy."

"Yes, ma'am. And you must be the wonder agent."

"That's right." Molly grins at him, then switches to business mode. "We need to get you to the signing room."

"Yeah. Okay." I glance at Nick.

"Go. I don't want to get in the way."

"Can he come with me?" I ask Molly, then to Nick I say, "I guess I should have asked you first. Do you want to come?"

"Definitely," he says quickly.

Molly thinks for a second. "Yeah. I can probably swing that. Give me five minutes to clear it and get him a badge. In the meantime, you two get to the signing room."

I take Debbie's badge from Nick. "Can you also return this? She's in the lobby."

With a nod, she reaches for the badge and then turns on her heel and power walks away.

Nick's smile slowly builds as he looks at me. "She's something."

"Right? I don't know what I'd do without her."

His hand finds mine and intertwines our fingers. All around us, people are moving and talking, but I focus on Nick. I still can't believe he's here. It's odd seeing him outside of Moonshot. We were in such a bubble this summer, and it crossed my mind once or twice since then that maybe our fling was a product of proximity and nothing else. I can easily cross that theory off now.

"I don't want to get in the way or interrupt. I just had to see you. I couldn't wait to see you again."

"Me too. I was seriously considering flying out to see you tomorrow."

"Really?" His grin is back, and though I can't see them, I know his dimples are buried under that beard.

"Yeah. I wasn't sure if you'd think it was charming or clingy."

"Hopefully my presence clears that up." He chuckles.

"Clingy, right?" I lean into him.

His head dips, and he brushes his lips against mine. When he pulls back, I can see the same emotion and questions in his expression that I've felt all week.

"We better get you to your fans." He opens up his stance.

I know he's right, but I want more time alone with him.

The signing room is a huge space with two entrances and hundreds of authors and vendors set up in booths with tables and backdrops. I'm sitting at my publisher's table with three other authors. There's a nameplate in front of my spot, and behind me is a banner for the upcoming book. I know the second Nick has seen it. He glances at me, mouth pulling up higher on one side.

"This is so cool." He walks around the table to get closer to it, then pulls out his phone and takes a selfie with it.

"Want an ARC?" I grab one off the stack and hold it up for him. "They had to rush print these for the event, but they turned out pretty good."

He takes it, then poses with it for another photo.

"I'm so fucking proud of you."

My face heats with the compliment.

"I loved the ending. It was perfect."

"You already read it?" I sent it out before I left for the conference, but I figured with hockey camp starting he'd be too busy to get to it anytime soon.

"In one sitting." He sets the book on the table and closes the distance between us. With one hand, he brushes my hair away from my face and lets his fingers linger at my neck. "It was funny and sweet. Sexy."

"I had some inspiration on that front." I beam up at him. All I want to do is kiss him and talk about what we're going to do next. When am I going to see him again? How will this work? I want him to be in my life every day instead of waiting months between weekend visits. But the other authors are coming in, and I know the doors will open soon for readers.

Nick looks around. "Where do you want me so I'm not in the way?"

Molly shows up with a badge for him, a bottle of water, and an extra chair.

"Wow. You're good," he tells her.

"Obviously." She winks.

Minutes later, it's chaos. Readers speed walk across the room, dragging their carts of books behind them. Nick's brows shoot up as he watches it unfold. I don't have long to capture his reaction before there's a line of people waiting with my books.

I smile and sign each one, sometimes adding a personalization or a quote. Other times I get pulled into conversations about the characters. I love hearing their perspective. It takes me back to when I was a kid and Olivia would read those first stories and tell me what she thought.

Several people recognize Nick. He's polite when they ask him for a photo or signature, but he waves it off and tells them he's just here to support me. Word must get around pretty fast because pretty soon

I have a line that gets so unwieldy the event staff start turning people away.

"Your fans are coming to see me just to get a glimpse of you," I whisper to him between people in line.

"Those aren't my fans, baby. Those are all yours." He sits off to the side, a foot behind me. He hands me fresh Sharpies when mine run out and reminds me to drink water by silently setting water in front of me, but otherwise, he just sits and watches, taking it all in with this proud look that I will remember forever.

We run out of early copies of the book well before the signing is over, but the line just keeps going. After the last person has left my table, I sit back and sigh.

"You did it!" Molly is giddy as she dances in front of my table.

"Now can I nap?" I ask hopefully. And by nap, I mean take Nick up to my room and get naked.

"You have thirty minutes." She waggles a finger between me and Nick like she knows exactly where my head was at. "Then we're meeting Doreen for dinner."

"That wasn't on the schedule."

"I know. She requested it an hour ago."

"Is that bad? It feels bad." My stomach dips with unease.

"Relax. Everything is fine. The promotions for the book went so well this weekend, she probably wants to talk about the tour schedule. We need to lean into the excitement."

"All right." I'm not convinced but I have other priorities right this minute.

Nick and I start to walk off and she calls after us, "Twenty-nine minutes!"

In the hallway, people are sitting along the walls, resting and recharging before the next event. There's a final party tonight, karaoke and dancing.

Nick takes my hand as we move quickly.

"Want to come see my room?" I ask.

"I want to be wherever you are."

"Me too." I stop, prepared to tell him exactly how I'm feeling.

He takes a step, then pauses and glances back at me. "Everything okay?"

Before I can answer him, Matt approaches us from the side, smiling like we're old friends. "Ruby, hey."

Nick tenses beside me, then steps closer.

"Who's your friend?" Matt asks, though I'm ninety-nine percent sure he already knows.

Instead of giving him any information, I cut to the chase. "What do you want, Matt?"

"Just being friendly." He holds up both hands defensively and shoots a befuddled expression like he can't imagine why I'm being so sharp.

"We're not friends."

Matt's gaze slides from me to Nick.

He holds a hand out between them for Nick to shake. "You're that hockey guy, right?"

Nick's jaw flexes as he glares at my ex-boyfriend.

Matt pulls his hand back, still somehow looking smug. He looks to me. "Genius move having him show up here. Did you come up with that or Molly?"

My stare narrows on him. "Not everything is a marketing ploy."

"No?" He shrugs. "Anyway, nice to meet you. I'm Matthew Rose."

"I know who you are." Nick's voice is low and gritty.

"Oh cool. Do you want me to sign something for you?"

"Why would I want that?"

"I'm kind of a big deal." Matt's brows pinch together, then he laughs it off. "I wrote a little book you might have heard of, *Becoming Alaric*."

"Oh, I've heard of it," Nick says. "And I also know you stole the idea from Ruby."

For only a second, guilt flashes on Matt's face but he recovers quickly. "You can't steal ideas."

"Can't and shouldn't are two different things."

Once again Matt laughs. He turns his attention back to me. "I wrote the biggest book of the year, maybe the century. Do you really think you could have said the same if you'd written it?"

I hate to admit that I've had that thought. Maybe the magic wasn't in the idea but in him. Either way, it was a shitty thing to do.

"What the fuck did you say to her?" Nick asks, grip tightening on my hand.

Matt hesitates, jaw moving back and forth as he considers us. Slowly, that sly grin returns. "You should be thanking me. Do you know how many people would kill to have me write their concept? I did you a favor. You would have turned it into some cheesy, chick-lit crap that only sells to women who want a one-hand read."

No sooner does he get the final word out, than Nick is lunging forward and punching him. Matt crumples to the ground, catching himself on one knee. He looks up, blood in his mouth, and sneers. There are a few gasps and wide-eyed looks, but no one comes forward.

"We have to go." I grab Nick's arm and pull him with me down the hall.

No one comes running after us, so when we turn a corner, I slow and face him. Then start laughing.

Nick's jaw is tight but slowly loosens, and as a smile finally stretches across his face, he laughs too.

"Fuck, I'm sorry. I shouldn't have done that."

"Are you kidding? That was the highlight of my entire year."

"I don't know how you kept your cool all this time, knowing damn well he stole it from you." His jaw returns to stone.

"It doesn't matter. He's going to spend the rest of his career striving to recreate something he doesn't know how to do. He has to look at himself in the mirror and reconcile who he is and what he'll do to get ahead. I sleep just fine at night. Though better when it was next to you."

"Same."

"Well, that was entertaining," Molly interrupts.

I open my mouth to ask her how she already knows, but she waves me off. "I was thirty seconds behind you. Good news. Matt's jaw isn't broken."

"Is that good news?" I ask.

She levels me with an unamused glare.

"Kidding," I say. I mean, kind of.

"That's on me," Nick says. "I take full responsibility, and I'll do whatever's necessary to make sure it doesn't blow back on Ruby."

"If anyone asks, we'll tell them you were in a jealous rage. Though I doubt Matthew will mention it. He went down like a sack of potatoes." She makes a face depicting her embarrassment for him. "But we have bigger problems."

"We do?"

"Doreen wants to meet with you now. She got a last-minute flight home and needs to leave soon."

"Go," Nick tells me.

Molly nods her head and angles her body for me to follow her.

"No." I shake my head. "I'm sorry. I'm sure whatever she wants is important, but I need five minutes alone with Nick."

Molly heaves a sigh then looks around. She tips her head to the left. "The green room is probably empty."

"Thank you."

I take his hand and lead him there.

"Five minutes," Molly reminds me.

The green room is, as Molly assumed, empty. I shut the door and lock it. I turn and lean against it. With one hand, I wave toward the table of drinks and snacks. "Want anything?"

"Yes," he says as he wraps an arm around my waist and drops his mouth to mine again.

I fling my arms around his neck, and he pulls me up, holding me against him as he walks over to an empty table and sets me down on it.

He stands between my spread legs, leaning down to keep kissing me. My hands slip under the hem of his shirt and trace over the hard, lean lines of his stomach muscles.

"Fuck, I missed you." His fingers glide up my thighs and under my skirt to settle on either side of my hips.

"I missed you too."

I did not wake up this morning with "have sex in the green room" on my bingo card, but all I can think about is getting closer to him. I push his pants and boxers down until his dick springs free.

As I circle the base with my thumb and forefinger, Nick groans against my lips.

He pulls back and looks me in the eye. "I didn't come here to punch your ex or for a quick fuck."

"I know, but that was very satisfying to watch. I've never been so turned on."

It seems that's all he needs to know because he hooks a finger on either side of my panties and tugs them down. I shift to help him, and he frees the material from my legs.

"We don't have a lot of time, and I've been dreaming of this since the second you left."

"Do your worst, Galaxy."

He chuckles then takes my mouth and pulls me to the edge of the table. I guide his cock to my entrance, and he wastes no time pushing inside.

We share a groan, tongues stroking together as we press our bodies as close as we can possibly get. Nick drives into me until I can't take any more, then pulls out and thrusts again. I'm already climbing. A week of longing and replaying every other time we've done this served as foreplay.

He's close too. I can tell by the way he moves faster and the slight shudder each time he fills me.

"Goddamn, you take me so good, baby."

"More." It's a beg and a plea. I'm teetering on the edge, and it feels so perfect.

His answer is to hook an arm around my thigh, lifting and wedging himself farther between my legs.

And as I finally get there, tears well in my eyes. Nick is right behind me, caressing my face and telling me how good I feel. I soak up every word and every touch. He comes with a nip of my bottom lip and a deep groan. Then he stays there, still inside me, holding me to him. His chest rises and falls, and I can feel his heart beating the same rapid pace as mine.

The emotion bubbles over. The tears slide down my cheeks, and it's so ridiculous that I'm crying right now, I also start laughing.

"What's wrong?" Nick's gaze is filled with a frantic concern.

"Nothing," I say, which I realize isn't very reassuring as I keep crying.

His thumbs swipe at the tears tracking down my face.

"I'm just so glad you're here," I manage to get out through a sob and a hiccup. "I missed you so much. I have slept in your jersey every night."

His lips twitch and pull into a smile. One dimple peeks through his beard.

"I'm sorry that I'm crying. I swear I'm happy."

He keeps that smile aimed at me as he brushes his lips over mine. It turns out kissing is the magic trick to stop the tears. His mouth is gentle and sweet, the kind of kisses that I could get lost in for days.

But unfortunately, Molly has other plans.

"Two minutes!" she calls from out in the hallway.

"She's relentless, huh?" Nick asks.

"You have no idea."

He pulls up his pants and then grabs napkins off another table to clean me up. The clover necklace I gave him hangs around his neck.

"You're still wearing it," I say, motioning with my head to his chest.

He looks down and then back to me. "Of course. It's my version of sleeping in your jersey."

I laugh lightly. Nick helps me to my feet and then holds out my panties for me to step into. His hands slide slowly up, leaving goose bumps in their wake.

"I wish you could stay longer. I hate not seeing you every day."

"That's partly why I came," he says.

"What do you mean?"

He pauses, staring into my eyes as his teeth work over his bottom lip. "I love you, Ruby."

Of all the things I thought he might say, that hadn't been on the list. "You do?"

"Yeah, Red. I do. I should have told you before you left, but I kept telling myself we hadn't known each other long enough for me to feel the way I do about you. But a week without you, and I know I wasn't mistaken. You stumbled into my life, and I'm pretty sure I fell in love with you right then and there. I was scared. I'm still scared. I've never wanted anything more than I want this."

Another laugh falls from my lips. I'm giddy, almost delirious with how happy his words make me.

"I'm not even sure if you want the same thing, but—"

"I want it," I assure him. "Whatever it is."

He nods and a half smile tugs at his lips. "I don't know what it looks like, but I want to make this work. I'm in. All the way. Whatever you want. I'll figure out how to visit you on every off day, though I'll be honest, those will be few and far between for a while with the season starting. You can come stay with us whenever you want too. Any time you want. For as long as you want. Or I can get you tickets to games and fly you out to watch or if you are sick of hockey, then we can spend every night on the phone, and you can tell me all about your day. And after the season is over, Aidan and I can come stay with you for the summer. I need you too, Red."

Molly's voice comes from the other side of the door as she knocks loudly. "It's showtime, Ruby!"

I don't want to go back out there, but I know Molly well enough to know she will break down the door if necessary. There are still so many things I want to say and things I desperately want to hear from him.

"Go."

"But . . ."

"You don't need to answer now. You know my situation and how I feel, but you should take time and think about it. Really think about it, Red. And whatever you choose, I don't regret a single moment."

I start to argue that I don't need time to think, but he keeps going.

"You have so many incredible opportunities coming your way with the book. I'm so fucking proud of you, and I want you to enjoy all of that. And your sister is about to have a baby. I know how much she means to you and you're going to want to make her a priority too. Maybe jumping into things right now is too much for you, and that's okay."

"No. I . . ." I shake my head. "I want to be with you too. We'll figure out how to make it work."

He rests one palm on the side of my face and presses his lips to mine once more before stepping back. He takes my hand, and we start for the door. Just before we reach it, he pauses.

"I almost forgot." He pulls a black box from his pants pocket and hands it to me.

"What is it?"

"Open it."

I flip the top of the jewelry box to reveal a stunning gold necklace with a diamond encrusted hockey stick charm.

"Aidan helped me pick it out."

The tears are back.

"I miss him too."

"Same. He's working on a new song for you."

Molly knocks again, and before I'm ready, Nick unlocks and opens the door to reveal my very anxious-looking agent on the other side.

"Oh, good." She smiles and her shoulders relax. "Ready?"

I'm not, but Nick steps away from me. He's smiling as he walks out the door. "Later, Red."

I'm in a daze as I follow Molly through the hotel. Nick *loves* me. He wants to make this work. He showed up today *for me*. I don't think I could be any happier. Maybe he thinks I need time to think about being with him, but I don't. I've known since the moment I left Moonshot.

Doreen is waiting for us in the hotel coffee shop. She stands as we approach. I blink away the happy-tinged haze as I greet her.

"Hi." My voice wavers.

"Thanks for meeting with me before I go." She sits and waves a hand for us to do the same.

"Of course. Is everything okay? I thought the reception of the book went over well."

"It has. We're all thrilled for you. I was right to trust my instincts," she says with only a tinge of "I told you so" in her tone. "You've proven you have what it takes to write across sub-genres, and your readers are happy to take the ride."

"Wow. Thank you. It all feels so surreal."

Her lips purse as she considers me. "The question now is, what do you want to write next?"

"I . . ." I start to give her the pitch for the *Love Bites* sequel, but I'm certain Molly has already sent it to her. "I'm not sure what you're asking."

Her red lips curve into a small, but satisfied smile. "I'll cut to the chase because I know you've had a long day. Whatever it is that you write next, I want to publish it."

"You do?"

"If it's the book you've already pitched, great. If it's more sports, that's fine too. Or perhaps you want to detour into time travel, fantastic. Whatever it is, I want it. I love the Ruby Madison universe. It's fun and unexpected. I think we could build something truly special together."

My jaw drops as I mentally press rewind and replay her words, turning them over in my brain. She looks to Molly while I process. "I'll send over my official offer for the pitch, as well as two additional books of your choosing."

"Holy crap." A huge smile spreads across Molly's face, and her voice lifts an octave. She schools her expression before speaking again. "I mean, that's great. I look forward to receiving it on behalf of my client."

I'm still frozen in stunned silence. She wants my book. She wants my book and *two* more!

Doreen pins her gaze back on me as she stands. She lifts her large purse onto her shoulder. "Congratulations on writing a fantastic book. I'm excited about the future, Ruby."

I get to my feet, still not quite sure that I'm not dreaming. "Thank you so much."

"No need to thank me."

"You took a chance on me when no one else did."

Her lips twist into one last smirk. "And every other publisher will spend the rest of their careers regretting it."

Chapter Thirty-Four

NICK

Training camp is in full swing. We've done medical reviews, on- and off-ice testing, small group practices, social media promotional interviews, as well as talking to the media.

The rookies just finished with their practice, and our veteran group is taking the ice to warm up before we start.

We have a full house: photographers, reporters, front office staff, and even some fans.

"Hey. How was the convention?" Travis asks as we circle around, shooting pucks and warming up.

"It was good. You should have seen how many people were there to see Ruby." I smile at the memory.

"And?" he asks with so much anticipation vibrating through him it makes me chuckle.

"I told her how I felt and now it's up to her."

Travis waits like he's hoping for more. Actually, his head looks like it's going to explode.

"Is she coming back?" he asks finally.

"She said she wants to visit, yeah. And I'll try to visit her too."

"Oh." A deep crease forms between his brows.

"Don't look so happy for me." My tone is dry, and another laugh slips free.

"I'm sorry. I am happy for you, but . . . I miss her too. I was hoping you'd convinced her to pack her shit and come back for good."

"I know, buddy." I pat him on the shoulder. "But she has stuff going on too. They're sending her on a book tour, and her sister's about to have a baby. And you know what it's like for us. Even if she were here, I'll be gone half the time."

He bobs his head like he agrees. "Maybe I should text her some pics of you in the locker room later. You're looking great, man."

"No," I say immediately.

"But—"

"No."

He grins. "I already sent her all the photos I had of you in my phone, including some cute ones of the two of you."

I should be touched, I suppose. "Aidan's at his mom's tonight. Do you want to grab a drink after practice?"

"And brainstorm wild, extravagant, over-the-top gestures to convince her Moonshot is the best place in the universe and you're the only man she wants to sleep with for the rest of her life?"

I open my mouth to say no, but what the hell. I'm already planning to do everything I can to keep showing Ruby how much I want this to work. Maybe Trav will have a good idea. Probably not, but maybe. "Sure."

He pumps a fist in the air.

"But I get full veto power," I warn him.

"Let's circle up," Coach Lenshaw calls as he steps out onto the ice with the rest of the coaches.

Trav and I fall into a line with the rest of the group. It's his third season at Moonshot, same as mine, so I already have a good feel for his coaching style. He's not big on small talk or pumping us up, but he's direct and honest, and when he tells us we're doing something good or bad I always know I can take it at face value.

"We're going to split up today and scrimmage. All out, don't hold back. I'll be switching up lines and groupings to see where we might make some adjustments. Coach Marigold has the groupings."

He steps back, and Coach M reads off the teams by line. Once I've heard my name, I head over to the bench to grab my mouthguard. I'm on the first line with D-Low and Travis. We were the starting first line last year with the most scoring and shots on goal. I'm sure Coach will swap in and out some other guys to see if he can make the other lines stronger, but there's magic in playing with these two, and I'm hopeful we can keep doing it.

Penn is on the bench, adjusting his gear and preparing to get in the net.

"How's the knee?" I ask him.

He flashes a cocky smirk as he pulls his mask in place. "Fucking fantastic."

All the anxiousness is gone after only a few minutes of play. The game takes my full concentration, and I'm happy to find I'm able to give myself over to it. Going up against other teams might still be a mental battle, but I'll take it as it comes.

The puck flies out of play, and Coach blows the whistle to stop the game. I circle around, preparing to take the face-off, when a crash somewhere in the stands pulls me out of my focus.

I glance over, finding the source by the commotion. Several members of the media have stood to help the woman to her feet. Someone picks up a yellow backpack and holds it out to her. My already speeding heart kicks up another notch.

Ruby's cheeks are pink as she composes herself. She smooths down the skirt of her dress and scans the ice, finding me and smiling hesitantly.

"Galaxy?" Coach calls my name as he stands at center ice with the puck.

"One sec, Coach."

He looks puzzled and a little taken aback by my request, but I'm already skating toward her. She continues down the steps, looking more beautiful than I remember. Less than twenty-four hours since I left Denver, but the relief I have seeing her is overwhelming.

We meet at the bottom of the stairs just off the ice. I take out my mouthguard and flip up my visor. I'm so happy to see her, I can't seem to say anything.

"Hi!" She lifts a hand in an awkward wave.

"Long time no see."

"Clingy, right?"

"Charming." I flash her a smile. "I'd hug you, but I'm sweaty."

She lets out a soft laugh. "Sorry to interrupt, but I have good news, and I couldn't wait to tell you."

"What's up, baby?"

"I sold my book proposal!" She raises both arms out to her sides and lifts her shoulders. "My meeting last night, the one that couldn't wait, was with the editor who bought it. She bought three books actually. I'm under contract for the next two years of my life."

"That's fantastic news. Congratulations!"

"Thank you."

My gaze shifts to the people on the ice and in the stands all watching us.

"I'm not complaining, Red, but is there a reason you came all this way to tell me that instead of picking up the phone?" I ask, grinning at her.

"Well, I had planned to wait until practice was over." She waves at the team and coaches. She raises her voice, "So sorry."

"It's fine. They can wait." Coach is surely going to have a talk with me later about distractions at practice, but I don't care.

She tucks her hair behind one ear and looks at her feet before glancing back up at me.

"Okay, here's the thing. I'm not sure I can write books anymore without the sound of hockey in the background. It also helps to have inspiration from my extremely hot and sexy boyfriend."

"Did you just call me your boyfriend, Red?"

Her face scrunches up as she aims a timid smile at me. "Yes?"

"I love it. And I'm happy to be your inspiration any time."

"Good, because I don't need time to think about what I want. It's you. I want you, and I don't care how much schedule juggling it takes. I'm all in."

"Me too."

Her smile is back and filled with sass. "Also, I was thinking . . . Since I'm going to be writing nonstop, and Hotel Fourteen is uninhabitable, maybe I could stay at Chalet Galaxy. You know, if it's available."

My smile spreads as wide as it's ever been. "For how long?"

"Three books, inevitable writer's block . . . It could take a while." She smiles back, mirroring my happiness. "I haven't worked out the details yet. I want to visit my family as much as I can and be there when Olivia has the baby. Then there's the tour coming up and . . . I want to stay indefinitely."

I pull her into my arms and kiss her. I'm vaguely aware of some chatter and laughter, then I distinctly hear Travis let out a whoop of excitement, followed by the rest of the guys tapping their sticks on the ice.

"Is that a yes?" she asks when I set her back on her feet.

"It's a yes. Stay as long as you want. Stay forever."

She squeals and presses her mouth to mine.

"Galaxy!" Coach yells. I can't find it in me to feel bad, even as I turn to face him.

"Yeah, Coach?"

"Care to join us, or are you taking the day off?"

"Sorry, Coach."

"Gotta go," I tell Ruby. I toss a wink at her before I finally take the ice. My teammates pat me on the back as I make my way to center ice.

Trav falls in beside me. “She stole my thunder. How am I going to top that?”

Laughing, I punch him in the shoulder. “I’m sure you’ll come up with something.”

Chapter Thirty-Five

RUBY

I wake up with Nick's arm thrown over my middle. I snuggle deeper into him, and his arm tightens.

"You're still here," I say, voice still gruff from sleep. We crashed at the cabin after I got moved back in, and then we celebrated . . . many times.

"Mhmm." He pulls me against his chest. He's warm and smells faintly of my perfume. His mouth travels along my neck and shoulder, dropping soft kisses that have me turning in his arms to celebrate again.

My stomach, however, picks this inopportune moment to growl. We skipped dinner last night in favor of sex, and I have no regrets.

"You need to eat some breakfast," Nick says.

"No. I don't want to go anywhere."

"Me either, but I have big plans for you today, so first . . . food." He brushes his lips over mine, then gets out of bed. I shift, pulling the blanket up around my bare shoulders.

I watch him as he pulls on his boxers and jeans. "I could get used to this."

He glances at me over his shoulder as he pulls his T-shirt on over his head. "Good. I like having you here."

We haven't talked through everything yet, but being here feels right.

"What happens when Aidan comes back?" I ask.

Nick looks to me like he needs more information to answer my question.

"If you don't want to tell him yet or think it would be weird to have me stay at the cabin, I found some apartments—"

Nick's expression shifts from confused into some grumpy scowl that I can't quite decipher. "I'm not hiding you from him. Plus, he already knows we had a thing this summer."

"He does?" I ask, then wince at the implication.

"Yeah, I mean, we weren't that subtle, so I guess I'm not shocked that he saw us making out at the rink."

"Oops. Your fault. All that padding really does something for me."

He leans forward with both hands on the mattress to kiss me again. "Better for him to see his dad acting like a horny teenager in love than wondering if he's taken a vow of celibacy."

"Did you say love?" My smile widens. He's already told me he loved me once, but I'm dying to hear it again.

"Yeah, Red. I'm in love with you."

I pull him back onto the bed—or most likely, he lets me pull him back onto the bed.

"I love you too," I say between kisses, sliding my hands under his shirt.

He hums and settles his weight on top of me. Breakfast can wait. He brushes my hair out of his face and guides his hand to settle at the base of my neck where my pulse point flutters under his touch.

I'm filled with so much happiness I feel like I might float away without him.

"I think I'm going to need you to sneak over here and wake me up like this every morning."

"You just want me to bring the good coffee from the house."

"That too."

He laughs against my mouth and then takes my bottom lip between his teeth. I let out a contented sigh.

I don't hear the knocking until Nick yells, "Go away!"

I freeze, listening for it now. "What if it's Aidan?"

"He's not due back for a couple hours. And he wouldn't have knocked."

The door handle jiggles, and then the knocking starts back up. "Nicky. Open up."

Nick groans and stands. "Perfect timing, Dad."

He picks up my shirt from the floor and tosses it to me. While he sees to the door, I jump out of bed and quickly get dressed. I come out, running my fingers through my hair, as Mike is setting a cardboard box on the kitchen counter.

"What's all this?" I ask.

Nick's jaw is tight. Uh-oh. This can't be good.

Mike smiles at me. "Welcome back, Ruby. We missed you around here."

"Thanks. Me too."

Nick sighs. "Dad, you can't move in. I told Ruby she can stay here while she writes her next book."

Heat blooms in my face. Of course. It is his place after all. I should have thought to ask him.

"I'm so sorry," I say to him.

Mike reaches out and gives my hand a reassuring squeeze. "Nothing to apologize for, darling. I thought you might prefer something a little closer to my son. I cleaned out the downstairs bedroom. It has an attached bathroom, even nicer than this one, and a deck that looks out to the lake."

"I don't know what to say." I look from him to Nick. "Do you want me under the same roof?"

He tugs me to him by my shirt and scoops me up in his arms, kissing me like we don't have an audience.

Behind me I hear Mike say, "That's what I thought."

"Ruby-Doo!" Travis's big, booming voice comes next.

He walks in, carrying more boxes. Conrad, Danny, and Penn follow after him.

"You recruited my friends to help?" Nick asks his dad.

"I'm not as young or as strong as I look." Mike winks at me.

Travis puts down the box then wraps me in a big hug, lifting me off the ground and stealing all the breath from my lungs.

"Need air," I wheeze.

He sets me down but keeps his arms around me, rocking side to side. "So fucking happy you're staying with us."

"Us?" Nick mutters.

I laugh. "Me too."

Danny is the next to hug me. "Congrats on the book deal. If you need a beta reader, let me know."

"I do, and you're hired."

Penn leans down to give me a quick side hug. "Glad you're back."

"Thanks, Penn."

Conrad shuffles forward with a shy smile. His hair looks like it's been cut since the last time I've seen him, and it's out of his eyes, which makes him look even more like he stepped off a runway.

"Hey, Ruby," he says as I wrap my arms around his shoulders. "Congratulations."

"Thanks."

"Should we get everything moved and then have a party?" Trav asks with a mischievous glint. "Good day to take the boat out. Probably our last chance."

"I just noticed you're wearing your trunks," Nick says, arching one brow.

"I always come prepared." He slaps him on the shoulder and then heads to the house, presumably to get another box.

"You sure you know what you're getting into?" Nick asks as he takes my hand and pulls me from the doorway.

"I have a pretty good idea."

"Still want to stay?"

I lift up on my toes to kiss him. "Definitely."

"Can we watch a movie tonight?" Aidan asks as we're cleaning up after dinner.

"Sure," Nick says. He looks to me, and I nod my agreement.

Mike pushes back from the table. "I think I'll leave you three to it. I have a new audiobook I want to listen to, and then I'm calling it a night."

"Night, Dad," Nick calls as Mike ruffles Aidan's messy hair.

"Good night." Mike lifts a hand in a wave and heads out the sliding door.

It's been two weeks since I moved in, and the nights are my favorite. When Nick doesn't have a late practice or game, we have dinner together followed by TV time or sitting out on the back deck. Fall in Arizona is really just extended summer, but here I've already had to break out my sweatshirts and leggings.

After the kitchen is clean and the dishwasher started, we settle in the living room, and Aidan scrolls through the options, calling them out one by one.

My phone rings while we're deciding between *Mighty Ducks 2* and *Sandlot*.

"It's Travis," I say, looking at the screen.

Nick and I share a concerned look. I accept the call and put him on speakerphone.

"Hey, Trav. Everything okay?"

"Yeah, yeah. I have a quick question for you."

"Me?" I ask.

"Yeah."

"O-kay."

"Is love at first sight a thing?"

"Excuse me?"

Nick groans and falls back onto the couch beside me.

"You're an expert on love and romance, so I trust your judgment," he says as if that explains this bizarre phone call.

"I don't know about *love* love, but yes, I think you can have chemistry with someone from the moment you lock eyes," I say.

Nick's lips pull up at the corners. "Me, right?" he whispers.

I'm transported back to the airport, me babbling and him with his grumpy, stoic expression.

"I definitely felt a spark of something," I whisper back, then lean forward and press my lips to his.

"Why?" I ask when Travis falls silent on the other end.

"Because I just met my new neighbor, and I'm pretty sure I'm in love."

Epilogue

NICK

The roads are covered with fresh snow, and the mountains look like something out of a postcard. I pull into the driveway and cut the engine. It feels good to be home. We had a three-game road trip. Two games in California and one in Washington. We won all three, but it still feels like the real trophy is waiting for me inside.

As I push open the front door and step inside, Aidan's voice calls out from the living room.

"Dad!" He stands, guitar in hand.

"Hey!" I aim my smile at him, then at Ruby. She's curled up in her favorite chair with several blankets wrapped around her and her computer situated on her lap. A fire is going, and she has a space heater next to her.

Aidan meets me halfway and stretches his arms around my waist.

"Did you grow another inch while I was gone?" Sometime over the past few months he shot up and doesn't show any signs of stopping.

"No." He giggles into my chest. I hug him to me, breathing deeper than I have since I left. There's nothing more grounding than getting to be his dad. Any time I leave for an extended amount of time, I'm hit with that reality all over again. Watching him grow and become his own person is such an honor.

Ruby gets up from the chair with one of the blankets draped over her shoulders. Winter has been an adjustment for her. She never leaves the house without at least three layers, including a hat, scarf, gloves, and long underwear. Doesn't sound sexy, but it's a lot of fun peeling her out of all of it.

"Welcome home." She rises up on her toes to kiss me. I circle one arm around her waist to pull her to me.

"Ooh, you're cold." She shivers into my mouth.

"Speaking of the cold, the lake froze over."

"Can we go skating?" Aidan asks almost as soon as the news is out of my mouth. He sets his guitar on the couch and brings his hands up in front of him, begging like he did when he was younger. I don't know how many more years he'll do things like plead to go skating with me, but I plan to take advantage of it for as long as he does.

"Definitely."

He rushes out of the room, a flurry of excitement.

"You must be exhausted," Ruby says quietly when my son is out of earshot.

"I am," I admit. "But I was able to sleep on the flight."

In fact, I'm sleeping a lot better in general. That might have something to do with the woman in my bed most nights. We've kept the downstairs bedroom as her room, but it acts as her office now. I like peeking in on her, watching her fingers fly over the keyboard or sitting in deep thought. She's already finished her next book and started another.

I've continued talking with the team psychologist too. I wouldn't say my fears and anxiety are gone, but I'm navigating it. Every day. Little by little. It's easier with Ruby by my side.

"You're a good dad," she says.

I swipe my lips over hers again.

When I pull back, she has a devilish glint in her eyes. "Maybe the two of you should hang. Boys' day."

"Are you trying to get out of skating on the lake, Red?"

"It's so cold out there." Her voice is part whine and part laugh.

"I'll keep you warm."

She groans, but then a smile tips up the corners of her mouth.

Twenty minutes later we're out on the lake. Aidan has his hockey stick and a few pucks. I drag out a net for him so we can shoot around. A few neighbors are outside, enjoying the little sunlight poking through the clouds. One of Aidan's friends down the street joins him, and the two kids fly across the ice, mostly messing around but occasionally taking shots at the net.

I stick with Ruby, holding her mittened hand and slowly circling the lake.

"It really is beautiful here." Her nose and cheeks are pink. "But I can't wait to visit Arizona next month."

"Me too."

I met her family in November when Olivia had her baby. The three of us, me, Aidan, and Ruby, spent a long weekend there. It was great meeting them, seeing Ruby so happy. Aidan and Greer hit it off and have been playing video games together every Saturday.

Dad comes out and gets the fire pit going, then brings out hot chocolate for everyone as we tire of skating and retire to sit around the fire. Aidan goes inside to grab his guitar, and his friend runs home to get his trumpet.

Dad grimaces as the two of them make noise that might be music. He sticks it out for a bit, but eventually goes back inside.

Ruby and I sit side by side in lawn chairs. Her head rests on my shoulder, and she has two blankets wrapped around her.

I don't remember ever feeling this happy. It's a thousand little dreams all wrapped up into one incredible life.

When Aidan's friend says he needs to get home, we say goodbye to him, and then it's just the three of us.

Aidan strums lightly, not seeming as interested now that he's alone.

"Did you learn that new song we talked about?" I ask him, breaking the silence. My breath is visible in the air.

He grins and nods his head rapidly.

"Another one?" Ruby asks, looking amazed and impressed by my son. "Can I hear it?"

Aidan looks to me for permission.

I had a slightly different plan, but this feels right. Just the three of us out by the lake, stars shining above us—and don't tell Ruby I said this—but even the bite of cold in the air is perfect. It guarantees she'll snuggle closer.

I give him the nod of approval, and Aidan gets settled with his guitar in his lap. Ruby sits forward, giving him all her attention. I love how much she supports him and cheers him on. She's been good for all of us.

Even Dad seems happier. During the day, she takes a break from writing, and the two of them have lunch and go for a walk. In no time at all she's become so essential to our lives that I can't picture it without her. Next month her book releases, and she goes on tour. It's going to be torture around here without her, but I can't wait to watch millions of people fall in love with her words.

As Aidan gets to the chorus, Ruby's eyes light up.

"Oh my gosh. I know this one!" She hums along to "Is This Love."

That night in the truck is burned into my brain forever. Just like a million other nights. I don't want to forget any of them. And I want to make a million more memories just like it.

He gets to the end, and Ruby claps so enthusiastically that Aidan looks bashful. He flicks his hair out of his eyes and then looks to me.

Ruby elbows me and shoots an outraged glare in my direction. "Why aren't you clapping? That was so good."

Then her gaze drops to my hand. I have the ring between my thumb and pointer finger. Her eyes go wide, and she gasps.

"Oh my god. Nicholas Galaxy, are you proposing to me while I'm wearing long underwear and mittens?!"

I chuckle. "I had planned to do it at Christmas, but I can't wait."

Her eyes well with tears. "You want to marry me?"

"Yeah. I want to marry you, Red."

She shucks off the heavy gloves and sets them in her lap. I hold out the ring to her. "I love you. I can't picture any life better than this one with you. And if you'll let me, I'll spend the rest of my life keeping you warm."

"Eww." Aidan scrunches up his face.

I flash him a wry smile. Ruby looks over to him.

"You're good with this too?"

"Yeah. You make my dad really happy, and you make the best cookies." He grins.

"You both make me really happy too." She turns back to me.

"That a yes, Red?"

She nods, and I slip the ring onto her finger. She's silent, staring at it for so long I'm not sure what to make of her subdued reaction. Then all at once, she jumps up from her chair and throws her hands into the air.

"We're getting married!" Her voice echoes into the night. She yells it again and again.

Laughing, I stand and circle one arm around her waist. "I think they heard you."

"I get to marry you," she says quietly.

Aidan starts playing the wedding march, and I hug her to me. "And I get to marry you."

How lucky am I?

Bonus Scene

RUBY

I wipe a tear from the corner of my eye and bite down on my bottom lip to stop a sob. I truly didn't think I would be this emotional. It's an exciting day, one that should be happy and celebratory, and yet here I am at Aidan's high school graduation trying not to cry like a baby.

I'm flooded with memories of him as a little boy, learning to play guitar, playing hockey, eating Froot Loops, playing video games, learning to drive, going to prom, and on his first date. It all feels like just yesterday.

"Aidan Nicholas Galaxy," the announcer calls his name. Three rows of family and friends in the gymnasium stand and yell as Aidan walks across the stage. He accepts his diploma, then faces the audience and moves his tassel from the right to the left. He still has the same head of messy dark hair and bright green eyes like his father, but now he's taller than his dad, and his boyish features are angular and defined.

Aidan's mom, Beth, is on one side of me, and we share a teary-eyed emotional smile as we take our seats again. Through the years we've become friends. At first out of necessity. I knew very little about being a stepparent, and she was so welcoming and gracious as I stepped into that role.

"It's okay, Mommy." Chloe places her little hand on my arm. She's only six but one of the sweetest, most empathetic humans I've ever met. I might be biased.

"Thanks, baby." I kiss the side of her head and promise myself I'm going to remember every second of the next twelve years with her. It all goes by so fast. More tears well in my eyes, and I choke back a sob.

Chloe sits half on my lap and half on Beth's. When Chloe was old enough to realize her big brother had another set of parents, she'd get upset when Aidan left to stay with Beth and Cory. They were so lovely about it and started inviting Chloe over too. She's been like a second mom to her.

Nick chuckles softly as I wipe tears as fast as they fall. It's useless to fight it. I'm happy, but I'm sad too. Aidan's leaving in a month, and things will be different.

Nick places an arm around my shoulders and pulls me into his chest. I glance up at him with a wobbly smile, and he drops his mouth to mine in a quick kiss.

"I love you," I whisper as I reach a hand up to the side of his face, letting my fingers slide down over his beard. It has the tiniest bit of gray in it now, and there are a few faint lines around his eyes. Still, he gets hotter with each passing year, and somehow, I fall even more in love with him and with our life and family.

"Get a room," Trav says from the other side of Nick. He smiles as he side-eyes us.

All the guys are here tonight. Travis, Conrad, Danny, Penn, and their significant others. Some have remained in Moonshot, others left, but they're all back this weekend to celebrate Aidan.

My family is here too. They're sitting in the row behind us, fighting the same tears as me. When I moved here, I worried that we would grow apart. Instead, they've been so supportive and really made an effort to be in our lives. From daily calls and texts to weekly video chats, and lots of visits. They come here in the summer to get away from the desert heat, and I go there in the winter when I can't stand the cold.

It all worked out better than I could have imagined. Everything has. It's hard to see what life might look like in five or ten years, but even if I could have seen us now, I wouldn't have believed it was possible to be this happy.

We've been through lots of changes. Nick retired from playing hockey and then took a year off before boredom set in and he went back as a broadcast analyst. As for me, I'm still writing. I slowed down a little when Chloe was born. I wrote early in the morning or late at night, during nap times (when I wasn't also napping). Now that she's in school, I'm finding my rhythm again.

When all the graduates have received their diplomas, the principal gives a short speech and then calls Aidan and a few other students to the stage again.

Nick and I share a confused look, but our question is quickly answered when Aidan and the others appear with their instruments. A drummer, a singer, a bass guitarist, and Aidan with his guitar. All that practice paid off. He's insanely talented. I have no doubt he could make a career of it if he wanted, but for now he's determined to follow in his dad's footsteps. He's already been drafted to a professional team, but he's attending college to get a degree first.

I'm a blubbering mess as Aidan and his musical classmates play an old Green Day song. I stop fighting it and cry through the rest of the ceremony.

As soon as it's over, the gymnasium is a flurry of activity. Families and friends weaving through the crowd to find their students and take pictures. Our group stands in the back. There's no way Aidan won't be able to find us with all these tall guys together in one spot.

"Ruby." Penn hugs me. He only got in this afternoon, and I barely was able to say hello before the ceremony.

"It's so good to see you," I say as I lift up on my toes to hug him.

"I heard about your book being turned into a TV series. Congrats. When will it release?"

"I'm not sure. I'm working on the screenplay right now." It's hard. Way harder than I ever anticipated.

"It's going to be great." Nick wraps an arm around my waist and pulls me to him.

"Of course it will be," Penn assures me.

"Mommy, I need to go to the bathroom." Chloe looks up at me with big, pleading eyes.

"I'll take her," Greer offers. My stunning niece is taller than me and all grown up. She's still playing softball and still winning championships. And Flynn still treats each one like the most important game anyone has ever played.

"Thanks," I say to her and watch as they go. Chloe's only six, but today it feels like I'm going to blink and she'll be gone too.

Nick kisses my temple. "You okay?"

"Yes," I say, then stick my bottom lip out. "No."

He chuckles. "Don't worry. He'll come back to visit."

Aidan chose a college in Arizona. My family is thrilled he'll be close. And I'm thrilled that I'll have another excuse to visit.

"I know." And I do, but I also know it'll be different. Not bad different, just different.

When Aidan finally makes his way to us, he goes through a series of hugs and congratulations that start with his mom and dad and end with Everly. When he started getting interest from pro teams, she was his first call.

"Remember when I was little, and I asked you if you'd be my agent someday?" he asks her with a smile that's half arrogant man and half shy boy.

"I do." She laughs. "And wow that makes me feel old."

Jack drapes an arm across her shoulders with a smile.

"Yeah, same," Nick mutters.

"But I'm very grateful that I was the first agent you ever knew, and you still chose me," Everly says.

"Of course he did. You're the best," Jack adds.

She beams at him.

It feeds my soul, having all my people in one spot.

"I'm going to go with my friends for a while before heading to the party. Is that cool?" Aidan asks when the conversation hits its first lull. He looks from his dad to his mom.

They both nod.

"Don't be too long," Nick says. "You're the guest of honor."

Everyone is coming to our house to continue the celebration. A lot of people are in town for the whole weekend, but some will have to head back to their homes later tonight.

The series of hugs starts all over again. I start crying when Nick wraps his arms around his son. He whispers something I can't hear to Aidan, but I watch as emotion crosses his face. Nick hasn't been a mess of tears like me, but I know he's sad too. Last night I woke up in the middle of the night and found him on the back patio looking through old photos on his phone. It'll be a big adjustment for all of us, but I can't wait to see all the amazing things Aidan does.

When it's over and everyone else has left, Nick and I start for the truck. Chloe walks between us, holding each of our hands.

I glance over at Nick and then at Chloe. She has his dark hair and dimples, but my blue eyes and my love of books. She started reading early and hasn't stopped.

Nick catches me staring and gives me a wink, then pulls a giggling Chloe up onto his shoulders. She's my mini me but a total daddy's girl. She adores him, and he's wrapped around her little finger.

"Should we stop for ice cream on the way?" he asks.

"Yes!" Chloe shouts with a lot of enthusiasm. She got her sweet tooth from her grandpa Mike.

"Everyone is waiting for us to get back to the house," I remind my husband.

"Dad's there," Nick says. "And Trav will keep them entertained."

"You're just avoiding the chaos," I tease him.

He grins in acknowledgment. "I want to spend a few more minutes alone with my girls. Time goes fast, you know?"

My heart squeezes. "I do."

He stops and leans down to kiss me, which has Chloe in a fit of giggles again. She laughs every time her parents kiss, like it's the most ridiculous thing two adults could do. And sometimes it feels ridiculous that life could be this happy. This good. This fun. And that I could be this lucky.

Acknowledgments

This book idea came to me when I was in the midst of promoting a non-hockey book and felt like all the world wanted was for me to write another hockey hero instead. That story went on to become my bestselling book, which should give you some clue how neurotic authors can be—or at least this author. Still, I liked the idea and Nick & Ruby's story was born! Thank you, dear readers, for following me down all the sporty paths. Sports puck forever!

Now for all the people who I need to thank.

To my husband who gave up sleeping in during his summer break so I wouldn't have to wake up alone while I wrote this book. He's the reason I write swoony heroes who are all green flags. And the reason that I'm always creating stories where heroines feel seen and loved in a way they never have before. Next summer, let's go on a vacation instead!

To my incredible team: Jamie, Kayla, Sahara, and Tori. I can't say thank you enough. I'm so fortunate that I get to work with each of you.

Sarah Jane, thanks again for the stunning cover illustration. Your art inspires me endlessly.

Lori, my cover designer, thank you for your willingness to try approximately one thousand different fonts and color variations!

Becky, Jamie, Katie, Sahara, and Sarah—this book is so much stronger for your suggestions and notes. Thank you for always treating my words with such care while still pushing me to be a better writer.

Everyone at Valentine PR and my agent and publicist, Nina, thank you for all that you do.

Brittney C. for helping me cast my audiobooks and coming up with the best marketing ideas!

About the Author

Rebecca Jenshak is the *USA Today*–bestselling author of the Moonshot Hockey series, among other new adult romance novels. When she isn't writing, she can be found cheering on local sports teams, hanging out with friends and family, or curling up with a good book at home in southern Arizona.